GOOD COP DEAD COP

BOB RUCHHOFT

AND

PHIL SMITH

AuthorHouse™
1663 Liberty Drive
Bloomington, IN 47403
www.authorhouse.com
Phone: 1-800-839-8640

First published by AuthorHouse 2/4/2010

ISBN: 978-1-4490-6186-9 (e)
ISBN: 978-1-4490-6184-5 (sc)
ISBN: 978-1-4490-6185-2 (hc)

Library of Congress Control Number: 2010900436

Printed in the United States of America
Bloomington, Indiana

This book is printed on acid-free paper.

Thanks

Phil:

First to, Larry and Joy Redman you two got me started, made me think it was possible, this whole story telling idea. And of course Laurie for putting up with my temper tants' over computers and everything else and the hours and hours of correcting and trying to teach the un-teachable.

Bob:

To my wife, Christine, whose support, encouragement and knowledge kept me at it when I needed a push.

About the Authors

Bob Ruchhoft moved around the Midwest as a youngster and then settled in Southern California for his high school years.

In 1960 he joined the Long Beach, California Police Department after a stint in the Army and a few odd jobs. He worked a radio car for a few years where he and Phil were partnered up. He then was assigned to an elite unit that worked the waterfront amusement zone known as the Pike. The two man crews walked 'the beat', made up of Navy bars, dance halls, tattoo parlors and locker clubs which were populated by the predators that followed the fleet. The beat was known as the toughest mile on the West Coast.

In 1964 Bob moved to the Los Angeles Police Department. He worked all the hot areas from South Central to Skid Row. After his promotion to Sergeant he worked Internal Affairs, vice and patrol. After promoting to Lieutenant, he worked in the prestigious Metropolitan Division, ran the Gang Squad for seven years and then was assigned to Robbery Homicide.

He was Commanding Officer of Hollywood Detective Division when he and Phil reconnected, after years of no contact. They quickly re-established their friendship.

When Bob promoted to Captain he commanded several detective divisions and closed out his thirty four year career as Commanding Officer of the Organized Crime Division.

Phil grew up as a 'Navy Brat' during World War II. He spent his high school years in Southern California, sailing and surfing and spent his college years doing the same thing. He joined the Long Beach Police Department, one of the larger departments on the West Coast.

After his police job he went to work for one of the large hotels in Las Vegas and after that a number of little adventures including deep sea diver, security consultant for a national firm, salesman, dishwasher and sundry other endeavors. After he got sober, he settled down a bit in the business world.

Now he lives on an old, but sturdy sailboat on a pretty bay in Southern California with a Springer Spaniel.

PROLOGUE

He felt the cold water as it flowed across the sidewalk and up against his face. As he lay there trying to understand what was happening the water ran onto his frayed, dirty shirt, soaking it. He raised his head up far enough to look around. The view through his bleary, bloodshot eyes revealed little. A few trash cans, an abandoned car, assorted debris. The narrow confines between the tall buildings suggested it was an alley in which he'd just spent the night. He pushed himself up and rolled over onto his buttocks. The change in position allowed for a better view of things; maybe 'better' wasn't exactly the right word. The water running from a rainspout proved to be the source for the wake up wash job of his shirt. This momentarily puzzled him, seeing as how it wasn't raining, but he let it go.

After a few moments of just sitting there, staring at the filth surrounding him, he shook his head and began to cry.

"I've really hit rock bottom." he muttered. “In fact, I'm beneath the rocks. How the hell did I manage to get this fucked up?"

He knew, of course. He'd asked the question of himself a thousand times and answered it pretty much the same way each time.

"Booze. I'm a hopeless alcoholic and that's that. Smart enough to realize it, not strong enough to quit. Nothing philosophical about it." he thought.

"Speaking of which, I could really use a drink. No, not use a drink. I need a drink," he said to himself. "Stop crying and go get one." he ordered. He rolled over onto his hands and knees and began to struggle to get to his feet. It was then he realized, struggling to stand up, that he couldn't. He also realized he'd placed his hand squarely on top of a pile of feces. He pulled his hand away and fell to his left and over onto his back. Laying there, staring up at the mid-morning sun, he could feel it's' warmth. Tears once again began to run down his cheeks. He held up his hand and looked at it, covered with dog shit.

"That's it", he concluded. "Today's the day". With the last bit of strength he could muster from his undernourished, thoroughly abused body he got to his feet. He walked to the downspout and rinsed off his hand. "I'm out of here", he declared, "for good."

Chapter 1

The man hated the sun more than he hated the committee. His power to change either was nonexistent.

The yellow sun, glaring down through the dust of the construction, sucked at his strength as he made the uphill climb from the huge excavation that he and ten thousand other souls had been working on for the last seven years. He, at committee decree, made the climb twenty-two times a day. The large bamboo basket, filled with forty or so kilograms of dry earth and rock, wore into his back. The pain in his legs and chest became unbearable a little sooner and further from the crest every month.

The giant construction project would take 11 more years.

The year was 1972 and his wife was about to gift him with their seventh child. The hope that this one would be a male child gave Fang the strength to struggle the last few yards to the top of the site. Of the six daughters he'd fathered, two died in the first week after their birth and one was given to a distant childless cousin in a large city. And the most beautiful was sold to the General for the equivalent of forty-three American dollars.

The General was a man to be feared. He held ultimate power over the workers. He always arrived at the project in an open car, a black 1948 Packard Phaeton, with two soldiers in the front seat armed with submachine guns. Always a truck followed with ten more soldiers. They would come roaring into the tented camp scattering the work force and coming to a stop in billowing clouds of yellow brown dust. The General was an albino, a condition that gave him a fierce, surreal appearance. Among his many enterprises was the buying and selling of young, pretty children.

Late in the evening Fang made his way through the encampment, bone weary. He heard the sound of a newborn crying. He hurried, anxious for news as to whether he finally had a son. The midwife emerged from the canvas tent and bowed her head to him. His wife was lying on the soiled bedding, holding the small bundle. The look of sadness and shame told him all he needed to know. They named their newest child Fang Ce Song.

Song was an odd looking baby. Her features seemed elongated and her nose was too thin, making her eyes seem too far apart. But her hair was beautiful, black, almost blue, and she was slender. By the age of two it became obvious she had inherited the genes of her great-grandmother, a renowned beauty in the village of the father's family---a village destroyed during the time of the Japanese incursions into China.

When Song was ten years old, as she walked along the dirt road bringing sticks back to her family for the evening fire, the General's car roared by. She stood there in the dust cloud and stared defiantly at the receding car. Because of the dust in her eyes, she didn't see the General turn in his seat and stare, stare at her until the car rounded a curve in the road.

Fang had little choice in the matter. He agreed that the price was more than generous and the money changed hands.

That evening Song's mother bathed her by the light of the fire while her father, with his back to her, finished his dinner. The night was warm and she and her mother sat outside the tent under a half moon. Her mother took one of her hands in her own.

"Daughter, you must leave the family now. A man of the Army is going to come soon and take you. It is best for our family and for you. It is promised you will be taken care of and given to a wealthy family as their own."

Her mother reached into the sleeve of her worn garment and brought forth a white bone pin about seven inches long. It gleamed a dull white in the light of the moon. Song stared at her mother with dull eyes and one tear pushed itself over the brim of her almond eye, running slowly down her cheek. It fell upon her mother's worn hand.

"Daughter of mine, we have no choice. This hairpin was your great-grandmother and carries a story of the women of the family in better times. I pray you will cherish it as I have and that your grandmother's spirit will protect you."

Still the child said nothing. Her mother stood and said, "Go and bid your father farewell. Then sit here and wait for the car."

Half an hour later a man dressed in a black suit came to the entrance of the tent and her mother, without a word, pushed Song gently to him. He took her by the hand and led her to an old sedan painted a drab green, the exhaust drifting into the air of the moonlit night.

Song sat in the back seat all night long, staring straight ahead and expressionless as the car bumped over the dirt roads. Shortly before dawn they entered a broad highway. By ten o'clock in the morning they'd reached a large city near the coast and parked in front of the medical building of a university.

While Doctor Wu examined her, the man in the black suit went to the Bureau of Records and certified that the child had been killed in an accident at the construction site. Fang Ce Song no longer existed, by decree of the Chinese Government. When the man in the black suit returned, Doctor Wu assured him that she was in good health and disease free. She was picked up at the university by a grim-faced woman and taken to a warehouse by the docks where she was put in a room with nine other children and given a bowl of rice and vegetables and some broth. The drug contained in the food worked quickly and she was soon asleep.

The trawler left on the morning tide. The Ministry of Fisheries had approved its departure the day before, allowing a four-month trip to the Marshall Islands. The paperwork was all in perfect order.

As the boat left, the General's adjutant made a note in the accounts receivable records that in four-and-a-half months a deposit would be made into one of the offshore accounts located in a small bank at the east end of the Panama Canal. The thirty-five thousand dollars brought the account to over three million. The General would be pleased.

As the trawler reached the halfway point in its voyage, a location at mid Pacific, Song's father was killed. Fang was especially tired and the giant earth mover crushed him under its huge wheels before he could get out of the way.

Fang's family, mother and remaining daughters no longer useful, were cast from the camp. All perished in the desert while trying to make their way to the village of a distant relative. The desert scavengers made quick work of the bodies of the mother and her two remaining daughters.

CHAPTER 2

The squat man slid his hand along the back seat of the patrol car searching for any contraband. His hand closed around a small baggie stuffed into a corner, and a smile came over his face.

The man was bald. Other than black, bushy eyebrows, not a hair grew on the block of a skull that sat on thick, powerful shoulders. His neck was barely discernible. He stared from beneath those bushy eyebrows at the six men answerable to him as he exited the beat-up black and white patrol car. He was dressed in tan khakis, starched and ironed to perfection. "Trustee" was stenciled in neat black letters on the front and back. His seniority as well as his imposing presence accounted for his unofficial position as the trustee in charge. The other four trustees who were assigned to fuel and clean the patrol cars accepted his authority without question.

The top of his head was grimly decorated with the tattoo of a spider web, and sitting just above his furrowed brow a black spider with red gleaming eyes held a miniature damsel in distress. For obvious reasons, everyone called him Spider. When not in jail serving sentences of thirty to one hundred and eighty days for various drinking offenses, he was a barber and at one time had been a merchant seaman. In his youth, at one of his more exotic ports of call, he had an old Asian tattoo artist apply the decoration to his bald head.

Spider's duties at the Long Beach Police Department jail included making sure the black-and-whites were clean and full of fuel after each tour of duty before going on to the streets. This position lent Spider much power in the social strata of the complex jailhouse community. Spider was never out of jail for more than thirty days. Spider was an alcoholic and one of the regulars in the wino brigade that made their way in and out of the "gray bar hotel," as the jail was fondly called. On those unpleasant occasions, when Spider's sentence ran out and he had to vacate the jail, he always made sure that a close crony occupied his position of authority. This assured that when he inevitably returned, usually within a week or two, he could easily resume his place at the top of the pecking order.

Spider always checked each car before he allowed the other prisoners to begin cleaning. First, he looked under the front seat and then he pulled the back seat from its metal clips. On an average day he'd find two or three bucks in change along with various items that arresting officers missed when searching suspects they'd arrested. The arrestees got rid of the evidence on the way to the station, working it out of their pockets and stuffing it behind the seats. This gave Spider the merchandise, knives, once a gun, drugs and money he needed to remain in charge of the jailhouse population. Being no fool, Spider turned the gun over immediately. A drunk arrest was one thing but guns could lead to hard time. The small baggie he'd just found would come in handy. As for the cops who drove the patrol cars, well, he actually liked most of the cops he knew.

Five black-and-whites were lined up at the gas pumps with the blue suits laughing and talking quietly as they waited for the tanks to be topped off. They were assigned the late three watch, so named for the hours worked - 6:30 p.m. till 3:00 a.m. Overlapping the district grids, they were called wild units and were on duty during the hot, high-crime times. The cops assigned to the watch were not hot dogs, necessarily, but they did like the work, the action, and that made for a strong sense of camaraderie among the troops.

Spider watched the two officers standing apart from the others on opposite sides of their assigned patrol car. Both were close to the same age, in their early twenties.

Mitch Thacker was six-foot-three and carried his two hundred and five pounds on a swimmer's physique. Close-cropped hair with a patch of gray that sprouted when he was twelve years old and hard blue eyes that seemed to miss nothing gave him an intimidating air. Jake, two inches shorter and weighing almost the same, was more muscular, with dark sandy hair and the same military crop, and intelligent eyes full of serious curiosity. He looked older than his twenty-three years. Both officers carried themselves with pride. Mitch looked sideways at Jake, a brand new rookie fresh out of the Academy, with approval. His uniform was freshly pressed and the leather gear shined with a recent buffing. Most importantly, the badge, Jake's badge, glinted in the blue fluorescent lights of the parking area.

Jake stared across the assigned unit car at his partner with curiosity and nervousness. This was his first night on duty since graduating from the Academy. He had decided a long time ago that law enforcement was his career of choice and he was excited about his first night on the street. Mitch was his partner, and from the gossip Jake heard in the Academy, a bit of a character, given to jumping into things, being out front on hot calls. And hard, very hard, on new partners.

"Want me to drive?" Jake said across the roof of the car. Mitch started at him for a second, and then shook his head no and climbed into the driver's seat and directed Jake to ride shotgun. The trustee finished cleaning the windshield. Mitch reached out and handed the prisoner a pack of cigarettes and said, "I hear you're doing okay, Burgers. You hang in there."

Mitch swung the car smoothly out of the parking lot and onto Broadway. He picked up the radio mic and checked them into service, then looked over at Jake.

"This your first night on duty, huh?"

"Yeah," Jake paused, "I've really been looking forward to this. I've wanted to be a cop for a long time. We're working downtown. Do you think we'll be busy?"

"Friday night, Navy payday, and it's warm. What do you think?" Mitch said without looking at Jake.

"Oh, well yeah. I guess, I mean, yeah." Jake felt that Mitch was trying to be a hard guy. They were almost the same age. 'Big deal'. Silence seemed a good idea. And for the next half-hour they drove the beat without a word.

Downtown Long Beach was a ten-square-block area made up of

bars and jewelry stores and pawnshops and locker clubs, all catering to the fleet. Long Beach was a Navy town and the fleet was in. At one point Mitch pulled behind a cab and beeped the horn. The cab pulled over and Mitch got out of the black-and-white. He directed Jake to stay put while he walked to the driver's side window and stood talking with the cabby. After a few minutes he got back into the car.

"What did he do wrong?" Jake asked.

"Nothing," Mitch answered. He pulled into an alley, cruising slowly, looking at the rear entrances of the various businesses without saying anything else. Jake was feeling a little resentful of the silence. He picked up the hot sheet and began studying the stolen car list, deciding it was going to be a long night. After ten minutes or so, Mitch broke the silence.

"Do you like hot dogs?"

"Hot dogs?" Jake asked, trying to understand the hidden meaning to Mitch's question. 'Is he trying to find out what kind of cop I expect to be?' Jake wondered. He'd heard in the Academy that Mitch was known as a bit of a hot dog by some of the guys on the job.

"Yeah, you know, frankfurters? In a bun, with mustard, catsup? Maybe chili or relish? Are you hungry? I wanna grab something to eat before we get a call," Mitch said, looking quizzically at Jake.

"Oh, sure. That'll be great," Jake answered.

A minute later they pulled into the parking lot of a small restaurant built to look like a trolley car with a neon sign proclaiming itself to be "The Hot Dog Show." They ordered food, a tuna sandwich for Jake and two chilidogs and a coke for Mitch. They took them back out to the car and ate in silence, listening to the radio squawking intermittently.

"Okay," Mitch said as he finished is second hot dog. "I'm going to give you my rookie speech. I will not take it personally if you don't want to work with me again, and please believe me, for the next few minutes anything you have to say will go no further than this car. Okay?"

Jake nodded his understanding. Mitch began.

"This job's a lot different than what they told you in the Academy. Some of the old timers tell you to forget everything you learned there. That's not true. However, I don't think they tell you that a lot of police work is bluff and a lot of times, sixth sense. You'll see as time goes by. Now, the safe way to not get in trouble is to get a quiet beat and do as little as possible. There are a lot of good guys that choose that way and that's just fine. I know what kind of reputation I have and some of it's true. I like action and it's great fun catching the bad guys and all that stuff. But I do get into, ah, situations sometimes that are a little hard to explain."

Mitch looked at Jake to see if he was paying attention. Jake nodded and Mitch continued.

"Look, I asked about you. A couple of your instructors say you are a good candidate to make a fine officer. Working with me is a little risky, but I think it's more fun than the safe way and maybe you'll learn a little quicker. A couple of rules: nobody gets hit when they're cuffed, never get on the take, and no pussy parties."

"Pussy parties?" Jake interrupted.

"Yeah. Some of the guys got nothing better to do. They like to sneak up on kids necking in their cars so they can see a little young stuff. It's a waste of time and a little weird. I guess they get their jollies that way. As far as free smokes and coffee, that's okay. It makes the storekeepers feel they're getting special treatment. I give the smokes to the winos and some of the other street people. It pays off in the long run." Mitch stared at Jake. "And cabbies. Try not to write them tickets. They are a great source of info, and if they see you jammed up they'll call in, just like the carnies down on the Pike. Anyway, when I come to work, I work. Assholes go to jail and the crooks know I'm out there. That's it. What do you think?"

Jake sat there for a minute thinking.

"Yeah, I'd like to work with you." Jake relaxed. It felt right. There were times over the next few months when Jake would question that decision; however, not often.

Mitch grinned, and as he pulled the unit car out of the parking lot he said, "Good," slapping the steering wheel. "Let's go fight crime. There's more, but you'll learn."

That first night on duty they made a couple of misdemeanor arrests and recovered a stolen car with two teenage joy riders inside. The next shift Mitch told Jake to take the wheel.

*****

It rained all day and finally stopped an hour or so before Mitch and Jake began their third night on duty together.

Fog had replaced the rain and Mitch figured a quiet shift, a few burglar alarms set off by the moisture and maybe a traffic accident report. He gave Jake a quick once over. Jake had a presence, an appearance of self-assuredness. There was a look in Jake's eyes of no nonsense. He wore his uniform comfortably, unlike most of the new officers who took some time to get used to the blue. An ever present toothpick, a habit he picked up when he quit smoking, was in the corner of his mouth.

Before they settled in to their assigned police car, Jake riding shotgun, checked the twelve-gauge Winchester and put it in the rack. He handled the weapon with familiarity, another good sign to Mitch. They left the police lot and drove along the quiet streets of downtown. The first few days of two new partners working together is always spent sizing each other up, finding common ground and getting to know each other. This is especially important when one of the partners is brand new. It didn't take long for Mitch to decide Jake was OK. Someone he would be comfortable with and able to count on in any situation. Up until ten thirty, the evening progressed as Mitch had thought it would, quiet.

The LA River parallels the Long Beach Freeway and runs into the Pacific Ocean. It is really a cemented over flood control. The river/flood control was full, the surface slick and brown with tan foam swirling in the racing currents. The normal debris, tree branches, trash from city streets dumped by uncaring citizens, old furniture and once in awhile a refrigerator or stove went crazily bobbing along. The water moved swiftly, fed by the cities above Long Beach all the way to the mountains.

"Whoa! Hold it!" Jake's voice tense. Mitch hit the brakes and the black and white slid to a halt at the Willow Street overpass. Jake had spotted a bicycle lying on the levee that the kids rode on. The little headlight was on, barely discernible in the fog. Under the circumstances, an excellent observation by Jake.

In the water, the twelve-year-old girl was clinging to a tree limb that had lodged against the abutment of the Willow Street Bridge. The cold current pulled at her and debris threatened to break loose her fragile grip. She was at least twenty feet from the safety of the cement embankment. Too far for either Mitch or Jake to swim to her rescue, given the strength of the fast moving water.

Jake turned and began sprinting up the levee away from the

exhausted little girl. As he ran he began pulling off his gear .About a hundred feet upriver he plunged into the icy water. Swimming hard and being carried along by the current, Jake managed to reach the child. Once he had her, he clung to the trash and debris gathered at the cement column of the bridge. Mitch clambered back on to the roadway and radioed the situation to communications, requesting help. Time was of the essence, it wouldn't take long for the cold water to sap Jake's strength. It was a toss up as to whether the fire department would arrive before the girl and Jake were swept away.

Then one of those lucky quirks that happen once in awhile occurred. A tow truck came driving over the Willow Street Bridge. Mitch jumped in front of it and quickly explained what was going on to the driver. He immediately got the truck backed up just above Jake and the young girl.

Mitch took off his gun belt and hooked the tow cable around his waist and the driver of the truck lowered him to the water and the two exhausted people. Fighting the strong current Jake and Mitch managed to get the semiconscious girl between them and signaled the tow truck driver to pull them up.

The fire department ambulance took the little girl to the hospital where she would be treated for exposure and subsequently make a full recovery. The two wet officers stood on the bridge staring at each other breathing hard from the exertion. Mitch smiled and said:

"If your uniform's a little too large, it would be a lot easier to have it tailored than shrink it like this." Jake smiled back; he got it.

It was an hour before they got into dry uniforms back at the station and by then their shift was over. They had coffee together and talked late into the night.

The next afternoon Mitch called the watch commander.

"Hi Lieutenant, Mitch Thacker here. Gotta' a request. I'd like to keep Jake Reed in the unit. He's got everything it takes to make it." A pause and, "Thanks, we'll do some good work for you sir." Mitch hung up with a big smile.

Three months and a little more after Jake first sat in a police car with Mitch, Moses Brinkers put his arm around his son, Amos, and said, "C'mon, boy. It's time to go to work."

Moses was a powerful man and as gentle as he was big. His parents had been sharecroppers and Moses had worked hard all his sixty-eight years. His head was almost devoid of hair except for a fringe of grizzly gray above his ears, but his eyes were clear and his six-foot, three-inch frame was muscled with years of hard work.

It was eleven-thirty in the evening and Amos was sleepy and cranky. Since losing his wife almost twenty years ago, Moses had devoted his life to caring for his son. Amos was as large as his father, forty-eight years old, and mentally retarded. He loved animals and his toy trucks.

Father and son walked down the drive of the neat yellow frame house that Amos proudly kept in good repair. He stopped and pulled a weed from the flowers that grew along the edge of the gravel driveway. The old delivery van was parked in front of the house. Moses had purchased the van from a local bakery. He'd painted it battleship gray and proudly put his company name in gold letters on the sides. "Brinkers," and in smaller letters underneath, "and Son." For years the father and son had cleaned the parking lots of small malls and markets, after closing time. The work suited them both. Moses liked the independence, and the methodical pushing of the wide broom across the asphalt satisfied the simple mind of his son.

At about the same time Moses woke his son, six men walked out of the Garden Club in Bell Gardens. About ten miles up the 710 Freeway from Long Beach, Bell Gardens was a rough town. Driving around Bell Gardens at night, or even during the day for that matter, could be an exciting experience. The criminal element seemed drawn to the sleazy saloons, cheap hotels and less-than-efficient police force. If one wanted to live dangerously, Bell Gardens would certainly satisfy the need for a thrill or two.

The six men climbed into a dull yellow Chevy station wagon, four in the back and two in front. Snake started the car.

"Okay boys, let's go. In an hour we'll all be in fat city." The driver spoke from the corner of his mouth; a trait he had picked up from a movie star he thought was especially good at being a tough guy. By default, he was the leader of the group--a gang of small time thugs that, collectively, couldn't muster up a three-digit IQ score. To toughen his image, he occasionally made reference to someone he had killed with a crossbow and told his cohorts that he was wanted in another state. In fact, there was a warrant for his arrest in Florida on a wife-beating charge. Small and wiry, he sported a thin black goatee that he often stroked while speaking to others.

All of them had, at one time or another, been in jail for

something, usually minor offenses. Now they were about to try the big time. Snake, a name the leader liked to be called, had planned the heist for almost a week. One of the gang had stolen the station wagon the night before. The rest of the gang had protested loudly about the six-cylinder, worn-out getaway vehicle, but Snake had decided the car would work out just fine, reasoning that the cops wouldn't figure it as suspicious. They pulled onto the 710, the Long Beach Freeway heading south. There were patches of fog. The traffic was light.

"Check your pieces, men," Snake said in the manliest voice he could muster. "These armored car guys are always ready to shoot it out." His crew nervously pulled out two pistols and one old shotgun and checked to make sure they were all loaded. As they drove south, Snake pondered his plan.

Mitch stretched and yawned, banging his knee on the shotgun bracket.

"Yow! Damn thing. Why'd they mount this under the dash? Pipe smoking engineers never have to use what they design. Shit!" he said, rubbing the knee vigorously. He had been grousing for the last two hours. Jake smiled to himself. After working together for three months he knew his partner's idiosyncrasies pretty well. Tuesday night. Their two days off would follow and Mitch had confided once that he didn't like his days off and would rather be working.

"Well, three more hours and we'll be done for the night. What are you doing tomorrow?" Jake said, needling his partner. Mitch stared at his partner, who focused on driving the car.

"Jeez, what a boring night," Mitch said, not rising to the bait. They had only made two traffic stops all evening and hadn't had a call. They'd spent the whole shift cruising their beat downtown. Even the bars seemed to be almost empty.

"It's the twelfth. Payday's three days away," Jake said, referring to Navy paydays that fell on the first and fifteenth of each month. Then things always got busy.

"Yeah, Friday." Mitch brightened perceptively.

Jake turned left onto Broadway and headed east towards one end of their beat. At Lime Avenue and Broadway there was a Safeway grocery store. At the far end of the parking lot was a nightspot, Henry's Whip, a favorite spot for the downtown crowd. The bartenders, the hookers, hotel employees, bookies and assorted others who worked the nighttime all gathered at Henry's Whip. Generous drinks and a loud jukebox seemed to be the main attractions. That, and a pizza joint across the street that stayed open until three or three-thirty in the morning.

It was a few minutes after twelve. Mitch waved to the Safeway manager as he pulled out of the darkened parking lot. The unit car crawled by Henry's Whip and both officers looked at the nearly empty lot.

"Even the Whip's quiet," Mitch said, staring out the window. Jake nodded and turned left, heading up Alamitos Avenue--a wide street with small businesses and run-down apartment houses running from the ocean all the way to the city limits. Half the yellow streetlights were burned out and the few trees along the sidewalks were half dead, their leaves brown and branches hanging listlessly. Two blocks up from Broadway the police cruiser and the station wagon passed each other.

"Don't look back!" Snake snapped. "The cops. What are they doing? Did ya' see them?" Two of the men in the back seat, startled by the police car, had in fact turned and stared at it. They jerked their heads forward at Snake's command. One of the men sitting in the middle sank down in his seat and looked out the back window of the car.

"Nothin'. They ain't doin' nothin'," he whispered. "Just drivin' down the street." He watched the taillights grow smaller as Snake turned onto Broadway.

"Jake, turn right at the next street, cut your lights and make a U-turn," Mitch ordered.

"What's up?" Jake said, coming alert to the sound of his partner's voice.

"That wagon that just went by." Mitch was turned in the seat, staring back down the street.

"Wait! They just turned right onto Broadway. Hang a left and go over to Atlantic. We'll come in behind them on Broadway."

Jake swung the police car smoothly onto the side street, turned off the lights and accelerated.

"Five or six guys in that wagon," Mitch said. "Just didn't look right. They don't belong in that car. When we catch up to them, just cruise along behind them for a while, okay?"

Jake nodded and turned left, heading down Atlantic towards Broadway. Both officers looked ahead, trying to spot the yellow wagon crossing the intersection, but the car didn't appear.

"Where the hell did they go?" Mitch said. "Punch it. They must have already cleared the signal."

When the black-and-white got to Broadway a moment later, both partners stared up and down the street, trying to see the car. The street was empty. They sat there at the intersection and looked in all four directions. Nothing. It was twelve-thirty and there wasn't a car on the street. Mitch picked up the mic.

"Unit 32..."

"32, go ahead." The dispatcher's voice came back over the radio immediately.

"32, a good shake, early model Chevy wagon, light color. Last seen west on Broadway at Alamitos about four minutes ago. Five or six white males, probably mid-twenties. 10-4?" Mitch said into the mic.

The dispatcher acknowledged and put the description over the air to all units immediately.

"Pull over here and let's just sit for a while," Mitch said, reaching over and turning down the volume of the radio and lowering the window. They sat there looking and listening. Mitch had shown Jake early on that sounds were too often ignored by cops.

"Look at it this way," he'd said. "Good hunters are always quiet."

What happened next would be a hot topic of conversation for years afterwards--in the Academy, in squad cars and in cop bars. It would form an iron bond between Jake and Mitch---the kind that occurs from time to time between cops.

The station wagon was parked in the shadows at one end of the mottled yellow Safeway building. Moses and Amos had finished cleaning the lot and were walking towards the old bread truck. Amos was carrying an old canvas sack filled with bottles and cans collected from the trash. They would be turned into cash in the morning for spending money.

As the father and son neared the truck, Snake and his gang jumped from the shadows and Snake shouted, "Drop the cash. Get flat on the ground, you mother-fuckers, or we'll drill you full of holes!" Another phrase he had picked up from the movies, no doubt.

Snake held the old shotgun in a menacing position, pointed at the two men. They stopped, bewildered by these crazy white men screaming at them. Snake moved in and pushed the barrel of the gun against Moses' stomach.

"Down! Get on the ground, you old fuck!" Snake was getting braver. The drinks they had consumed before beginning their venture helped. Moses did not like being told what to do. Never had.

Reflexively, he grabbed the barrel of the shotgun with his left hand and pushed it aside. Simultaneously he took Snake by the throat with his powerful right hand, squeezing mightily. The shotgun discharged, sending buckshot into the front tire of the Chevy that one of the gang had driven out from the shadows.

Jake and Mitch both jumped at the sound of the shotgun.

"Parking lot. It came from the parking lot!" Jake shouted, putting the police car in gear and squealing around the corner, bouncing over the curb and into the lot. Both officers saw Moses and Snake in a wild dance, their shadows eerily jumping from one pool of light cast from the overhead lights to the next. Moses was swinging Snake around, trying to wrest the shotgun away from him. Snake, in turn, was frantically trying to hold onto the gun and breathe at the same time. Amos was crying loudly, jumping up and down with fear for his father and not understanding what these white men were doing.

Snake finally broke loose from Moses' grip and screamed for his crime cohorts to shoot. At the same time, the police car jumped the curb and accelerated towards the group. Snake, of course, meant for them to shoot Moses. However, seeing the headlights of the police car heading at them, they assumed he meant the black-and-white and opened fire. One round went through the windshield of the police unit and imbedded itself in the front seat between the two officers. Several other rounds were later found in the grill.

"Holy shit! Run 'em down. Don't hit the black guy!" Mitch shouted, grabbing the twelve-gauge riot gun from its rack. Jake floored the accelerator and pulled slightly to the right. The right front fender caught two of the suspects and they fell backwards and bounced off the side of the yellow get-away-car. As the unit car came to a stop, Mitch rolled out the passenger side, and Jake, drawing his weapon, jumped from the driver's seat.

Moses turned his head as Jake fired one round at the suspects. Snake pulled the shotgun free and turned to fire at the police officers. He fired too soon, however, and Amos, without a sound, slammed to the asphalt parking lot and lay there, not moving. Mitch was pointing the riot gun at the other three men, one was firing wildly in the general direction of the police car. Before Jake could return fire, Snake's second shot caught Mitch in the left side, lifting him in the air and dropping him to the pavement.

For Jake, everything went into slow motion. Slow motion, just as

Mitch had told him it would if he ever found himself in a gunfight. With a cold, deliberate stance he brought his weapon around and fired twice at the man who had shot his partner. Snake, hit twice in the chest, fell backwards into the van that he thought was a Brink's armored truck. He died amidst the mops and brooms. A gallon of floor wax tipped over on one of the shelves and the lumpy fluid poured down onto his face as he gasped his last breath.

Mitch, still conscious, rolled over and managed to fire one round from the riot gun, catching one of the standing suspects in the knees. At such close range, the damage from the double-ought pellets was considerable. Four of the pellets hit the suspect's right leg, almost tearing it off. The other three lead pellets hit the left leg at the kneecap, destroying it. The scream from the man gave his two companions a start, and the one with the gun stopped firing to look at him. Jake calmly fired his last four rounds and both men dropped to the ground. One of the two would survive.

Jake ran to his fallen partner. Mitch was ashen and moaning with pain. "How bad? How bad is it?" Jake knelt by Mitch, who slowly shook his head.

"Hurts. My arm and chest. Get some help. See how the victim is."

Jake looked over to Moses, who was kneeling next to his son and moaning, big tears coursing down his cheeks. He ran to the police car and got on the radio. "Citizen shot, officer needs help," he exclaimed. "Officer down." He followed that with his location and then ran back to Mitch.

Unit cars began arriving, followed closely by the paramedics.

Soon the parking lot was filled with emergency units, the red lights flashing, reflecting against the pale yellow of the building. Jake stood beside the gurney as the uniformed medics loaded Mitch and Amos into the ambulance. Mitch smiled a weak smile and winked as the gurney slid forward. "Good. You did a good job, partner. Thank you."

Snake had used a worn-out old twenty-gauge shotgun loaded with equally old, worn-out birdshot. Neither Amos nor Mitch suffered any permanent injuries.

Snake, on the other hand, had died within moments of his injuries. The two that were slammed against the car survived and served long sentences for armed robbery and murder. If anyone dies during the commission of a felony, that's murder in the first degree. The fellow that survived Jake's bullets was more than happy to be a witness for the prosecution against his surviving cohorts.

Three weeks later Mitch was back on duty. He and Jake climbed into the unit car and Mitch checked them in with the dispatcher. Twenty minutes later, without looking over at his partner, Mitch asked, "Miss me?"

“It was a living hell without you, Mitch.”

"Yeah, yeah, let's go get a hot dog."

CHAPTER 3

Jake and Mitch worked a unit together for a year and a half. They had great fun as well as some sad and stressful times. Two young cops all bushy tailed and feeling invincible. The brass liked them working together. Good arrests and clean beats with minimal amount of heat from the public.

One night after shift, Mitch put his arm around Jake's shoulder as they walked to their personal cars in the parking lot next door to the station.

"Well, partner, this Friday is the first of the month."

"Yeah, and?" Jake said looking at his friend and partner with a raised eyebrow and shifting the ever present toothpick from one side of his mouth to the other.

"I told the 'Sarge' to detail you to Unit Seven. I'll be working with Schmeling from now on."

"What the hell! What's your thinking? We're doing a great job together." Jake stepped back from Mitch, spitting out his toothpick.
They stood there facing each other.

"Well, we are. Good police work, good team. That's the problem.

Nothing more I can show you. You gotta' work with some of the other guys. Learn from them. Hell, we'll work together again. You're going to turn out to be the best cop on the beat, wait and see." Mitch gave him a thumbs up and turned and walked to his car before Jake could mount an argument.

Outside of cop circles, most cops don't talk much about the dark side of the job. They all recognize it, by some unwritten rule or tradition something limits any real sentiment to light comment. Sometimes the bitter reality of the job swallows up one of them and serves as a harsh reminder to the rest that they're vulnerable, too.

Police work, especially in a big city, is one long roller coaster ride of exhilarating ups and depressing downs that wind you up and let you off at the end of your watch. Slowing down the mental and emotional machinery enough to relax and forget about the previous eight or so hours becomes a real challenge. Depending on one's mind set, it may mean going home and thrilling the little woman with tales of your exploits, going to a bar on the way home and having a few with the boys, or engaging in some other mind-expanding exercise. To be sure, some do just go home and go to bed, but, for at least the first few years on the job, most cops are far too wound up for that. And when it came to unwinding, Mitch, unfortunately, wrote the book. In one rather momentous six-month period, Mitch's exploits became the stuff of legend as he plodded steadfastly down his own personal path to self destruction, trying to free himself from the grasp of a demon that was squeezing the life out of him.

Jake had been told that when Mitch came on the job the consensus among his academy classmates was that he had what it took to be the Chief of Police someday. Mitch, at 6-foot, 3-inches, steely blue eyes, black curly hair and an imposing physical appearance, was a natural athlete. He was good looking and had the personality and charm the rest of his peers admired and resented all at the same time. Most of the carhops and waitresses on his beat had the 'hots' for him, and, within reason, he tried his best to accommodate them, at least the good-looking ones.

Mitch was more than just another pretty face, however. He was college educated at a time when most cops weren't, and his interests revealed something of a serious side. He was actually interested in the more genteel aspects of life: art, literature, music, classical of all things. He played tennis avidly, had close friends at the local yacht club with whom he sailed regularly and he played golf as well. In other words, Mitch was not your average cop. At least not in the beginning. In fact, it was a bit of a mystery why he had become a cop at all. A real mystery man, Jake thought.

After breezing his way through the Academy picking up the basics of the job, Mitch went to work in a radio car on the "late three" shift. Before very long it was apparent to his partners and supervisors alike that Mitch had a natural talent for police work. His instincts and mental acuity seemed always to put him in the right place at the right time. A lot of criminals went to jail courtesy of Mitch, and because of his rather imposing, self-confident appearance, not many put up much of a struggle.

There were exceptions. One morning about 1:00 a.m. Mitch and Jake got a hot call to respond to a gay bar, aptly named "Just Us Girls," on the north side of their area. The radio operator advised them an assault was in progress. However, by the time they got there the situation had deteriorated into an attempted murder by a notorious homosexual baiter named Bobby "Boots" Trask.

Trask was aptly nicknamed. He wore heavy leather boots that were studded around the soles with nail heads. "Boots" enjoyed dropkicking people, especially homosexuals who objected to his crass remarks. He was reputedly able to kick an average-sized man in the face while standing flat footed in front of him. It was this particular talent that "Boots" had just demonstrated when Mitch and Jake walked in the front door of the bar.

"Boots" was heading for the door and apparently still flush with success when he decided to demonstrate just one more time how deftly he could kick. Mitch, who was quicker and a whole lot 'defter', caught Trask's boot in mid air and turned it 90 degrees to the right. Unfortunately for "Boots," the rest of his body was going 90 degrees to the left at the time. His agonized scream muffled the sound of his knee dislocating. The spontaneous cheers from the bar's patrons helped, too. Trask went limping off to prison and Mitch became something of a hero to the gay community. A few of them even asked him out, Jake recalled.

Mitch and Jake worked the hottest areas in the city. They were assigned to a radio car that only responded to hot calls rather than the more mundane report calls, family beefs and the like. Mitch thrived on the excitement and anticipation of dangerous confrontations with all manner of criminals. He loved what he was doing and did it as well as any cop on the job. Commendations were routine, and because he was highly disciplined, Mitch rarely required any supervisory attention. Citizens he came in contact with never had anything but praise for his conduct.

Then one night it all began to come apart. Mitch had been in court all day for the third day in a row and he was dog-tired, actually looking forward to the end of his shift. It had been an unusually quiet night when the radio burst forth with a call:

"Burglar there now, on the roof." The location, an industrial building was not far from where they were. Mitch, working a one man car, acknowledged the call and began to roll. Jake who was in a sister unit, made a U-turn and took off Code 2, get there as quick as you can with no lights and siren. When they got within a block of the location, Jake killed the lights, idled up to the front of the building and saw Mitch at the other end of the building. Mitch gave Jake thumbs up and cradling the riot gun in the crook of his arm, disappeared around the corner into the darkness of an adjoining alley. Jake went to the rear of the building and deployed at the diagonal corner so they could watch all four sides of the building until another unit arrived. Jake and Mitch stood quietly in the dark, listening for any indication of activity. While in this position, Mitch heard the sound of breaking wood coming from above him and concluded that someone was up there, probably trying to get into the building through the roof. Mitch quickly moved to the rear of the building and waved at Jake to get his attention. He then pointed to the roof and Jake nodded, indicating he understood. Mitch returned to the front of the building to await the next unit.

Standing alone in the dark, late at night, in a deserted industrial area waiting for something to happen makes the best cop a little nervous. When you realize there is someone else in your immediate vicinity, it adds to the tension, especially if they're involved in criminal activity and may be armed. Mitch, who controlled his anxiety as well as anyone, listened while the activity on the roof continued on and off for several minutes. Then another black-and-white pulled up with the lights off and two more cops jumped out and deployed to cover the rest of the building.

When another unit arrived and the building was well covered, Jake began climbing a fire escape ladder to get a look at the roof. By now the burglar sensed something was amiss and crept towards the edge of the roof to get a look. Jake spotted him first and shouted "He's on the roof." All the cops on the ground looked up and waited, including Mitch. The burglar, crowbar in hand, took off on a dead run across the roof, directly away from Jake, and as he got to the opposite edge he leapt for the roof of the adjacent building, a distance of about six feet. The burglar's leap was almost directly above Mitch, who reflexively swiveled his shotgun up from his hip and fired one round, hitting the burglar in mid air and blowing him twenty feet down the passageway between the two buildings. He was dead when he hit the ground.

There was complete silence for several seconds, then a lot of running and shouting before everyone figured out what had happened and determined that none of the cops at the scene had been shot. One cop went to his patrol car and requested an ambulance and a supervisor, while two others approached the burglar and handcuffed him--a standard procedure. Then Mitch walked up and looked down at the suspect. He knew immediately that the burglar was dead and in all probability he would have been able to deal with it, except for the fact that the burglar appeared to be about sixteen years old. As it turned out, he was fourteen.

The climate at a police shooting, especially one at which there has been a hit, is a complex mix of emotions. Cops, by the very nature of their job, are generally involved in the saving of lives, not taking them. Protection of the weak and helpless is the essence of the job. It helps to keep things in balance and offsets all the negative experiences that cops undergo every day. At the same time, however, and consistent with a desire to protect, is an equally strong wish on the part of many cops to test their manliness by confronting a dangerous, armed suspect and calmly shooting it out with him, *ala* Wyatt Earp. Maturity and time on the job tend to diminish this 'cowboy' mentality.

Mitch was not like a lot of other cops. Jake thought it highly unlikely that Mitch ever harbored any strong desire to get in a shooting. When he found himself in a confrontation with the armed suspect who shot Amos Brinker and himself, Mitch acquitted himself well. But shootings were not the career experience Mitch routinely longed for.

As Mitch stood there staring at the burglar, someone took the shotgun from his hand. Jake walked up and asked Mitch if he was all right, and Mitch nodded. One young cop with all of two months on the job and a 'ghetto commando' attitude slapped Mitch on the back and said, "Nice shot." Mitch looked at him and said nothing. The kid walked off.

Mitch appeared calm and in control; however, his silence and the look of desperation in his eyes told another story. Mitch looked scared to death. At that point, Jake thought Mitch may have felt he had started a sequence of events that would inevitably lead to a terrible end. Ambulances, supervisors and the news media all began arriving at the scene. After officially declaring the burglar dead, the paramedics covered him up and left. The coroner was notified to come and get him. Detectives arrived at the scene and tried to identify the body. They found a variety of papers in the cheap plastic wallet he had in his pocket, including an ID card from a local high school. They then set out to notify the parents, not a pleasant task.

In the meantime, Mitch had been allowed to stand around and hear a variety of remarks, some sympathetic and some tinged with the black humor of cops trying to sustain a facade of cold indifference to death. Mercifully, Mitch was finally taken to the station by a sergeant who, though woefully unqualified to do so, nevertheless tried to provide Mitch with advice on how to deal with the shooting. None of it, of course, helped. After writing a report on the sequence of events leading up to the death of the young burglar, Mitch was given a pat on the back, reminded that burglary was a felony in California and the Penal Code said it was okay to shoot felons. None of that helped a bit of course. Mitch was sent home, alone, to work it out for himself.

The following day two detectives from the burglary unit conducted a follow-up investigation at the shooting scene and then went to Mitch's apartment to interview him. After talking to Mitch briefly about the incident, they told him it looked like a good shooting to them and left. 'Good' simply meant that circumstances of the incident were within the legal constraints of the Penal Code. It didn't alter Mitch's dark view of the matter--a fact that became stunningly apparent as time passed.

Mitch had indelibly imprinted an image in his mind of the fourteen-year-old boy landing in a dead heap at his feet, and nothing would erase it. From that point on, Mitch was never the same. For the first few months following the shooting, he confined his increasingly negative behavior to his off-duty time. After-work drinking bouts with anyone willing to accompany him, or alone if necessary, became the norm. He'd drink until the bar closed, drink on the way home, and continue until unconscious. Along with the drinking came a variety of interesting capers that most of his fellow cops thought were hilarious, and Mitch, who clearly didn't seem to care much any more, concurred.

One night Mitch was sitting in a saloon and well on his way to booze oblivion when he realized that the holster with his two inch .38 revolvers in it had slipped around to the small of his back. He reached around to pull it back and accidentally fired a round, hitting himself in the left buttock. Mitch remained seated on the barstool, insisting the bullet missed him and demanding another drink. After several minutes, one of the barmaids noticed a puddle of blood on the floor below Mitch's stool. He was loaded into the bartender's car and driven to the hospital where the bullet was removed and given to Mitch as a souvenir. Everyone, including Mitch, laughed like hell over that one. His exploits became the hot topic in every roll call as one story after another was recounted, more often than not with Mitch sitting there laughing along with everyone else.

Soon, Mitch began screwing up on duty. It really wasn't hard to understand why, considering his usual hangover condition and deteriorating pe. Mitch drifted away from his previous recreational pursuits and most of the friends he had enjoyed. He spent most of his off-duty time at home and drunk, except for those rare occasions when he would stay sober for a few days as though he was trying to help himself. A few days were about the best he could do, however, and then he was back to the routine. The remarkable thing about it all was that, although everybody saw Mitch self destructing, no one really tried to help him. Most guys took the position that he was a big boy and he could take care of himself. He was tough. After all, he was a cop and, well, if he wanted to become a buffoon, what the hell, it was his business.

Jake had thought about that often. He and Mitch had been close. Not just partners but friends. When Mitch began to lose it, Jake thought, he should have tried harder to help him. Mitch told him on a number of occasions that he didn't want or need any help. Jake took him at his word, but realized later that, in spite of what Mitch wanted, he should have pressed the issue. Jake thought about that a lot over the years and he knew why he hadn't tried harder to help Mitch. Jake realized that his lack of compassion had come from his own encounters with an alcoholic father who dumped a lot of crap on him during the course of his adolescence. His old man had let him down with regularity, always because he was boozed up. Ugly scenes that were burned into Jake's memory, capped off with a drive across country in a broken-down Ford with a shot wheel bearing and brakes that barely worked. With the old man drunk in the back seat, Jake drove 2,100 miles to his grandparents' home. His father was institutionalized, and Jake, an emotional wreck at the age of fifteen, lacked any sympathy for people who couldn't control their cravings. Those childhood memories had made him unbending on the issue. If he'd only known then what he knew now, Jake thought.

Minor screw-ups at work became the norm for Mitch as he went through the motions. He was obviously no longer interested in what he was doing but apparently was afraid to let it go. Mitch, always so independent, had now come to desperately need the department and his brother officers. As he plodded along, most of his mistakes were covered by his partners, or in some cases, his supervisor. They all believed they were doing the right thing. Inevitably, the screw-ups got to be big things--too big to cover.

Finally, Mitch was taken out of the field and assigned to the booking desk because somebody thought it would be a good idea to watch him a little closer. There was a sergeant at the booking desk virtually all the time. That job worked out well for Mitch, at least for a while. Then one night a previously undetected facet of Mitch's personality, probably unleashed by the trauma of the shooting and the subsequent drinking, revealed itself. A motor cop brought in a guy he'd originally stopped for jaywalking. Rather than sign the ticket, the arrestee had refused and then gotten indignant, threatening to kick the motor cop's ass "all over the street." Two more cops happened by at the time and helped get the guy under control and transported to the station for booking. After they explained what they had to the booking sergeant, he approved the booking. Mitch stood nearby, listening. Based on what he heard, he formed an immediate dislike for the arrestee who was getting more obnoxious by the minute. As he stood facing Mitch across the booking counter he kept up a steady flow of insults about small-time cops in general and Mitch in particular. Seeing that he was getting to Mitch, he turned up the volume and got nastier, finally bragging that he'd done "hard time" in state prison for "kicking the shit out of a cop." That did it! In an instant Mitch was over the counter and in one punch laid the guy out on the floor. Mitch's face was ashen with rage as he began to alternately kick and punch the semi-conscious arrestee, all the time shouting, "You think you're bad? You think you're bad?" It must have been a rhetorical question because Mitch wasn't waiting for the answer as he advised the guy that he, Mitch, was the baddest son of a bitch this guy was ever going to meet. Clearly completely out of control, Mitch was restrained by a couple of other cops who were now more than satisfied that the con got the ass kicking he richly deserved. Mitch finally calmed down about the time the sergeant, who'd excused himself to go to the head, returned to the booking desk. He was briefed on how Mitch was viciously attacked by the con that then had to be forcibly restrained.

This little event, though not deemed a matter worthy of discipline or perhaps a little counseling, did lead to Mitch being reassigned to the graveyard shift. His reputation obviously preceded him because he was immediately assigned to a one-man foot beat. The sergeant in charge of the foot beats told Mitch in no uncertain terms that all he wanted him to do was walk back and forth on his beat all night and not do any police work. The second night out, Mitch got particularly annoyed at that mandate and decided to write a parking ticket, a relatively minor act of defiance. Considering how things had been going for Mitch the past few months, however, he probably should have left well enough alone. The car he ticketed belonged to the wife of the Mayor who, upon discovering the ticket, drove directly to the station to dispose of it. After appeasing her and canceling the ticket, the foot beat sergeant left the station to find Mitch and determine why he was doing police work. When he finally found him, Mitch was sitting in the Star Café, an all night hamburger joint that catered to the less affluent. He was drinking coffee and talking to the cook, John, an old wino who was temporarily on the wagon. The sergeant, a notoriously unsympathetic sort named Huber, asked Mitch to step outside so he could speak to him. Mitch sensed immediately that he was not about to be commended for any recent accomplishments and concluded that any one of a number of recent screw-ups must have come to the good sergeant's attention. Looking as contrite as possible, Mitch stood there waiting to get his ass chewed out. However, when Huber revealed the source of his annoyance, Mitch got indignant. He argued that if he couldn't do any real police work he ought to at least be allowed to write a ticket once in a while. Anyway, how was he supposed to know the car belonged to the Mayor's wife? Mitch's protests fell on deaf ears, however, as Huber stood listening impassively. When Mitch was finished Huber informed him that since his beat assignment wasn't providing him sufficient job satisfaction, he would be given an additional daily task. Maxine!

Of all the things the cops on the graveyard shift didn't like, Maxine duty was, by far, the thing they didn't like the most. Maxine was the Chief's secretary and it was generally believed that she had all the power the Chief had, but that she was more likely to use it. It was generally believed that Maxine was at least 75 years old. There were more than a few cops who were totally convinced that she was the Chief's mother and that she was using her maiden name to conceal the fact. There was an equal number who were certain she wasn't the Chief's mother, but rather his mistress. He simply had a fetish for old, wrinkled women. There was a small group of sickos who jokingly suggested she was one and the same.

In any event, for as long as anyone could remember a police car had to go to Maxine's house each weekday morning at 8:30, pick her up and drive her to the station. This wouldn't have been a particularly difficult task under normal circumstances. But it wasn't simply a matter of pulling up in front of her house, honking the horn and waiting for Maxine to hobble out and climb into the car. No, nothing that easy.

The cop assigned the task was expected to go to the front door, announce his presence and then escort Maxine to the car, open the door and help her in. He was then expected to make small talk all the way to the station. Since things rarely went that smooth, each morning's call to Maxine's was an experience. Maxine was quite unpredictable, primarily because she had a fondness for gin which she often satisfied to excess. So, some mornings she responded to the door in fairly good shape, ready to go, pleasant and communicative. Other mornings she responded in conditions ranging from slightly hung over to blind drunk. Some mornings she didn't respond at all. Those were the worst because it meant having to go inside her house and then trying to find her. Not many cops savored the idea of finding a 75-year-old woman lying face down, much less face up, on the bed, floor or, on one occasion, curled up on top of the stereo. Waking her up was distinctly unpleasant because, embarrassed; she was generally nasty as hell. Coupled with this fact was the added delight of having to deal with three nasty little half-pint dogs that barked incessantly while dashing around the room looking for the opportunity to dart in and bite the ankle of the unsuspecting.

Once having awakened Maxine, one was required to wait while she went through the morning ablutions, a process rarely completed in less than half an hour. This meant working overtime, in addition to all the other fun. And acting pleasant on top of it all! Needless to say, avoiding Maxine duty was the preferable option.

When Mitch was assigned to Maxine duty, he was highly indignant. Everyone else on the graveyard shift was delighted as hell. Mitch griped about it for a while and then began the ritual duty grudgingly, but surprisingly efficiently. Even he could see that it wouldn't pay to get on the wrong side of Maxine, and before long he had her thoroughly charmed. Catering to her eccentricities and treating her as though she was as important as she imagined herself to be, Mitch and Maxine got on famously.

Then one morning, the Chief arrived at his office at the usual mid-morning hour and discovered that Maxine was not at her desk as usual. After asking around and learning that no one else had seen her and after phoning her house and getting no answer, the Chief suggested someone get the hell over there and find out what happened to her. The Day Watch Commander, Morton Tubbs, ever eager to please the Chief and improve his own chance of promotion, decided to handle the matter personally. When he got to Maxine's house, Tubbs found Mitch's police car parked in the driveway. He walked up to the door and was about to ring the bell when he heard the voices of Mitch and Maxine inside. They were alternately singing and laughing hysterically. The laughing followed each line of a thoroughly filthy song and it didn't take a genius to realize they were both drunk. Letting himself in, Tubbs walked into the kitchen where he discovered Mitch and Maxine sitting on the floor, whooping it up. Tubbs ordered Mitch to his feet although to accomplish that Tubbs had to help Mitch more than a little bit. Maxine, dressed in a slip and high heels, managed to struggle to her feet unassisted. She then proceeded to assail the good lieutenant with a variety of threats, not surprisingly all related to her influential position as the Chief's secretary. Ever vigilant to those things that might either help or harm his career, Tubbs decided his best course of action was to make a graceful exit and deal with Mitch later. That is precisely what he was doing when the three dogs caught sight of him and began chasing him down the hall to the living room, barking and nipping all the way. One of them got a temporary hold on the heel of one of Tubbs' shoes and it was all he could do to keep from kicking the little bastard across the room.

Needless to say, Mitch was unassigned Maxine duty and transferred to the Day Watch where Tubbs could deal with him directly. As funny as this incident seemed at the time, it was indicative of just how far Mitch had slid. The guy, who for many had epitomized the true cop in every respect, had now become a self-destructing buffoon who provided a daily dose of laughs for those former admirers. Mitch was fast approaching the time when the department's tolerance of his behavior would run out. In spite of knowing that his termination was becoming inevitable, Mitch pressed on.

On a cold day in October, Mitch finally squeezed the last drop of compassion from the department and effectively brought his career to a close. By that time, though, he really didn't give a damn about much at all. The job had only been providing him a place to be for part of the day. It disciplined him, marginally, and kept him in touch with reality, more or less. Maybe more than he wanted to be. Mitch probably didn't think about the job much or what it meant to lose it. In looking at the rest of his life, however, it's clear that Mitch's departure from the ranks of the 'thin blue line' was akin to a non-swimmer losing his life jacket while floating in the open sea.

Considering all the capers Mitch got involved in over those last few years, the one that got him fired really didn't amount to much. He showed up for work drunk. Nothing new. When one of the sergeants on the watch took exception to his condition, Mitch told him to shove it. This response from Mitch was a little out of the ordinary. Normally he was apologetic and contrite, but this time he snapped back, hostile as hell and indignant over being confronted about his condition. Given the circumstances and his past performance, Mitch's position was a little weak, to say the least. When that was pointed out to him by a couple of his brother officers as well as the sergeant, his response was about the same. After overlooking years of screw-ups and misconduct that would have gotten most people fired, the axe finally fell and Mitch found himself out on the street and without a job.

Jake didn't see or hear anything from Mitch for a very long time. He'd dropped out of sight, as they say. Then one day one of the cops on the watch told Jake he'd seen Mitch. He was part of a work crew of county jail inmates picking up trash along the freeway a few blocks from the station. Jake checked and found out Mitch had been arrested for beating the hell out of some bartender. He was given thirty days in jail.

It was shortly after Mitch's firing that Jake decided to leave Long Beach and pursue his law enforcement career with the Los Angeles Police Department. He tested and was hired a few months later.

Jake didn't give Mitch much thought as he began his career with the L.A.P.D. However, from time to time Jake would run into some old acquaintance that had recent news about him. It was always bad and generally included some jail time for something related to booze or fighting.

A time came when Jake made Sergeant and was working downtown patrol on the Day Watch. A beat cop asked for a meet with Jake near sixth and Main, almost the heart of skid row. He told Jake that there was this beat up old wino that kept telling him that he was an ex-cop who had a partner named Jake Reed. When Jake asked the patrolman what the guy looked like, the officer pointed down the street to a man leaning against the wall of a boarded up business. Jake stared at the figure for a long minute and realized it was Mitch. Jake took a deep breath and started down the sidewalk towards his old friend and partner.

It was no reunion of long lost buddies. Mitch was pathetic. His hair was dirty and stringy and hung down over his bloodshot eyes. He was barely coherent, mumbling about an old girlfriend who was coming to pick him up and take him to Palm Springs. Jake didn't think Mitch even recognized him and felt only disdain for his old partner.

As far as Jake was concerned, Mitch put himself in that condition and had only himself to blame. Reflecting back on the incident and his own strong feelings about it, Jake came to realize it wasn't really that cut and dried.

CHAPTER 4

Many years later…

The nagging ring of the phone finally awakened Jake enough to realize what was interrupting his sleep.

"Jake Reed here, speak to me," he answered.

"Lieutenant, Sgt. Holloway here, Hollywood station."

Jake's less than cordial reply, "I know where you are, Holloway," didn't seem to faze the Seargeant in the least.

"Gee, I hope I didn't wake you," Holloway responded snidely.

"No problem, pal. I had to get up to answer the phone anyway."

"I've got a homicide for you, Lieutenant."

"Tell me about it."

Holloway began to fill Jake in. "Young female, apparently raped and strangled. Up in the hills, inside her apartment. There's a patrol unit standing by. I took the liberty of notifying the homicide standby team. They're on the way and will meet you at the scene."

"Your usual competent response is, as always, impressive," Jake told Holloway. "I'm on my way. What's the address?"

Holloway replied with the address, which was up on a winding road in the Hollywood Hills. Jake thought he'd to check his map book on the way when Holloway offered him directions.

"I'll call you from the car," Jake told him and hung up. He noted the time on the bed stand clock: 6:00 a.m. 'About the time I get up anyway. At least it's not the usual middle-of-the-nighter,' Jake thought. He leaned over and kissed his wife, Edie, on the shoulder and headed down the hall to the bathroom.

After almost twenty years with the Los Angeles Police Department, eight of those as the Commanding Officer of Hollywood Detective Division, Jake was familiar with callouts, particularly in Hollywood. A quick shower and shave, and Jake was out the door. He climbed into his department vehicle, a plain color, two-door Chevy, and headed for the freeway. Once on the freeway, Jake called on the car phone and got directions to the crime scene from Holloway, who also advised him that the lead detective at the scene, David Kilgore, had requested a criminalist and a photographer--basic procedure at any homicide scene. Contrary to most cop movies, however, the coroner isn't called right away. The coroner's investigator generally wants to examine the body, move it around, take the temperature, and more and than remove it from the scene. This tends to annoy the detectives at the scene, so they simply wait to call the coroner's office until they're pretty much done.

David Kilgore was a very interesting guy. It's likely he could have promoted to the department's upper ranks had he chosen to do so. He was college educated and very bright. With 24 years on the job, he had opted instead to work homicide for the past 17 of them. Jake was glad Kilgore made that decision. He was as good as they get when it came to murder investigations. Kilgore ran the division's homicide unit. The people who worked for him respected and admired him. They jokingly refered to him as "Dr. Death." That seemed to go hand in hand with the unit's slogan, which was displayed on a large sign on the wall: "Hollywood Homicide. Our day begins when your's ends."

Jake and the Station Commander, Captain Hughes, had a few discussions about that sign. Hughes doesn't think the sign reflects an appropriate message. Cop humor is hard to explain, especially among homicide cops. Captain Hughes was a good guy, and if he pressed the issue Jake would have the sign taken down. The Captain, mostly, had left the issue alone.

After wending his way through early morning traffic that was typically Los Angeles, Jake exited the freeway and headed up into the Hollywood Hills. Thanks to Holloway's thorough directions, Jake got to the crime scene without getting lost once. The Hills being what they are, this was quite an accomplishment. He parked the police car across the street from the crime scene, got out and spoke briefly with the uniformed officer who had been assigned to keep a log of everyone who responded: who they were, what time they arrived and their assignment. This officer had also been the first one to respond to the scene. He filled Jake in on what he'd observed initially.

Jake thanked him and crossed the street, putting a fresh toothpick in his mouth.

He went up the walk and entered the open front door. The apartment was bright and airy with a wonderful view of Hollywood and the city beyond to the south. Even though it was in the throes of remodeling, the place was comfortable and livable. An old-fashioned, movie-land, Hollywood-type of place with small French doors opening out onto a small balcony. Old-fashioned swing-out windows let in a breeze that was billowing the makeshift curtains--sheets really--lightly away from the sill. Bright sun shone on the bare wood floors and equally bare walls. There was no furniture to speak of--only an old stuffed chair, some boxes, a milk crate with a television on it and one glass-fronted, old-fashioned cabinet. There were some boxes of books and a few clothes hung in the open closet. Not much else except two big, nosy, gray cats that obviously had the run of the place and were letting themselves in and out through the unscreened, open front window.

Jake looked around and spotted Kilgore standing in an adjacent room, apparently a bedroom.

"Morning, Dave."

"Hi, Jake. Victim's in here."

Jake looked the floor over thoroughly before walking across to the bedroom. As was his habit, he'd stuck both his hands in his pants pockets. He learned years ago that hands in the pockets didn't touch things that might have evidentiary value at the crime scene. He was there to observe, not conduct the investigation. As he crossed the room, he noticed some magazines scattered around which suggested the occupant wasn't the usual aspiring actress who had moved to Hollywood to try to catch a break. News magazines, architectural guides and designer periodicals all indicated to Jake that someone serious and thoughtful about life had lived here. Piled-up bills suggested things weren't going all that well. She was hopeful, ambitious, thoughtful, intelligent, loving and, now, dead.

She was lying on the floor on her stomach with her back arched and her chin resting on the edge of the bed's box spring. The mattress was pushed partially off the bed, the apparent result of a struggle. She was nude except for a silk blouse that was pulled up under her arms. A towel was wrapped tightly around her neck, and dried blood traced two ribbons from the corners of her mouth. Her face was the ashen shade of death. Her eyes were closed.

In death she had been denied her dignity--left lying exposed to the world, sexually assaulted and strangled, perhaps not in that order--by someone who crept into her home in the middle of the night. Someone who had no regard for her, for who she was, or for her plans, hopes, dreams. Someone with no interest in what she meant to those who cared for her, loved her, and needed her. One of the predators who haunt the city, opportunistically preying on those who are too trusting, too naive, unaware of the realities. Jake thought of his own daughter and the pain the young woman's death would bring to her father. A father who will have to make do with memories and tell himself she died easily and peacefully. That she didn't suffer.

She lay there as detectives, print technicians, photographers and, finally, the corner's deputy stepped over and around her trying to find some clue to identify the son-of-a-bitch who took her life, a life the department tries so hard to protect.

Then she was finally, unceremoniously, taken away.

After a brief conversation with Kilgore, Jake took one last look around for something to jump out at him--a clue, anything--and seeing nothing he left and headed for the station. The Hollywood police station, where Jake's office was located, was in the heart of tinsel town. Fifty or so detectives were assigned to the station, depending on the department's personnel situation. Detectives are the first to go when there is a shortage of people. Fill up the patrol units first and then worry about the detective positions. This policy usually resulted in several vacancies in the detective division. Clearly, the criminal element didn't sympathize with the problem.

Jake pulled into his parking space and walked into the station. Entering a detective squad room is an interesting experience. The squad room looked like the scene of a major paper explosion. Not that that condition is unusual at all. Police work is 90 percent paperwork, and cops, conditioned to this undeniable fact, develop a phobia about throwing away or otherwise losing a piece of paper that they may have to produce at some time in the future. They've all learned that the report you throw away today is the one that someone will ask you for tomorrow. So every cop's desk, in-box, out-box, top, middle and bottom desk drawer and locker is jammed with paper. All of it is, of course, critical to his or her career and likely to be kept until retirement. With that much paper around it's not surprising that a substantial amount finds its way to the floor, the top of file cabinets, window ledges, and the term *paper explosion* provides a pretty accurate description of the place. And despite several strongly worded lectures by Jake at the behest of the Station Commander, nothing seemede to change. Jake actually liked it that way, all cluttered. It's the way a squad room ought to look. That's police work.

As Jake sat down in his office to write a few notes before briefing Caption Hughes about the latest murder, his secretary, Rene, stuck her head in the door to tell him that he had a call.

"Do you know who it is?" Jake asked. She told him it was someone by the name of Mitch Thacker.

'Oh, great! Just what I need,' Jake thought to himself. 'A phone call from Mitch'. It had been years since the last time he called. He babbled incoherently in a drunken stupor about some huge criminal conspiracy he knew about. Jake didn't need it right now.

"Take his number and tell him I'll call him back." Jake told her. He was reasonably certain that in five minutes Mitch would forget he'd ever called. At least that was the outcome he hoped for. He didn't want to hear how bad his old partner had become. It saddened and angered him all at the same time. What a waste of a good man.

'Oh, well,' Jake thought, 'I've got more important things to take care of right now.'

Jake went to the Station Commander's office to brief his boss on the homicide in the Hills. The boss, Captain Ed Hughes, was a good man to work for. He understood cops and appreciated their efforts, unlike a few captains Jake had worked for over the years. Jake gave him all the details and assured him the case would get plenty of attention, despite a heavy homicide case load. They discussed a few other high-profile cases Jake's detectives were handling and then Jake returned to his office. As he walked in Rene said, "Oh, there you are. I was just going to look for you. There's a Captain Anderson from the Long Beach P.D. on the phone. He wants to talk to you."

"Okay. I'll get it in my office." Jake walked to his desk, sat down and picked up the phone. "Jake Reed. How can I help you, Captain?"

"Jake, it's Mitch Thacker. Can I talk to you for a minute?"

"I'm not sure I know who you are. The only Mitch Thacker I know probably died some time ago." Jake's voice was guarded and distant.

"No, I didn't die. Should have but didn't. It's me."

"Yeah, okay, it's you. What do you want, Mitch?"

"I'll make this short. I know you're busy. I haven't had a drink in a long time now, eight years, and I want to come by and have a cup of coffee or something," Mitch paused for a moment. "I only need about five minutes, Jake. I need to do this in person."

Mitch waited in silence.

Finally, "Be at my office tomorrow at eleven thirty. Can you do that?" There was a resigned tone to Jake's voice.

"I'll be there," Mitch answered. "Thanks, Jake."

CHAPTER 5

Jake finally got up from his desk to go home about 6:00 p.m. As he headed out of the station, he passed by the front desk and said goodnight to his two Night Watch detectives who were both busy on the phone. They waved as Jake passed. One of them, Charlie Parker, rolled his eyes and looked at the ceiling with a pained expression on his face, apparently running out of patience with the caller on the other end of the phone. Jake smiled his sympathies, walked out the front door and around to the parking lot where his department car was parked.

'Its good being the Detective C/O, he thought. 'Got my own parking space and a company car to drive back and forth to work. Now if I could get them to stop calling me in the middle of the night to respond to all those homicides, things would be perfect.' Jake knew that was bullshit. He didn't mind the callouts. He liked his job and he liked being where the action was. Edie, his wife of fifteen years, on the other hand, preferred a night of undisturbed sleep. She never complained, though. Jake was thankful for that. Some of the guys who work the homicide team catch a lot of flack from the little woman when the phone starts ringing at three in the morning.

As Jake drove home that evening, he thought about Mitch and those days in the early sixties when they worked together at Long Beach P.D. Jake recalled graduating from the Academy and being assigned to Mitch, who was his training officer. Jake had heard about him. His name had come up during Jake's training, usually connected to some arrest or other activity that was deemed to be an excellent example of how police work was done. When Jake found out he was assigned to Mitch, he was delighted.

They worked well together and stayed partners for almost two years, and by the time they split up they had become fast friends. Jake recalled more than a few adventures they'd been involved in. The caper on the roller coaster, down at the beach, was one to remember. So was the shooting of old man Brinker's kid, Amos, when Mitch got shot. The rescue of the kid from the flood control had been quite an experience for them, too. 'All that fun and they paid us, too,' Jake thought. That was probably the best time he'd had as a cop. At least up to a point.

But there were some bad times as well.

It hurt Jake more than he was willing to acknowledge. The way Mitch changed, the drinking and what he became. He could see in his mind's eye that time on skid row. Mitch filthy and drunk, dead drunk. Jake asked the beat cop to put Mitch on a bus and send him back to Long Beach.

The last time Jake heard from Mitch was about ten years before. Jake was working an organized crime unit at the time. Mitch called him and said he had some information on some organized crime figures in L.A. He said he had a lot of stuff the police didn't have that he wanted to pass on. Jake was skeptical but agreed to meet him. They met at a small restaurant in Chinatown a few days later. Mitch showed up for the meeting bearing little resemblance to the man Jake had known years before. He looked as though he'd aged another ten years. He was bloated and flushed, typical of an alcoholic nearing the end of his life. Mentally he had become paranoid and delusional, totally out of touch with reality. To make matters worse, he had a woman with him who was at least seventy years old, wrinkled and only slightly more coherent than Mitch. She was Mitch's current roommate and an alcoholic as well. Mitch explained that she was a well-to-do widow he'd been living with in her Newport Beach ocean view home. She hung on Mitch like a cheap suit, kissing and fondling him. Thoroughly disgusted with the whole situation, Jake excused himself and got up to leave. Mitch tried to persuade him to stay and listen to what he had to say but Jake wasn't having any of it. That was the last time Jake had heard anything about Mitch, and he frankly had assumed Mitch was dead by now. What a hell of a surprise to hear his voice. He actually sounded sober.

Jake was dubious, but he figured he owed it to Mitch to meet with him. Jake thought the most it would cost him was lunch and an hour or two of his time. He certainly had no plans to re-establish the friendship. Mitch had an arrest record now and probably wasn't the best guy to be associating with. Which reminded him; first thing in the morning he'd have his adjutant Kelly McBride run Mitch's record for him so he'd know just what Mitch had been up to. Any dope dealing or sex crimes, rape, or such would mean lunch was out.

'We'll see.' He thought as he pulled into his driveway.

Jake walked in the front door, threw his sport coat over the chair in the living room and headed for his den. He removed the 9 mm pistol and holster from his belt, along with a set of handcuffs and a pouch containing an extra magazine of ammunition. He placed them in his desk and locked the drawer. An old habit that he developed when his daughter Jenny was little and like most kids, prone to play with things they shouldn't. Now she was married and raising three kids of her own. Three perfect grandchildren, if anyone asked.

Jake walked through the house, grabbed a beer from the refrigerator and headed for the patio to relax. He sat down and put his feet up on one of the patio chairs, loosened his tie and popped the top on the beer. A long swallow, followed by another and he put the can down. It had been a long day, highlighted by the rape and murder of the young woman in the Hills that morning. Kilgore had briefed Jake earlier that afternoon when he'd returned to the station. She'd apparently come to Los Angeles about six months ago and was trying to develop a career as an interior designer. Not much more was known about her, at least not yet. She'd been doing all right. Not great, but making a living and attempting to succeed here in the City of Angels. She lived alone in the house where they'd found her. Several of the detectives from the homicide unit were looking for her current boyfriend.

The murder disturbed Jake more than most. The nature of it, the rape apparently committed while the killer slowly strangled the girl, was sick and perverted. It was the work of a real, evil, subhuman son-of-a-bitch. One who could strike again if not caught.

'That could have been Jennie,' he thought. He tried to imagine how the victims parents must feel. A shiver ran through him as he thought about it.

Jake was still thinking about the case when he heard his wife pull into the driveway. The squeal of her tires sent a subtle message to him that she had probably just spent an hour or better in rush hour traffic and was either fed up with her fellow drivers or had to go to the bathroom. It was after 6:00 p.m. She'd had another long day, as usual. People who had the mistaken idea that teachers only worked six or seven hours a day ought to follow Edie around for a week. Ten-hour days were the norm. Add an hour each way for the freeway commute and it made for a hell of a long day. Two to three hours at home grading papers and getting ready for the next day was a part of the routine as well. Once, Jake sat down and figured out how much Edie made an hour. He decided not to tell her. Not that it would make any difference to her. Teaching was more than a job to Edie. 'God bless her for that,' he thought. She had a commitment to her students that continually amazed him. She taught in a high school miles from home, in a minority community for a below-average salary with very little parental support and a school board whose members had no clue about anything other than how to get re-elected. Yet she steadfastly refused to move to another school because she believed she could make a difference and always would. The occasional visit from a former student who had succeeded, and there were many, bolstered her belief in her convictions. She'd made a difference to scores of kids and that was good enough for her. Money wasn't everything.

She came in carrying the usual bag full of papers over her shoulder.

"Hi, honey," he called from the patio. "How was your day?"

"Frantic!" she replied. That meant typical, he'd come to realize.

"You high school English teachers have all the fun."

"Yeah. All that fun and the big bucks. What could be better?"

"Oh well. Only six more months and school's out for the summer," Jake reminded her.

"Six months! I'll never make it!" she said, collapsing into one of the other patio chairs.

After some more small talk about the events of the day they retired to the kitchen where Jake put together a light dinner. He enjoyed cooking for Edie. She spent as little time as necessary in the kitchen and was glad to let him handle it. The first few years they were married, Edie cooked most of the time. However, Jake began taking up the culinary responsibilities after it became apparent Edie's skills lie elsewhere. After almost twenty years of marriage they both preferred the arrangement.

During dinner, Edie asked Jake about the callout he'd gotten that morning. Jake preferred to keep Edie isolated from the realities of the world and rarely discussed any of the cases he was involved in with her.

"Murder up in the hills," he said. "Not a pretty sight. The victim reminded me of Jennie."

She could see he didn't want to talk about the case, and realized that it was because the details would probably upset her. She appreciated his concern and loved him for it.

Almost in passing, Jake told her that he'd heard from an old partner, Mitch Thacker. He gave her a brief rundown about Mitch and his abbreviated police career, advising her they were going to meet for lunch. She sensed his reluctance at meeting Mitch, but let it go.

After dinner, Edie retired to her office-den and began working on papers. Jake grabbed a toothpick and sat down to read the paper that he'd never gotten to that morning. On the front page of the second section he found an article about the Chief of Police. He'd announced his retirement, indicating he was planning to leave and move to Hawaii in the next few months. 'Only a short time away,' Jake thought. 'Now all the big shots in the department's upper echelons will be maneuvering for position. The next few months are going to get interesting.' The news article went on to say that there were three men considered to be the top candidates within the department. All three were Deputy Chiefs at the present time. One in particular got Jake's attention immediately: Walter Burnett, Chief of Detectives. "Jesus, that's all I need," Jake said.

"Did you say something to me, honey?" Edie yelled from her room.

"No, I'm just expressing my delight with the news that Walter Burnett may be the next Chief of Police."

Edie got up from what she was doing and walked to the living room where Jake was sitting.

"What!" she asked. "Walter! He could be the next Chief? That ought to be enough to get you to retire."

"No chance. I'd never let that bastard think he'd driven me from the job! I'd hang around just to piss him off. Of course, if he transferred me to Property Division or Communications or some other equally exciting job, I'd probably have to rethink my position on the matter."

"Do you think he has a chance to get the job?" Edie asked.

"Under normal circumstances, no. But I'm not too sure the powers to be have the sense to see him for who he really is. For that matter, I'm not sure they wouldn't hire him anyway. Time will tell. He's the consummate politician and all-around, pardon my language, asshole."

Jake and Walter Burnett went back a long way. At one time, they had been friends. They both worked Intelligence Division, occasionally together. They got along well and seemed to share a common point of view on most issues.

Intelligence Division was responsible for monitoring the activities of organized crime figures that were identified in the City of Los Angeles. This meant intercepting them at the airport when they came to town and suggesting they leave on the next plane back to wherever they'd come in from. On those occasions when they elected to stay, it meant haunting their every move, jacking them up whenever possible and arresting them for the slightest step outside the law. The whole idea was to make their lives so miserable they'd finally pack up and leave. The tactic worked relatively well, for the most part. There were, of course, a few stubborn gangsters who didn't get the message and stayed well after the welcome mat had been pulled out from under them. One in particular, a porno-dealing maggot from Chicago, became a personal challenge for Jake. Burnett, on the other hand, didn't share Jake's passion. Burnett preferred the high rolling thugs that were regularly depicted on the front page of the newspaper, usually hugging some would-be starlet. It was apparent to Jake that Walter was hoping to nab one of these high profile gangsters and thereby enhance his own career.

Over lunch one day, Jake suggested to Walter that perhaps he ought to pay more attention to the less visible element of the underworld and those who inhabited it and less to trying to grab attention for himself. Walter accused Jake of being obsessed with 'dirty pictures', inferring that his interest in the Chicago pornographer was for reasons other than throwing him in jail. At that moment Jake considered kicking Walter's ass; however, the restaurant in which they were eating wasn't the place for a brawl. Instead, Jake got up to leave. Before he did, he advised Walter that the restaurant full of patrons was the only thing saving him from an ass kicking.

The next day two guys from Internal Affairs confronted Jake. They advised him that Walter initiated a complaint alleging that Jake had threatened him. Jake told them that he had, in fact, done exactly that and, the truth of the matter was he would have done more than threaten Walter had the situation allowed it. After the complaint process ran its course and the Division Commanding Officer reviewed the investigation, Jake was suspended for three days. Jake and Walter hadn't spoken since.

"Come on, Honey. Sit with me and watch some TV," Jake said. She sat down and Jake gave her a big hug.

CHAPTER 6

The next day was bright and sunny. The traffic was moving smoothly, unusual for Sunset Boulevard. Mitch actually saw people smiling and saying hello to each other. Nothing about the day matched his mood.

He was on his way to the Hollywood Division of LAPD. On his way to see Jake for the first time in what? At least ten and maybe twelve years?

It was hard to decipher the feelings he was having. Anxiety, for sure. Unsure he was doing the right thing. Why bring up bad memories for someone else? Was he being selfish? He checked his motives once again as he drove along. Too complicated for his mind; he would rely on an old-timer's guidance.

It started with a dream. One of those dreams you can't shake, that hangs there just below the surface of the conscious mind, nagging and chewing. He hadn't thought of Jake for years, hadn't seen or spoken to him in what seemed like maybe ten years, and then the dream. He went to an old man he knew who was a hell of a lot wiser than he was and asked him what he could do to get rid of the bad feelings.

"Make amends." One of those short simple answers that always seemed to work for him, now that he was sober.

*****

It had taken two days for Mitch to get through to Jake. Finding out where, in the vast reaches of the L.A.P.D. Jake worked was one thing. Then, after learning he was the Commanding Officer of the Detective Division in Hollywood, Mitch had a few officers screening calls and such to deal with. The first phone call Mitch made proved fruitless. He finally got through to Jake's secretary. He had the distinct feeling from the secretary that a return call from Jake was unlikely. A light subterfuge worked.

"Lieutenant Reed's office," Rene, the secretary, answered.

"Yeah, Captain Anderson, Long Beach P.D. here, for Lieutenant Reed."

"Just a moment sir." She didn't recognize his voice. After a moment, Jake came on the phone.

Mitch knew from the tone of Jake's voice that he wasn't thrilled to hear from him but he pressed on, explaining the reason for the call and stressing that he only needed a few minutes. He explained that he'd been sober for eight years and finally got Jake to agree to meet. He was actually surprised that Jake wanted him to come to the station.

Now he was on Sunset Boulevard, on his way to the station. As Mitch drove along he went back in his mind twenty-five years, to a time when he and Jake were partnered up on the Long Beach Police Department.

Jake stood out above all the cops he worked with over the five years Mitch was 'on the job'.

The Pike ... with the carny workers and the Navy and the run-aways and all the grafters and hookers that followed the fleet.

The Avenue ... the ghetto with the shootings and stabbings and all the good people of the neighborhood trying their best to keep it together.

Vice ... the small time bookies and the pimps and the children hurt for life.

A shootout that connected Jake and Mitch like brothers ... late and quiet and then the violence.

Then another shooting, a kid ...

The end of the job ... drunk and more drunk.

Bodyguard at Las Vegas New Frontier Hotel...

More drinking and finally, decline onto skid row. Phone calls to Jake about organized crime. Some good information but offered in a stuporus haze that left Jake both saddened and disgusted. Jake wasn't interested in the ravings of a lunatic. And who knew what other buffoonery.

As Mitch drove along, all those thoughts and more came unbidden to his mind and all too soon he found himself at his destination.

*****

Hollywood Division was on Wilcox just off Sunset Boulevard. A white, two story rambling building with a big parking lot on the south side. The lot was filled with black and whites and plain cars. A normal police station with cars and officers, in and out of uniform, coming and going. Mitch drove on down the street and found a parking spot a half block away. He'd been sober for eight years but still drove a drunk's typical car-- bent front bumper, crunched fender and a paint job by 'rust and sons'. He didn't want anybody to see him driving that beater, especially Jake. He stood on the sidewalk and appraised his appearance for the twentieth time. He could not figure out the high state of nervousness he was experiencing. He stared at his hands, noticed a slight trembling as he lit another cigarette. Mitch took a deep breath and began walking towards the entrance to the station.

The desk sergeant was polite enough and told Mitch to take a seat while he called back to the Detective Division. In a few minutes a female officer in plain clothes came through a door and introduced herself. "Hi, I'm Kelly McBride, Lt. Reed's Adjutant. Are you Mr. Thacker?"

Mitch nodded yes and she said, "Come with me, please. The lieutenant will be with you shortly."

He followed her down a hall and into the detective squad room.

A busy room. Desks covered with files and coffee cups and computers. Bulletin boards with wanted posters, calendars and the occasional joke from a magazine or editorial that meant something different to cops than was intended by the writer. Detectives working at the desks or coupled up talking quietly. That intense undercurrent barely discernible. Mitch experienced something akin to the feeling he always got crossing the Canal to Cape Cod, a feeling of coming home.

Jake's office was a glassed in cubicle in one corner of the squad room. He stared through the window of the closed door at Mitch as he talked on the phone. Mitch knew he was sizing him up, seeing if he was sober. And something else. Jake's countenance had an almost sad look. 'Still chewing on toothpicks though' Mitch noted. Jake motioned Mitch into the office and pointed at a chair.

"Well, you don't look too bad. What's this about Mitch?" Jake's voice was as stern as his eyes. Mitch sat there looking back. Jake, he saw, had aged remarkably well. He was well muscled and had a lean hardness to him, both physically and mentally. Mitch smiled to himself. Jake still had his customary toothpick in the corner of his mouth.

"Well, you look great Jake. It's been a long time and I, well..."

The phone rang and Jake held up his hand as he answered. He talked with someone about overtime cards and records and then after hanging up, stared at Mitch for a moment and then seemed to come to a decision.

"Come on, Mitch, we'll go have some coffee or lunch," he said, standing up and walking past the seated Mitch without waiting for an answer.

They rode in Jake's plain car down Santa Monica Boulevard in silence. Jake seemed at ease and Mitch's nervousness increased. He felt an energy he couldn't understand. He had made harder amends than this, but never with so many feelings.

Jake pulled into the parking lot of a small cafe and parked.

"This place serves a pretty good lunch. Hungry?" Jake said looking over at Mitch.

"Oh yeah, a little lunch sounds good." Eating was the last thing on Mitch's mind. He did a quick mental inventory of his finances on hand.

He had forty bucks in his wallet. No problem.

The cafe was nicely decorated, flowers on each table and colorful pictures on the walls. The waitress greeted Jake as though he were an old friend and seated them in a corner away from the other patrons. They studied the menus silently, and then Mitch took a deep breath and began:

"I appreciate that you would give me this time Jake. God knows, you don't owe me anything." Mitch could feel an energy, almost as though the world and time had stopped. Like the feeling on a nighttime sea when everything gets quiet, when you just know nature is getting ready for a major change. Jake just stared and nodded slightly for Mitch to go on.

"Anyway, I need to acknowledge to you that I know what an asshole I've been. That I had no right to..." Mitch paused as if gathering strength and then continued in a rush of words. "See, I got sober a couple of years ago and part of the process is to make amends. I know I can't do anything for you. But well, I'm not looking for forgiveness or anything like that. I just need you to know I realize how, well, how it feels like I let you and a lot of other people down and I want you to know if the day ever comes when I can, I want to make amends. That I'm sorry for the things I did and the trouble I may have caused you over the years." Mitch paused again in thought and then continued. "You know I feel selfish about this in a way. I mean part of this is so that I can stay sober. I guess that's selfish."

Jake sat quietly for a few moments and then looked at Mitch.

"Why after all these years? What's it been, twenty or so years?" He shook his head slowly. "Why now?"

"Well, I know this is going to sound kinda', well, stupid, I guess. I had a dream about you last November, one of those dreams you just can't shake, it hangs there at the back of your mind and gains power, I suppose. You know what I mean?" Mitch looked at Jake.

The two men sat there in a corner of the small cafe. One an ex-cop and ex-skid row drunk, the other a hardened police lieutenant. Neither given to believing anything that wasn't solid. The slight edge of cynicism that came with the lives they had led.

"Mitch," Jake's voice was low and somber. "Mitch, we were good partners and good friends. It bothered me a lot to see you go down hill like you did." Jake paused and looked at his old partner. "You don't owe me anything. It's good that you're sober and I suppose I can assume you've gone straight?" Jake raised an eyebrow and stared intently at Mitch.

"Straight? Straight as in crime?" Mitch picked up a spoon and twirled it in his hands. "Look, I got booked a lot of times, Jake, but never for a felony. I did some bad stuff but not violence, not hurting anyone. Well, except for this one asshole who ... never mind."

Jake didn't respond. His mind went to the rumors from years before that Mitch had worked for the mob when he was in Las Vegas, after he was canned from the Long Beach PD.

"What are you doing now? Where are you living?" Jake asked.

"Oh, I'm a live-aboard down at Alamitos Bay, an old sloop, and a sailboat. Live in a million dollar neighborhood on a twenty five thousand dollar boat."

"Work? What are you doing?" Jake raised that eyebrow again.

"Mostly boats. I take short deliveries once in awhile and bright work, I like doing bright work, you know, varnishing teak and a diving job when I can, if the money's right. You, I've heard great things about you. I still run into the guys from those days on Long Beach P.D., Arnie and Chester some and others, they tell me you're one of the best."

"Well, it was a good move to come to LAPD, I've been lucky. Married to a great woman and have been for about twenty years now."

And they spent the next hour catching up on their lives. Jake chose not to ask about Mitch's Las Vegas days.

Chapter 7

At two a.m. the next morning, Mitch came awake with a start. His dog, Briney by name, was washing his face vigorously with her tongue in a manner suggesting she needed to pee, and right now. He got up, stuck his head out the aft hatch and looked at the bay. It was a warm evening and the moon was just peeking over Saddle Back Mountain to the east. He sighed, lifted Briney over the rail onto the dock and began fixing coffee. Sleep wouldn't be coming back this night.

He sat in the cockpit, sipping the hot coffee and listening to the light slap of the rigging of the boats in the small marina, as if talking to each other. The boat was his home. He'd been living aboard for the last nine years with his Springer Spaniel. Lighting a cigar, he made a mental list of the necessary maintenance he would do that coming week. The boat was built in 1968 and needed constant care, but he liked the traditional design, the full keel and simple rig. The boat had taken good care of him over the years. So had the dog. Back aboard, she lay in the V berth forward, her eyes glowing in the light of the lamp in the main cabin as she watched her master sitting on deck.

As always, his mind wandered around in the middle of the night.

He liked sitting in the night and thinking. His thoughts drifted to the previous day. It was good seeing Jake. It was another step on the long road back from oblivion.

Once again, he thought how blessed he was. Couldn't get to where he was--from where he'd been, was a phrase he used quite often.

After Long Beach P.D. tired of his antics and sent him packing, he found himself, after a few minor arrests, working in Las Vegas for the New Frontier Hotel. A high school buddy's father referred him to the hotel and they hired Mitch as Security. It was fun for a while. The hotel gave him an advance to buy a wardrobe, and they gave him a room at the hotel. All he had to do was keep an eye on the big spenders. Make sure they got everything they wanted and that their stay was happy and safe. He sometimes worked three or four days, on call for twenty-four hours and then had several days off. He'd taken up with a couple of different showgirls and drank steadily on his time off.

In the sixties, the mob still had a strong influence in the gambling Mecca and Mitch's background with law enforcement came in handy from time to time. One of the Captains on the Las Vegas Police Department was a constant visitor to the hotel, and it wasn't long before Mitch and the Captain became drinking buddies. It was through the Captain that Mitch made friends with Tony. Tony was, to all outward appearances, an employee of the hotel. He had a position as public relations representative. A five-minute conversation was all Mitch needed to know Tony was a mob guy, there to oversee the skim operation and keep things running smoothly.

Tony was treacherous. His eyes were cold and without emotion. He was a year or two older than Mitch. Short, 5'-10" or so and he weighed at least two hundred and twenty pounds. He always wore the same outfit. Black silk suit with red lining and white on white shirts and ties. He always smelled like Wild Root Hair Crème Oil.

Mitch remembered his first move to the inner sanctum. Tony walked up to the cocktail lounge where Mitch was sitting and watching the flow of people in and out of the casino.

"Here." Tony handed Mitch an envelope. "Give this to your buddy, the Captain, when he comes in." Tony stared hard at him. There was more to this than a simple delivery. Tony was letting Mitch know the Captain was on the pad. Mitch took the envelope and nodded his head slowly.

"Right. Anything you want him to know?" Mitch was implying

he had some control over the Captain. Not true, but Mitch couldn't help but play the game. He was bored with babysitting rich patrons.

"No, not right now." Tony nodded his head and strutted away.

Two things occurred in the next six weeks that gave Mitch new status in the hotel and Las Vegas.

The Captain had called and asked to meet with Mitch in a bar a few blocks from the police station. He was sitting in a corner booth when Mitch got there. They exchanged a few stories; the Captain telling some war stories of when he worked patrol and then:

"Listen, I got a small problem and maybe you can help me out here." The Captain paused and looked at Mitch expectantly.

"Sure, Captain, what can I do for you?"

"Well there's this broad, a dancer. She's, ah, she's kinda' taking something a little more seriously than she should. You know what I mean?"

"No, but I'm sure it's nothing that can't be worked out. She work at the hotel?" Mitch asked.

"Yeah, she's, well I've been seeing her once in awhile, and now she's threatening to call my family, make trouble. I never promised her anything and now she's getting ready to shake me down." The Captain stopped and stared at Mitch to see his reaction.

"Uh huh, well I can talk to her," Mitch said.

"Good, I don't want to have to go to Tony with this. I don't want her hurt or anything, you know what I mean?" The Captain looked around to see if anyone was listening and then he finished with, "Us cops have to stick together, right?"

"You got it, Captain. I'll see what I can do." Mitch smiled. He knew the man sitting across from him couldn't care less about the girl. The Captain didn't want to weaken his position with Tony. Mitch knew something else. He had seen the girl and Tony several times in recent weeks, talking together. The way he had it figured Tony was setting the Captain up. A few hours later, he was sure of it.

As soon as Mitch got back to the hotel, he found Tony and apprised him of the conversation he'd had with the Captain. Tony seemed pleased.

"OK, here's what we do. I'll move the broad to the west coast and, you tell the man everything's under control." Tony stopped and thought for a moment, "He don't need to know you told me anything, understand?" Mitch nodded in agreement. 'That should make the

Captain happy', he thought.

A few weeks later Mitch was walking through the large parking lot of the hotel late one evening when he heard a commotion a few rows from where he was walking. He walked toward the voices he heard.

He saw two black men bent over a woman lying on the ground between two parked cars. The woman moaned.

"Hey! What tha' fuck's goin' on?" he asked. Mitch didn't carry a gun, but he did have a rather large leather sap with him. A remnant from his days as a street cop. The two men stood up and from the parking lot lights Mitch could see the woman was bleeding.

"Get your hands in the air and turn around or I'll blow ya' into the next world." Mitch pointed the sap at them, figuring they couldn't see whether it was a gun or not.

"Oh wait man. We was just try'n to he'p the lady, c'mon man, take it easy." The two men started backing away as they talked.

"Your choice, flat on the ground, now! Or flat on the ground for good." Mitch put the bluff in his voice, the good old cop bluff. The men hesitated and then assumed a kneeling position. From where he stood Mitch, asked the woman what happened. In a feeble voice she pointed at the men and said:

"They, they hurt me. Please help ..." Then she laid back down.

One of the men, still on his knees, bent forward quickly in order to get to his feet. Mitch moved in and kicked him hard in the face sending him over backwards. As the second man tried to gain his feet, Mitch sapped him twice at the temple and he went to the ground as well. He turned his attention back to the first, and was kicking him in the ribs when the uniformed security people pulled up on a golf cart.

"Hey! Hey! Hold it!" The two private cops shined their flashlights on the scene. "Oh, Mitch, what's up?"

"You guys got cuffs, hook these two pricks up and call the police. They were mugging this lady," Mitch said, turning to the woman who was now sitting up pulling her skirt down over her exposed legs. One of the security cops put his light on her.

"Oh, man! Miss Montini are you alright?" Miss Montini was Tony's first cousin; the daughter of Tony's uncle; the reputed boss of the Boston mob.

Mitch thought about the situation for a minute.

"Don't call the police. Bring these two fucks to the security office." Mitch knelt by the young woman, "You just sit right here, you're safe now. We will have a nurse here in a second," he said, motioning to the security men. One of them quickly got on his hand held radio and contacted his office; advising them of the situation and requesting the hotel nurse immediately,

The next morning, Tony called Mitch to his apartment in the penthouse.

"I'm indebted to you. So is my Uncle. He sends you his thanks." Tony stopped and looked seriously at Mitch. "I appreciated the way you came to me about the Captain's problem. I figured you for a guy that would side with him, you bein' an ex cop and all. I made a recommendation to the General Manager. He thought it was a good idea. You, from now on, are ... let's say, special security. You just wander around and watch things, OK?"

"Whatever you say, Tony," Mitch answered.

"Good. There's more money for ya', of course. Here's something from my uncle to express his thanks for what you did for my cousin." Tony handcd Mitch an cnvclopc that turncd out to havc twcnty fivc onc hundred dollar bills in it.

Mitch spent the next year at the hotel. He did a number of 'favors' for the Montini family. Nothing that he felt was evil, although there were a few things that certainly fell into the gray areas of the law. He had a chance to meet the uncle himself. When told by Tony that Mitch was the man that saved his daughter from the two black assailants, he grabbed Mitch in a big bear hug and gave him two big wet, garlicky kisses on each cheek.

Mitch never did ask what happened to the two rapist muggers, and no one ever mentioned them. He didn't really care.

He stood up in the cockpit and rubbed his face, and then went below and to sleep.

CHAPTER 8

It had been raining. Not a heavy rain, one of those drizzly gray all over rains. Now the sun was out and the day was nice. Mitch sat at an outdoor table at the Koffee Kup waiting for Jake. After that first meeting, they agreed to get together occasionally for lunch or at least a cup of coffee. The color of the day and an old wino hitting Mitch up for a buck brought back some old memories.

*****

Las Vegas lasted for about two years. The Captain got indicted over some drug deal that didn't involve the hotel. Mitch always suspected Tony had some part in it. Tony's uncle had come back out a week after the Captain got busted and stayed for one day. The day after he went back to New England, Tony came to Mitch:

"I got some business back East." Tony stared at his cigar, "I don't think I'll be coming back. I miss the East Coast, the food, the people, you un'erstand." Tony paused and stared at Mitch, "I like you OK for an ex cop, here's a little piece of advice for you. Watch your drinking, it's gonna bite you in the ass one of these days." Tony stood up, patted Mitch on the back and walked away.

Two months later, the new management told Mitch his services would no longer be needed. They gave him a very generous severance check and Mitch came back to the West Coast with no idea of what he would do next.

He rented a single apartment in Hermosa Beach, a smaller city up the coast twenty miles or so from Long Beach. There were several beach bars within walking distance, so he fell into a pattern of walking the beach in the afternoon and then hitting the pubs about seven in the evening. The five grand was a lot of money back in the seventies and he figured he had enough to last him close to a year if he was careful.

Mitch was sitting in his favorite bar at his spot down at the end of the long bar when the FBI agent came up to him.

"I'm special agent Trimble," giving Mitch a quick glance at his credentials. "I want to talk to you about the Montini family."

"Sure. What can I do for you?" Mitch answered.

"You worked for them. What did you do?"

"No, I worked for the New Frontier Hotel. Not for them. I knew Tony, he worked there too," Mitch answered.

"Mitch, we know you did some work for them, let's don't BS. each other. You came out here to the west coast several times, what were you doing for them?"

"Are we talking about them or me?" Mitch said, taking a sip of his drink.

"What are you doing now Mitch? We've talked with some of the people you worked with on LBPD. They say you were a good cop." The agent turned on the barstool so as to face Mitch. "We don't want Tony, he's small potatoes. Your name came up in some tapes we have of the uncle talking. We think you might be able to get next to him."

"Next to him?" Mitch smiled, "Next to him? Why? He's senile. You want to know what kind of diapers they use on him? That old man doesn't know his name, never mind anything else."

"This the way you want to play it?" Trimble said, "We're offering you a chance to get back on the job. The uncle runs the New England mob, you could do something important."

"Look, the hotel gave me a good bonus check when I left and no, I wasn't a good cop. If I was, I'd still be one." Mitch stared down at the bar. "I'm doing OK, not doing anything wrong. Just walking on the beach and," Mitch held up his drink, "having a couple of cocktails in the evening. There's nothing I can do for you guys."

Trimble kept probing and talking and Mitch kept putting him off. Finally Trimble got up and said:

"I'll keep in touch Mitch, you keep your nose clean, understand?"

Three days later the phone rang in Mitch's small apartment.

"Hello?"

"You doin' OK?" It was a voice with an East Coast accent.

"Who's this?" Mitch asked.

"It doesn't matter. Your Uncle thought it was pretty funny that you called him senile. He sends his regards. Call him sometime."

That was when Mitch realized the mob was even trickier than he thought. They had sent one of their people to check on him posing as a Fed.

So he drank and he walked and the money got low.

He called the East Coast and asked if there was anything he could do for the Montinis. The voice on the phone said someone might be in touch. A week later he found himself working as a bartender. A bartender at the Garden Club in Bell Gardens.

Bell Gardens was one of the toughest cities on the West Coast back in those days and it didn't take long to realize the Garden Club was connected to the mob on the East Coast. Besides tending bar, Mitch picked up some extra money, occasionally by walking to an attorney firm down the street from the bar and picking up a briefcase which he delivered to San Francisco. Once he sat at a meeting between the attorney and a representative of an outlaw biker gang with the assignment of protecting the attorney from any harm.

And the drinking got worse and it turned out the bartender job was his last steady job except for a short stint with Kreske Company catching shoplifters and thieving employees.

Mitch was arrested on his thirty-second birthday. It wasn't anything very dramatic. He was staggering down the street and got booked for drunk in public. The attorney bailed him out and let him know he was no longer welcome in Bell Gardens and phone calls to the East Coast would be a bad idea.

He couldn't remember how, but he ended up at the Greyhound Bus Depot in downtown L.A. where the cops picked him up and put him in detox rather than booking him. He made some friends, the jailhouse buddies kind of friends, and couldn't seem to leave skid row. He kept telling himself he was going to straighten up and, just like everyone else, he made the decision every morning and was still there every night. Had to have that one drink first. A year later, Mitch was still there, living in an alley behind a dumpster.

Mitch shook his shoulders in revulsion. There was an image that would come to him, unbeckoned, even after all those years. An image that summed up just how low he'd gotten in those days. He remembered Union Station. The old station had been built in the thirties and had old-fashioned stalls in the men's bathroom. The doors had been removed because of security. He could still see the fancy tile floors and fogged mirrors over the stained sinks. The high ceilings amplified every sound and the comings and goings of the passengers created a constant hum. Mitch would take off his old combat boots and the several pairs of socks he had on and put first one foot, then the other in the commode to wash them. As he did so, he held the flush handle down to create a steady flow of water. Somehow, in his addled mind, he wasn't like the others if his feet were clean.

One morning, half drunk he looked up through bloodshot eyes, with one foot in the toilet and saw a man staring at him. It was what he saw in the man's eyes that stuck with him, that showed him what he'd become. Disgust and something worse. A look that said he was a derelict, not even worthy of pity.

Mitch wasn't sure but about a week later an L.A. cop, who walked a beat on the row, took him to the station and gave him some clean clothes and let him take a shower. Then he put him on a bus to Long Beach. Just before he left the cop put his arm around Mitch's shoulder and told him to try to quit drinking and get straight.

Mitch shivered again, recalling the past. He took another sip of the now cold coffee. He hoped that someday he'd run across that beat cop. He'd like to thank him, to tell him about that man he found at Union Station. How a short time later, because someone cared, that man finally found help.

*****

Jake pulled the plain car into the parking lot of the Koffee Kup on Sunset Boulevard. He found himself looking forward to seeing his old partner every week or so. It was a bright sunny morning and the yellow and blue building with the white fenced patio glistened in the sunlight.

He saw Mitch sitting at one of the patio tables kibitzing with a waitress, a tattooed spike-haired young thing with an earring in her left nostril.

"I'd like a cup of coffee, please." And as she left to fill the order, Jake smiled at Mitch, "Nice girl, are you going to take her home to meet the folks?"

"Dead. My parents are dead, so I can see her anytime I want. I'm thinking a farm and three kids, she'll cook and I'll plant and harvest, what do you think?" Mitch answered deadpan. "Her name's 'Moon in Waiting' and she turned eighteen yesterday and nobody can tell her what to do anymore and she is going to be a famous singer as soon as she gets a break." Mitch smiled and took a sip of coffee. "She reminds me of the Pike. Remember all those run-aways, all the hamburgers and room rent girls?" He was referring to the girls, young girls that would end up in the 'Jungle' turning tricks for small amounts of money to eat and a night in one of the flophouses. Many a romance between a green young sailor from the Midwest and a run away girl blossomed from those somehow innocent trysts.

"Oh yeah, those were the days," Jake said, watching the waitress putting his coffee down.

The two men sat there quietly, each with their own fond memories.

"The roller coaster! Remember that night? Damn that was funny! What a night that was." Jake laughed, breaking the silence. Mitch nodded, a big grin on his face.

*****

They had been working together about three months when the detail sergeant grabbed them before the squad room meeting and told them Vice needed two uniforms to walk the Nu Pike. The regular detail was working the Miss Universe Pageant as bodyguards to the contestants. Mitch readily agreed, and as he and Jake walked the four blocks to Pike and Cedar Avenue, the center of the amusement area, Jake asked:

"Seemed like you really wanted to do this, how come? I mean a walking beat? Isn't there more action in the car?"

"No, this is one of the best jobs on the department. You'll see." Mitch waved his arm around him. "This whole area is sailors, hookers, small time cons and bikers and a whole bunch more ding-a-lings feeding off the fleet. Never mind AWOL sailors and guys on the run. You just wait and see, I bet we get a good felony bust tonight."

They spent the first two hours walking the beat. Past the carny booths. Booths of stacked metal milk bottles, dart games, hit the cup with a coin and more, all with the seedy men or women standing in front of each booth calling out:

"Three balls for a quarter! Three for two bits! Knock 'em down and win a teddy for your girl! Two bits!"

And the under-inflated balloons tacked to the plywood wall waiting to be popped with the dull unbalanced throwing knives. 'Same price, a quarter and win a gold watch, guaranteed!'. Thirteen bars and hot dog stands and that sweet smelling cotton candy, all pink and fluffy nothing.

And the rosy cheeked young Navy boys. Some in uniform, most in civvies with their packs of cigarettes rolled up in their tee shirt sleeves or stuck in the socks so as not to interrupt the perceived sleek lines of their tailored uniforms or tight clothes, many showing off new tattoos.

And the group of conventioneers, all florists, gawking. Teenagers on a date. Middle-aged marrieds on their way to the Hollywood on the Pike for an evening of dancing.

And the rat-eyed predators looking for the sailor that would give a month's pay to get laid and would end up waking in one of the dimly lit hallways of one of the cheap hotels looking for the room number that didn't exist. The chicken hawk searching for a baby run away. The bikers with the serious intent of knocking over the head a merchant seaman and taking three months' pay, paid in cash by the steamship line in accordance with Federal law.

All of them wandering aimlessly. Looking for something, not sure what. Walking and looking on the midway.

Jake and Mitch were walking away from the photo stand, where you could stick your head in a plywood cutout of a jail and prisoners and have your picture taken as a jailbird or sitting astride a wooden donkey with a sombrero and send the pictures home to your folks showing them what a great time you were having in the home port of the US Navy in the City of Long Beach.

"Hey! Hey, officers, quick! He's stuck up there! Hurry up I think he's hurt." The carnie was running towards them, the faded blue canvas change bag flopping at his waist.

The old wooden roller coaster touted itself with a brightly colored sign as the fastest and steepest ride in the world, and at one time it was.

The first car and the last car were for the bravest riders and, as the cars clacked their way up to the highest summit, the manliest of all would let go of the metal safety bar and put their arms above their head for the take-your-breath-away swooping first dip. On occasion a rider, out of very poor judgment or more often tipsiness, would stand up in a show of extreme bravado. This was why the carnie was rushing at the two officers. A very drunk sailor in uniform, fresh out of boot damp and on his first liberty, had met one of the Pike girls and, trying to show her what a fine specimen of manhood he was, had stood up and fallen out of the last car at the very top of the wooden structure. He was hanging upside down, one leg bent at a very unusual angle around a cross member, keeping him more or less in place.

"Shit!" Mitch stood there hat in hand staring up at the hapless sailor. Jake stood beside him looking in the same direction.

"What now?" Jake asked his partner.

"He looks unconscious, or asleep maybe! Yeah, maybe he's asleep and he'll have a nightmare and wake up and climb down. What do ya think? Should we stand here and wait and see?" Mitch seemed upset, unlike his normal behavior in stressful situations. Jake stared at his partner with one eyebrow raised.

"Dumb fucking sailor, I hate heights, dammit!" Mitch took off his Sam Browne belt with all the gear and motioned Jake to do the same. "Come on, we got to go up there, stupid bastard's gonna fall. We don't have time for the fire department to get here. Damn, I hate this."

Jake spit out his toothpick and followed Mitch into the maze of wooden beams at the base of the creaky old structure. Then they both began to climb, first up the old metal ladder and then, about sixty feet off the ground, out onto the wood beams to the main brace which went straight up to where the sailor still hung upside down. Iron spikes were nailed into the brace every foot and half or so as a way to climb up to the top. Jake, taking pity on the obviously nervous partner, pushed past him and grabbed the first spike.

"I'll go first, you follow me." Mitch didn't argue and they both climbed the last twenty feet and sat straddled on the highest beam, the unconscious young man between them. Mitch pulled the belt from his pants.

"Give me yours and we'll tie this stupid prick to the girder and let the fire department take it from there. If we try to carry him down, I'll drop him."

The two of them reached down and Jake got hold of one of the sailors limp arms and pulled him closer to the beam. Mitch linked the two belts together and after several tries swung the belts under the man and tied him firmly to the underside of the beam.

"There, now pull his other arm around here and cuff him in case he wakes up."

"Cuff him?" Jake said, not seeing the wisdom of locking the sailor to the beam for a moment and then, "Oh yeah, he can't fall no matter what, right?"

"Right, and I'm sure he's broken some law anyway and besides I gotta get down. I can't take it up here," Mitch said, and turned and started sliding back along the wooden girder to the beam that would bring them back to the safety of the ground.

That is when it happened.

Now Mitch never really thought about having children, perhaps because he had been shifted about from family member to family member as a child or from some other deep psychological wound, but when the splinter pierced his flesh in the region of his manhood he reacted as any man would. He yelled and instinctively reached for his crotch, letting go of his precious hold on the wooden beam. Of course he fell.

With remarkable reflexes, Jake wrapped his legs around the beam and lunged forward grabbing Mitch by the collar and necktie and there they were; Jake upside down and holding onto Mitch, all two hundred and five pounds of Mitch swinging back and forth.

"Ok, I'm going to swing you over to that beam. Grab a hold of it, OK?" Jake said to his terrified partner. Equally frightened of falling and of having a splinter stabbing one of his testicles, Mitch nodded, gurgling for air. Jake swung and Mitch grabbed the beam. Then the sailor came to and began screaming.

The next few seconds were filled with much yelling, lots of profanity and several threats of bodily harm once the three men got to the ground, in the event they were lucky enough to do so, still alive.

About then, the first of the firemen arrived and, with big grins under their fireman's hats, helped all three men to the ground. Fortunately for the sailor, the shore patrol arrived on scene and rescued him from a much-harried Mitch. The old Chief Boson's Mate in charge assured Mitch that the Navy would mete out a suitable punishment.

The splinter in fact had merely stabbed Mitch in the left cheek of his buttocks and required no medical attention. Jake yanked it out in the back of the Shanghai Cafe.

As they walked along a half hour later Jake felt that silence was the best approach to take after the roller coaster incident. Finally, Mitch spoke:

"Well, that was interesting. Let's go over to the jungle."

The 'jungle' bordered the west side of the amusement park. Made up of rundown two- and three-story buildings that were once deluxe resort hotels, it was an area of cheap one-room apartments and bars and liquor stores and one or two pawnshops that attracted the ex-cons and run-always and other low lifes of downtown. Downtown in a sailor town.

West Seaside Avenue separated the trash-strewn sand of the beach from the jungle. The Rainbow Room was a bar on Seaside that catered to the predators and vultures of the area. The only Navy personnel to be found there were the 'We can get you Government supplies cheap' profiteers and thieves of the military community. "Not a nice place," Mitch explained to his partner as they pushed through the front door.

The noise in the bar diminished noticeably as the two uniformed officers entered. The patrons stole glances at the two cops, mostly in the cracked mirror reflecting the lined-up bottles and the room from behind the back bar. The bar ran the length of the room with the customary red vinyl and torn bar stools and on the opposite side, booths of matching fabric and condition. Jake stood at the entrance and Mitch slowly walked the length of the establishment nodding his head to the customers and tipping his hat to the three or four heavily made-up females.

On his way back to the front of the bar, he stopped at one of the booths and stared down at the sole person sitting in the booth with a tall drink in front of him. The man was large shouldered and muscular. He was wearing an expensive sport coat and a silk shirt unbuttoned halfway down his chest exposing several gold chains. There were tattoos peeking from under the cuffs of the black coat. He stared sullenly into his drink. Jake watched Mitch stand there for a full minute, not saying anything. Finally the dark-haired man looked up at Mitch.

"There a problem?" He spoke with a southern accent.

"Gee, I hope not, let's see some ID," Mitch said quietly.

The man was at least ten years older than anyone else in the bar, including the two officers. He had the hard eyes of trouble. An ex con,

Mitch thought.

"ID? Go bother somebody else sonny, I'm clean so..."

Before the man could finish, Mitch had him by the back of his jacket. He pulled him from his seat and pushed him into the mahogany cap rail of the bar. Then he swung him around and cuffed him.

"C'mon asshole, let's go down to the station and see what you're about."

Three of the local bikers stood up and blocked the exit. One of them held his arms out from his side and in a guttural tone said to the officers:

"Wait a minute man, that guy didn't do nothin'. I think..."

He didn't get a chance to express his opinion. Jake moved quickly burying his nightstick in the biker's mid section. "You're interfering. Want to join your buddy here?" The tough biker dropped to his knees and fell forward. Jake turned and grabbed one of the other two bikers by the throat and squeezed his Adams apple. "What about you?" The fight was over before it started.

They took the fellow in the booth to the station. Mitch went upstairs to the detective bureau and told one of the detectives the guy felt dirty and asked him to do an out-of-state check on him. Turned out he was an escaped con from Mississippi.

*****

"You guys want a refill?" The spiked-hairdo waitress interrupted the two men reliving, with great pleasure, the old days. Mitch nodded yes and she topped off the cups.

"Those were the good old days, as they say," Mitch said.

"How do you figure that?" Jake asked.

"Assholes screwed with you, a little street justice straightened 'em right out."

"And that was good, in your opinion? I mean looking at it now, you think it was good?"

"I sure as hell don't see anything wrong with it, in the appropriate situation."

"Who determines when the situation's appropriate?"

"Well, the cop who's dealing with the asshole. Who else?"

Jake stared at Mitch for a long moment. "You know, Mitch, I guess I kicked as much ass as anybody."

"That's putting it mildly," Mitch said, grinning.

"That sort of crap doesn't happen much anymore though. And when it comes to the department's attention, people lose their jobs."

"That's a shame. There's still a need to drop some dirt bag from time to time. It's the only thing the dipshits understand," Mitch said with confidence.

"You're full of shit, Mitch," Jake replied.

"I'm surprised to hear you say that, all things considered."

"Yeah, well I guess I see things a little differently now. Maybe I matured."

"You mean you're just getting old," Mitch kidded.

"No, seriously, Mitch. Think about this for a minute. We were cops out on the street and we were supposed to protect people, right?"

"Well, yeah, the good people."

"Good people. Bad people. The Constitution doesn't make those distinctions."

"The Constitution! What the hell does the Constitution have to do with it?" Mitch wanted to know.

"Shit, Mitch, it has everything to do with it. Our job isn't, or in your case wasn't, just to throw assholes in the slammer. Cops have a legal obligation to protect peoples' rights. I never gave it much thought until several years after we worked together. The people give the government its authority. The Constitution defines that. It's a contract, a social contract that government's supposed to abide by. Nowhere in there does it say the police get to kick some jerk's ass if he doesn't behave. Every time we did we were denying some poor bastard his right not to be screwed over by the government. Considering the number of times you've been booked over the past few years, I'd think you, of all people, could appreciate that."

"Actually, I probably needed my ass kicked on those occasions when it happened. I did tend to get a little obnoxious after a quart or two."

"I see I'm getting nowhere with you. But I'll tell you this, Mitch, we're both lucky we didn't wind up getting hauled in by the Feds over some of our capers."

"Yeah. You're probably right," Mitch replied. "But personally, I think a little ass kicking can go a long way toward getting an asshole's mind right. Why do you think the gang problem's as bad as it is? Back in the sixties we never would have let that get out of hand like it is now.

Those punks don't understand anything that doesn't have a little pain attached, just to get their attention."

"I can see this is hopeless," Jake replied. "See if you can get Moonbeam or whatever her name is to bring us some more coffee, will ya?"

"I'm sure she'd be delighted," Mitch said as he waved at the waitress.

"I don't mean to sound holier than thou, Mitch. It's just that that the 'kick ass and take names' mentality we operated with in the sixties is no good. Wasn't then and sure as hell isn't now. It just took me a while to realize it."

"Yeah, yeah. I get the point, even if I don't agree with it. As for holier than me, well you probably are, but I'm working on it."

The two men stared at each other, one with a slight grin, and the other with a resigned look. The funny young waitress laid the bill on the table and walked away with an exaggerated swing to her hips. Both men watched her and then Jake picked up the bill and said:

"Well give me a call and we'll hook up again next week, OK?"

"Yeah I'd like that Jake, call ya' Monday or Tuesday."

CHAPTER 9

Chief of Detectives Walter Burnett leaned back in his very large swivel chair and looked out the window of his office, enjoying the commanding view of Civic Center. Turning to look around his spacious office, he scanned the memorabilia adorning the walls and cabinet tops, pleased with what he saw. His career was represented by all of these things, including the large office with the grand view. He'd worked hard for the last twenty-eight years to get to this point and he enjoyed his position immensely. When he spoke people listened, especially the 1,800 detectives under his command.

Today was a particularly good day to be the Chief of Detectives. He'd just finished with a telephone conversation with the Mayor. He and the Mayor had developed a close relationship over the past few years. Not without sacrifice of course, but it was all worth it. The Mayor, Charles Knowles, had, from time to time, run into little potholes on his road to City Hall and on more than a few occasions Walter had paved them over, figuratively speaking. The Mayor was particularly beholden to Walter for arranging the release of his daughter after her arrest for shoplifting and then fighting with a security guard who ultimately wrestled her to the ground, breaking her nose. Several other less dramatic situations required some phone calls, all of which served to save the Mayor from the embarrassment of rude questions from the press. The Mayor was grateful and considered Walter one of his confidants. That, of course, is exactly what Walter had hoped for. Chief of Detectives was fine but Chief of Police was better.

Recent conversations with the Mayor left Walter with the distinct impression that he was in position to be the next Chief of Police. With the current Chief's departure only six weeks away there was no time to be wasted in getting oneself on the "A" list of candidates. The Mayor would make the final selection and Walter intended to be at the top of his hit parade. As he sat pondering his future, Candy Warburton, Walter's secretary and Girl Friday walked into the office.

"Phone call. Your outside line," she said.

"Do you know who it is?" he asked.

"It's Mistcr Calarasi."

"Okay, thanks. By the way, if you don't have any plans I'd like to take you to lunch."

"That would be nice," she said as she walked out of the office.

Walter picked up the phone. "Hello, Arlo. How's the movie business? Booming, I assume."

"The movie business is always good. Right now it's exceptional."

Arlo Calarasi was a good friend of Walter's and a business partner. A good friend in the movie industry in Los Angeles was very beneficial to one's hopes for future success, especially if that good friend was Arlo Calarasi. Arlo donated large suns of money to the political party currently in power in the city and county of Los Angeles. His generosity was rewarded with an impressive degree of influence among the movers and shakers, as they liked to call themselves, throughout Los Angeles. A little money goes a long way. A lot of money, as in Arlo's case, goes right to the seat of power. Walter knew that when the time came, Arlo would let the powers to be known that he, Walter, should be the next Chief of Police.

"Is everything all right?" Walter asked.

"I'm going out of town for a week. Back east to visit some friends. Will you have someone, a patrol car maybe, keep an eye on the house?" Arlo said.

"Yes, I can arrange that. I'll call Hollywood station and have a vacation check set up for you. They do that sort of thing all the time.

When are you leaving and returning?" he asked.

"We're leaving the day after tomorrow and getting back the twenty-third," Arlo told him.

"Done. I'll make the call today. Anything else I should know?" Walter asked.

"No," Arlo responded. "Anything new regarding the Chief's spot?"

"Well, it looks to me like the competition for the job is down to only two or three of us right now. Charles Collins, Brad Michener and me. Michener is probably not really in the running since his recent encounter with the Highway Patrol. They nabbed him for drunk driving according to the latest rumors. He hasn't been to court yet but that can't help his hopes for the job."

"Probably not. I think you're in the driver's seat, Walter. I'll be at a luncheon tomorrow. I think the Mayor will be there. I'll remind his Honor of my sentiments."

"Good. Call and let me know if you hear anything interesting."

"I will, Walter. And thanks for taking care of the check on my house while I'm gone."

"No problem. Have a nice trip if I don't talk to you before you leave," he replied.

Walter hung up the phone. Who would have thought that a little partnership in a dry cleaners shop would turn into such a successful venture? Walter met Arlo at a cocktail party a little more than ten years ago. Walter sensed Arlo was a person who would become 'someone' in the L.A. social strata and in Walter, Arlo recognized a man who would do anything to get ahead. Some discreet checking with friends proved Arlo's first impression to be correct. Walter was a climber, both professionally and socially.

Arlo called Walter and invited him to lunch at one of the in spots in Beverly Hills. After some sparring around, Arlo suggested Walter might be interested in a joint business venture. Arlo knew of a dry cleaning shop that was just put on the market at a bargain price. He told Walter that for a small investment he could be half-owner. When Walter learned that he would be a silent partner, he readily agreed. Within three years there was a chain of fourteen shops spread out across the county. Walter always received his proceeds in cash. Arlo explained that the dry cleaning business was an almost all-cash business and that he had a very proficient accountant.

Arlo bought several other businesses and the arrangement with Walter was lucrative for both. Walter had kept his role as silent partner in these various ventures to himself. Not that he was doing anything wrong but it was just better if the department thought you were only involved in police work, with nothing distracting you from your duties to the citizens of Los Angeles. Very occasionally, Arlo would ask Walter for an extra sensitive favor. A police record check on someone, pull some pressure off a nightclub, or very rarely a heads- up on some pending investigation. These favors started slowly enough, and, on face value, seemed harmless. After all, Arlo, and to some degree Walter, had become involved in the entertainment industry. Everyone knew there were plenty of flakes in that business and information helped weave your way through the sharks. Walter felt he had been a real help in Arlo's success in becoming one of "the" producers in Hollywood.

Walter picked up his phone and spoke to Candy over the com line. "Candy, will you get me the Watch Commander at Hollywood on the phone, please?"

CHAPTER 10

"Andy, honey, will you be home for dinner?" his wife asked. Andy stopped in the open door and thought for a minute.

"I don't know. I'll have to call you later," he replied as he went out the front door. He walked to his car, which was parked in the driveway. He took careful note of the location of the various toys his two boys, Jeffrey, age 8, and Ben, age 6, had scattered around the area. In spite of his efforts, he nearly ran over Ben's red trike as he backed out of the driveway. The two boys waved from the front window and Andy waved back. Then he slowly drove off, looking at the house he and Melanie bought only a few years ago. Their dream home; their upper, middle class, two story, suburban dream home.

It didn't help, he thought. Nothing ever seemed to help. Not really. Nice home, great wife, two perfect kids and, on top of that, I've got a good job. Make pretty good money, he thought. But nothing helped. He knew he didn't deserve it. Never would. He was sure of that.

Tears began rolling down his cheeks as he drove through the up-scale development toward Madison Boulevard. Once on the boulevard, it was just a few blocks to the freeway. The northbound on-ramp would take him into downtown San Jose, to his office. Dunn and Krutcher, Stock Brokers, it said on the door. Below that was Andy's name in smaller letters, along with the names of two other junior partners. He'd done well for himself. At least as far as his wife was concerned. Only thirty-one and a junior partner. I'm glad she's happy about that, he thought. I want her to be happy. She's a wonderful person who deserves to be happy.

But Andy drove past the northbound on-ramp and entered the freeway heading south. South, toward Los Angeles. The large overhead sign said 'Los Angeles-351 miles'. Andy stepped down on the accelerator, merging with the traffic flow. He loosened his tie and thought about where he was going and what he was going to do when he got there. The tears continued to run down his cheeks.

He drove all day, steadily southward toward his destination, stopping once for gas and a large cup of coffee.

Andy had considered calling Melanie from the gas station. He'd like to hear her voice. He'd like to explain. She deserved an explanation. How many times had he tried to talk to her, to tell her the things that ... it didn't matter.

‘Maybe I'll write her a letter, try to explain,’ he thought. But he knew he wouldn't, couldn't ever hurt her by burdening her with all of that. He feared she'd feel responsible, guilty somehow for not realizing something was wrong. He knew there was nothing he could do about that, although the thought saddened him further. A not unfamiliar wave of despair swept over him. And although his involuntary response to cry came strongly, he was unable to produce but a single tear. ‘None left,’ he thought. Finally dried up.

Andy drove on, stopping only once more. He bought a second cup of coffee he really didn't want at a quickie mart so he wouldn't feel guilty for using the restroom.

Late in the afternoon, right in the middle of rush hour, Andy arrived in Los Angeles. However, crossing the city limits still left him forty miles from his destination. Seeing the familiar signs, streets and what passed for landmarks in the sprawling, overcrowded metropolis evoked only unpleasant memories. He took the freeway toward West Los Angeles and exited onto Sunset Boulevard, almost an hour later. The sun had nearly set. Andy took off his sunglasses and tried to push them into his shirt pocket. The hinge on the glasses caught on the pocket and after a couple of tries he muttered, "Fuck it," and threw the glasses out the side window.

He drove west on Sunset toward the beach. A mile or so before he got to the coast he turned right onto a narrow, two-lane street and then onto a still narrower lane that wound up a canyon where it eventually ended. Large estates occupied the hillside on both sides of the canyon. Andy pulled the car over onto the narrow shoulder and stopped about a block short of the lane's dead end. He sat, staring out the window at the huge house that occupied several acres at the end of the canyon.

As the last of the daylight waned, the canyon darkened and grew cooler. Time to get on with it, Andy thought. He got out of the car and, after retrieving his briefcase from the rear seat, walked up the road toward the big house. The driveway entrance to the house had a large gate denying entry. Andy removed a plastic card from his briefcase, inserted it into the gate control and, as the gate opened, he entered. After a few seconds, the gate closed behind him. Andy walked up the drive toward the house, dark emotions sweeping over him. He walked toward the front door and then changed direction, turning instead and going through a small, unlocked gate on the side of the house. He walked through a large, well-maintained garden to the rear pool area. Adjacent to the pool was a bathhouse. He reached up to the top of a large beam over the door to the bathhouse and retrieved a key. Andy used the key to open the bathhouse door and he entered. He then walked through an inner door into the house. Although it was dark inside, he turned on no lights, comfortably familiar with his surroundings.

Without looking around, Andy walked through the empty house to the staircase in the living room and proceeded upstairs to the second floor. He walked along the upstairs hall towards the rear of the house, his footsteps muffled by the heavy carpet. As he neared the end of the hall he realized he was beginning to shudder, almost uncontrollably. He forced himself to stop shaking, taking a deep breath as he paused at the door to the room at the end of the hall. Then he opened the door and entered the huge master bedroom.

'The Master's Bedroom,' Andy thought. He walked to one of the nightstands, turned on the Tiffany-shaded lamp and set his briefcase on the oversized, canopy-covered bed. He opened the case and removed a videotape, which he placed in the VCR on top of a television set that sat on a table at the foot of the bed. He turned both devices on and began removing his clothes as the picture appeared on the screen. Once naked, Andy got into the huge bed, covered himself and lay there watching the videotape. Tears once again rolled down his face. After several minutes he sat up in the bed and pulled the briefcase over to him. He opened it and removed two small handguns and a folded piece of paper. After pushing the briefcase off onto the floor, Andy laid back down. He opened the paper and read it carefully. Satisfied, he folded it back and placed it on the pillow next to him and leaned over and turned off the light. He then took a pistol in each hand, aimed them both at his chest and pulled the triggers. After only a moment of pain Andy died. And no more tears ran down his cheeks.

CHAPTER 11

At one a.m. on a Tuesday night four days later, the moon was a silver half heading towards full with high wispy clouds racing across the sky on the jet stream. The mansion at the end of the lane was well back off the street and the wide expanse of lawn had bushes and small trees interspersed with flowers and walkways. The property was surrounded by a six-foot stucco wall. A wrought iron gate blocked the main drive at the street. Lamps at each side of the gate cast a dull yellow glow into the night. The stucco wall presented only a minor impediment to the two burglars. The taller of the two boosted his much shorter partner over and then pulled himself over after him. The two-story colonial house was dark except for a light in one of the upstairs front windows. The light went off and then came back on in thirty, exactly thirty, seconds.

"There, it's on a timer. Tha' lights on a timer, it turns off and then back on. Let's go."

Two men broke from the shadows of one of the larger trees and moved quickly to the corner of the house furthest from the street. One of them carried a small dark bag. They weren't dressed in a fashion typical of burglars. Both had on sport coats and ties, loosened at the neck. The taller of the two was wearing jeans and the other tan slacks. The short one took a penlight from his pocket and, shielding it with his hand, moved the beam around the sill.

"No wires. Give me the pry bar," he said. The shorter of the two fumbled in the bag and handed him a short metal bar. Wedging it under the window he tried to force it open. After several tries, he looked at his cohort:

"Here, you try. I can't get the damn thing to budge."

The short man tried several times as well, to no avail. He sneezed and banged his head against the wooden sill.

"Shh!" the tall man cautioned.

"Can't help it, I got a damn cold," the other answered, wiping his nose.

"Fucking thing's painted shut. Let's do the back door," the tall one whispered.

"We did a door last time, remember?"

"Oh, so what? You want we just forget it? We do windows next two times, okay?" the tall man said in a louder, angry whisper. He turned and, without looking back, walked around the corner to the back of the house. The other followed obediently.

"Hold it!" The tall man held his hand up and was standing flat against the wall.

"What?" the short one said, sidling alongside the other.

"The bathhouse door," putting a finger to his lips.

"Yeah, so?"

"Look!" in a hoarse whisper. "It's open."

The two men stood there without moving, barely breathing, staring at the open door in the shadow of a large tree close to the house.

"What do ya' think?" the short one asked. "Think somebody's home?"

"Quiet. How tha' hell do I know? Do you hear anything?"

"No. Don't see anything either. They musta' forgot to shut it when they left," the short man whispered after peeking through another window.

"Okay, then. You go in and I'll be right behind you." The tall man pushed at the other as he spoke.

"Why me first?" he asked.

The tall man thought for a second and then said, "Because I'm taller than you and I can see over your shoulder."

The other man had no answer for that logic and moved to the door and into the bathhouse. From there, they entered the dark house. They stood silently in the kitchen area for several moments and then the taller one said, "You take the upstairs and I'll work down here."

"Right. Uh, if I run into anybody, then what?"

The man reached into the bag his partner was carrying and fumbled around for a minute, finally pulling out a black canister, saying, "Mace 'em and run like hell. I'll meet you at the car, okay?"

"Yeah, okay. But I don't like it. What if it's somebody else pulling a job?"

"Mace 'em anyway. C'mon, let's get going. We've been here too long." He gave the short man a push of encouragement and moved out of the kitchen into a hallway leading to the front of the house.

The shorter one stood at the foot of the wide staircase, listened for any noise for a minute and then moved slowly up the carpeted steps. Looking back down the stairs he could see the beam of his cohort's flashlight moving back and forth in the parlor.

He moved from the top of the stairs and down the hallway. The smells of furniture polish and wax mixed in the dusty odor of emptiness. The short man relaxed slightly. The place felt empty. He pushed open a door to a bedroom and began the business of burglary.

He went first to the bathroom. It was surprising how many people hid their valuables in the medicine cabinet. He shook each bottle he couldn't see into and then looked inside the toilet tank. Finding nothing, he moved into one of the bedrooms and began rummaging through the bureau drawers and the bedside tables. He was rewarded with a watch and two nice rings that he stuffed into the pockets of his sport coat. A look under the bed and between the mattress and he moved on to each of the other rooms, repeating the process quickly and efficiently.

Finally, he came to the last door at the end of the hall. He stood there waiting, staring at the yellow light showing through the crack at the bottom of the door. After a minute or so the sliver of light went dark. He waited a few minutes and then pushed into the large room. Its size suggested it was the master bedroom.

With the light off, the room was bathed in the soft blue glow of a television that had been left on, buzzing quietly in the emptiness, the screen blank. He stood there trying to spot the lamp that was on the timer, knowing it would be coming back on in a few seconds. Before he could locate it, it came on.

"Oh, oh shit!" The man stumbled backwards, fumbling at his waist, and fell over a footstool with a loud thump. The lower half of the body was spread-eagled beneath the bed covers. A large pool of coagulated blood spread across the chest of the corpse and on to the mattress. The eyes were open, staring at the ceiling. The body was unclothed and bloated with the gases of decay. It had begun to change to the greenish-blue color of rotted beef.

Downstairs, the noise of his partner falling startled the other man, who immediately started for the back door and then stopped and cautiously began making his way towards the staircase and the sound from the second level. He climbed the stairs, walked down the hall and peeked around the door of the large bedroom. He saw his cohort standing at the foot of the king-size bed.

"Pssst! What the hell!" he said in a hoarse whisper.

"I dunno. He's dead. Crap! We walked in on a homicide, ya think?" The short man rubbed his head nervously as his partner moved into the room and leaned over the body on the bed.

"Man, he's ripe. Been laying here at least a couple 'a days." The taller man held a handkerchief to his face. "Can't you smell him?"

"Naw, I told ya' I got a cold," the short man said, still staring at the body.

The second man walked around the bed and then bent down and picked up a piece of stationary and, after scanning the paper, looked at the other man.

"Note. It's a note. The guy offed himself," he said, and turned to the TV. "It's on VCR. What the hell was he watching?" referring to the corpse. "Push the eject button."

The first man walked over and did so, and with a humming noise the VCR spit out a tape. He took it from the machine and, holding it in front of him, looked to his partner with his eyebrows raised in a questioning expression.

"Take it with us." The man stuffed the note into his pocket, "And this, the note."

"Should we call? Uh, report this?" the short man asked.

"What? What? Call the cops and what? Hi, officer, we were doing a burglary and found this body and we'd rather not be here when you get here, so could you take your time. You know, give us a chance to get the hell out of here?" The tall man shook his head. "Right, you do that. Just wait a few minutes while I get the fuck out 'a here, okay?"

The short man hung his head, effectively chastised, and they both moved out of the bedroom and left the house, much as they found it--with the exception of the jewelry, the videotape and the note.

An hour and a half later the two culprits sat in the apartment of the tall one, side by side on the ratty old couch, staring at the TV set, blank now as the tape finished playing. Finally, the tall one spoke,

"Okay, here's how I see this." He stood and pulled the tape from the VCR. "This is a lot of money for us, a lot. The guy on this tape is Arlo what's-his-name. Movie producer or something. I've read about him in the papers. He's a big society guy, knows the mayor and hangs around with all the Hollywood mucky-mucks. Rich guy, finances movies and all that shit. We sell him the tape. Believe me, he don't want nobody knowing what's on this," holding the tape up in the air. "Two hundred thou' easy."

"Oh, man, isn't that pretty risky? We're talking extortion," the other interrupted.

"It's worth it. I'm telling you this guy will pay. And we'll keep the note for insurance. Won't mention it, just the tape. I'm telling you, it'll work. I got a good feeling."

The short man shrugged his reluctant agreement and they spent the next few hours planning how to relieve Arlo of some of his money. Extorting Arlo, the tape for the money, was obvious. Should be a piece of cake. They had to figure how to contact him and make the exchange.

"Not to worry. This guy is a Hollywood pussy. It's a sure thing, a walk in the park," the tall one said.

CHAPTER 12

Jake and Mitch sat down at the Koffee Kup for the once-a-week get together. They'd gotten past reliving the "good old days" and now spent time discussing more contemporary matters. The department was a topic that interested Mitch and he was always ready to listen to the latest goings- on. Jake, now comfortable enough with Mitch to share some of the inner workings of the job, kept Mitch up to date on a few cases they'd discussed. Mitch was particularly interested in the Hollywood Hills murder case involving the young woman who'd been strangled. They discussed it at some length and Jake realized Mitch would like nothing better than to be working the investigation. Jake also realized that despite Mitch's years of brain cell destruction, he still had a cop's sixth sense and could probably do a credible job of investigating the murder.

Jake also told Mitch about the current jostling for position that was going on within the department as the top brass tried to move up in the pecking order and get more visible; all to better their shot at the Chief of Police opening that was imminent. Jake, of course, told Mitch about Walter Burnett and his past experiences with him.

"What happens to you if that jerk takes over the top spot?" Mitch asked.

"Nothing. He'll be too busy to screw with me. At least I think he will. I doubt he gives me much thought. We haven't seen each other in a long time and he's got more important things to worry about than Lieutenant Reed. Besides, if he wanted to screw with me, he'd have done it long ago. But I sure hate to see him as Chief of Police. Particularly with guys like Collins around."

"Collins, who's Collins?" Mitch asked.

"A hell of a lot better candidate than Burnett. Unfortunately, he's a low-key, no-nonsense kind of guy who'd never consider, much less do, any self-promoting. He probably doesn't stand much of a chance. Too bad."

"Yeah, it is. He sounds like the right guy," Mitch said. "Oh, by the way. I forgot to tell you what happened. The Audubon Society will probably want to give me an award or something. I was taking a walk yesterday when I found this baby crow. He was cowering on the sidewalk, the poor thing. Fell out of a nest, I guess. I took him back to the boat and fed him. He's doing real good. Cool, huh?"

"A crow, what are you going to do with a crow? What about the dog?" Jake asked, shaking his head. 'What next?', Jake wondered to himself.

"She's in the car," Mitch said.

"Who's in the car? The crow!"

"No, the dog."

Jake stared at Mitch. "What I meant was. What about the dog getting after the crow?"

"Shouldn't be a problem. She doesn't know she's a bird dog."

"Well, that's a relief. I suggest you not tell her."

"Yeah, I…"

"Hold it," Jake interrupted. He reached for his beeper. He looked at the number displayed on it and then said, "Got to call the office." He got up and went to the phone in the hallway of the restaurant. After a brief conversation he walked back to the table. "That was Kelly."

Before he could continue, Mitch interrupted. "Ah yes. The lovely Ms. McBride. I'd sure like to get…"

"Yeah, I bet you would. Forget it, Mitch. She's not your type and, more to the point, you're not hers. No way, Jose. Not going to happen."

"Okay, okay. I get the picture. But it's her loss, poor girl."

"Yeah, right. Anyway, to get back to the police work for a moment. I have to respond to a call. Sounds like a suicide over in the hoity-toity part of town, up above Sunset."

Mitch looked rather wistfully at Jake.

"You want to come along?" Jake asked him.

"Yeah, but is it OK?"

"Sure," Jake told him. "If anyone asks who you are, tell 'em you're a professor doing a study on suicides. Here, stick a toothpick in your mouth. It'll make you look like a regular guy." Jake said, handing Mitch one from the supply in his pocket.

"Okay, great. Let's go."

*****

It was the typical crime scene. Uniformed cops standing around waiting for directions and hoping the brass would notice their professional demeanor and transfer them, on the spot, to a job at Robbery/Homicide Division. A plain clothes assignment, every beat cop's dream. Mitch took note of the deference shown to Jake as the two of them entered the palatial home. Not only the other officers, but also the techs and people from the coroner's office all showed Jake an affectionate respect. One of the officers directed them to the stairway.

"Upstairs and down the hall to the end, Lieutenant. You can't miss it," he said.

Jake and Mitch followed the young officer's directions to the top of the stairs. From there, the master bedroom could be seen. It was clear that that was where the action was. They walked down the hall and into the room where several officers, both uniformed and in plain clothes, were standing around. It was apparent to Jake that most were there out of curiosity rather than need.

"Those of you who don't need to be here, please get the hell out so that those who do can do their job," he directed. All but three left the room hurriedly; the two detectives who were handling the investigation and a third man who was examining the body closely. The TV. at the end of the bed was on however; it displayed only snow, no picture.

Jake shoved his hands in his pockets as he walked into the room. It was a habit he'd picked up a long time ago from an old detective named Steckle who told him it kept him from touching anything at a crime scene. It gets a little embarrassing when the detectives in charge of the crime scene get returns on prints that were lifted, only to find they belong to their boss.

"Looks like a fairly routine suicide, Lieutenant." The man speaking was wearing thick horn rimmed glasses and had white rubber gloves on his thin hands.

"Kid shot himself right in the chest." He pointed to his heart with both of his fore fingers as he spoke. "Twice," he said.

"From the smell I'd say it's been awhile. Maybe a week."

Mitch figured him for a coroner.

"Uh huh, find the gun?" Jake asked. "Or should I say guns?" as he stared at the corpse lying on its back, both arms flung wide to either side. There was a parade of ants moving from some unseen cranny in the large bedroom, across the carpet and then onto the bed, feasting on a large mass of dried blood.

"Yah. One's over in the corner by the lamp. The other's under the bed. Must have bounced off the wall. It looks like two guns, one shot in the chest from each. Never saw that one before..." Horn rimmed glasses said, pointing. "No note. Funny, he chose this room, isn't it? It looks like his parents' bedroom."

"How do you arrive at that conclusion?" Jake asked.

"Pictures," he replied, pointing at the photos on one wall.

Jake glanced at the photos then turned to Joe Seagar, one of the two detectives examining the body. "Have we identified this guy yet, Joe?"

"Well, not for sure yet, Boss, but there is a picture of him on the wall. He's with two older people, probably his parents. For the moment, it looks to us like this is his parents' house. If it is, this is their bed. And that makes this one for the books. Killing yourself in your folk's bed is pretty weird," Seagar replied.

Jake grunted and walked over to look at the weapon on the floor near the lamp.

We may have to call Behavioral Sciences to explain this one," Jake said. "Seems like there should have been a note though, doesn't it?"

Seagar agreed.

"It stands to reason that if someone crawls into Mom and

Dad's bed and kills himself, he's sure as hell trying to tell them something, doesn't it?" Jake added.

"I have to agree with you, Lieutenant. We've looked the place over pretty thoroughly and there's no note so far. We'll keep looking. Maybe one will turn up."

"Maybe the circumstances speak for themselves. This guy may have figured that when the folks found him in a rotting heap in their bed, the message would be pretty clear. He probably didn't have to say anymore. It'll be interesting to hear what his parents have to say about this, won't it," Jake mused. While thinking about that, he walked over to take a look at the picture Seagar had referred to earlier. Jake took one look and recognized the man in the photo immediately. It was Arlo Calarasi. The woman, a fashionably dressed and rather stunning redhead about forty, was undoubtedly his wife.

Jake turned back to Seagar and told him who they were. He whistled his surprise. "No shit! This will give the press something to do today, won't it?" Jake agreed and told Seagar to try to find out where the Calarasis were, maybe by contacting the neighbors. The decomposing condition of the body suggested the house's residents hadn't been home for some time.

"By the way, Joe, how did we happen to get notified about this? Did someone call it in or what?" Jake asked.

Seagar said he didn't know but he'd find out.

Meanwhile, Mitch wandered down the upstairs hall, tired of being in the same room with the body. A uniformed officer nodded hello and Mitch nodded back. An open door beckoned and Mitch went into another bedroom. It felt like a child's room. The pillowcases had cartoons on them and there was a tinker toy set in one corner in disarray as though recently played with. Several stuffed teddy bears sat slouching on top of a chest of drawers. Mitch looked in the closet. Men's clothing hung there. Several gaudy sports coats, slacks and dress shirts as well as some iridescent jump suits. The room made Mitch uncomfortable, it was out of sync.

He wandered around the room picking up an item here and there, opening a dresser drawer and looking. He pushed a calendar aside and stared at a picture.

The boy appeared to be about sixteen years of age. He was standing next to two adults that Mitch surmised were his parents. The boy was dressed in a pair of pajamas with a little hood thrown partially back from his face. The pajamas were a costume, a little yellow duck costume. The boy was dressed like a little yellow duck.

Mitch stared at the picture. The boy's expression made him feel uncomfortable. That old warning tickle hit his gut. The boy looked dead, dull, no life in his eyes. The woman was looking away from the camera with a bored expression. The man stared straight ahead, a slight smile on his face. His arm hung loosely over the boy's shoulder. Mitch shook his head, walked from the room and back down the hall to the death scene.

Jake was finishing up, talking to the investigating officers.

"Keep on top of it, fellas. The media's going to have a feast on this one." Jake looked over at Mitch. "Ready? Let's go." Mitch followed Jake from the mansion. They climbed in the plain car and headed out through the front gate and on to the road.

"I gather you know who lives there," Mitch surmised.

Jake headed rapidly back the way they'd come.

"I'll drop you off at the coffee shop. I want to get back to the station. The brass will want to be briefed on this one right away."

"The parents are important, huh?" Mitch asked.

"Oh, yeah," Jake replied. "Arlo and Maureen Calarasi. Arlo is a big wheel in the movie business. He's part of what passes for high society in L.A. Does the charities and is in with the Mayor and all that. You get the picture." Jake shook his head. "If the stiff in the bed is their son, and I assume it is at this point, it's not too hard to imagine how he wound up like he did. Couldn't live up to the old man's expectations. Or couldn't handle the dope. Or had so much he got bored or who the hell knows. Maybe we'll find out, maybe we won't. Happens a lot with these kids of the rich and successful. Suicide or drugs or run away to a commune with the 'Yamatsun Gurunga' or some such thing."

The two men rode along in silence for a few blocks and then:

"Uh, I don't think so," Mitch said.

"Don't think so, what?" Jake asked.

"That guy was troubled in a different way. That family's kinked." Mitch stared straight ahead.

"Well maybe. What makes you say that?"

"The kid's room, it just feels wrong. You ought to have a look at it." Mitch was hesitant to go any further. He didn't want to look foolish in front of Jake. A few minutes later they pulled up in front of

Mitch's old Mustang.

"Give me a call first of the week, OK?" Jake said. Mitch nodded.

"Can I ask a favor, Jake?" Mitch asked.

"Yeah, what is it?"

"I don't know if you remember but I have a daughter, Missy."

"Sure, I remember. She's living with your ex, isn't she?" Jake asked.

"Well, she was but she's 23 now. I doubt if she's still living with her mother. I have no idea where either of them is, actually. That's what I was going to ask, if you could help me find her. Missy, that is."

"I'll see what I can do, Mitch. Kelly, my adjutant's pretty good at tracking people down. I'll have her see what she can do. Why don't you give her a call with the particulars. I'll tell her to expect your call. Okay?"

"Thanks Jake, I really appreciate it. I haven't seen my daughter in 16 years."

"We'll find her, Mitch. No problem."

Mitch slid behind the wheel of the Mustang, waved to Jake and drove off. Jake left in the opposite direction, headed for the Hollywood Station.

*****

The brass and white ceramic telephone sat on the polished maple desk, a tiny blue light flashing impatiently at its base. The distinguished, silver haired man reached over with a manicured hand and picked up the receiver.

"Yes?"

"Good evening, sir. Could you call me back on the 573 number?"

The man replaced the receiver without response, reached under the desk, brought out a second phone and dialed number six. The call up-linked to a satellite, which transmitted the signal back down to Italy and from there across two continents and an ocean, back to Los Angeles.

"Thank you" a tinny sounding voice said.

"Good evening," the silver haired man replied.

"I am catering a dinner party. There are some delectable pomegranates, they will be picked just in seven more days or so. I thought of you,"

" Yes?" and after a pause, "the price?"

"A little higher, however the flavor is exquisite. Two fifty a pound," the tinny voice said.

"That will be just fine. Let's say a week from today in the evening." The man broke the connection without another word. He sat back in the green leather chair and rested his jaw on top of his cupped hands. His thoughts were broken a few minutes later by a light tapping at the door of his study. His wife pushed the door ajar and asked,

"Are you ready to retire Clinton?"

" No, you go ahead. I have some cases to review," he responded without looking at her.

CHAPTER 13

Jake pulled into the station parking lot, leaving his car in its assigned stall. He walked through the rear door and down the hall adjacent to the jail. The holding cells were all fully occupied, he noted. The usual assortment of gang bangers, hookers, petty thieves and street-savvy runaways who find Hollywood irresistible. 'At least until they get here,' Jake thought. Several more arrestees were handcuffed to the benches along the wall.

All those in the cells, as well as those sitting on the benches, were waiting to be booked. Although most of them were probably arrested for misdemeanor offenses, there were a few hardcore assholes in the group. Jake recognized some of them, including a gang banger from the notorious 16th Street gang, Chuy Mendoza. Chuy was hard to forget. He had "16th St" tattooed across his forehead in 1" block letters. No one could question that Chuy was committed. 'Chuy ought to be committed,' Jake thought, 'to the psycho ward at County'.

As he walked into his office, Rene handed him several phone messages and told him that Kilgore had been in to see him earlier. Jake thanked her as he browsed through the messages. "I'll see him in a few minutes."

Jake sat down at his desk and put the phone messages in order; the one's he needed to respond to immediately and then those that could wait. Before he could pick up the phone, however, Kelly walked in. "Anything I can help you with before I go to lunch?" she asked. Jake thought a minute.

"Yes, there is but not right now. Mitch is going to be calling you with some information about his long lost daughter. I told him you'd be glad to help him find her. He hasn't seen her in a long time, 15 years or so and he has no idea where she is. Do what you can for him, will you?"

"Sure, Boss, but who's Mitch?" Kelly asked.

"You know that tall, gray haired guy who was in here the other day?"

Kelly nodded.

"Well, that's Mitch. Old friend of mine who, incidentally, thinks you're pretty hot. I tried to straighten him out by telling him you're a lesbian but I don't think he bought it."

"Thanks! That's all I need."

"Go have lunch. I'll talk to you when you get back," Jake told her. "Oh, by the way, would you please bring me the morning report before you go?"

Kelly brought Jake the report and left. He threw it on top of the pile of reports already in his 'in-box.' Jake reached for a fresh toothpick and the phone. He made the calls he didn't figure could wait. As it turned out, they could have. Hanging up after the last one, he pulled a legal tablet from his top desk drawer and began writing a few notes before briefing the Station Commander, Captain Ed Hughes, about the suicide.

Hughes would want to brief the Chief of Detectives, Walter Burnett, as soon as possible and definitely before Burnett heard about it from the media. Nothing pissed the Chief of Detectives off more than learning about some major incident over the radio or, worse yet, from some news reporter, rather than from one of his own people. In fact, repeated failures on the part of a Captain to keep the Chief fully informed have occasionally resulted in re-assignment to less desirable positions, such as traffic or supply. Neither Jake nor Captain Hughes wanted to see that happen.

Jake finished his notes, threw the toothpick in the trash and walked across the hall to the Captain's office. Hughes motioned him in and Jake sat down while the Captain finished up a phone call with his wife. "She's a good woman and I love her dearly but she can talk longer about nothing than anyone I've ever known," Hughes said as he hung up.

"I know what you mean, Captain. I've got a screwball who calls me about once a month, former reporter for the local throw- away paper, who can put your wife to shame. I'll be glad to refer him directly to you next time he calls so you can make the comparison, if you'd like," Jake offered.

"No thanks. I'll take your word for it. What have you got?"

"A suicide. Got the call up yesterday. Up in the hills above Sunset. Very ugly. Identification on the body indicates it's Arlo Calarasi's kid. Male, 32 years old, named Andy. Nobody at the house so we weren't able to positively I'd. him. My detectives are trying to find his parents, but the neighbors tell us they're in Europe somewhere."

"Arlo Calarasi. He's a movie producer or something, isn't he?"

"That's him. Big mover and shaker. Buddies with the Mayor. I've heard he has some friends in the upper echelons of the department, however I don't know who they are."

"Well, I don't either, but I better let Chief Burnett know. He'll have a shit-fit if the local press calls him before we do. Thanks, Jake. I'll call you if Burnett's got questions I can't answer."

"Okay, Captain. We'll keep working on this, trying to locate his parents."

"By the way, Jake, how did we get on to this? If no one was home, who called the police?"

"I don't know Captain. We're looking into that, too. When I get an answer I'll let you know."

Hughes nodded and reached for the phone as Jake walked out and returned to his office. Jake sat down at his desk and lifted the pile of reports from his in-box. 'Now for the mundane side of the job,' Jake thought as he browsed through the first few. 'On second thought, I better return some more phone calls first'.

Half an hour later, Jake hung up the phone after completing the last of the calls. Finding no way to avoid it, he finally began to go through the stack of reports. A quick review of the Morning Report revealed that nothing of earth-shattering importance had occurred over the past twenty-four hours. The usual rapes, robberies, burglaries and assaults, a few stolen cars and a significant number of arrests kept the guys in the radio cars busy. Vice had had a good night. The Trick Task Force had been in the division and arrested seventeen men, all looking for a good time. Unfortunately for them, the women they solicited were all police officers. Among those captured was an off-duty deputy sheriff. "What the hell was he thinking?" Jake wondered aloud. Life is full of surprises.

The balance of the report contained administrative information. On-duty traffic accidents, officers on sick days, overtime used, people loaned to other divisions, any other personnel information and, it seemed, on and on. Reviewing the report, Jake noted that Jeanie Leeds had begun her maternity leave, the third time in as many years. "I wonder if she can remember what it's like not to be pregnant." Jake said to himself. Further down the report Jake noticed several people were off sick. The flu had been running rampant through the division for the past week. 'No wonder we're falling behind on follow-up reports,' he thought. Seven detectives had called in sick, two from the Burglary unit, three who were assigned to Robbery and two from the Juvenile section. 'This keeps up,' he thought 'and I'll have to start carrying cases, too'. The two guys from the Burglary unit were partners, Pritchard and Landers. "I hope for their sake they aren't off fishing again," Jake mumbled.

About four months before, the two of them took a couple of sick days to go deep-sea fishing. Unfortunately, the boat they were on capsized near the Long Beach breakwater and the Coast Guard had to come to the rescue. They made the six o'clock news and blew their sick story. They were both given a minor reprimand.

Jake also noted that Thorney Parsons, his long-time deskman, had announced his retirement. 'Now there's a real problem', Jake thought. Getting anyone to work the desk was going to be a challenge. Detectives want to detect, not sit at the desk and answer the phone all day. Thorney had been placed on 'light duty' status due to a heart problem, and he really had no choice but to man the phones. 'Maybe I'll put Jeanie Leeds on the desk,' he thought. 'She's pregnant all the time anyway. She probably shouldn't be in the field.'

It suddenly dawned on Jake that Kilgore wanted to see him. Jake called Kilgore on the com-line.

"Dave, this is Jake. Rene said you were looking for me earlier.

What's up?"

"Glad you called, Boss. I've got a friend of yours here at my desk. He says he has some info for us that we might be able to use. It has to do with the Hilltop case."

"Really. Who is it?" Jake asked.

"It's Earl Entwisle," Kilgore replied.

"You mean Earl the Girl?" Jake chuckled.

"The very one. And looking quite lovely, I might add," Kilgore replied.

"Well, why don't you two waltz on back here to my office and let's see what Earl has to tell us," Jake said.

Kilgore indicated that he and Earl would be right there; not waltzing, he added.

'Earl the Girl. What a piece of work he is,' Jake thought. Earl thought he was a female trapped in a man's body. Nothing unusual about that. A lot of mcn think that, cspccially among thosc living in Hollywood. Earl dressed in women's clothes and hung around the clubs that cater to those of a similar persuasion. About a year ago, Earl had a run-in with a macho male from south of the border who he'd been dancing with at one of the clubs. The guy, who became indignant when he realized he'd been dancing with a male rather than a female, beat Earl within an inch of his life.

Jake and two of his detectives, Terry Calder and Wynn Adams, had responded to the scene just as the ambulance crew was hauling Earl away. His condition had led them to believe that the investigation would soon be for murder but Earl fooled them and survived. After a month in the hospital, Earl was back on the scene. He'd lost some of his sex appeal and wasn't as attractive as he once was but Earl was coping.

As for the suspect, the two detectives located him in Mexico. They managed to extradite him and get him convicted of a felony assault. Earl declared his undying devotion for Hollywood Detective Division and Calder and Adams, in particular, for their efforts. In fact, Earl drops by the station regularly with cookies or cakes that he's baked especially for his heroes.

Kilgore walked in with Earl and they all exchanged greetings. Earl was decked out in all his feminine finery and trying to appear as demure as possible. However, at 6 feet and 190 pounds, that wasn't easy. Earl shook hands with Jake and sat down.

"Still chewing on those toothpicks, huh?" Earl said.

"Yep," Jake replied.

Jake noticed that Earl wasn't as 'cute' as he once was. A result of the savage beating he'd sustained. Jake also noticed that Earl's voice was deeper. Probably made it tougher for him to pass himself off as a woman. 'We all have our problems,' Jake thought.

"So, what's up, Earl?"

"Well, honey, I have some information for you that might be helpful. It's about that young girl who was killed up in the hills a few days ago. The one the paper said was raped and strangled?"

"You know something about that, Earl?" Jake asked.

"Well, I think I might."

"I appreciate you coming in Earl. Tell me what you've got."

Earl crossed his legs and leaned forward, lowering his voice as though he was afraid someone might overhear him. "What I've got is a conversation I had in the restroom of the 'Sassy Lassy' the other night. I don't hang out at the 'Classy Lady' anymore since my unfortunate encounter with that asshole from Mexico City. Anyway, I'm doing my ablutions, taking my time before rejoining my gentleman friend when this little, sawed off, son-of-a-bitch comes barging through the door, yelling and screaming like he was nuts. Imagine that! A man in the ladies room!"

"Shocking," Jake agreed, wondering if it ever occurred to Earl that, in spite of what he thought, he is also of the male persuasion.

"That's what I thought and I told him to get out immediately. He called me a bitch and told me to shut up. Imagine! He looked around like he was looking for someone and then he turned and walked out. As soon as the door shut, I hear this voice from one of the stalls ask if he's gone. I didn't even realize there was anyone else in the bathroom. I opened the stall door and here's this chick standing up on the toilet seat. I guess she was hiding from "Shorty." It was obvious that she was real scared of him. She told me that he'd just gotten out of prison and she thought he'd already killed one woman. She said he was a real weirdo and she wanted to get away from him. Well, I'd just read about the woman up in the hills and had a feeling that she might be the one he killed."

"Really, why?" Jake asked.

"I just have this feeling. I've always felt that I was psychic. Maybe that's it. I don't know, Lieutenant. I've just got this feeling."

Kilgore asked Earl what he could tell them about the girl who was hiding in the stall. He admitted that he couldn't tell them much but he said he was going to go to the "Sassy Lassy" every night until he found her. Earl said he was certain she'd show up and when she did, he'd see what he could find out about her for them.

Kilgore looked skeptical but, like Jake, he realized that a lot of cases have been solved by some pretty unlikely bits of information from some pretty unlikely characters. This certainly fit that criteria.

Jake and Kilgore thanked Earl for coming in and assured him they'd appreciate anything he could come up with on the female. Earl left and after a short conversation about the information he'd provided them, Kilgore went back to his desk and Jake went back to his in-box.

"Paperwork! I love it," Jake muttered.

An hour later Jake decided he'd had all the paperwork he could stand for one day. He retrieved his shoulder holster and 9mm Berretta from his lower desk drawer and put it on. He took his sport jacket from the closet, threw it over his shoulder and headed out of his office. As Jake walked past the detective desk, he stopped to talk to Thorney Parsons.

"So, you're going to pull the pin. How many years have you got on the job, Thorney?" Jake asked.

"Well, I'm gonna have thirty on in about a week. I think that's enough for me," he replied. "You know Jake, I've got a heart problem. I want to spend more time with my wife and my grandkids. And less time parked on the fucking freeway everyday. You know what I mean?"

Jake nodded. "Yeah, I know what you mean. We're going to miss you around here, though. When's your party?"

"Haven't set a date yet, but I'll let you know Jake."

"O.K. See you tomorrow."

An hour of freeway traffic later, Jake finally pulled into his driveway. "Thorney's got the right idea," he muttered. He went in and changed into his running gear to go jogging and ease the stress a little. As he ran, he thought about the suicide of Andy Calarasi. Definitely a weird one, he thought. The guy was certainly trying to send a not so subtle message to his parents. Killing himself in their bed is bad enough. But doing it knowing he was going to lie there and rot for a week suggests he was more than a little upset with them.

"I'd like to know what that's all about," Jake said to himself.

"I'd also like to know who called the police."

Just as Jake got back to the house, Edie drove up, wrapping up her forty mile commute for the day.

"Well, you've had a long day, as usual," Jake said.

"When you make the big bucks you have to give 'em a big effort," she replied, a bit sarcastically. "How was your day?"

"Not bad. The usual crap."

"I just heard on the radio that the son of some Hollywood biggie committed suicide. Were you involved in that?" she asked.

"Yeah, I was at the scene. Interesting," Jake replied.

He gave her a sanitized version of the suicide as they walked into the house.

"Why do you think he killed himself? Did he leave a note?" she asked.

"Haven't got a clue. No note, nothing at all. It'd sure make our job easier if these suicide victims would leave a letter of explanation," Jake said, smiling at Edie.

Jake stripped off his running gear as he headed for the shower.

"I'm going to get cleaned up before I start dinner. That is unless you'd like to go out to eat," Jake suggested.

"Let me think about it."

Much to Jake's delight, Edie joined him in the shower a few minutes later. After thoroughly washing one another, they made love under the warm water. Between the twenty minutes in the warm water and the love making, Jake felt exhausted.

"Well, if you want dinner tonight honey, it's going to be pizza from the freezer or a restaurant someplace. After that little interlude I'm too weak to cook."

"How about Marino's?" Edie asked and Jake agreed.

"Splendid idea. Let's go."

Marino's was a favorite of theirs. It's a small, neighborhood restaurant they'd been patronizing for years.

They made the short drive, parked and, in a few minutes, were seated and sipping glasses of Chianti at a table in a quiet corner. As they waited for their meal they talked about the latest department scuttlebutt and Walter Burnett's prospects for gaining the Chief's job.

"I've got a nasty hunch that Walter's already got things pretty well in place," Jake said. "The guy's got connections inside and outside the department. He's been campaigning like a politician for the last year."

"But it's not a political position, is it?" Edie asked.

"Never has been, but Walter seems to have made it one. He's out glad-handing everyone in sight. He's gotten real close with the Mayor and the Mayor's the one who has the last word on the selection."

"Well, the Mayor's no dummy, is he? He certainly can see when he's being operated, can't he?" Edie asked hopefully.

"I don't know, honey. Let's hope so. I'd sure rather see Collins in the top spot. But if running around stroking all the 'powers to be' is necessary, he doesn't stand a chance. Poor guy's saddled with too much integrity. He apparently believes that doing your job efficiently counts, in the end. I'm afraid that won't get it these days."

Dinner arrived and they ate casually, dropping the discussion about the Chief's job and chatting about nothing in particular. After dinner, they each had a cup of coffee. Edie asked Jake about Calarasi's house, how it was decorated and how big it was. Jake had to admit that he hadn't paid that much attention to the décor. As for the size of the place, he told her it was huge and not particularly pleasant. Jake told Edie that the place was dark and furnished like an old European mansion, kind of like the house in the movie "Dracula."

"I guess that figures, doesn't it?" she said. "The guy is a Hollywood producer and with a name like Calarasi, he's probably eastern European. Maybe he's from Transylvania."

They both laughed and got up to leave. Jake left a tip on the table, paid the bill, grabbed a handful of toothpicks and they left. They drove the few blocks back to the house, parked and went inside. Before going to bed, Jake checked the answering machine and there was a message from Mitch. His crow was missing. Jake stood there, pondering that when the phone rang. He picked it up, expecting to hear someone from the station advising him of a callout, but instead it was Mitch.

"Jake. Mitch. Listen, don't worry about the crow. I found her. She was hanging around with some seagulls at the end of the pier."

"Rest assured that I wasn't especially distressed over the matter. But thanks for calling." Jake got ready to hang up the phone when Mitch said:

"Man, that was some weird suicide today, huh?"

"Yeah. I've had a few that were pretty strange but that was

one for the memoirs."

"Did you find out who called it in?"

"No, not yet. That remains a mystery. Probably some hired help, a gardener or a cleaning lady. Something like that. We'll find out. Anyway, good night Mitch. I'll be able to sleep now that I know the crow is safe and sound."

CHAPTER 14

The Armbruster was typical of the area. Between Wilshire and Sunset in West Hollywood, there were blocks of old stone and mortar fronted six and eight story apartment buildings. Built during the thirties, most of the units were one bedroom and singles. In the thirties, they were upscale. Now they were old, marginally livable, worn out, each barely distinguishable from the other. The Armbruster was no exception. Long hallways, dark and quiet, with worn flowered carpeting; the door of each apartment identified with tarnished brass numbers. The short burglar knocked softly at Number 422. His partner in crime opened the door immediately, holding the morning paper in his hand.

"You called 'em didn't you," the tall man said in an angry voice the minute the door was closed, waving the newspaper in his partner's face.

"What? What are you talking about?" the short man said.

"Look, you dipshit. Read that." He was holding the Metro section of the L.A. Times. "Better yet, I'll read it to you."

The article was half way down page one and told of the police finding the son of a prominent Beverly Hills couple. He was found in their bedroom, the apparent victim of suicide. The article went on to describe Arlo's successful business career and his many charitable activities.

"So? So what's that got to do with me? What're you all pissed off about? What do ya' mean I called them?"

"Oh, well listen to this, you asshole. The police were alerted by an anonymous phone call. That was you, wasn't it?" The tall man slammed the paper down on the old stained coffee table, knocking an empty beer bottle onto the hard wood floor where it rolled to a corner of the small front room and lay there. Both men stared at it. The short man broke the silence in a whiny voice.

"Ah, you know, I felt sorry for the kid. I waited a couple of days before I called. Hell, what could it hurt? I mean the cops'll probably not even notice we hit the place. They'll be too busy with the, you know, the stiff." The tall man stood there staring at his cohort and then turned and walked to the kitchen saying over his shoulder,

"You better hope so, that's all I got to say. You want a beer?"

"No, it's too early," relief in the short man's voice. "Got any tea?"

"Tea? What's the matter with you? Do you really think I'd have any tea around here?" waving at the dirty kitchen, dishes in the sink and the trash basket overflowing with bottles and frozen food cartons. "What a pussy."

The two men sat at the Formica table and the tall man laid out what he thought would be a good plan to contact Arlo.

"I'll call him. One good thing about the news article, we know he won't be back before tomorrow. I got his office number this morning from information. Called and talked to his secretary. She says he'll be home soon. Told her I was an old friend and wanted to tell him how sorry I was. So what we do is call him and set up a meet. Not gonna tell him about the note, we keep that as insurance. I'm tellin' you, we are going to hit big on this one." He stopped and looked at his partner who shrugged and said:

"Well, I don't know. We're talking extortion. That's big time all right. Big jail time. Are you sure about this?" He stared at his hands nervously.

"It's gonna work, I'm telling you, trust me."

The short burglar stopped at a 7-11 the next morning and picked up a cup of hot tea. Back in his car, he sipped at the foam cup with a frown on his face. He thought he could taste more cup than tea. Convinced the hot liquid pulled the foam of the cup into solution, he rolled the window down and splashed the contents out and onto the side of the car. He rounded the corner and pulled up to the curb at the Armbruster and honked the horn. His partner came out the front door and walked down the sidewalk. He got in, sat down and said:

"Morning. I called his office. Secretary said she thought he'd be in in an hour. Let's go to a pay phone and I'll make the call."

"Maybe we should wait, uh, wait 'til tomorrow," Shorty said, still nervous.

"No way. We catch him right when he gets in, shock value," his partner said. He reached over and turned off the radio. "Get over on Wilshire and find a pay phone."

He pulled the light blue Ford into traffic and a few blocks over turned onto Wilshire and into the same 7-11 where he got his tea earlier. The pay phones were in a row along the front of the building. The passenger jumped out and chose the one furthest from the entrance and motioned to his cohort.

"Change. I need some change." He held out his hand and the second man got out of the car and gave him a handful of coins. The tall burglar began stuffing them in the phone.

"Yeah, I called earlier. You said Arlo would be in, I'd like to speak with him." He paused, listening. His partner pressed in, trying to hear every word. He frowned and pushed him back. "No, I don't have a name. You just tell him it's a new friend that has something he'll want very bad. Got that? Very bad."

They stood there for almost a minute, one with the phone to his ear and the other nervously standing on one foot and then the other, wrapping and unwrapping his arms around his chest.

"Yeah, yeah, good morning pal, good for me." The tall burglar paused and then, "No! You listen! We were in your house. We have something you don't want anybody to see, you fuck, so pay attention." A pause and, "Listen, you Hollywood fag. I couldn't care less what you do with your dick. We got a tape your kid was watching when he offed himself, and it's for sale. We figure you want to be the highest bidder. Let's just say we got..." he stopped talking and then, "we have a bid of a hundred and ninety grand and you are going to bid two."

The burglar looked at his partner and winked and then said into the phone:

"Good, I'm glad you're a reasonable man. You figure it out and I'll call you in say, two hours. We want to be out of town by tomorrow morning." A pause and then, "Fine then." He hung up and turned to the second man who asked,

"What do you mean we're leaving town? We can't leave town. I got a house and..."

"No dummy, we're not leaving town, I just told him that so he'd be comfortable that we're not gonna keep hitting on him. Get it? You gotta think on the run. Gotta always be thinking ahead." He tapped his temple. "Come one, we got a lot to do."

Both men got in the car and headed east on Wilshire.

Two hours later, the two burglars pulled into a Shell station and parked by the air and water machine.

"You stay here. I'm gonna call him," the tall man said, pointing at a payphone by the sidewalk. He was at the phone for at least five minutes and then got back in the car, a satisfied look on his face.

"We're in, man. We hit it. The big one."

"Why? What did he say?" the short one asked.

"Tonight, we meet tonight, he'll have the money."

"Meet where?" Shorty was nervous. "When?"

"The '507,' downtown. At eleven tonight." The tall man slapped the dash. "Two hundred thousand! Oh, man."

Sixth Street in downtown was quiet. The only business open, the '507' with a small red and blue neon sign sputtering in the window announcing 'co ktails,' the 'c' burned out. An old woman with her nylons all wrinkled and bunched at her ankles wandered down the dirty sidewalk muttering to herself and stopping every few feet to search through the pockets of the two old raincoats she wore before shuffling on down the lonely street. It seemed as though every other street lamp was burned out.

At eleven thirty, the light blue Ford pulled up, and sat idling, down the street from the '507.'

"OK, here's how we'll do it." The tall man sat in the passenger seat. "I go in and make the deal and you stay here and keep an eye out."

"I dunno. I don't like this. This guy's rich, big time mucky-muck. Why this dive? It don't make sense," the short man said, fidgeting with the steering wheel.

"What? Ya' think he's gonna want to meet at the Biltmore? Or maybe a church? I bet his secretary found this joint in tha' yellow pages. He's probably thinking about one of the movies he's made. Don't sweat it," the tall man said.

"Well, be careful, that's all I got to say."

"Yeah, yeah. Just sit here and keep your eyes open, OK?" The tall man climbed out of the car and winked. "I'll be back in a few." He walked rapidly down the block with a swagger and disappeared into the skid row bar.

The '507' was just as he expected. There were a couple of small tables and chairs in the middle of the room and three old vinyl covered booths against the wall. The bar ran the length of the room on the far side. The bartender was leaning over the bar talking to one of the three old men seated at the bar. One old, heavily made up woman was asleep in one of the booths. He looked around and could see no one that could be Arlo. He looked at the bartender with a raised eyebrow. The barkeep beckoned:

"You the guy supposed to meet here?" he asked.

"Yeah, I'm looking for…"

"He's back in the office. Gave me twenty to use it. Tell 'em to make it quick. The owner sometimes comes in before closing," he said, pointing down the dimly lit hallway where the bathrooms were located, according to the sign above the doorway.

The tall man walked to the hallway and looked. At the far end, a door was slightly ajar with a thin shaft of light reflecting off the wall. He walked down the hallway.

"This should be easy," he thought. "These Hollywood bigshots are all a bunch of pussies. He'll fold as soon as I get in his face. If he tries to play the tough guy with me he'll be in for a hell of a surprise. He's got no idea who he's dealing with."

CHAPTER 15

The boy was born in a small hamlet in the southeastern corner of Lithuania in 1938. He was named after his father, Josef Shustis. Josef, an evil man with a fierce temper, got along with no one in the village. He was relegated to the communal pig farm where he spent the day cleaning the pens, feeding the animals and, on occasion, kicking those that came near him. He returned home most nights to vent his anger on his wife, his only child, or both, for some imagined transgression. In vain, Josef junior looked to his mother for protection. She had her own way of coping with her dismal life and spent most of her time in a drunken stupor or screaming at her small son, taking out her hatred for her husband on the child.

On the morning of young Josef's thirteenth birthday, his father slapped him in the face at the breakfast table, causing the boy's bowl of mush to fall from the table and spill onto his father's soiled work boots. Josef senior made Josef junior lick the porridge from the dirty boots and the filthy wooden floor.

That night the son waited until his mother and father were both asleep in their bed. He crept into the alcove where they slept and poured boiling water onto his father's face and, as the large man thrashed about, he stabbed him repeatedly in the chest until he ceased the struggling. He then calmly slit his drunken mother's throat.

Josef took his parents' small savings from the porcelain tea kettle in the kitchen cupboard and fled to the coast where he found a Chinese merchant vessel whose accommodating Captain cared less about paperwork and more about young Caucasian boys.

Josef worked on the ship, suffering the abuse of the Captain until he turned eighteen. Then, late one evening in the hold of the ship, Josef drowned the Captain in the bilge and jumped ship in Boston harbor where he soon became an accomplished mugger.

He came to the attention of the Montini crime family, and they began to use him on occasion as an enforcer. He was arrested a number of times, once for suspicion of murder. He was convicted of a few lesser crimes and served a three-year term in state prison. He never sniveled, and never used the Montini name to try to cut a deal. Uncle Montini saw Josef as a 'stand up guy.' He also recognized Josef's cold, violent nature and believed that, with a little maturing and personal attention, he could be put to good use. But first he'd have to make a few changes. A new identity would be the first order of business.

*****

Arlo Calarasi was born about the same time as Josef junior, in a small village in Romania. He was a beautiful baby although somewhat delicate. His mother doted on him. His father was rather frail. He fancied himself an artist and so did little in the way of work to support his family. He died an early death, falling into some pots of paint one morning following a stroke. This was fine with Arlo's mother. She was a strong, dominant woman who immediately browbeat the local general store owner into selling her his business. She was feared by the townspeople. It was understood that her grandfather was head of one of the Gypsy clans, and she lived under the protection of that strong hand.

Arlo was different from all the other children of the village. By the time he was fourteen, it was common knowledge that he was one of the soiled ones, as the homosexual men were known in that area of the world. His mother's strength protected him from any insults or harassment, other than the occasional sideways glance from one of his peers and frequent giggles behind his back.

Making his beloved mother dresses was one of Arlo's greatest joys. He was talented with a needle and thread, and when he became a young man his mother had an addition built onto her store and set him up with his own dressmaking shop. The women of the village didn't condemn him, and he patiently built his business to three or four dresses a month. He was quite content sewing and living with his mother.

Arlo's comfortable existence changed abruptly one cold fall afternoon. His mother, on her way from the town hall, was run over by a wagon and team of horses hauling coal. She died immediately in the middle of the muddy street.

It took only a short time for the town's resentment of his mother to focus instead on Arlo. For all his mother's protection, she left him very naïve in the ways of the world. He didn't know to bribe the tax collector from the capital, and within six weeks the properties of his mother were confiscated. People in the village would have nothing to do with him, other than to insult and, on occasion, mete out a sound thrashing.

One day, two men from his dead grandfather's gypsy clan paid him a visit and offered to help him by sending him to the United States where his talent for sewing would be appreciated. Arlo jumped at the chance, and in short order, he found himself on a small tramp steamer heading for his new life in America.

One of the two gypsies had taken him to the capital and after an exchange of money, Arlo was given a passport along with a permit to leave the country. Romania was a backward country and, other than school records, the only official recognition of Arlo's existence was the birth record at his village. His fingerprints had never been recorded. This made Arlo a prime candidate for one of the clan's numerous business ventures.

When the tramp steamer docked in Boston harbor, two men were allowed to board the ship. They went immediately to Arlo's cabin, knocked him unconscious and stuffed him into an old steamer trunk. One of the men found Arlo's papers and carefully replaced Arlo's photo on the passport with another. The two men left the cabin and departed the ship. Much later that night another man came out of the fog and climbed the ship's ladder to the deck. He handed one of the ship's officers an envelope and disappeared into the superstructure.

The next morning Josef stepped off the boat and handed an immigration officer Arlo's passport and papers. He was fingerprinted and walked into the United States as Arlo Calarasi.

As for the real Arlo, he and the trunk were removed from the ship just before it sailed. It was buried in a swamp that was soon to become an extension of the runway at Logan Airport.

Josef, now Arlo, waited at the end of the neighborhood bar for Uncle Montini to beckon him to the table for his new assignment.

*****

The old man sat at a table in a corner of the bar for an hour before he beckoned to Arlo. Arlo stared for a moment and then picked up his half empty drink and slowly drank it down, got up from the bar stool and strolled to the old man sitting at the table in the corner. Uncle Montini seemed not to notice the insolence and motioned Arlo to sit down across from him. He picked up a bottle of wine and poured a small amount into a glass sitting in front of Arlo.

"Let me see your new papers." Montini said, holding out his hand. He stared at the documents for several moments and then handed them, back saying, "They are good. In six months, you will apply for citizenship. We will smooth the way." Arlo nodded his understanding and the old man continued:

"My nephew is on the west coast now. He and a trusted attorney are putting things in motion." The old man reached across the table and patted Arlo's hand. "You are a good earner and have gained the family trust. This new identity was an investment we think will be very profitable. This is what I want you to do."

And the old man detailed his plan to Arlo.

There were experts in the legal profession who strongly believed that some Supreme Court decisions were soon to be handed down that would clear the way for adult porn to be legitimized. With the advent of video tapes and VCR's, the Montini family felt they should be in at the beginning of this business. Arlo was to remain an upstanding citizen. He was to become an influential member of the community in Los Angeles, active in charities and politics. First, through several corporations, he was to open a chain of dry cleaning shops. The attorney would handle the details. The Family would introduce Arlo to some influential people in the community and, at the right time, Arlo would begin to finance some independent films. The funds necessary would be filtered through several union pension funds available to the Montinis. Harry Becker was a small time pornographer on the west coast who owned a movie production company called Blue Bird Pictures. Harry would be the front for the family and would answer to Arlo by phone and hand carried messages, under no conditions was he to know Arlo or the family connection. Controls on Harry were in place. An infusion of cash would be put into Blue Bird, and a larger studio and better equipment would be purchased. In addition, a number of videocassette stores would be opened in the greater LA area owned by several different corporations. The attorney and a CPA firm would handle all transactions and the nephew would be available to nudge anyone reluctant to cooperate in the business venture. Arlo was to stay at arm's length and make sure things ran smoothly. The video rental and the dry cleaners were largely cash businesses and would be used as money laundering operations. There were a few rules. One was that the businesses would show a small profit and pay their taxes. The nephew would handle any and all enforcement. Arlo would break no laws. Arlo was to marry, for appearances' sake. This operation was a ten-year plan.

The old man sat back and stared intently at Arlo.

"Is there anything you do not understand?"

"Who do I answer to?" Arlo asked.

"You will answer to me. My nephew is separate," the old man said in a quiet voice.

"This plan. It seems very complex for so simple a thing. Make movies and rent them." Arlo held his hands open, palms up. "And married? I do not wish to be so encumbered."

"Being married is a requisite. I have a woman in mind. She is to know as little as possible about our business. She will have duties to perform, charities, church events, high society things. She is controllable. I have, shall we say, private information of a harmful nature to her. The West Coast has long been a problem. We have not been welcome when we have tried to do business. The larger police departments seem to want to catch people rather than make money. The politicians are politicians, nothing more. They drift with the currents. It is not an easy area to do our business. They build and then tear down. People move to the area and then leave. There are no communities of people like we have. No Italians, no Slavs, no Polish. Only the Blacks and the Mexicans seem to stick together and they are not trustworthy." Uncle Montini stopped and stared at the ceiling in thought.

"We have some influence with the unions and, because of that, some with the entertainment community. These are two of the most powerful groups out there. I think our strength will grow in those areas." The old man watched closely Arlo's reaction to his discourse.

"I understand." Arlo said, tilting his head in respect at the old man.

With a wave of dismissal, Uncle Montini said:

"The attorney will be in touch. I will be watching closely your progress."

Arlo understood the meaning of those words and smiled inwardly. He was smarter than the family.

Montini sat at the small table for ten minutes after Arlo left. He motioned with the small finger of his right hand and instantly one of the men seated at the bar came over and leaned down to listen to the man's instructions.

“Have the girl on a plane right away. I wish to speak with her.”

The man nodded his understanding and hurried away.

Chapter 16

Arlo stood next to a desk in the surprisingly richly furnished office at the rear of the seedy '507' bar. The extortionist stood just inside the door, staring. He reached inside his coat just as the crowbar smashed down on his shoulder, knocking him to the floor. The two men had come out of the ladies' room in the hallway and followed right behind him as he came down the hall.

One of the men knelt down with one knee in the small of the back of the fallen man and quickly patted him down, pulling a snub nosed revolver from his waistband. Holding it up he said:

"Gun, Boss."

"Get his wallet. Let's see who this fuck is," Arlo said.

"Hey, what tha' fuck man. Who do ya…" The man twisted, trying to get up. The squat man swung the crow bar again hitting him in the side of the head. Arlo threw a roll of duct tape to the other man.

"Boris, put him in that chair and cinch him up." Arlo pointed to a wooden chair that seemed out of place with the rest of the furniture. Both men lifted the now bleeding burglar to his feet, sat him roughly in the chair and taped him in place.

"Here's his wallet, Boss." Arlo took the brown leather case.

"Listen you guys you're making a big mistake. Do you know who I…"

"I'll tell you who you are," Arlo interrupted, standing over the bound man. "You are a man with a very serious problem. You should be careful who you try to shake down." Arlo began looking through the wallet as he talked. He looked at the man through half-closed eyes. "I want that video tape, now. Where is it?"

"Who the fuck are you?" the man in the chair said. One of the henchmen hit him in the mouth breaking two of his front teeth.

"I ask, you answer," Arlo said in a low voice. The man in the chair spat some blood and a broken piece of tooth.

"Fuck you."

"Tape his mouth," Arlo said, taking a yellow pencil from his desk drawer and pushing it into the electric sharpener. He held it there, letting the small motor whir quietly for a few seconds. Then, in one smooth motion, he thrust the sharp point into the sitting man's shoulder just above the collarbone. He twisted the pencil against the bone until it broke. The extortionist pulled against his bonds, he head thrashing back and forth, he eyes wide in pain and fear. Arlo turned back to his desk, and the sound of the sharpener whirred again. With no expression, Arlo turned back to his subject and thrust the second pencil into the man's other shoulder. The man made muffled sounds through the duct tape.

"Boss! This guy's got a badge! The son-of-a-bitch is a cop. Says on his I.D. card his name is Landers." One of the henchmen held a black leather case in his hand. Arlo looked at the shiny badge and then back at the seated man. He began sharpening a third pencil saying "Some cop. Trying to squeeze me for 200 grand. You really fucked up." He took the pencil from the sharpener.

"I find every day items are just as effective as the more dramatic tools for pain." He held the pencil in front of his victim. "Can you imagine what this could do in other areas of your body? Boris, pull the fuck's pants down."

The hood complied, pulling the man's pants and underwear down to his knees, exposing his genitals. Arlo leaned over and placed the point of the pencil under the man's testicles and against the flesh just above his anus.

"I want you to nod yes if you understand my question. You

have no choice. Got that?" The wide eyed man nodded his head rapidly, the two pencils sticking out of his shoulders, blood beginning to soak though his clothing.

"When I take the tape off your mouth, you are going to tell me where the tape is, if there are any copies and who you are working with. Do you understand?" The man shook his head up and down and tried to pull his hips away from the pencil. Arlo reached down and ripped the tape off the man's mouth.

"Oh, oh please." Arlo put pressure on the pencil. "No wait! I'll tell you. It's outside in the car. My partner's in the car. The trunk, in the trunk, no copies."

Arlo stared down at the man, thinking. Deciding if he was telling the truth. He pushed on the pencil, penetrating the flesh and then wiggling the pencil back and forth. The man screamed as the sharp point broke off against the prostate.

"Are you sure? Sure you've told me everything? What color and what kind of car and where exactly are you parked? What's your partner's name?" In a rush of words he told the cold-eyed man what he wanted to know, including his partner, Marty Pritchard's, name. Arlo taped his mouth again and turned to his two henchmen:

"Go get his friend and search the car." The men turned and left the room without a word.

Arlo smiled at the broken man in the chair, patted him on the head and then moved behind the desk. He sat down and began going through some paperwork.

It was his addiction to tea that saved him. He had been fidgeting for the last fifteen minutes, watching for his partner, staring at the front of the '507'. He kept looking at his watch. It was taking too long and his bladder was full. Finally he climbed from the car and walked down the sidewalk to an alley a few store fronts from the parked vehicle. After looking back at the car and the '507', he moved down the alley and, with a sigh of relief, unzipped himself and began peeing behind some trash cans.

As he stepped from the alley onto the sidewalk, he saw two men come out of the bar. They had the posture that triggered the short man's survival instincts. They looked like bad news. He faded back into the shadows of the alley and peered around the corner as the two men walked quickly to the car. Both of them drew weapons from under their loose shirts. That was all he needed to see. Something had gone very wrong.

He turned and moved rapidly away, down the alley and onto the next street over. Without any hesitation, he began walking quickly down the empty street out onto the busily trafficked Wilshire Boulevard.

As he trotted along looking over his shoulder he saw a bus coming down the street. He stepped from the curb and waved the bus down and climbed on board. He held a dollar towards the driver who said:

"Exact change please," pointing at the coin receptacle.

"All I got is bills."

"Sorry. We don't make change sir, security you know," the driver responded.

"Aw, shit! Here." Pritchard handed over a five dollar bill. "Keep the change." He moved to the rear and sat down, slouching low in the seat and staring out the window.

He was scared and hadn't any idea what to do, other than get away from the area and find someplace to rest and think. He figured Landers was dead, or 'as good as'.

*****

"Here, Boss. There wasn't nobody in the car." The hood, Boris, a Russian Mafia associate, held out a package wrapped with a brown paper bag. "This was in the baggage place."

"Only this?" Arlo asked as he opened the bag and removed the tape. "Did you look for the other man? Did you search well?"

"Yes, we looked carefully. Ivan is still searching."

Arlo looked back at the man taped in the chair, his chin resting on his chest.

"Where would your friend go, asshole?" Arlo tore the tape from the man's mouth.

"I, I don't know." He flinched as Arlo moved towards him. "Wait! Maybe home, he might go home. He lives in the valley. On Roscoe. Yeah, no place else to go, he'd go home. It's 12111 Roscoe. I don't know anywhere else he could go. Please."

"Boris, go get Ivan and go there. Wait. Put this piece of shit in the bathroom first." Arlo pointed to a door at the back of the room. Boris did as he was told, dragging the chair with the extortionist into the white tiled bathroom. As he left to find Ivan, Arlo handed him a piece of paper with the address written on it.

"Call me here when you get to the house."

Arlo sat at his desk and leaned back in the upholstered chair. A cop, a twist he hadn't anticipated. He picked up a glass paperweight and absentmindedly moved it from one hand to the other. He stared at the closed bathroom door.

*****

"This is the end of the run, mister." The bus driver was looking back over his shoulder at the lone rider. Pritchard looked out the window. They were on Sunset Boulevard in Westwood. It was 2:15 AM and still a few late night people were strolling along the sidewalks, mostly college kids from the UCLA campus. He sighed, got up and walked down the aisle of the bus with no idea where he was going or what he was going to do. He was sure his partner was dead or under arrest. He only had one person to turn to, and he couldn't tell him about the extortion plan. That would be admitting they were holding out.

He walked down Sunset and slipped into an all night café and took a booth in the very back of the restaurant. He ordered a cup of tea from the old waitress with food stains on her tan uniform. When the tea arrived it was tepid. He motioned to the waitress and told her. She frowned at him, took the cup and walked slowly back to the counter. She returned five minutes later with a slightly warmer cup and asked him if there was anything else he wanted, with a sarcastic tone.

He pulled out his wallet and took stock of his assets. A credit card with $230.00 available, two twenty dollar bills and four singles. He had to make the call. He had to get some money and hole up until he could figure out what was happening. He walked back to the pay phone on the rear wall and stood there, thinking. Nope, he couldn't make the call. There was nothing he could say that wouldn't get him deeper into the mess. If the cops weren't after him, they would be soon. The two men he saw come out of the '507' looked like hoods. Arlo had connections. That made sense to him. Rich guys always had connections. The more he thought about it, the more convinced he became that his partner was dead and that he'd probably told Arlo and his friends who he was. He sighed and left a dollar on the counter and walked out of the restaurant and back to the bus stop.

*****

Arlo stood up from the large, ornate desk, reached into a drawer, took out a twenty-two pistol and checked to make sure it was loaded. He pushed the cylinder closed and looked at the door to the bathroom. The man tied to the chair was moaning softly, the sound muffled by the closed door. Arlo had made up his mind. He stood in front of the bound man and pulled the tape from his mouth.

"I have a few more questions."

"Oh shit, listen we can work somethin' out here. I'm a detective I can…" Landers whispered in pain.

"This is what I want to know. Where do you work? Who else knows about the tape, and most importantly where would your partner go, if he didn't go home?" Arlo asked.

The detective told him everything. They, he and his partner, worked the burglary detail. They targeted rich homes and broke in, stealing only cash and jewelry. No one else was involved except a fence in Las Vegas and he swore there were no copies of the tape. His partner was married, but about to be divorced and the wife knew nothing. The telephone on Arlo's desk rang. He moved to the desk and picked it up.

"Yes?" He listened for a moment and then said, "Leave Boris there in case the other one shows up. Are you sure you searched the house thoroughly? Good. You go to this one's apartment. Look there and call me again." Arlo gave him the address, hung up and said to detective Landers:

"He hasn't come home. Where do you keep the stuff you steal before you get rid of it?"

"Behind my bureau in the bedroom. There's not much there right now. Some watches and a couple of items from your place. Ya' know, jewelry," the detective answered.

"What kind of car do you own? And your partner, what does he drive?"

"We don't have cars. I live near downtown and he, he drives a city car. The one parked outside."

Arlo was satisfied he had all the information he needed from this man. He placed his foot against the side of the chair and pushed the man over sideways into the tub.

"Hey, hey! Wait. What are ya'…" the detective said, twisting his head to look up at Arlo.

Reaching for the towel rack, Arlo took a white terry cloth towel and holding it against the side of the man's head pushed the barrel of the small pistol against the cloth and fired twice in quick succession. The rounds entered the detective's brain and spun through the soft tissue. Death came instantly. The towel protected Arlo's expensive clothes from any blood spatter.

Arlo closed the bathroom door quietly and resumed going through his paperwork.

CHAPTER 17

Walter arrived at his office at eight a.m. sharp. He sat down at his desk with a satisfied sigh. He called to his secretary on the intercom and ordered some coffee to be brought in to go with the bagel and cream cheese he picked up at the Jewish deli on the way in. She brought a steaming mug along with the summaries of the police actions of the night before. Walter took a big bite of the bagel and began perusing the reports, a glob of white cream cheese stuck to the corner of his mouth. He looked up at his secretary standing in front of his desk and waved her out of his office.

A half hour later his private line rang.

"Yes?" Walter said.

"It's me."

"Good morning Arlo. How are you?"

"Walter, we have a problem. We need to meet as soon as possible. At my other office."

"Why there? You know that's never a good idea, for me to be seen in that area."

"No choice, Walter. Let's say in an hour." Arlo's tone indicated no room for argument.

"Don't tell me an hour. I have things to do here. Impossible, maybe this afternoon." Walter knew how to play the control game.

"An hour, Walter." Arlo hung up without waiting for an answer with a loud click. Walter stared at the phone in his hand.

An hour and twenty minutes later, Walter pulled into a parking place a few doors down the street from a church on Seventh street. It was an old church, made all the more modest by forty years of accumulated grime from the heart of the city. Walter entered through the wooden front doors and made his way down one side of the chapel and through a door that led down a dark hallway and through a second door that exited into an alley, directly across from the back door of the '507'. He pushed a trash can out of the way and pulled at the door. It was locked and he had to knock quietly for several minutes before the door swung open. Arlo stood just inside, in the shadow of the dark hallway.

"You're late." And without another word, or a chance for Walter to respond, Arlo turned and walked down the hallway and into his office. When Walter entered, Arlo was already seated behind his desk. Walter put his hands flat on Arlo's desk and leaned forward:

"I don't take orders Arlo, I give them. Don't ever talk that way to me again, do you understand?"

"Sit down." Arlo pointed to a chair behind Walter. Walter stood there glaring. Arlo motioned to the chair with a bland expression. After a moment, Walter sat.

"What is this about, what's so damn important?" Walter asked.

Arlo sat staring at Walter with no expression. Then he spoke in a quiet voice:

"Walter, do the names Pritchard and Landers mean anything to you?"

"What? Who?"

"You heard me."

"Let me think, why?" Walter said. Arlo didn't answer.

"Well, there's two detectives by that name, work Hollywood. Why?"

"Did you send them to my home, Walter? Did you decide to switch sides? Change our relationship?" Arlo said.

"What? What the hell are you talking about?" Walter said in a loud voice.

"What else am I to think? These two men break into my home while I'm away, steal and then contact me and try to shake me down."

"What! They what? Explain, I don't understand." Walter said leaning forward in the chair.

"This Landers, he calls me the day I get back. The day I'm making arrangements to bury my son, and tells me he has information he knows I'll want. Two hundred thousand dollars worth of information. When he tells me what he has, I agree to meet him here and pay."

"What did he have, what information?" Walter interrupted.

"Fortunately, it is very harmful to the both of us. If it weren't, I would be sure you were involved."

"Involved? Involved how?" Walter sputtered.

"They are cops. They work for you, right?"

"No, not for me. I have some eighteen hundred men under my command, I don't think I'd know them if I saw them." Walter said. "Hollywood division, they work under Reed."

"Who?"

"Jake Reed," Walter answered, "a real prick, can't stand him. We had a run in years ago. Doesn't matter. What? Tell me what the hell happened."

"This Landers, he and his partner have been doing break ins. They hit my house," Arlo paused and then, "They found records, records of all our transactions. Records of the business we are in. Neither of us could afford this kind of information made public. He said he had a friend in the press, I had no reason not to believe him. He came here and I tried to give him the money."

"What, what do you mean tried?" Walter said.

"He refused to part with all the records. I think he figured I couldn't remember how many there were. He became antagonistic and pulled a gun and I had to shoot him."

"Shoot him? You shot a cop?" Walter shouted, coming out of his chair.

"Calm down, Walter. I had no choice, I didn't know he was a cop, we found his badge afterwards."

Walter slumped in his chair, his mind was racing. A dead cop, he had to maneuver to get out of this. Murder wasn't something he could be a party to; even though it sounded faintly like self defense, he was sure that wasn't the case.

"This is bad Arlo. What's your defense going to be? Self defense? Of course I'll do what I can, but you've got yourself in a real mess here." Walter said. Arlo smiled.

"No, Walter. You and I have a small problem. This whole incident will be put quietly away. This Landers, before he died confessed only his partner was involved. I had some people search both homes. Landers apartment and Pritchard's house. There are no copies of the records. Pritchard has gone to ground. We need to find him to clean up any loose ends. He appears to be the only loose end."

"I can't be a party to this, Arlo." Walter said.

"Walter, you are involved. We have no choice. We have to get rid of Pritchard. Think what would happen to the both of us if it came out that we are major pornographers, not only adult but child porn. Firstly our careers would be over and jail would be preferable to what the people that sponsor me, us, would do. The people I answer to are very serious people. This child thing is very profitable, but they have a very strong policy against this business. I do not have the power to bring them to refrain from taking action. Their actions would be most unpleasant."

"Child porn?" Walter said in a choked voice.

"Yes, among other endeavors. Do not tell me you didn't know that, Walter. Where do you think those films you so dearly enjoy come from? The library? And the monies? The thousands a year, all that from run of the mill fuck films?" Arlo stopped and stared at Walter.

"Oh, Jesus, what a Goddam mess." Walter put his head in his hands. "What do we do?"

"Find Pritchard and get rid of him and continue as before. You'll be Chief of Police and I will be an upstanding member of the community. Those two cops were dirty anyway. They deserve nothing more. Right?"

Walter nodded slowly. They were crooked cops. Who cared whether they were dead? He took a deep breath, he had to face the fact about the child porn. In the back of his mind, he'd known for awhile, probably a long while. He had always assumed there might be some mob action in the distribution. He was too far removed for that to be a problem. His mind was already beginning to look for solutions to the problem.

"The body, what did you do with Lander's body?" Walter asked.

"It's been handled, and we can do the same with Pritchard. We just need to find him. There will be a way to point any investigation to the fact they were burglars. The perception will be they are on the run. It will all work out, Walter. Keep me informed. That is all you have to do."

"Wait, they hit your house. What if the trail leads to there? I have to be careful, I can't seem interested."

"There is nothing to indicate they came to my home. There is nothing to tie them to us. They disappear and they're crooks. How bad is your department going to want to dig? The old Chief isn't going to want that." Arlo stood up and came around the desk and put his arm around Walter's shoulder, smiling, "and, the new chief won't want to start off with a scandal, right?"

Walter gave a weak smile back, and, after agreeing to keep an eye on things, left for the station.

Arlo sat at his desk. He was satisfied. He had Walter involved and the child porn was in the open between them. The other operation was best kept hidden from Walter at this point. The video that had caused the whole incident was destroyed and no one was the wiser. If the Montini family knew about his fondness for children, both in business and pleasure, it would be over. These old mustache Petes and their old codes, fuck them.

Arlo smiled. Nobody was smarter than Arlo.

Chapter 18

The next morning, just before 8 a.m., Jake pulled into his parking space and walked into the station. The detectives at the front desk greeted him as he walked by on the way to his office. Jake said hello to Rene and Kelly, grabbed his coffee cup and headed for the coffee maker at the back of the squadroom. Weaving his way through the crowded aisles, Jake said hello to those detectives who were still at their desks. Many had already been in, gone through their reports and headed off to the jail to interview arrestees from the previous night. Those not dealing with arrestees were out filing cases at the D.A.'s office or trying to track down victims and witnesses for interviews. Hanging around the squadroom was a luxury few could afford.

Jake went back to his office and began going through the stack of reports piled in the middle of his desk. 'Crime marches on,' he thought, chewing on the ever present toothpick. As he glanced over each report Jake realized that even after twenty some years in the business, he was still continually amazed at the things people did to one another. Every time he thought he'd seen it all, someone came along to show him a new one. 'That little caper over on Yucca last week was one for the books." He thought.

It had been about three in the afternoon. Jake was at his desk when Kelly came in and told him that the Homicide Unit was at the scene of a murder in a parking lot at 661 N. Yucca, an old thirty unit apartment building. Jake responded to the scene where he met Kilgore. Dave directed Jake's attention to a large cardboard box sitting on the ground next to a large trash bin. As they walked up to the crime scene tape which surrounded the immediate area, Jake could see that a large amount of blood had flowed from the box and congealed on the asphalt. Jake and Kilgore stepped under the tape and carefully approached the box, cautious of anything that might be of evidentiary value. At the box, Kilgore carefully raised one of the flaps, then a second one. Inside the box, clearly visible, was a human foot. Next to it, was what appeared to be an arm. Kilgore and Jake speculated as to whether or not the box might contain an entire body. When the Coroner's Investigator got to the scene, about an hour later, it was determined that it did.

The manager of the apartment building identified the victim, based on several visible tattoos, as a tenant of one of the units. A check of his apartment turned up nothing unusual. There was no sign of anything amiss.

Meanwhile, one of Kilgore's detectives noticed, through the blood, that there was an address on the box. It had been shipped to the same building but a different unit. He and his partner went to the apartment where they found the tenant, a nineteen year old guitar player from Michigan, passed out on the couch. When they looked in the kitchen, what they found bore a strong resemblance to a butcher shop.

The investigation ultimately revealed that the guitar player had come to Hollywood three months before to attend music school. He struck up a friendship with the guy in the box who had been a small time cocaine dealer. He was also a homosexual with a penchant for young men. After getting the kid strung out on cocaine, he often took payment for the coke sexually. The kid, who was terribly addicted, gave in to the dealer when he had no money and an uncontrollable craving.

The day of the murder, the kid went to the dealer's apartment to buy a fix. The dealer was in the mood for sex and told him to keep his money, he wanted some action instead. The kid got angry and returned to his apartment, followed by the dealer who tried to convince him to give in. The kid, desperate for some coke, apparently couldn't bring himself to accede to the dealer's lust and instead took a butcher knife from the kitchen and killed him. He then helped himself to the coke dealer's stash, took several hits and then began dismembering his former tormentor. Once he completed the job, he placed the various parts in a large box he'd received in the mail from his mother. The box had contained some clothes, cookies, a birthday present from his girl friend back home and pictures of the family. After cramming the dealer into the box, he dragged it down to the trash bin. Realizing it was too heavy to lift into the bin, he set it down next to it for the trash collector to pick up. Unfortunately for him several stray dogs found the box first and began enthusiastically licking up the blood that had flowed out and then they began pulling on the cardboard looking for more. That attracted the attention of the building maintenance man who checked it out and called the police. That particular homicide was, as they say, a self-solver. Unlike most of them, Jake thought.

As Jake continued plowing through the paperwork, Ed Marquez , the supervisor of the Burglary Unit, knocked on the door jamb.

"Hey Boss, gotta' minute? We may have a problem."

"Yeah, come on in Ed." Jake said. "What's up?"

"Yesterday, Marty Pritchard and Frank Landers worked late. They came in about 4:00 in the afternoon. They were working on a hot prowl burglar and thought they had a handle where he might be doing his thing. They had a little surveillance set up, just in case. Anyway, I saw 'em when they came in. They hit the street about the time I was leaving so I know they were out there, at least for awhile. When I came in this morning I noticed their plain car wasn't parked in the lot. I tried reaching them on the radio when I got into the office, but they didn't respond. Just a few minutes ago one of the Day Watch patrol cops came by and told me they found one of our cars, the one Pritchard and Landers were using, parked on a side street, out of the division, down off of Main. One of the doors was hanging open and the inside was a mess, according to the patrol guys. Marty and Frank weren't anywhere around. I'm not sure just what the hell's cooking but I'm going down there to check it out. Just wanted you to know. I'll let you know what's up as soon as I figure it out."

"Yeah, O.K. Ed. Keep me posted. Let's hope there's a

reasonable explanation for this."

"I'll call you as soon as I know anything," Marquez said as he turned and walked back toward the squad room.

Jake pondered the situation. 'Those two seem to require an inordinate amount of supervisory attention,' he thought. 'If it isn't taking sick days every time they want to go fishing it's overdue follow-up reports or personnel complaints or something. Probably time to split 'em up before they get in real trouble.'

Thirty minutes later, Marquez called on Jake's inside line.

"Jake, we've got a serious problem. Someone got into the police car, went through the trunk and the glove box. It looks as though whoever it was, was looking for something. Pritchard and Landers aren't around. Some of their personal stuff is still in the car. I don't know what the hell to think."

Jake thought for a moment. "Stay put, Ed. I'll be down there in a few minutes. Meanwhile, get a couple of patrol units to begin a search of the area. Get me on the radio if you come up with anything. O.K.?"

Marquez acknowledged Jake's directions and hung up.

Jake told Kelly where he was going and then left the station to meet Marquez.

While driving to meet Marquez, Jake ran the situation over in his mind.

'My first instinct is to think these two characters are, or were, up to something,' Jake thought. 'And Frank "Fuzzy" Landers is probably the one who dreamed up whatever it is they were up to. I hope they haven't gotten themselves into serious trouble.'

Jake pulled up to the location a few minutes later and got out of his car. Across the street, next to Pritchard and Lander's car, Marquez, stood talking to a pair of uniformed officers. He broke off his conversation and walked over to Jake.

" Doesn't look good Jake. The car is trashed inside. The trunk, too. Somebody really went through it, obviously looking for something. Whoever it was left all their police gear alone. Didn't take any of it. It doesn't add up," Marquez told Jake.

"Any wits? Did anyone see anything? "

"Nope. Nothing. We haven't located anyone who saw anything. Of course, considering the neighborhood, I'm not surprised."

"No, I'm not either. What do you know about the case they

were working on, Ed?"

"Not much. I was planning on going back to the station and going through their case packages to see what I could dig up. Maybe one of the other guys in the unit knows specifically what they were working on."

"How many people have we got involved in looking for these guys?' Jake asked.

"I have three black and whites and one detective team at the moment. They've been door to door, a block in every direction. Nothing. I was just getting ready to request a citywide broadcast when you drove up."

"O.K., but hold off on the broadcast until I call the Station Commander. He needs to be briefed first. I don't want him hearing about this over the radio and not having all the details. And he'll want to brief the Chief of Detectives first, too."

"I'll wait to hear from you," Marquez replied.

Jake turned and walked over to the detective's car. He took a brief look and then turned to Marquez. "I want this car printed inside and out, Ed." Marquez told him the print team was on the way. Jake gave him a thumbs up, walked to his own car, got in and left. He arrived at the station several minutes later.

Jake went straight to Captain Ed Hughes' office.

Jake spent fifteen minutes briefing Hughes who then got on the telephone and called Walter Burnett. Hughes asked Jake to stick around, just in case there were any questions from Burnett he couldn't answer. When he hung up Hughes thanked Jake and told him to keep him informed. Jake assured him he would. As Jake was walking out, Hughes said, "I gather there's no love lost between you and Burnett."

"Really. Why do you say that?" Jake asked.

"The tone of his voice when I told him you were handling the situation."

"Walter and I go way back, Captain. And you're right, there's no love lost. I think he's an asshole, and he shares similar sentiments about me."

"Well, we'll keep that between ourselves, Jake."

"Yes sir, Captain."

Jake went to his office and told Kelly to get in touch with Marquez and have him call. Jake returned a couple of phone messages and then got a call from Marquez.

"Alright, Ed. Go ahead and put out a broadcast. After you do, come on into the station. We need to discuss this situation and where we need to go from here. O.K.? "

Marquez agreed.

"By the way, we have contacted their homes, talked to their wives or whoever they live with, haven't we?

Marquez confirmed that he had phoned each of their residences. He told Jake that Landers lived alone, but he phoned there anyway. No answer. Pritchard's answering machine was on, so he left a message. Jake told him he'd see him when he came to the station and hung up.

Jake called Kelly into his office. He explained what was happening and told her that if she got any calls from the media to take a number and not comment. She nodded and asked him if he wanted her to prepare a press release. Jake told her to hold off until the Press Relations people insisted on it.

Jake told Kelly to get the home addresses of the two detectives for him. She left the office and returned a short time later. As he looked at the addresses, Marquez walked in the office.

"Anything new, Ed?"

"Nothing. I just got in. I'm going to go through their case packages and the log. If I find anything helpful, I'll let you know."

Looking at the addresses of the two detectives, Jake told Marquez to have one of the other supervisors go to Pritchard's house, which was forty miles from the station in Ventura County.

"I'd feel better knowing for certain that he isn't there and not just refusing to answer the phone. You know what I mean? Or maybe he's fallen ill and can't. Whatever."

Marquez said he'd get Jerry Larson, the Robbery supervisor, to do it.

"Good. In the meantime, I'll run by Fuzzy's apartment and see what's up there," Jake told Marquez.

Marquez walked out of the office. Jake called Kelly and she stepped in.

"Kelly, are you busy? he asked.

"Not really," she replied.

"Good. Get your purse. We're going to do a little police work."

*****

As Jake and Kelly pulled out of the station parking lot and turned south on Wilcox, Kelly asked Jake where they were going.

"Fuzzy Lander's place. I just want to look around, satisfy myself he isn't there, dead drunk or sick or something. With that guy, you never know."

"True. Fuzzy doesn't strike me as the most professional detective in the division. Marty, on the other hand, seems like a pretty decent guy."

"Yeah, I think he is, but I'm not sure teaming those two up was a great idea. Fuzzy needs a partner who'll tell him when he's off base. Marty tends to go along with the show. Although they've both managed to stay out of trouble, lately. And they have made some pretty good arrests in the past few months."

A short drive later, Jake pulled up in front of the Armbruster and looked at the old building curiously.

"Are you sure you wrote down the right address?" he asked Kelly. "This doesn't look like a joint even Fuzzy Landers would live in."

"That's the address we have in our file. Apartment 331."

"I'm beginning to think Fuzzy's even flakier than I thought he was," Jake said.

"This place was probably real nice at one time," Kelly observed.

"Yeah, back before either one of us was born," Jake said skeptically.

Jake and Kelly entered the building and found the manager's apartment. Jake showed him his identification, explained why they were there and asked for the key to Lander's apartment. The manager, an overweight, unshaven hulk who was preoccupied ogling Kelly's legs, gave them a key and offered to personally escort them to the apartment.

"Not necessary. We're trained detectives, you know. We can probably find it all by ourselves," Jake said, somewhat sarcastically. "Would I be correct in assuming that Apartment 331 would be on the third floor?"

The apartment manager sensed it was time to go back to his

T.V.

"Yeah, third floor." He took one last look at Kelly's legs and closed the door.

"I think you have a potential suitor there, Kelly." Jake said as they headed down the hall towards the stairway to the upper floors.

"Seems like. I'll probably have to let my chance for love go, though. You know the department's policy about converting on duty contacts into off-duty relationships. Damn the luck," she replied.

They climbed the stairs to the third floor, turned right and walked down the hall over the threadbare carpeting to Apartment 331.

"What the hell does Landers spend his money on, I wonder?" Jake remarked. "It sure isn't on rent."

"To each his own. Maybe he's saving for retirement."

"Yeah, or maybe he spends it on furniture. Look at this joint," Jake said as he opened the door. "It looks like he gets most of his stuff from the Goodwill."

"Fuzzy's got a reputation for being a little tight with a buck, you know," Kelly said.

"I'd say it's well deserved, from the looks of this place. Let's look around."

Jake walked to the kitchen while Kelly went to the bedroom. After just a few moments, it was clear that Landers wasn't in the apartment.

Jake went into the small bathroom, checked behind the shower curtain and then, for no particular reason except, perhaps, the natural instincts bred by experience, he removed the lid from the toilet tank.

"Well, you never know, do you?" Jake said as he reached into the tank and removed a plastic ziplock bag. "What do we have here?"

Kelly heard Jake and asked him what he was talking about as she walked into the bathroom.

"Take a look at this."

As they examined the bag, Kelly said, "Looks like it's full of jewelry. Maybe it's the Landers family jewels."

"Yeah, no doubt. My wife keeps all of her jewelry in the toilet, too."

Jake opened the bag and examined its' contents. Two Rolex watches and some loose diamonds, a number of rings and diamond bracelets were in the bag. Jake dumped the bag out onto the bathroom rug.

"I'm no expert but I have a hunch we're looking at some expensive stuff. What do you think, Kelly?" he asked.

"Well, I know Rolex watches don't come cheap. And those diamonds look real to my well trained, female eye."

Jake thought for a moment. Then he scooped up all the items and dumped them back in the bag.

"Kelly, I don't know what the hell Landers is doing with this stuff but I've got a hunch it isn't good. When we find the guy he's going to have to explain a few things. Assuming, of course, that we do find him. This looks suspicious as hell to me."

"I agree, Jake. If I were going to offer a wild guess, I'd say it's probably stolen. But what would Fuzzy be doing with stolen stuff? I know he's a little flaky but I don't think he's a thief. Do you?"

"Frankly, I don't know what the guy is capable of, Kelly. We'll give him the benefit of the doubt, for now. Time will tell, as they say. Let's go back to the station and check this out," Jake said.

Kelly nodded. "Before we do, though I want to show you something kind of interesting. We may want to take it with us. Come here for a minute," Kelly said, gesturing toward the bedroom. She showed Jake a notepad that was on top of the night stand, next to the bed.

"I noticed this," she said. She picked the pad up and handed it to Jake. "If you look at it on an angle you can see some impressions on the paper. Something was written on the previous piece of paper and the impression was left on this one. I think I can run a pencil over it and bring it out so we can read it," she said. She got a pencil out of her purse and in a few seconds the writing was clear. 507.

"Well, that's helpful," Jake said. "Did you learn that at Detective School?" He asked.

"As a matter of fact I did," she replied. "This could turn out to be something."

"Well, bring it along and we'll ponder its' meaning later."

"Wait, there's more. I found this list in the drawer. It's a bunch of addresses, about nine or ten of them. They're in some pretty high end neighborhoods. Interesting, don't you think?"

"Yeah, they are. And I don't like what I'm thinking. Bring those things along and let's go back to the station.

Kelly picked up her purse from the bed where she'd laid it and slung it over her shoulder. As she turned to leave the room, a white envelope fell from her purse and fluttered to the floor. Jake saw it and started to retrieve it for her.

"I've got it," Kelly said, stepping quickly in front of Jake. As she picked it up Jake noticed she'd blushed.

"Love letter, huh?" he quipped.

"Yes, as a matter of fact."

"You certainly do keep those affairs to yourself. I haven't even heard a good rumor about your love life."

"Good. That's the way I prefer it," she replied.

They left the apartment and went back down the stairs, stopping at the manager's unit to return the key. As they walked out the front door of the building, Jake looked back and saw the manager ogling Kelly.

"You've got a real fan there," he told her.

"I'll call him later," she said.

*****

Back at the station, Kelly followed Jake into his office.

"What now, boss?" she asked.

"Well, Detective McBride. Given what we have here, what do you think our next step should be?" Jake asked as he sat down at his desk and looked at his overflowing in-box.

"Well, in my opinion and with all due respect to Fuzzy, there's enough here to make me think he's up to something. The stuff we found in the plastic bag looks stolen and the address list is suspicious, to say the least. Let me do some checking on the computer. I'm going to talk to the guys in the Burglary Unit, too. They may recognize the watches and jewelry from one of their jobs."

"Okay. Sounds like a good start."

As Kelly turned to leave the office, Mitch walked up to the doorway.

"Mind if I come in?" he said. Then, looking over Kelly's shoulder at Jake, "Are we still on for lunch?"

"It slipped my mind until you walked in, but sure, why not?"

"You forgot about lunch? I'm crushed."

"Things have been a little frantic around here this morning. In fact, Kelly and I have been out in the field on a case." Jake said.

"Yeah. That's right. I had a chance to hone my detective skills and show the boss what a thorough investigator I am," Kelly told Mitch.

"Really. And what did you do to impress him?" Mitch asked.

Before she could reply, Jake interrupted, "Show him your handiwork with the pencil on the note pad. That clue should clear up the whole case in no time," Jake joked.

Kelly looked at Mitch. "Well, there you are. You try to teach someone something and…"

"Raising something indented on paper isn't exactly a new, scientific breakthrough," Jake replied, chuckling. "And even if it was, the writing you raised, '507', doesn't tell us much."

Mitch spoke up. " Well, for what it's worth, back in the bad old days I used to drink in a joint called the 507. Down in the skidrow area."

"Yeah, and '507' might be a lot of other things, too. Maybe Fuzzy was keeping track of the number of beers he's had this month."

Jake grabbed his coat from the closet, stuck a toothpick in his mouth and said, "Let's go to lunch and we'll talk about it."

"Kelly. Why don't you come, too?' Mitch asked. "I'd be happy to buy."

"I never pass up a free lunch. That is, if it's okay with the boss."

"Sure, come on. Maybe we can get him to buy us both lunch."

*****

Over lunch Jake, Mitch and Kelly discussed the mornings' events. The missing detectives' story had been on the radio news during the drive to Louie's Pizza and Pastrami, an eatery popular with the cops from Hollywood station. Jake knew this meant his afternoon would be spent either on the phone or meeting personally with the news hacks from the local media. This time, however, he was grateful for their attention. It could lead to something helpful. Maybe some information from the public; some observation or an anonymous tip regarding their whereabouts. 'You never know', he thought.

"Well, what else do you have Jake?' Mitch asked. "I mean, besides the '507' thing, which, by the way, I'm going to check out. I haven't been down to my old haunts in years. It'll be interesting to see how things have changed. I may find some old acquaintances who know what's happening."

"Well, we have a zip lock bag full of watches and stuff that's probably stolen. That was hidden in the toilet tank. We've also got a list of addresses that might be burglary locations. We haven't checked our crime reports yet. Other than that, not much. We're waiting to find out what turned up at Marty Pritchard's place. One of my detective supervisors is there now," Jake replied.

Over their food, they discussed the case and various scenarios that might explain what happened to the two missing detectives. Burglars or not, they were still cops and the search would be intense and persistent, Jake told them. "It looks bad but until we find them, I don't want to jump to any conclusions. When we get all the facts, we'll figure this thing out. Finding them is the number one priority."

They finished lunch and returned to the station. Kelly began researching the address list to determine if any of the locations had been burglarized while Jake began returning phone calls to the media. Mitch went to get coffee for himself and Jake, stopping to chat with a couple of detectives who worked the Auto Theft Unit. Mitch loved the 'cop talk' and the detectives, who were getting used to seeing him around and knew he was an ex-cop, spoke freely.

Within twenty minutes, Kelly was back in Jake's office. As soon he hung up the phone, she told him that all but one of the addresses on the list had been burglarized. In every case, the homeowners were on vacation at the time the burglaries occurred, she told him.

"That's interesting. More than a coincidence, I'd say."

"That's certain. I also matched up two of the watches to one of them. I'll check the serial numbers to be sure but the description fits," she said.

Mitch walked in, catching the end of the conversation.

"What's up?" he asked.

Kelly told him what she'd found, including the fact that the victims had all been on vacation at the time they were hit.

"Isn't that interesting. How do you explain that?'" he asked. "How would they , the burglars, know when people were on vacation?"

"Good question," Kelly said as Jake picked up his ringing phone.

Mitch thought for a minute. "Kelly, when I was a cop,

admittedly more than a few years ago, we kept a vacation book in the Watch Commander's office. When people went on vacation, they'd call in and let us know when they were leaving and when they'd be back. Then the Watch Commander would have the car in the area keep an eye on the house, as time permitted. Do they still do that?"

"Sure we do. I'll go get the book and check the addresses. You never know." Kelly walked out as Jake hung up the phone.

"What are you two doing?"

Mitch explained and Jake agreed that the vacation book was a good possibility.

Kelly returned in a couple minutes with the book and she and Mitch began comparing addresses.

After a few minutes she turned to Jake. "Every one of the burglarized locations is in the book. Isn't that just great. People call us to watch their houses and two of our detectives use the information as their own handy little shopping guide."

"I hate to think that's what they were doing but it sure as hell looks like it. I better go fill the Captain in on this. He'll want to keep Burnett informed. And Burnett will probably come gunning for me. I know he'd like to deep six my career, given the chance. He may think this is it. I am responsible for these two jerks.

"Oh, Lieutenant," Jake stopped at the door and turned to Kelly with a raised eyebrow, "Tomorrow's Friday. If it's OK, I'm going to take an overtime day for a long weekend."

Jake nodded his approval and walked out of the office to talk with the Captain.

"Cap, I need to brief you on the latest regarding Landers and Pritchard. You aren't going to like it."

Hughes motioned him in. Jake took a seat and filled him in on what he, Kelly and Mitch had discovered. After he finished, Hughes shook his head.

"Those assholes," he exclaimed. "Talk about betraying the public trust. When we find those two, I'd like to be there to personally hook 'em up."

"Believe me, Captain, when we find them, and we will, I'll make sure you get that opportunity." As Jake turned to leave Hughes said,

"Jake, I'm glad you're running the Detective Division. You'll get this thing figured out and the I know you'll deal with whoever's involved the way they need to be dealt with."

"Thanks, Captain. You better call Burnett and bring him up to speed. He might want my head. These guys do work for me and he may see this as an opportunity to kick me out of here and down to communications, or worse."

"We'll see about that," Hughes replied as he reached for the phone.

Jake walked out and back to his office while Captain Hughes picked up the phone and dialed Burnett's number. Sandy Warburton answered in her usual officious tone. Hughes told her who it was and asked to speak to Burnett. She informed him that Burnett was on another line and asked him what he wanted to speak to the Chief about. He told her it was confidential. Hughes knew that Burnett would tell her anyway but he preferred giving a first hand account to the Chief. That way he knew the facts were straight.

Sandy put him on hold and within a few moments Burnett came on the line.

"Good afternoon, Ed. How's things in glamorous Hollywood? Which actor's been booked now?"

"Well, Chief, for a change it's not the movie industry that's keeping us in business. It's the two missing detectives, Pritchard and Landers. It's beginning to look like they may have taken up an alternate line of work."

"Do tell," Burnett replied. "How so? What were they up to?"

"Unless we've misconstrued the facts, it looks very likely they were pulling burglaries all over Hollywood. If we're correct, this may help explain why they're missing. Here's what we've got...."

Hughes described the situation to Burnett. After he finished, Burnett asked a few questions and concluded by saying "Ed, we've got to keep this out of the media. The Chief of Police is about to retire and we don't want him going out on a sour note. He's had a distinguished career and corruption of this sort will certainly taint it. Let's just keep this in-house and handle it quietly."

Hughes reminded him that the media was already aware of the missing detectives. They'd been asked to help in trying to locate them by running photos and descriptions. They certainly wouldn't let the matter drop, now.

"I realize that, Ed. But let's at least keep this latest development away from them. Those vultures would have a field day with it. And frankly, Ed, as the Chief of Detectives, I don't want a story like this getting blasted all over the news."

Hughes got the big picture immediately. Burnett had himself penciled in as the next Chief of Police and this would seriously diminish his chances.

"Okay, Chief, I understand," he replied. "We'll keep it quiet."

"Good. And make sure Reed understands. He tends to ignore directions he doesn't agree with."

"I haven't noticed that particular trait. I have noticed that Jake isn't shy about telling you what he thinks. And he doesn't like dirty cops any better than you or I do. Frankly, I'm glad he's working for me. There's not a better man for the job." Hughes threw in the last few comments to let Burnett know that Jake had his full support and respect. And just in case Burnett was planning to suggest Jake might need to be reassigned.

"Yeah, yeah. Fine, Ed. But one other thing. Be sure you keep me fully informed. I want to know every development. And I want to know it as soon as you know it. Call me any time, night or day. Is that clear?" Hughes thought he was getting a little intense and assured Burnett he'd be the first to know anything.

"Be sure Jake Reed understands too." Burnett hung up before Hughes could respond.

'Man, he doesn't like Jake very much.' He thought, hanging up the phone.

*****

"Chief, you have some messages." Walter's secretary held up several of the pink forms and began looking through them as she spoke. "Captain Martin wants . . ."

"Later." Walter said over his shoulder as he went directly to his office. "I don't want to be bothered. No one for the rest of the afternoon." He pushed the door shut behind him and sat down heavily behind his desk. He swiveled in his chair and stared at the pictures on the wall behind him. In times of stress, the images served to comfort him.

Walter and President Nixon at a ceremony honoring a cop hero, a newspaper heralding Walter breaking a famous case, a number of movie celebs and Walter, the Mayor, Arlo and Walter at a pool party with their arms around each other, big smiles on their faces. He craved the world in which he traveled, the rich and well placed, the people who wielded the power. He was part of that strata and he planned to climb to the upper levels. His appointment as Chief of Police was only one step.

As he stared at the pictures, he went back in his mind, back to the beginnings of his relationship with Arlo.

He'd been a cop long enough to realize Arlo was more than he showed himself to be at that first lunch. Intuitively he sensed the violence, the cunning and cold nature that lay below the surface. The buying and selling of the dry cleaning businesses seemed legitimate enough and the profits were rewarding. He ignored the fact that a movie producer wouldn't normally be involved in such a business. Back then, Arlo had already established himself as an independent money man in the film industry. He was traveling in the circles that Walter wished to join.

He wasn't surprised when, after a year or so, Arlo disclosed that eventually the dry cleaning shops ended up under the ownership of a Nevada holding company. Walter was given silent shares in the company. Arlo assured him the operation was squeaky clean. The eleven shops were a real asset in that the business was almost all cash transactions.

And, at about four years into their business relationship, Walter and Arlo branched into the porn business. Arlo again reassured Walter that their participation was well hidden, that neither could afford to be known as pornographers. Soon another corporation held over twenty porn shops in Los Angeles county.

Walter's profits in these ventures were always in cash. He felt comfortable he was safely hidden from any public scrutiny. If nothing else he was a cautious man. He had made a number of discrete inquiries as to Arlo when it was first suggested they become business partners. Arlo was clean, he was what he said, an immigrant from behind the iron curtain who had made good in the great country of hope, the United States.

Walter's participation had been up until now limited to the occasional record check or some other information gathering his position as a cop afforded. As he was promoted through the ranks, he would steer an investigation in a different direction and two or three times gave warning to Arlo about a case that might be coming close to a business associate. Nothing that could be pinned on Walter. Although neither Arlo nor Walter acknowledged one part of their business, it was understood kiddie porn was too lucrative a field to ignore. Walter justified this part of the business with the thought that the 'models' were really of age, 'they just looked real young'. Walter had his own collection. He enjoyed the pictures. 'Lots of powerful men had their foibles, didn't they?'.

Walter turned back to his desk and put his meaty hands down with a sigh. He had to come to a decision. He accepted that Arlo had to keep a second set of books. Arlo could not use this against him, he was satisfied there was no way to pull Walter down without Arlo sinking as well. Too bad the detective had to be killed. 'So be it' Walter thought, 'he would have done the same'.

They had to find the second detective before the department did, of that he was sure. Walter picked up the telephone on his desk and dialed.

"This is Chief Burnett, let me speak to the Captain." And after a brief pause, "Yes, good afternoon Captain. The two missing detectives, are we sure they are dirty?" Pause. "OK , I want to remind you again, we don't want the press to get wind of that, our official position at this point is they are missing, nothing more. The Chief of Police is a week away from leaving. We don't want him to go out under a dark cloud, understand? And of course whoever comes in doesn't need to start with a big story about dirty cops. I want to be kept current on this, Captain. The Mayor's office has already called twice, we want this tight. Am I clear?" Another pause. "Good. Who's handling this in your division, is it still Reed.?" Walter frowned. " Well, I guess. What about internal affairs? Oh, all right then."

Walter sat there thinking. 'Too bad this happened in Hollywood, of all places.' Jake Reed was smart. He'd been around and he was persistent as hell. Walter frowned even deeper, Jake Reed could be a real problem.'

Then Walter's face took on a smile. He was smarter than Jake. Jake was a
Lieutenant. Walter was Chief of Detectives.

*****

The '507' was named for its' address. 507 East 7th street, right in the middle of skid row. Mitch had parked the old Mustang several blocks away and made his way through the old familiar alleys of his drunken days to the doorway of a closed pawn shop, across the street from the bar in which he had spent so many days and nights drinking. Just down the street was the alley where he'd occasionally taken up residence in those days, sleeping behind a dumpster. He sighed. Those times didn't bring pain any more; he looked upon them with a kind of bemused puzzlement.

It hadn't taken Mitch long to make himself look like he fit the neighborhood. He'd stopped at a thrift shop after parking the car. He spent seventeen dollars on an old knit cap, a worn dress shirt and a 'too' large pair of brown pleated pants. A stained brown raincoat, two sizes too small and a scuffed up pair of saddle shoes completed the ensemble. As an afterthought he added a pair of sunglasses, taped together at the bridge. As he walked through the alleys, he scraped his fingernails in an oil puddle and wiped his hands on a piece of newspaper from a trashcan. The same can yielded a wine bottle, not quite empty, that provided the necessary 'cologne' to round out his disguise.

'Yup,' he thought. 'Just like the good old days, dirty and smelly. It sure helps me remember why I'm sober.'

He slouched in the doorway across from the bar for more than an hour, watching the patrons entering and leaving. The old gray pensioners, the bag lady clutching a dollar bill and the younger, homeless types. He watched the occasional old hooker with the heavy, garish makeup, trying to look attractive but not quite accomplishing it. The street all seemed the same, familiar and surprisingly, sort of comfortable.

'Well, so much for Memory Lane,' he thought, stepping out of the doorway and starting across the street.

He pushed through the red velvet curtain at the entrance, walked over to the bar and took a stool.

"What'll it be, pal?" The bartender was a mean looking young thug with a teardrop, jailhouse, tattoo under his left eye.

"How much is a glass of port?"

"A buck. You want one?" The man's eyes continually shifted around the room, dismissing Mitch as of no consequence. Mitch nodded and reached in his pocket and counted out coins in the exact amount. The drink was served and the bartender moved down the bar.

Mitch began looking around.

The '507' was different. The lighting was lower, the music louder, the jukebox playing the current punk and rap music. Given the music, Mitch wasn't surprised to see the clientele had changed, as well. Where there used to be friendly camaraderie among the regular customers, the patrons in the bar were mostly loners, quiet and sullen. Mitch didn't recognize anyone. The smell of Lysol, smoke and beer was the same. Mitch moved to the hallway and the restrooms.

At the end of the hallway, the door to the storeroom had been replaced with one that had security hinges and double dead bolts. Mitch moved to the door and rapped against it. It felt solid, too solid, compared with what he remembered as a wooden door with a bad latch. Mitch moved back to the stool and motioned for a refill, the first drink poured on the floor in the hallway.

"So, you been working here long? I used to come in here a long time ago. I was hoping I'd hook up with some old friends." Mitch said to the bartender.

"That'll be a buck, champ." The bartender said.

"Oh, sure, here. So how long you been here?" Mitch asked and asked again.

The bartender put his hands on the bar and leaned forward.

"What's your problem, pal? I don't need any friends and I don't like questions. Who are you, anyway?"

"Hey, no trouble," Mitch spread his hands in supplication. "Just back in the area and trying to look up some of my old buddies, you know." Mitch smiled nervously, "Used to know the owner, Bleek, Bill Bleek. Who'd he sell the place to anyway?"

The bartender stared at him for a minute and then moved away without saying anything.

Mitch sat there, looking around. He noticed a row of liquor bottles at the end of the bar. There were two bottles of Haig & Haig scotch and two bottles of Grey Goose vodka. The bottles were about half full. Mitch looked around, poured his second drink on the floor and motioned with the empty glass. As the fresh drink was put in front of him, he asked, pointing at the bottles:

"Expensive stuff. Place must have a high roller or two coming, huh?"

"Out. We don't like nosy people in here. Hit it, jerk."

The bartender picked up Mitch's full glass and pointed at the door. Mitch started to say something, thought better of it and left before there was any trouble.

Once outside, on a whim, Mitch went around the corner and into the alley to check out the dumpster where he'd once resided. He stood there next to the tall metal box, thinking. Then, from down the alley, Mitch heard a door creak as it was opened. He looked over the top of the trash bin and watched a well dressed man walk across the alleyway. He reached into his overcoat pocket, removed some keys and unlocked the backdoor of the '507' and entered. Mitch waited a few minutes and then walked to the door from which the man had emerged. It was the back door of the old church that faced the next street over from the '507'.

Mitch hurried around the corner and reentered the bar, however the man wasn't there. The bartender glared at Mitch and started around the end of the bar as Mitch beat a hasty retreat. He hid in the alley by the bin for almost an hour, but the man he'd seen earlier did not reappear.

When a light rain started Mitch gave up and decided to drive by Jake's house. If the lights were on, he'd stop and tell him about what he thought he'd found out. On second thought, he decided to stop, regardless. Jake would want to hear what he'd found out. Something was going on at the '507', that's for sure.

An hour later Mitch walked out the front door of Jake's house, shaking his head. As he got into his car he muttered to himself,

"You try to help a guy out! I don't understand it. I give him some hot clues to solve this case and he thinks I'm off on a tangent. Geez! Why do I bother?"

Mitch drove off through the rain.

CHAPTER 19

"Ah, the dawn of a new day," Jake said, as he got into his department vehicle and headed for the station. No callouts the previous night meant he and Edie had both had a good night's sleep. He was glad for that. Edie was giving final exams all week and needed all the rest she could get. "What a job," he muttered. "Considering all the extra time she works in the average week, she must be making all of $2.00 an hour."

As he crept along the overloaded freeway, he pondered the events of the last few days. How long had Landers and Pritchard been doing burglaries, he wondered? Using the 'vacation check' book in the Watch Commander's office. That takes some balls. Imagine walking in there and going through the book, apparently unconcerned about who might notice what they were doing. 'Those bastards were brazen as hell,' he thought. 'Unless, of course, they had someone else helping them out. Maybe someone on the midnight to 8:00a.m. shift. Someone who could easily go through the book when the Watch Commander is out.'

Unlike the Day Watch, when Landers and Pritchard were

normally working, the Watch Commander's office on the A.M. shift was unoccupied much of the time. No clerical personnel or desk officers are assigned, so when the Watch Commander goes out, anybody can walk in and go through the 'vacation check' book.

'I'll have Marquez check that possibility out,' Jake thought. The whole situation troubled Jake. He was the man in charge and what happened in the division was his responsibility. After the current matter is resolved, he thought, he'd have the inspection and control people come in and do an audit. "That's better than waiting for something else to go wrong," he said aloud, exiting the freeway at Hollywood Boulevard. Ten minutes later he pulled into the parking lot. He walked into the station, past the front desk and into his office, saying "Good morning" to those he passed. Jake hung up his coat and was reaching for his coffee cup and a toothpick when the inside line on his phone rang. He picked it up and said "Reed".

"Licutcnant, Kilgorc hcrc."

"Hello, Lieutenant Kilgore," Jake replied, trying a bit of wit to loosen up the usually stoic Kilgore. It didn't work.

"I'd like a minute of your time, Lieutenant. The information we got from Earl the Girl is beginning to look pretty good."

"Are you at your desk, Dave? I'll come back there. I need a cup of coffee."

"Come on back. There's a fresh pot on."

Jake walked back to the corner of the squad room the Homicide Unit called home. He poured a cup of coffee and sat down next to Kilgore's desk.

"So, what have you come up with, Dave?"

"Earl called me yesterday. He tracked down the woman he told us about. The one who was hiding in the bath room. Her name is Jessica Banks. She was back in one of the joints up on the Boulevard the other night when Earl found her. He talked to her long enough to find out that she's been staying with a friend up in the hills. It's only about a half a mile from our victim's place. She has a boyfriend named Darryl Sherman. Apparently he's the one who stormed into the bathroom looking for her, the night Earl was there."

"Jessica told Earl that Darryl is as mean as they come. She says he particularly likes to abuse women. From what she says, he kicks her ass with regularity. She's been trying to stay away from him, staying with friends, but he always seems to find her. He found her at her friends' place in just a couple of days. She said he just got out of jail about a month ago. One of the guys ran him through the computer. We have a workup on him."

"Yeah, and..."

"And Jessica's right. The guy's an animal. Four page rap sheet. Nothing but felonies, most of them for beating the shit out of someone. I'm betting most of the victims are women. Additionally, he's been popped twice for rape. He got a 'not guilty' on one of them and the other one is pending somewhere in the system. On top of all this, Jessica told Earl that the guy has some strange little quirks when it comes to sex. She didn't elaborate. Lastly, the guy's been in the area of the murder. Oh, yeah, don't forget. Earl, our favorite psychic, says he has a feeling about Mr. Sherman. What more do you need?"

"Well, I'm convinced." Jake said. "Let's hold off on booking this guy for murder, though, until we get a little more. Like physical evidence, or..."

Kilgore grinned at Jake. "If you insist. Seriously, I think Darryl is a good suspect. I have a team out talking to Jessica. After they've talked to her, we'll see if we can track Darryl down. He's definitely worth a look and an interview. I'll let you know what it looks like after we've given him the once over."

"O.K. Dave. If he is the guy, we need to get him off the street. Guys like this are never satisfied. We sure as hell don't want some serial killer/rapist running around out there."

*****

The rest of the day was pretty routine as Jake handled the administrative tasks required of his job. He fielded several calls from the media, despite the fact that Press Relations was supposed to be handling that particular function. Most of the calls were from news reporters he'd known for years. People he'd met and found to be trustworthy and honest. A few he counted as close friends. They reported the facts, left out the dramatics and when asked to hold off on a story that might jeopardize an investigation, they did. Jake discussed the missing detectives, leaving out their possible involvement in the burglaries. Jake had no intention of revealing that information, at least not for the foreseeable future. Captain Hughes had made it pretty clear that Walter Burnett didn't want that all over the news. Jake, however, had already decided that, long before he got the word from the Captain.

Ed Marquez spoke with Jake several times during the day, keeping him up-to-date on the search for Pritchard and Landers. Basically, Marquez had little to report. Aside from getting in contact with Pritchard's wife, who was in Las Vegas, there hadn't been any progress.

Marge Pritchard told Marquez that she'd gone to Las Vegas the day before the two detectives turned up missing. She had no idea where they might be and was understandably worried about Marty. She told Marquez that if they were in any trouble, he could bet it was Fuzzy Landers doing. She clearly was not fond of Fuzzy. Marge told Marquez she'd be home that evening to help, however she could.

At the end of the day, Jake walked out of his office and sat down next to Kelly's desk. She was on the phone but wrapped up her conversation quickly and hung up with, "I'll see you tonight."

"Hot date, eh?" Jake asked.

"Not exactly. I'm going up to the Academy Club for George Ryan's retirement party. You're going, aren't you?"

"Damn! I'd forgotten all about it, frankly. The last few days have been a little distracting. Yeah, I'm going. I wouldn't miss that little getogether. After 41 years as a detective, the guy's an icon. There's probably not a detective on the job who'd miss his party. Except the ones who're working tonight. I better call Edie and remind her I won't be home. Would you get her on the phone for me, Kelly? If she's not there leave a message on the machine for her, will you?"

"You got it."

*****

Jake left the station and headed towards downtown. He caught a glimpse of the freeway, saw that it was in it's usual 'parking lot' condition and opted for Sunset Boulevard. It wasn't a lot better, but at least it moved steadily, if slowly. After twenty minutes or so Jake left the boulevard and began winding his way up through Elysian Park, home to Dodger Stadium and the Los Angeles Police Academy. Jake loved the old academy. He, like most of those on the job, thought of it as their alma mater. It had been there since the thirties and a lot of legendary cops had walked through its' doors. The training had been only twelve weeks long when Jake came on. Now it was six months. 'Times change,' he thought. And so do the people who graduate from the Academy. Now, many more women were coming on the job. There was an increased emphasis on social and cultural issues; more attention to the sensitivities of those whom officers were likely to encounter.

'Overall, probably not a bad idea,' Jake thought. 'But it could be overdone. Ultimately, in a lot of cases, bodily force is the only thing some people understand. Just don't try convincing the A.C.L.U. of that'.

Jake pulled into the parking lot of the Academy. It was jammed with cars. Obviously George Ryan's retirement party was going to be the major event he expected. Another half an hour and they'll be parking people at Dodger Stadium, he thought. Jake slipped into one of the last spaces, got out and walked up the long stairway to the main building. The Club was on the far end, upstairs, above the restaurant. Jake walked up the stairs, through the entrance to the club and looked around. The place was packed with detectives, both retired and active, who'd come to pay their respects to George. Jake was pleased to see that a lot of the department brass were there, as well.

Jake shouldered his way through the crowd, looking for the guest of honor. Over near the large fireplace he finally spotted George, decked out in a tuxedo. The tux was becoming a tradition with retiring cops. They want their last hoorah to be special and the tux seems to add just that little touch of formality to the occasion. In most cases, it was both the first and last time most detectives would ever wear one.

Jake walked over and, after a few minutes, was able to edge through the crowd, reach out to George and shake his hand. Chatting briefly, Jake recalled what a hero George had been to him early in his career. They shared a couple of stories and George told Jake how pleased he was to have known him.

'Just like him,' Jake thought. 'A good word for everyone.' He couldn't recall ever hearing George say anything bad regarding anyone on or off the job.

Jake moved away to allow other well wishers a chance to speak with George and he headed for the bar to get a beer, shaking hands with several people he knew on the way. As he pushed his way up to the bar, cajoling a few detectives to "make way for your superiors", he noticed his boss, Captain Hughes, standing at the far end of the bar, talking with his favorite Deputy Chief, Walter Burnett. Jake was about to change direction and head for the opposite side of the horseshoe shaped bar when Hughes spotted him and waved him over.

"Shit," Jake muttered. He liked the Captain well enough but had no desire to stand around and chat with Walter. Particularly, when there was a roomful of detectives with whom he had much in common and many he wanted to talk with.

"Oh well, I'll make this as quick as possible," he said to himself as he approached the pair.

"Evenin' Captain, Chief. Nice party, huh?"

"Hi, Jake. Yeah, it is. Nice turnout," Captain Hughes replied.

"Hello, Jake," Burnett said, reaching out to shake hands.

Jake shook hands with him.

"Rumors are that you're the front runner to replace the Chief of Police, Walter," Jake said. "What do you think?"

"It's a nice thought. Time will tell. When are you gonna get serious and promote to Captain, Jake?" Burnett asked.

"I'm pretty happy doing what I'm doing. As long as the Captain wants me there," Jake said, looking towards Hughes, "I think I'll keep running Hollywood Dicks."

"You've got a job," Hughes assured Jake.

Jake glanced around the room, preparing to excuse himself when he saw Kelly coming through the front door. Jake almost dropped his beer when he saw that she was accompanied by Mitch. She had him by the hand and was leading him across the room in Jake's direction.

"Well, here comes your adjutant, Jake," Hughes said. Who's her friend?"

"Uh, he's a friend of mine. I didn't know they were…seeing each other," Jake replied, thoroughly shocked and not altogether pleased. Kelly walked up and said hello to the three of them. Burnett and Hughes said hello.

Jake, still somewhat shocked and slightly annoyed at the two of them for not previously mentioning they were seeing each other, nodded. Then, before Kelly could say anything, Jake introduced Mitch to Hughes and Burnett.

"This is Mitch Thacker. He's an old partner of mine from my days on the P.D.in Long Beach. Mitch, this is Chief of Detectives Walter Burnett and my immediate boss, Captain Ed Hughes." Both men nodded and shook hands with Mitch.

Walter said "Well, Mitch, I'll bet you've got some stories about this guy, huh?"

"Actually" Mitch said, "he's got a hell of a lot more on me than I have on him. Jake always played things pretty straight. Regular Mr. Clean."

"I'm not surprised to hear that," Hughes said.

Jake said, "I'd like to stay and chat but…" and started to move away.

Burnett spoke up, "Jake, before you leave I'd like to talk with you."

Kelly took Mitch's arm and pulled him toward the end of the room where George Ryan was holding court. "C'mon, Mitch. Let's go say hello to the guest of honor." Mitch nodded his goodbye and followed dutifully after her.

Captain Hughes started to walk away, as well. "You don't have to leave, Ed. It's nothing confidential," Walter said. Hughes indicated he needed to go to the restroom and would be right back.

As Hughes walked away, Jake asked, "What is it Walter?"

"What's new with the case of our missing detectives? Are we making any headway? Anything new?"

"Frankly, not much. We haven't come up with anything helpful, at all. Those two have basically vanished. I'm not sure if their disappearance is directly related to their apparent involvement in the burglaries, but it certainly seems likely as hell. Maybe they thought they'd been found out and decided to run for it. We did learn that Marty Pritchard's wife was in Vegas to get a divorce, but she swears that had nothing to do with him being a burglar, which she also swears she knew nothing about. Fuzzy Landers is single, lives alone. It was his place where we found the burglary evidence."

"Remember Jake, we don't want the media getting the story on the burglaries. We haven't proven that they're crooks yet. Besides, I'd rather not have a scandal like this just as the Chief of Police is retiring. The media would make it look worse than it is and sully the reputation of a fine Chief who's given the department thirty three years of his life. Don't you agree?"

"I guess I do, Walter. At least for the time being. At some point though, the public has a right to know what the people whose salaries they pay are up to. Don't you think?"

"Don't start that shit with me, Jake. I'm not suggesting we cover anything up. Just hold off for a while. Don't make me get nasty. Besides, what the hell do we care if a couple of detectives turned burglars and extor..., burglars, disappear. They're probably down in Mexico somewhere, sunning themselves on the beach. If we don't find them, who gives a shit?"

"I do, Walter. Those two worked for me and I take it real personal when my detectives are committing the crimes they're supposed to be investigating. I'm gonna find those two assholes if it takes me from now until the day I retire. This is personal."

"Okay Jake, do what you can. And make sure I'm kept informed. I want to know the minute anything, anything at all, turns up. Are we clear on that?" Walter asked.

"Certainly, Chief," Jake said, assuming a formal tone in his voice. "When I get it, you get it."

"Good."

Jake excused himself to mingle with his cronies, just as Hughes walked up. He began to look for Kelly and Mitch, then thought better of it. He decided that the next morning was soon enough to speak to Kelly about her choice of male companionship.

'Apparently Walter doesn't have enough to keep him occupied, ' Jake thought, ruminating on his toothpick.. 'He sure has taken an interest in this case. Unlike the Miller case a few years ago.'

Miller was a robbery detective who worked in Wilshire. He got hooked on heroine and was robbing banks to support his habit. Jake was working as the Assistant Commanding Officer at the time. When they got onto Miller he fled and was the subject of a two week manhunt until he was captured in San Diego. Jake recalled contacting Burnett to fill him in on the progress of the investigation and being told to give the information to his secretary. 'He sure as hell didn't seem too interested in that case. Now, he's got the 'hots' to be Chief of Police so he wants to be in the middle of everything. Phony bastard.'

Jake stayed at the party for an hour or so, mingling and chatting with old friends. He thoroughly enjoyed the company of his fellow detectives, especially the retired guys who he only saw occasionally, at parties like this one.

Then he left the Academy and headed back to the station to see what, if anything, had developed on the Hilltop case or his missing detectives. Nothing had and Jake headed for home. Half an hour later he pulled in the driveway, garaged the car and went in the house. Nearly eleven o'clock and there was Edie in her den/office working away, grading papers. He knew it was hopeless but nevertheless suggested she stop for the night and come to bed with him.

While he waited for Edie, his mind wandered to Kelly and Mitch and their apparent closeness. How close are they and how did he feel about that? Never mind how they managed to keep him in the dark. In fact, about ten days earlier . . .

*****

Castagnola's Restaurant sat on the pier at King harbor with a bar and a number of booths looking down into the swirling waters around the pilings. The atmosphere was quiet and the food was good and plentiful. Mitch had anguished over where he should suggest they meet. 'Romantic' and yet not too obvious. Classy but not too show 'offy'. He normally didn't have all these "before the first date jitters", but somehow this felt different.

He had called Kelly the day before, and after some small talk, had taken the plunge and asked her if he could take her to dinner.

"When?" She had asked with no hesitation. He had at first seen that as a good sign. Of course, then his mind took over and he began to question her motives. Did she accept because of his relationship with Jake? Was she after something, would she want him to do something? He couldn't accept that she might like him, might be interested in an old barnacle like himself. Finally, he wore himself down and called her back and suggested tonight and the restaurant.

" Great," she said. "I'll meet you there."

Mitch sat at the bar and sipped a plain tonic and lime watching the front door of the restaurant. He had arrived for his date a half hour early and taken a seat at the bar with a good view of the area. There was the normal mix of tourists and locals from the four marinas in the harbor.

"Hi sailor. Buy a girl a drink?" Mitch jumped at the sound of her voice behind him. Kelly had come in the back entrance.

"Oh, Kelly. Hi, I'm glad you could make it." Mitch said, standing and smiling nervously.

"I'd like a martini. Does it bother you if I have a drink?" Kelly asked sitting on the stool next to Mitch. She was wearing a simple summer dress. Her hair fell down over her shoulders, the soft light of the bar picking up the auburn highlights. Mitch tried not to stare at her legs, the dress came above her knees when she sat, it was difficult.

"Naw, let's get this out of the way. What bothers me is when people don't have a drink around me. That bothers me." Mitch looked away and motioned to the bartender.

They sat at the bar and made the small talk, feeling each other out, as first time dates will do. When Mitch asked her if she wanted a second drink she said, “No, let's eat, I'm hungry.”

They were seated at a booth overlooking the harbor with two sail boats anchored just off the pier.

"Is your boat like those?" Kelly asked.

"No, well those are both ketches and mine's a sloop and..." Mitch launched into a description of his boat and a history of sailboats, starting with the Phoenicians and moving forward. He stopped talking in mid sentence, realizing he was rambling like a school boy and looked at Kelly with a rueful grin. "Damn, I must be boring the hell out of you." Kelly stared at him and smiled.

"No, I like boats." She paused and looked into his eyes, disconcerting him even more. "You're nervous. Why? Is this your first date?"

"Oh well, no, I go out a lot. Well I mean not a lot, like all the time, I . . ." Mitch stopped knowing how foolish he sounded. 'Damn, what was it with this girl?'

"Is it because I'm a cop?" Now Kelly had a serious look.

"Not at all." Mitch took a deep breath. "It's, it's you're so darn pretty and young. I feel, well, I feel like a school kid. Kind of like, why would a girl like you go out with an old broke down sailor, ex cop like me?"

"I tried going out with the people I work with," Kelly looked out at the harbor, "Doesn't work. And the 'normies' are boring. The Lieutenant likes you; he says you were a good cop. And you do have an interesting life, don't you?" She turned and looked at Mitch. "What do you do? I mean now. What do you do for a living?"

Mitch stared down at the table. He didn't know why but he felt comfortable with this woman, comfortable and nervous at the same time. There was something about her; he sensed she was a kindred soul, a bit of a loner. He began telling her about himself, the truth instead of what he usually did with women-- telling them what he thought they wanted to hear.

"Oh, I do this and that. I don't like being told what to do so I work for myself. I'm good at bright work . . ."

"Bright work?" Kelly interrupted.

"Varnishing boats, the wood work. I like it, it's Zen like. So occasionally I'll take a varnishing job from one of the 'yachties'. Oh, and I was a commercial diver for a while, so I'll do a survey or recovery and some of the rich guys that own boats will hire me to, ah to 'resolve a dispute', sort of." Mitch stopped and looked at her, "I'm not sure Jake would approve of some of the odds and ends. I've acted as kind of a bodyguard a few times, not licensed you know. Does Jake know I asked you out?"

"What I do on my own time is my business. He is sort of protective of me, I like the Lieutenant, he is a good man. But you don't have to worry about me saying anything to him about what we talk about." Kelly paused. "Unless you tell me you are a felon, or serial murderer."

"Right. Well, let's don't mention this dinner, OK?" Mitch said. Kelly put her hand over his and smiled her agreement.

And they talked the evening away.

Mitch told her of his life leaving out hardly anything. Drinking his way to skid row, the arrests, his times in Las Vegas.

And she told him. Of being a loner. Living in foster homes. Working as a waitress to get through college and going on the department. Mitch asked her what happened to her parents and she told him her father had been a beat cop and her mom a cocktail waitress.

"They didn't want to get married and they put me with the sisters of Merciful Hit ya' with a Ruler and as soon as I could I ran away and they kept finding me and putting me in protective custody in another foster home." Kelly said this in a rush of words, staring down at her drink, and then, as she finished, looked at Mitch for his reaction.

"How did you find out that much background about your birth parents? I thought all those records were sealed." Mitch asked, that feeling of nervousness returning.

"Well, after I got on the department it wasn't too hard, a friend here and there, never found out who my dad was, but I did find my mother. We met about a year ago and we're working things out, getting to know each other." Kelly said.

"I have a daughter. Her mom left me. She was only three years old when her mom divorced me. Good idea too. I was no good." Mitch said, sadness in his voice. "Lost touch a long time ago."

"She'll find you, daughters always want to know their father." Kelly said.

"She doesn't even know I exist, I don't think. She was so young and her mother was a wise person, the way I was then, the smartest thing she could do was forget I existed."

"No! You should find out, it's important." Kelly said intensity in her voice.

"I know, I think about it all the time. I just don't think I have the right to interfere in her life. She's twenty now."

"Got to try. Gotta' try to find her." Kelly said with absolute knowledge in her voice.

"Well look, would you help? I mean if I gave you what I know, birth date, place, and all the other stuff, do you think you could do some checking?" Mitch asked hopefully.

“Sure, Mitch. Jake already mentioned this to me. Give me what information you have, and I’ll get to work on it as soon as I have time. How’s that sound?”

“Sounds great! I’ll write down what I’ve got right now.”

They talked some more. He found her easy to talk with and fun. And then it was late and Mitch walked Kelly to her car. He wanted to kiss her but instead hugged her for a moment. As she got in her car, he asked,

"Ah, I had fun tonight Kelly, could we, I mean do you think…"

She smiled up at him, "Call me. I'd like to see your home and that dog and crow. I like animals." He stood there feeling all happy, trying to hold on to the feeling of her body against him as he watched her taillights disappear into the late evening traffic.

*****

"What a pretty day." Kelly was leaning back against the cushions in the cockpit with the dog laying by her bare feet. It was a nice day. One of those blue skies, white puffy cloud days that make for perfect sailing. The warm light breeze moved Mitch's boat past the end of the Long Beach breakwater and the first gentle swell lifted the bow as he set the auto pilot to put the sailboat on a beam reach. The jib filled with a soft 'pop' and the boat steadied on a course past the oil islands and headed out towards the East end of Catalina Island.

Mitch and Kelly had been out twice since that first dinner at King Harbor. Once they went to a movie and, on the spur of the moment, he had called her at work and they met at Pinks on La Cienaga for a chili dog lunch and she had laughed at him when he spilled chili all over his brand new white shirt. He asked her if she would like to go sailing and she suggested today, Friday, saying she would take a personal day off. He spent the whole evening last night 'spiffing' up the boat.

She arrived right on time at 8:30 in the morning, carrying a red canvas bag and wearing a light jacket and pale blue shorts that showed off those long legs. Mitch nodded approvingly at her white canvas shoes. As women will do, Kelly inspected the cabin with curiosity, trying to discern the man from his home. She moved comfortably about the boat and put the canvas bag in a secure place in the sea berth aft and then with a hot cup of coffee in her hand, settled down in the cock pit.

"The bird, what's the bird's name?" Kelly pointed at the one legged crow that had taken it's normal perch when the boat was under way, on the teak arch over the hatch that commanded a view of the cockpit. The bird was turning it's head one way and then the other, staring at Kelly.

"Well I'm not sure, either Cheryl or Russell." Mitch smiled looking at the crow who was now preening it's feathers. "Mostly I call him Mister Crow. He's pretty good company."

"How did you end up with a crow?" Kelly asked.

"Well, I was walking on Main Street in Seal Beach about four months ago and I see this little pile of black feathers huddled in a corner by the book store and they're shivering so I know it's alive. And I'm going like, survival of the fittest and I can't take care of a baby bird that fell out of the nest and all that stuff and then it gave a little chirp and, well, that was that. So I brought it to the boat and I guess it likes it here because the son of a gun won't fly away." Mitch finished and smiled affectionately at the bird. Kelly stretched and said:

"It's getting warm, would you put my jacket below?" She unzipped the jacket and pulled it off handing it to Mitch. She was wearing a blue tank top that matched her shorts. "Just throw it with my bag and shoes." Mitch took the jacket, trying to figure out if Kelly could see his eyes behind the sun glasses. He couldn't help himself, her body seemed perfect to him. She wasn't wearing a bra under the tank top and, although not large, her breasts were full and the nipples poked against the thin material. Her legs were long and the shorts were loose at the waist hanging slightly off her hips. Mitch had to make a conscious effort to maintain eye contact as they talked, even with the sun glasses. She knew and smiled with a coquettish expression.

"Am I making you nervous?" She leaned back and looked down at herself. "I thought this would be a nice outfit to wear sailing, is it OK?"

"Are you kidding? You look great. I'm sorry, I can't help staring." Mitch paused and then blurted, "I really like you Kelly. I think about you. The first time, the first time I saw you at Jake's office I was attracted to you. Never, I never thought we'd be sailing like this."

Kelly stood up and smiled, a smile with just a touch of sadness and touched the side of Mitch's weathered face and they kissed for the first time. The crow cawed at a pelican gliding by just above the wave tops.

They spent the rest of the day tacking back and forth outside the breakwater under the bright yellow sun.

As he walked her to her car, Mitch shyly asked if she would like to sail to the 'Island' some time. She looked out the window of her car and slowly nodded yes and then drove away.

He called her at home that evening and asked:

"This coming weekend, great weather report and the Island won't be crowded." He trailed off afraid he was pushing things too fast.

"Uh huh and . . ." A teasing note in her voice.

"Oh, well, I mean I was hoping we, I mean you. The island--want to go to the island with me this weekend?"

"Sure, I'd like that."

They made plans, what she should bring, what time and all the stuff people talk about when planning something neither wants to acknowledge out loud.

*****

He reached down and slid the brown and tan deck shoe from

her pretty foot. She only resisted for a moment. The boat rolled gently to a small wave and a shaft of sunlight, coming through the port, moved from the cabin floor to her bare foot and along her leg. They both watched, transfixed.

Mitch and Kelly had set sail the night before heading to Catalina Island and Emerald Cove. The evening had been warm and clear and the stars, once away from the lights of the mainland, gleamed in the summer night sky. They sat quietly listening to the burble of the wake, the occasional soft click of the auto pilot, and once or twice the distant horn of a merchant vessel making port. Mitch put his arm around Kelly's shoulder and kissed the side of her neck; she was so pretty sitting there, the dog's head in her lap sleeping the trip away, the dim light of the cabin on the side of her face.

This was their first 'overnight' date. Kelly had added an overtime day to her two scheduled days off and Mitch suggested they leave for the island around seven in the evening. “You get off at five, I'll meet you at the boat as soon as you can get there. Sailing at night is plenty safe and that way we'll have two whole days before we have to come back. OK?' She agreed and here they were, underway.

They anchored about midnight, just on the lee side of Church Rock, a few hundred yards off the beach. Mitch put the tea kettle on the alcohol stove and they were soon sipping hot chocolate and smiling nervously at each other. Neither had mentioned sleeping arrangements. Mitch was strongly attracted to Kelly, but still had that 'school boy' feeling around her. They had kissed and hugged good night over the last few weeks, but nothing more.

Mitch moved to one of the lockers and pulled fresh bedding out and turned to Kelly, saying:

"'I uh, I laundered the bed stuff. It's nice and clean. You get the V berth and I'll sleep on the settee here in the main cabin."

"Oh, I'll sleep out here. I don't want to take your bed." Kelly said quickly.

"No, no I always sleep out here when I'm anchored. Need to get up and check the anchor during the night." Mitch said over his shoulder, making up the berth.

"Oh. Ok then." Kelly said, with what Mitch took to be, relief in her voice.

The dog and the crow watched the two of them with great interest. This was their first overnight guest in a long time.

"I'll go up on deck and smoke a cigar while you change and get in bed." Mitch said climbing the stairs and sitting in the cockpit, looking at the stars and the sea. Kelly was in bed in a few minutes and called up to Mitch:

"I'm all snuggled in. This is really cozy but what's the matter with Briney?" The dog was standing at the door to the forward state room whining softly.

"Aw, she's spoiled, she wants to get in the berth with you." Mitch called to the dog. "Briney. We sleep out here tonight. C'mon girl leave Kelly alone."

"Oh please, let her sleep with me, it's OK."

"Are you sure? She snores sometimes. She will keep you warm though." The dog looked at him as he spoke and wagged her tail in agreement.

Mitch, as was his nature, got up several times during the night to check the boat, to make sure the anchor was holding. He smiled affectionately as he watched the girl and the dog breathing quietly in sleep, Kelly's arm draped gently over the dog.

Kelly awoke in the morning to the smell of perking coffee and jumped from the V berth and stretched:

"God, I don't think I've ever had a better sleep." She pointed at the coffee pot, "Black please. Oh boy, that smells good." Mitch smiled and handed her a cup and told her he would be on deck for a while straightening up.

The morning sun was warm and the waters clear. They took the dinghy ashore and sat by a tide pool and ate their breakfast of muffins and juice and then spent the next few hours exploring and swimming.

Back at the boat, Kelly rinsed her self off with the surprisingly warm sun shower and, while Mitch puttered on the bow, changed into shorts and a halter.

The small shaft of sunlight moved back down her leg as the boat rolled back the other way and Mitch moved to her side and traced the path of the golden light on her leg with a light touch of his fingers. She sighed and moved to him. They kissed, a long and most passionate kiss. Both were trying not to breathe so hard. They pulled back and looked into each others eyes and Kelly stood and pulled her halter over her head, slowly keeping eye contact with Mitch. He reached out and pulled her back to him.

The next morning Mitch made a breakfast of fruit and muffins and a large carafe of chocolate flavored coffee. He went to the V berth and gently shook Kelly awake.

"C'mon sleepy girl, it's a great morning, the sun's already warm and there's no breeze, the sea's like glass, c'mon get up."

She opened one eye and stared at him. He stood there with a big silly grin on his face and his eyes looked down upon her with an expression of affection and excitement.

"Oh boy, I slept great." She said as she stretched and the light cover fell away from her. Her breasts accented in the morning light coming through the hatch. Mitch's smile even broader at her nude body. Her nipples became erect as she watched his eyes roam her body.

"Well, uh yeah, the boat rocks me to sleep every, ah every night . . .Oh you're so pretty, Kelly I . . . " Mitch turned away, "I made breakfast, let's take the dinghy and go off the island and eat." She could see his feelings were making him feel awkward.

They climbed in the dinghy with the dog and, in a few minutes were a half mile off the island. Mitch turned the outboard engine off and spread the meal out on a cushion. They ate quietly while the little boat lifted and fell to the gentle blue swells. The dog hung off the bow sniffing the small zephyrs of wind for any interesting scents.

"So Kelly, how'd you end up being a cop?" Mitch asked, breaking the easy silence. Kelly sat there her back resting against one side of the dinghy, her long shapely legs resting on the other bulwark. She tilted her head back and sighed:

"Oh, it's a long story."

"I like long stories." Mitch paused, "I, that is , I guess I want to know about you, I mean your life . . .I really like you, Kelly."

"Well, my real father was a cop."

"No kidding, who was he with?" Mitch asked.

"I, I don't know. My mother had me when she was young. She was trying to get into show business and she didn't want to get married. She sure didn't want to get pregnant so my grandmother kinda' raised me." Kelly stopped talking a sad look came over her face. Mitch took her hand:

"I'm sorry, I didn't mean to, to, you know pry or make you sad."

"No, no it's OK. I don't talk much about all that stuff." Kelly sat there, as a matter of fact she never talked to anyone about her childhood, the father she had never seen. But Mitch, he seemed a loner himself and she knew about his background. She knew she could trust him, he wouldn't make judgments, she just plain sensed this. Besides that he was infatuated with her, that she knew for sure. And she felt some degree of fondness for him herself.

She went on, telling him about school when all the kids teased her about having no parents. Her grandmother, old and cranky, making her read the Bible and do all the house work. Her mother, all glamorous, coming by once a year with an envelope full of cash at Christmas and never even a hug. Some college and then moving to Los Angeles and just drifting from job to job and occasional dates. And finally joining the cops. She felt for the first time like she belonged somewhere. Her mother had married well and she still wished they were closer but that seemed as though it would never happen. Kelly let out a deep sigh:

"At least I see my mother fairly often. She lives in a fancy home in the hills. Her husband's a creep but he's very successful and she has every thing she wants. Enough about me, what about you?"

And they spent the next few hours drifting along with the slow current that moved along the Island, talking and sharing as new lovers will do. Mitch telling her about being a loner and how special it was to him to have renewed his friendship with her boss.

They spent a wonder filled two days and nights making love and swimming and eating and playing with the dog and the crow and soon it was time to set sail for home.

*****

"Just a few more and I'll be along," Edie called breaking his train of thought about Kelly and Mitch. He laughed and said:

"I won't wait up." He knew she'd be at least an hour, maybe longer. When she got on a roll it was hard to get her to stop. He went to bed without her.

CHAPTER 20

The Chinese fishing trawler, one hundred ten feet in length, with a sixty-three ton displacement, lay hove to in the early morning light. Her bow rose slowly to each swell generated two thousand nautical miles to the northwest. Her rusted hull and dirty superstructure gave no hint of the clean and orderly interior.

Abaft and below the Captain's quarters, several steel bulkheads had been torched away, making one large room. The walls were painted gray and several pictures of cartoon animals hung about. There were six small beds along opposing sides of the room. A woman in a nurse's uniform sat at one end of the room; her black, almond shaped eyes moving from bed to bed. The Asian children, all girls aged from five and a half to nine years, were sleeping quietly. A mild narcotic had been served with their canned peaches an hour earlier.

The trawler was forty-one miles southwest of Catalina Island off the Southern California coast.

It was exceptionally clear, clear and warm and dry. The sea was flat, reflecting the crescent moon off the starboard quarter of Abner's boat. He watched the large fishing trawler maneuver a few hundred yards away. It would be another fifteen minutes before the transfer could be made. Abner nervously checked the engine gauges for the fourth time. The Bertrum lay dead in the water, idling engines the only sound in the darkness of the midnight sea.

This was Abner's ninth trip to rendezvous with the trawler. The two boats were forty-five miles out to sea from Catalina Island and seventy or so nautical miles from Abner's home port in Redondo Beach. An easy four hour run at the sport fisher's cruising speed of twenty knots.

Abner was nervous about the weather.

The old timers along the Southern California coast knew that when the decks are dry in the early morning it is best to stay in port. At certain times of the year, mostly September through November, high pressure areas out in the desert, coupled with cold low pressure air near the ocean, create the Santana winds. As the warm air of the desert moves through the canyons it is compressed and heated and blasts out onto the low lying areas of the coast and then to sea. It's common at these times for winds of seventy miles an hour and more to blow furiously across the Catalina Channel.

Abner sat on the fly bridge waiting for the signal to come alongside the trawler. He thought about the Reverend he'd met almost a year ago.

Abner was thirty eight years old and had inherited his mother's good looks. He wasn't very tall and compensated for his short stature with daily workouts. He had the blond, surfer cut of the early eighties and striking blue eyes. He always made sure he was dressed in the current fashion and kept up on the current catch words and phrases of the younger bar crowd at the beach. Unfortunately, Abner had also inherited his mother's brains. His father was a very successful land developer and amassed a large fortune. He was an avid fisherman and competed in tournaments all along the West Coast. When Abner was thirty years old his father suffered a massive heart attack while sitting in the in the fighting chair of the Bertrum. He had just hooked up to a large thresher shark off San Clemente Island.

It took just six years for Abner to run through his inheritance. His gambling success was matched by his business expertise. Luckily for Abner several large apartment houses were locked in a trust, along with the sport fisher, which gave him just enough income to get by. Although not enough to live the life he thought he deserved. One of his most prized possessions was a twelve year collection of Playboy Magazines and the first edition of Hustler. Abner had changed the name of the boat from Warrior to the Barbi, after one of his favorite playmates.

When the Reverend strolled by the boat that morning a year ago, Abner's life was at a low ebb. He was being harassed quite severely by a loan shark over some gambling debts and he was ready to accept any help, including the Lord's. The Reverend was short and stocky with slicked back, black hair and an unshaven look. He wore a black suit, somewhat rumpled, with a cleric's white collar. After some small talk about boats and fishing, he broached the subject.

"My ministry is dedicated to saving the waifs, the forgotten children of the world. There are many people here in this rich country that would love to adopt. But the laws are so complex it's almost impossible."

He went on to explain that there was an underground organization that brought orphans into the country, mostly from Asia. “Would Abner being willing to help?” The large sport fisher would be perfect for picking up these children at sea, from a larger vessel, he said. A vessel that couldn't come into U.S. waters.

It was the twelve hundred dollars per passenger that the adoptive parents would be willing to pay that brought out Abner's compassion. A deal was soon struck and now Abner's boat was lying off, waiting for the ninth pick up and another twelve thousand dollars.

Two hours later, the big Bertrum powered through the swell and cleared the Palos Verdes Peninsula just as the sun came up, peeping above the cloud layer in the L.A. basin. Within minutes it sat there, a huge orange ball shining through the dust laden air caused by the desert winds. Three and a half nautical miles to go and Abner would be safely tied up at the slip at King Harbor. He hadn't gone below even once to check on his passengers and now, as the seas and boat calmed down, he wondered how they had fared in the rough seas.

Twenty minutes later, Abner glided into the slip and cut the powerful diesels. He spied the Reverend standing at the top of the gangway and waved. Without returning the greeting, the stocky man walked down the gangway and stood at the bow of the sport fisher. As Abner stepped off the boat and began to tie the bow line, the Reverend's greeting was less than cordial and certainly not of a spiritual nature.

"Ya' little turd. Do ya' see it's day light? What the fuck!"

"It was very rough out there, I couldn't make…" Abner began to explain.

"Fuck that! At night, always at night. That's what you're paid for, right?" the Reverend said.

"Listen, you shit head, it was rough out there," Abner waved his arms at the strong wind still blowing. He had decided to take the offensive. "Feel that? It's wind, in case you didn't know. Wind means boats have to go slow. It's called a storm shithead!"

Slap! The Reverend hit Abner open handed along side his head, knocking him to the dock. The Reverend stood over him.

"Listen, stupid. What you do is, you climb back on your fucking boat and you make sure those kids are okay. Then you stay there and keep 'em hidden until tonight. Then I'll come back and get 'em, after dark. And everything better be OK or I'll squeeze your brainless head like a pimple, you prick. Understand?"

Abner nodded his understanding while rubbing the side of his head. The Reverend strode off the dock muttering to himself, "Shit head? I'll show him shit head."

The winds died down in the early afternoon and an hour after sunset a fog bank rolled into the harbor. Abner sat in the cockpit, sipped on a beer and waited. Waited, as he had done all day, for the Reverend to return. The nurse had only come up from below once to request that Abner get the children something to eat. He ordered three large pizzas and two six packs of soft drinks from a pizzeria a few blocks from the marina. The nurse seemed less then pleased with his choice of dinner. 'Fuck her,' Abner thought, 'what'd she want? Fried rice?'

By ten o'clock that night and after a number of beers, Abner came to several conclusions. The Reverend was definitely not a minister. The operation, as he had come to think of his trips to pick up the children, was in fact a black market adoption scam. Most importantly, Abner was entitled to more money and would confront the phony minister when he came back. He tossed several figures around in his mind. 'Two thousand, no twenty five hundred!' and back and forth until he fell asleep in the main salon.

At one-thirty a.m., the fog still lay heavily in the marina. The lights on the docks glowed wetly and the decks were covered in heavy dew. All was quiet. Any stray sound, a gull's squawk, a foraging rat or the slap of rigging on a nearby sailboat, was muffled by the fog.

Abner pulled himself awake to the sound of knocking on the hull. He looked through the port window and jumped back at the image of the Reverend staring at him, his face distorted by the moisture on the glass. The boat listed ever so slightly as the Reverend climbed aboard.

"Everything OK, stupid?"

"Well yes, I had to get them lunch and dinner. About time you got here. What time is it anyway?" Abner asked. The Reverend didn't answer and went forward to where the children were. Abner could hear the man and the nurse in whispered conversation. He moved closer to the companionway, trying to hear what they were saying. As he stuck his head around the corner, the reverend came back up into the main salon, bumping into Abner.

"Sit down over there," the squat man pointed at the settee, "and shut up."

"Listen we need to talk, I..."

"I said shut the fuck up," the reverend said without looking at Abner.

The nurse began carrying the children up from below one at a time and handing each child over to a man standing on the dock. They all appeared to be asleep. All except for the last little girl, who looked back at Abner as the nurse carried her across the salon. She had beautiful wet black eyes and no expression on her pretty face.

When all the children were off-loaded, the Reverend stood in front of the still sitting Abner.

"You wanna talk? Be here tomorrow night." The man turned and walked through the aft door.

"Listen. I know what you're up to and we gotta renegotiate." Abner said in a loud voice to the man's back. The man stopped and stood there for a second and then in a quiet voice,

"Yeah. Be here when I said, tomorrow." He disappeared into the foggy night a moment later.

*****

"We got two problems." The Reverend was standing in a phone booth at the corner of Melrose and La Cienega, holding the phone against his ear with his shoulder while he lit a cigarette and talked at the same time.

It had been three hours since the children had been picked up in the van at the marina. He'd followed the vehicle out Pacific Coast Highway and then halfway through Malibu. The small caravan had followed a winding road into one of the canyons to their final destination, a small house sheltered from the road by Eucalyptus trees and an old grape stake fence.

Boris and the nurse climbed from the cab of the van. The nurse began guiding the groggy children from the side door of the vehicle and onto the front lawn. Boris stood to one side, keeping an eye on the pajama clad group.

"Hey, wait! There's only eight! What the fuck?" Boris rushed to the open door of the van and frantically looked inside. The nurse stood there counting the children in disbelief, shaking her head slowly.

"What? What's the matter?" The Revered walked up from where he'd just parked the Lincoln Town Car.

"One of the kids. Gone," Boris said.

"Gone? Whad' ya' mean, gone? Gone where? Which one?" The Reverend was standing with his face inches from Boris, who stepped back with a bland look on his face and turned to the nurse.

"I don'no, ask her."

The Revered turned to the Chinese nurse who shrugged and said:

"The girl, Song, is not here. At boat, must be when at boat. We hurry then, too hurry. She must run away from boat." The nurse nodded her head yes, agreeing with herself.

The Reverend stood there thinking, "When things go to shit, they all go to shit. Boris, go back to the marina and look around, see if you can find her. And don't talk to that little fuck Abner. Got it?" Boris nodded, climbed into the van, backed up and turned the van around and took off down the dirt road.

The Reverend motioned for the nurse to get the children inside the house.

"Try not to lose anymore of them, you idiot," the Reverend said over his shoulder as he headed back to his car.

Once back in the city, he called Arlo.

"Two problems? And what would they be?" Arlo asked.

"One, the prick that owns the boat wants more money. He thinks we're a black market adoption agency. He thinks it's worth more, the greedy bastard."

"And problem two?" Arlo asked, his voice low.

"Well, one of the kids, a girl, got away. We lost her."

"You lost her! What do you mean you lost her?" Arlo's voice took on a hard edge. "That is not acceptable, I don't pay to lose items. You're getting sloppy. I don't like it when people get sloppy. Find her. Now."

"Don't play hard ass with me, Arlo. You an' me, we're partners, remember? I don't answer to you, so ease up."

"All right then, what do you suggest?" Arlo said.

"I don't think the kid's that big a problem. If she gets found, what? What can she tell anybody? Those kids are knocked out for the whole trip. Shit, she don't even know what country she's in. What's she gonna tell anybody? She was in China and she woke up here on a boat and somebody was gonna take her someplace. She doesn't know a damn thing. She doesn't know where, who or what. It'll take the cops a day just to find some one who can talk to her. And besides that, maybe your boy, Boris, will find her," the Reverend finished in a rush.

"And our boat captain?" Arlo asked.

"Well, that's another matter. With the kid gone he becomes a loose end. I told him I would see him tonight. He may have an accident."

"Yes, that's not a bad idea. I need to rearrange some of the deliveries of the…items. I'll talk with you in a day or two. Good-bye."

Uncle Montini's nephew hung up the phone slowly. It had been a long day and he decided a drink and a late dinner was in order. He was not a man inclined to worry. Everything would work out. He snorted as he thought of Arlo trying to hard ass him. 'That punk's starting to push his luck with me,'he thought.

The fog came rolling in around eleven o'clock. The dock lights and the occasional cabin porthole of a boat lit by an oil lamp glowed fuzzily in the night. Abner staggered slightly as he rounded the gangway to his boat. He had spent the last hour at the Lobster House bar drinking and trying to come up with a scheme by which he could increase his take in the little black market adoption ring he'd become involved in. The so-called 'Reverend' made him nervous. His demeanor suggested that he might be prone to violence. Abner reflexively reached to his waist and felt the small automatic pistol shoved down inside his waistband. He nodded his head assuredly and walked the last few yards to his boat.

He never had time to reach for the gun. Strong hands gripped him around the neck from behind and forced him down onto the wood of the dock. He struggled and let out a small grunt.

"Ow…" His face was pushed against the rough wooded planks. More hands grabbed his ankles and he felt a sharp pin prick in his forearm. Before he could react any further, he was dragged to the edge of the dock and his head and upper torso were forced into and under the water. It took less than a minute for his struggling to slow down and then stop.

The Revered held Abner under for another thirty seconds or so while the squat Russian held his legs.

"Bon voyage, you fuck. Let's go." The Reverend stood and motioned to the other man as Abner's body drifted slowly to the bottom.

CHAPTER 21

Michael "Moonie" Miller was feeling pretty good about things. The day was beautiful. A little breeze, nice and warm, was blowing in from the desert as it often does this time of year in the Los Angeles basin. Two days before Halloween and it's 81 degrees, mid-afternoon. It can't get much better than this, he thought. "Moonie" acquired his nickname years ago but it was hardly relevant anymore. In his early, rebellious years when he'd first moved into the Hollywood area, "Moonie" was simply known as Michael. Without a dime in his pocket and no intention of working too hard to get one, Michael simply hung out; depending on his wits and the generosity of strangers to get by. In other words, he begged, borrowed or stole what he needed. A dry place to sleep, some warm clothes and a bite to eat were all he required, or wanted.

Moonie had few friends. He saw himself as a rebel who shunned any involvement with society. The only exceptions were other denizens of the street who had adopted a similar, antisocial philosophy. However he never developed what you could call a warm, loving relationship with anyone. Aloof pretty well described his attitude.

Shortly after arriving in Hollywood, "Moonie" staked his claim on a stretch of Santa Monica Boulevard which became his territory, for all intents and purposes. He rarely left the six blocks or so he called home. The bus kiosks became his home in rainy weather and the dumpsters and trashcans located in the alleys adjacent to the boulevard became his source for most things necessary to his daily survival. When things got a little tough, "Moonie" would resort to panhandling, a practice he found particularly distasteful. Not because he felt this behavior was particularly degrading but rather because it meant he had to come in contact with "polite society," an accommodation he disliked intensely.

Wanting to make certain that none of those he put the touch on ever walked away smugly believing they had provided something to an otherwise helpless street person who doubtless would have starved without their generosity, "Moonie" always graphically displayed his disdain. He did that immediately after he had the money in hand and was a comfortable distance away. He'd bend over, drop his drawers and bare his buttocks to the donor. While this seldom resulted in any repeat donations, it made "Moonie" feel pretty good about himself. On occasion he mooned those who refused to give him any money but that became a lot of work as the numbers who didn't were significantly higher than the numbers who did. He also mooned an occasional bus, particularly enjoying the tour buses full of out-of-towners searching for the magic of Hollywood. On a few occasions he made the tactical error of mooning passing police cars. This generally resulted in his arrest; a not altogether bad thing on cold, rainy nights. Anyway, that was how Michael came to be called "Moonie" by all of his fellow street people. Having mellowed with age however, "Moonie" hadn't dropped his pants in years.

On this particular day, warm and lovely as it was and feeling good, as "Moonie" was, he was quite sure he was going to find some good, useable or sellable stuff as he dug through the dumpsters in the alley south of the boulevard. He had to maintain a pretty good pace to stay ahead of the trash trucks that were only a few blocks away. It was past noon and he had high hopes they would stop for lunch soon. Either way, "Moonie" was moving briskly from dumpster to dumpster. Pickings weren't too bad so far. He'd half-filled his shopping cart with aluminum cans and some redeemable bottles and he still had three blocks to go before he'd cross the boulevard and start down the other side. "Moonie" wasn't particularly tall and it was, therefore easiest for him to climb up on his cart and get right down into the dumpster. He could then rummage through the loose contents and open any trash bags that were there, as well. The particular dumpster "Moonie" was going through was behind the Jack Rabbit Theatre; a strip joint that couldn't possibly pass as a theatre anymore. He noted there were several green, heavy-duty trash bags inside. All were closed tightly at the top with plastic ties. The size and weight of the bags suggested to "Moonie" that the contents might well be a real find. "Moonie" decided that rather than fool with the ties around the top of the bag, he'd simply rip the side of the bag and inspect the contents. That way, if they looked promising, he'd empty the bag out. He got a firm grip on the first plastic bag and tore it open. Suddenly, "Moonie" didn't feel so good anymore.

*****

"Any calls while I was out?" Jake asked Rene as he walked past her desk and through the door to his office.

"None," she replied. "How was lunch?"

"Lunch with Mike? What do you think? The guy takes life too seriously. He's putting in twelve-hour days, working on the weekends and refusing to take a vacation. Work's his life and, it's probably gonna be his death. But, he's a lovable workaholic and he's probably the best prosecutor in the D.A.'s Office. I hope his boss appreciates that as much as our detectives do."

"Yeah, he's something alright. When he calls here, he always sounds like he's out of breath," Rene said. "A real man on a mission."

"That's Mike." Mike Gattis was a close friend of Jake's. They'd been involved in several cases together when they were assigned to an anti-gang task force years ago. They kept in touch and met regularly for lunch, usually at the Academy Club. Now Mike was in charge of the D.A.'s Major Crimes Unit. They got all the high profile cases and had a remarkable conviction rate. Jake often thought how fortunate it was that guys like Mike stuck to prosecuting criminals rather than defending them.

Jake sat down at his desk, stuck a toothpick in his mouth and began reviewing follow-up reports. The first one he picked up was from two of his robbery detectives, Manny Velasquez and T.J. Baxter.

They'd been involved in the ongoing investigation of a string of super market hits by a pair of shotgun wielding thugs. Over the past month, the two robbers hit five markets and gotten almost fifty grand. During two of the hits they'd beaten a couple of store employees who failed to respond quickly enough for them. Velasquez and Baxter figured it was probably just a matter of time before someone got shot and they'd been digging hard to find the suspects first. Their efforts paid off.

The follow-up report described in detail how the suspects were identified and subsequently arrested. Over twenty thousand dollars was recovered, along with two sawed off shotguns.

"One hell of a nice piece of police work," Jake thought. "It definitely calls for a written commendation."

Jake got up from his desk and started out of the office. He wanted to talk to Jerry Larson, the Robbery Detail's supervisor, to discuss the investigation and, if they were there, to compliment the two detectives.

Jake had barely gotten into the squadroom, however, when Rene called him.

"Lieutenant, phone," she said. "It's one of the patrol Sergeants. He's in the field and says he has something important."

Jake turned around, returned to his office and picked up the phone.

"Jake Reed. What can I do for you?"

"Lieutenant, this is Sergeant Bricker. I'm out here at 7156 Santa Monica Boulevard. I'm actually in the alley to the rear of that address. Anyway, there's a trash dumpster here. A homeless guy was picking through it. He tore open one of the plastic trash bags that was inside the dumpster and there was, er…is, a head. A human head! No shit, Lieutenant. A head."

"You're sure you saw a head, Bricker?" Jake asked.

"Yessir. No doubt about it. I know a head when I see one."

"Okay Sarge. I'll be out there in a few minutes with one of my homicide teams. Secure the location and hold on to the guy who found the head."

"You got it," he replied.

Jake called Kilgore on the com line. He explained to him what he had and Kilgore said he'd round up some of his detectives and meet Jake at the scene. Jake told Rene where he was going and left the station, taking Kelly with him.

As they drove out Santa Monica Boulevard, Jake told Kelly about his conversation with Sergeant Bricker.

"We haven't had a dismemberment case, if that's what this is, since that kid sliced and diced his coke supplier over on Yucca. Let's hope this one's as easy to solve."

The location was just a few blocks from the station and they were at the scene in a couple of minutes.

Jake pulled the police care into the alley that ran parallel to and south of Santa Monica Boulevard. A few yards into the alley, yellow "Police Line – Do Not Enter" tape was stretched from one side to the other. A uniformed police officer was standing at the tape to ensure its warning wasn't ignored by curious onlookers and the inevitable Los Angeles news media.

Jake got out of the car and walked up to the officer, pulling his jacket open to expose the badge on his belt.

Before he could say anything the officer said, "I know who you are, Lieutenant. The Sergeant's down the alley there at the dumpster. Moonie's there, too."

He raised the tape up as Jake and Kelly stooped and walked under it. They walked about fifty yards to the scene. Sergeant Bricker said hello and nodded towards the dumpster. Moonie stood silently.

"That's it. The bag's right on top, right where Moonie found it."

"I take it that's Moonie," Jake said, looking in his direction.

"That's him," Bricker responded.

Jake looked around the alley.

"Who's been in the dumpster besides Moonie? Anybody?"

"Well, I climbed up on that milk crate you see there and pulled the bag open just enough to confirm that there was an actual head in there," Bricker explained. "No one else has been near it."

"Good." Jake walked carefully over to the dumpster, examining the ground for anything that might be of evidentiary value. He stepped up on the milk crate and looked over the edge at the assorted loose debris and two green trash bags. The bag right in front of him was torn open and what appeared to be human hair was clearly visible. Jake removed a pen from his shirt pocket and asked Kelly for one. She removed one from her purse and handed it to him. Using both of the pens, Jake carefully opened the tear in the bag. He could clearly see that the object was a head. Jake leaned further over the edge of the dumpster and tore some more of the bag, exposing most of the face. His toothpick dropped from his mouth as he stared in disbelief.

"Well, it looks like we've found one of our missing detectives. It's Fuzzy Landers."

Jake stepped down from the milk crate and turned to Kelly.

"I want you to locate a phone and call the Captain. Tell him what we have here, that it's Landers. Tell him the location's secure and the media's not aware of the situation. I'd like to keep it that way for as long as possible. Come back as soon as you've done that." Kelly nodded that she understood and walked away.

Jake turned to Sergeant Bricker. "Sarge, I want you to get some more units here. We're going to go through every dumpster in the area. Both sides of Santa Monica, six blocks in either direction. If that doesn't turn up anything we'll go further. A cop's been murdered and another one's missing. He may very well be in this dumpster, too. If he isn't he may be in some other one. I want you to have one of your units track down the trash company that handles this area. When they do, find out if they've picked up in the last few days. If they're out in the area today, have them stop what they're doing and hold the trucks until we can go through them. They'll probably scream like hell but that's the way it's going to be. O.K.?"

Bricker assured Jake he'd take care of it and reached for the radio on his belt. Moonie Miller, who'd been standing near the dumpster, walked over to Jake.

"I heard what you said about the guy in the trash bag. I'm sorry he's one of your people. That ain't right. Killing someone and throwing 'em in the trash. That ain't right."

"It sure as hell isn't, Moonie," Jake said. "We're going to find out who did it. You can depend on that."

"Maybe I can help. I'll ask around. Maybe someone saw something."

"Yeah, you do that, Moonie. I'd appreciate it," Jake told him. Jake knew that good information often came from unlikely sources. The local street people were usually pretty well aware of what was going on in their territory.

As Jake finished speaking with Moonie he saw Kilgore pull up. Behind Kilgore, a second car also parked. Inside were two of Kilgore's detectives, Joe Trask and Michelle Berry.

Kilgore, Trask and Berry got out of their cars and walked to Jake's location.

"What have we got, Boss?" Kilgore asked.

"What we've got is 'Fuzzy' Landers. Or at least part of him. In the dumpster. There's a green trash bag in there and 'Fuzzy's' head is inside of it. I don't know what else the bag contains. Maybe the rest of him." There are a couple more bags that look the same. They may contain parts of 'Fuzzy' or, maybe, his partner. This is as ugly as it gets."

Kilgore nodded his agreement and asked Jake who found 'Fuzzy.' Jake filled Kilgore, Trask and Berry in on Moonie and how he'd found the head in the bag. Jake nodded in Moonie's direction and Trask and Berry walked over to speak to him. Jake turned to Kilgore.

"Dave, I don't know what the hell's going on here. It seems likely that Pritchard's probably bagged up and laying in some trash container like his partner. I don't know how much you know about their disappearance and what we've learned about their off-duty activities, but I need to fill you in. The two of them…"

"Let me tell you what I already know, Jake. The word's pretty much out on these two characters. I know they were doing burglaries on their off-duty time. Most of us figured they learned that the jig was up and decided to split, rather than go to jail. Fuzzy had no reason to risk doing time. He has, had, no family so taking off was a logical decision. Marty Pritchard's wife is dumping him, getting a divorce. That's why she was in Vegas. He knew it and we assumed he decided to join Landers on the open road."

"Well, given the current situation, it looks like whatever they planned didn't come off."

"That's putting it mildly, Lieutenant. At least as far as Fuzzy's concerned. I better get going on this situation," Kilgore said, turning and looking at the dumpster. "Have you called for photos and prints yet?"

"No, I haven't. You can take care of that. The old man just pulled up and he's going to want some details so he can brief the Chief. I'll be back in a minute." Jake turned and walked towards Captain Hughes' car. Hughes was getting out as Jake approached.

"Captain," Jake nodded.

"Kelly gave me the basics, Jake. What have we got?"

"I'm not sure I can give you much more at this point. We've definitely got Landers' head in a trash bag. What else is in there, I can't say. Seems likely we'll find the rest of him, either in there or in the general vicinity. We've got a search of the other trash containers in the area. I'm thinking we'll find Pritchard somewhere, bagged up like his partner, too."

The subsequent search revealed the rest of Fuzzy Landers stuffed in two more bags in the dumpster.

"These guys sure must have pissed someone off, Jake," Hughes said.

"Looks that way. I think it's likely this is connected to their extracurricular activity. Maybe they got caught trying to burglarize the wrong house. In spite of the high rent situation in the Hills, there are some real thugs up there. High rolling dope dealers, organized crime types who generally take care of people who screw with them, themselves. Maybe these two jokers unknowingly tried to rip off some gangster and got caught."

Hughes agreed that was a possibility. He then turned and walked over to the dumpster where he spoke briefly with Kilgore. He looked over the top of the container for a second and then walked back over to where Jake was standing, talking to Sergeant Bricker. Jake finished his conversation with Bricker, who acknowledged the Captain and left.

"Bricker has his people going through the other dumpster in the area looking for Pritchard. I'll let you know the minute we find anything, Captain."

"Alright Jake. I'll be at the station. I'm going back to brief Chief Burnett. By the way, is there anything new on the other side of the investigation? You know, the burglaries?"

"Not much. We're still trying to find where they were fencing the stuff they stole. We've also got that '507' thing to pursue. The more I think about it, the more I think it may turn out to be something. I think I mentioned, there's a '507' club down on skid row in Central. An acquaintance of mine told me about it. Given the area, sounds like it could play into this mess.

"Keep me posted," Hughes said as he got into his car to leave.

"I will," Jake replied.

*****

"Hello Chief, Ed Hughes here."

"Hello Ed. How are things in tinsel town?" Burnett replied.

"We've had better days. I'm afraid our little burglary scandal has gotten a lot nastier than expected."

"Really, how so?"

"We've turned up one of our missing detectives."

"Who…,where, er…which one?" Burnett asked.

He sounds a little flustered, Hughes thought. Maybe his politicking for the Chief's job has him on edge.

"It's Fuzzy Landers. He's dead. He was found in a trash container in an alley off of Santa Monica Boulevard. His remains were in a trash bag. He'd been cut up, in pieces I mean. His head was in the bag and we assume the rest is in there, too. Jake Reed and his homicide guys are at the scene now, waiting for the print and photo people. I gotta tell you Chief, it's one of the uglier murders I've seen. Burglar or not, no cop deserves that."

"Well, that's a hell of a development, Ed. Have they got anything to go on? Any clues?"

"They'd just started to go over the scene when I left. Jake will keep me informed and I'll do the same," Hughes assured Burnett.

"I guess Pritchard's probably out there in a dumpster somewhere, too. Or it may be his body's already in the local landfill; in which case we'll probably never find it," Burnett suggested.

"It might be but Reed and his team are pretty tenacious. If Pritchard's out there, dead or alive, I'd bet they'll find him. And I'd also bet they'll solve Landers' murder. You know Jake, he hates unsolved crimes. Especially murders. And when the victim's a cop, well…"

"Yeah, yeah I know, but it doesn't sound like they have much to work on. At least not yet."

"There is one thing they're going to pursue. Jake told me he had some info on a club over in Central that might be connected to this whole mess. Apparently the name of the place turned up on a piece of paper they found in Landers' apartment. He didn't think it was anything at first but I guess some guy he knows, a civilian friend, told him about the place and he thinks it looks like a possibility. Time will tell."

Walter felt beads of perspiration forming on his forehead.

"What's the name of the place?" he asked, trying to sound as casual as possible.

"The name was some number, like an address. 707 or 227 or 5…I'm not sure. I'll think about it and call you back," Hughes said.

Walter thanked Hughes and hung up. "Aw, Jesus," he whispered, "this is not good."

Walter sat and pondered this latest development. 'It's better they found Landers dead than Pritchard alive,' he thought. 'But now that Jake Reed has something to dig into, it's just a matter of time until that son of a bitch figures out what the '507' has to do with things.'

Walter's com line rang. He picked it up and Candy told him Ed Hughes had called back. He'd asked her to tell Walter the name of the club was 'The 507.'

"Okay, thanks Candy," he said and hung up. "That's what I figured," he thought.

Walter turned back to his desk and put his meaty hands on the desk with a sigh, he had to come to a decision. He accepted that Arlo had to keep a second set of books. Arlo could not use this against him, he was satisfied there was no way to pull Walter down without Arlo sinking as well. Too bad the detective had to be offed. 'So be it' Walter thought, 'he would have done the same.'

They had to find the second detective before the department did, of that he was sure. Walter sat there thinking. He didn't like Jake Reed being involved. Walter frowned even deeper, Jake Reed could be a real problem.

"I've got to call Arlo."

Walter walked out of his office, advising Candy he was going to lunch. He took the elevator to the underground parking garage and walked to his car. It was parked in the stall nearest the door; the one reserved for the senior Deputy Chief. One of the little perks of the job. "Soon, however, I'll be parking in the Chief's spot," he said.

Reflecting on current developments, however, Walter wasn't as sure about that as he had been. The whole situation with he and Arlo was going south fast, through no fault of his. He had no intention of letting Arlo screw things up any worse than they already were. Walter also had no idea how he was going to prevent it.

He drove to his favorite China Town restaurant where, after a short chat with the owner, Norma Chow, he ate alone. After he ate and paid the bill he walked to the rear of the restaurant and used the pay phone to call Arlo. They spoke briefly, agreeing to meet later in the day to continue their conversation. Walter hung up and felt a little better about things. He'd filled Arlo in on the situation and Arlo seemed fairly confident that they had nothing to worry about. For the time being, at least, Walter was able to forget about Jake Reed and focus on his impending interview with the Mayor which was scheduled for the following week.

Driving back to his office he went over the things he planned to present to the Mayor. He had his opening comments all prepared and memorized. He knew exactly how and what he was going to propose to do, to streamline the department and improve its efficiency. Walter believed he was the right man for the job and was pretty certain the Mayor felt the same way.

'Should be a piece of cake,' he thought.

It was nearly five-thirty when Walter walked in Sharkey's Grill, an upscale dinner house in the financial district. He and Arlo agreed to meet at five, however Walter intended to make a point with Arlo. Let Arlo sit and stew when he didn't show up on time rather than the other way around, as it usually was. Walter looked around, Arlo wasn't there.

"That asshole," Walter muttered to himself. "He does that on purpose."

Just then Arlo walked through the front door and up to Walter.

"Been waiting long, Walter?" Arlo asked, clearly pleased that Walter had arrived ahead of him.

"Nope, just walked in," Walter replied. "Let's get a table."

The Maitre'd seated them at a quiet table. Arlo appeared unconcerned over his brief conversation with Walter earlier that afternoon.

"Is there anything new since we talked?" Arlo asked.

"No, nothing. But it's only a matter of time before Reed gets his nose into the '507.' Then we've got trouble for sure. I'm telling you Arlo, this guy is no dummy. When he digs around and figures out you own the joint he's going to know he's on to something."

"How do you figure? What the hell does my owning the '507' have to do with anything? Why should it mean anything, one way or the other?" Arlo asked. "It's just a joint on skid row. Bums hang out there and, obviously, Landers was a bum. So what?"

"Shit Arlo. For an intelligent guy you ought to be able to see the problem here. Reed knows Landers was a burglar. He also knows that your house was on the hit list that Landers and Pritchard were using for their burglaries. Then he finds out you own the '507,' and he will. He's going to figure Landers wasn't killed just because he ripped you off. One things going to lead to another and…"

"Hold it. Okay, I get the picture. Personally, I think you're giving this guy too much credit for smarts but you know him better than I do. I'll…"

"No, you hold it," Walter interrupted. "There's one other little problem. Pritchard's still running around out there. You know, the other guy who knows what's what. If he shows up it's really going to get sticky. When Ed Hughes called me and told me they'd found one of the missing detectives I damned near had heart failure before he told me it was Landers."

"You worry too much Walter. I'll take care of things, trust me."

"Bullshit Arlo. You're not going to take care of Jake Reed like you took care of Fuzzy. That can't happen. No way. What do you think I am? I can't live with that. Don't even think about it."

"For Chrissake, will you settle down Walter. I don't solve all my problems by knocking somebody off. I'm a businessman, a pretty successful one. You know that very well. It'll be taken care of and nobody's going to get hurt. Believe me."

"It better be. I'm not shitting you Arlo. Don't do anything to make matters worse than they already are."

Arlo bristled for just a moment. He didn't like Walter's tone but he decided to let it go, for now.

"And what about Pritchard? He's gonna turn up and then what? He's out there somewhere, waiting for who the hell knows what. Sooner or later he'll contact somebody, probably Jake. Won't that be helpful."

"Take it easy Walter. My associates are looking for him. They'll find him soon. He's scared, obviously, or he would have contacted someone by now."

"How do you know he hasn't? Maybe he's talking to Reed already and Jake just hasn't decided to tell anyone," Walter suggested.

"Does that really seem likely, Walter? That he'd hold that back from his Captain, or from you, his Bureau Chief?"

"Well, no. I guess not. He'd have no reason to. You're

probably right, Arlo."

They got up from the table without ordering and walked toward the front door. Arlo handed the Maitre'd a twenty, explaining that they had to go and they left the restaurant. In front, they spoke briefly about Walter's upcoming interview. Arlo assured Walter he'd put in the good word for him with the Mayor. They shook hands and as Walter turned to leave, Arlo held on to his hand.

"Look Walter, don't worry. Stay focused on the prize. Chief of Police. The rest of this will work out. Believe me."

"I hope so," Walter replied, looking slightly relieved.

*****

Pritchard sat on the edge of the bed and stared at the same stain on the wall he had been looking at for the last two days. His face was haggard with worry. He rubbed the grainy stubble on his face and tried, for the hundredth time, to think of a way out of the mess his life had become. The choices seemed to be, one: go to jail, or two: get offed by Arlo's henchmen. He had to find some money and get to another state or even Mexico. His rent on the cheap motel room was up at noon and that was an hour away and he was flat broke. He reached in his pants pocket and stared at the only money he had. Two quarters, a nickel and three pennies. Enough to buy one more package of cheese twists. One more package of the crispy yellow curlicues he had been eating for three days and then what? Hungry and on the run.

The soft knock at the door startled Pritchard. He moved to the window and peeked through the dirty curtains. The Korean manager was standing outside.

"Yeah?" Pritchard said to the door.

"You pay for 'nother day?" the voice came through the door.

"No, I'm outta' here in an hour."

"Now, you pay now or leave," the voice demanded.

"It's only eleven, I got an hour right?"

"No. Eleven, time check out, you pay now. Not, you leave." The voice showed no mercy.

"Yeah, yeah, OK give me a couple 'a minutes, OK?"

"Five minutes, you leave." Pritchard could hear footsteps as the manager walked away. He pulled on his wrinkled pants and dress shirt and wiped his shoes with a corner of the reddish pink blanket.

He stared at himself in the cracked mirror over the dresser and sighed at his reflection. His eyes were watery and red and his pale complexion set off the black stubble. He ran his fingers through his unkempt hair with little positive result. Then he slipped out of the rundown room, stood on the balcony and looked at the traffic on Hawthorne Boulevard. As he got to the bottom of the stairs he glanced at a newspaper rack. On the front page of the L.A. Times, barely visible through the hazy plastic, was a photo of Fuzzy. Pritchard searched frantically in his pockets for some change and finally ripped open the flimsy box holding the papers. He stood there reading the article about Landers. In a dumpster! They'd found his head in a dumpster the previous day. A chill ran through him and he hurried down the sidewalk away from the seedy motel.

He had no plan. No idea what to do. He only knew he had to run. He just didn't know where or how.

A half hour later he was walking along Hawthorne Boulevard. The area of Inglewood he was in was low income. The storefronts reflected the neighborhood. Thrift shops, rent-to-own furniture and appliances, liquor stores and pawnshops, beer bars, and temp services. Pritchard stared at his image in the store windows as he walked along. He looked like a man coming off a weekend drunk. He needed to change his appearance. In the reflection of a flower shop window he saw an Inglewood black and white cruise slowly by, sending a jolt of adrenaline through his body. For a brief second he thought about running but the police unit cruised on down the thoroughfare.

He entered a thrift and war surplus store and grunted a greeting to the clerk who looked Pritchard up and down, appraising the potential sale:

"What 're ya' looking for?" the short and balding store keeper asked.

"Uh, some work clothes. I uh, gotta do some gardening. Some ah …" Pritchard couldn't think, questions were too big a burden. "Just some old clothes."

"How much you wanna spend?"

"What? Spend?"

"Ya, you know, money, how much money you want to spend, what's your budget?" the little man said.

"Oh," Pritchard looked down at himself and held open his sport coat, "maybe could I trade you for this coat. It's a Polo, you could sell it for a hundred easy."

"Right," the man smirked, "get all kinds of people in here with a hundred dollar bill they don't know what to do with." He pointed to a large cardboard box with a hand printed sign on the side stating 'GRAB BOX.' "There, pick out three items from there. Let me see the coat."

Pritchard pulled off the blue blazer and handed it to the man. Then he began rummaging through the box. Ten minutes later he walked out of the thrift shop wearing a gray sweatshirt with a torn cuff, a pair of bib overalls with the hammer strap hanging loose and a stained canvas fishing jacket of a rather greenish hue, faded by many washings. At the end of the negotiations, he had traded his wristwatch for a worn pair of work boots and a surprisingly clean white tennis hat.

He reached in the pocket of the jacket and pulled out a pair of sunglasses he filched when the storeowner had been looking the other way. As he looked at himself in yet another storefront window, an idea came to him. He knew somebody he could call. Somebody who could help him.

All he needed was a pay phone that worked and some change.

*****

Manny sat at one end of the bar. The end farthest from the entrance. 'Freddie's' was a neighborhood bar located a half block off Sunset on Bixel. Most of the regulars were middle aged and lived in the apartment houses in the area and worked in downtown Los Angeles. After five o'clock in the afternoon, business picked up but now there were only three people in the establishment. The resident bookie, Manny and the bartender.

The bar served as Manny's office. He tipped the bartender two dollars every day and he, in turn, took messages for Manny and let him use the phone behind the bar. Manny thought of himself as an information broker. He lived in the nether world of the professional snitch.

He sat reading the paper and sipping coffee. Manny never drank before six p.m. He was in a very good mood. A narcotics cop had just left and Manny was one hundred and fifty dollars richer. A quantity dealer had turned Manny on to a competitor's delivery location and Manny sold the information to one of his favorite officers. He turned the page of the newspaper with a contented sigh. The cop was happy with the arrest, the drug dealer was happy having a competitor out of business and Manny was happy because he got no heat and the dealer owed him, big time. It was Manny's way of doing business, playing both sides of the law. Only once had his business caused him a problem. A stick up man figured out who fingered him and Manny moved to San Diego for a few months.

The phone under the bar rang and after a moment the florid faced bartender held up the phone and asked:

"You here?" Manny nodded and reached for the phone.

*****

His American cousins didn't accept him. Even before he scurried from the dock, with the roaring trucks and shouting men moving cargo from the giant ships to the warehouse adjacent to the working areas, three of them snapped and bit at him, their yellow eyes gleaming in the night.

Before crossing Anaheim Street and entering the junkyard, the rat had escaped a pack of feral dogs and several cats. He'd almost been run over by cars speeding along the street he'd crossed trying to find food. The docks and surrounding areas of the American harbor were far different from the Korean port where he'd begun his journey and survival would be difficult.

Driven by hunger and fear, the rat huddled behind some rotted flares in a locker of the whale boat.

The rat carried within its blood, Streptobacillus moniliformis, well known in the Orient. The common name in the States was 'rat bite fever.'

*****

Wilmington is a waterfront community. It borders the Los Angeles-Long Beach harbor. The air is dusty and the streets dirty from all the truck traffic leaving the docks with their loads. Most of the residences are low-income family dwellings and the businesses are primarily related to the maritime trade.

At the east end of the small city, which is actually a part of Los Angeles, is a street which stretches for several miles that is wall-to-wall junkyards on both sides. They occupy most of the side streets as well. Most of them are filled with mounds of rusted autos and the debris of the harbor; winches and parts of cranes, cable spools and lengths of anchor chain, dented and rusted containers and industrial outhouses thrown away when the stench becomes too strong. And throughout the area, old boats of every sort. Landing craft from the Second World War, wooden sail and power boats beyond repair, lying on their sides rotting away and even an occasional small tug, everything of value stripped from her hull. Narrow dirt alleys separate the junk yards.

It is a very dangerous area after dark. When the sun goes down, people, mostly men, emerge from the yards, from inside the old hulks where they nest. They stand in the dusty, dirt alleys or lean against the fences and trashcans and wait. Pirate construction contractors, as well as those looking for low cost workers in a variety of pursuits, legal and sometimes illegal, come and do business. On occasion, the denizens of the yards supply materials stolen from the yards and the surrounding areas. And if someone is needed to steal a car or get rid of one this is the place to find a willing conspirator. Small quantity drug dealers and the occasional, very ugly hooker also ply their trade in the area. As can be expected, bodies turn up with some regularity in the area. Some of them die of alcohol and drug abuse and some are killed in territorial disputes and some are the ill informed who accidentally wander into the area.

Whatever else, it's a good place to hide.

Pritchard had been walking for more than six hours. Now, as dusk approached, he crossed Alameda Boulevard and the railroad tracks and turned up a side street into the yards. When he was a young cop, many years before, he had patrolled the junk yards as part of his beat. He knew the area and knew enough to keep his head down and find a place to hole up for the night. He reached into the pocket of the canvas jacket. He had some packages of soda crackers and little packets of sugar he'd lifted from a coffee shop when he had made the call to Manny. In the other pocket he had half a pint of cheap vodka he'd shoplifted at a liquor store. He went into the center of one of the junk yards and climbed into an old Navy whale boat lying upside down. He made a place to sleep out of some old cork life jackets with USN stenciled on them. He was set for the night and tomorrow held promise. A rat crawled over his chest during the night and tried to get into the jacket pocket containing the soda crackers, its nose and whiskers twitching. Pritchard, in his sleep, swatted at the rodent and was rewarded with a bite to his left hand.

Manny had been a snitch for Pritchard for years. He always gave good information. From Pritchard's point of view, Manny owed him. Pritchard had pulled him out of more than one jam, never mind all the money he had given him over the years. He'd called Manny about eleven that morning.

He'd explained to him that he had a little problem. When he told Manny that he was more or less on the run and that some people were looking for him, he was surprised to learn that Manny already knew that. He told Pritchard that Marquez had been by the bar looking for him. Manny, who knew nothing about what was going on with Pritchard, couldn't help Marquez. He assured Pritchard that he wouldn't say anything about their current conversation.

Pritchard told Manny that he needed some money and a car so he could get out of the state. Manny told him that a car would be no problem but that getting any large amount of money might be. Pritchard reminded Manny that he'd helped him out on a number of occasions and it was payback time. Manny told him he'd do what he could and Pritchard assured him he'd get the money back within a month. He asked Manny to meet him as soon as possible with the car and money. Manny wanted to know where he was but Pritchard told him it didn't matter. He told him to meet him the following day in Wilmington. He told Manny he'd be at the lunch stand at the corner of Anaheim and Henry Ford Avenue at ten o'clock in the morning. Manny agreed and asked Pritchard if he'd drive him back to the bar after he gave him the car. Pritchard assured him he would.

Pritchard hung up the phone, satisfied that his immediate problems were solved. He'd worry about the long range ones as soon as he got the car and got far enough away to think things through.

Manny also hung up the phone. After thinking for a minute, he picked it back up and dialed a number.

*****

Song had feigned sleep and watched through half closed eyes as the nurse sat reading at the forward end of the cabin. The children had been fed a dinner of very strange food they were unfamiliar with.

Hard, baked flat bread with a mix of cheese and meat in red sauce and a brown fizzy drink that was much to sweet for her simple taste buds. After dinner the nurse brought fruit juice around to each of the children. Song managed to pour hers behind the berth where she was resting with another of the girls. Now all the children were in a deep sleep except for her.

Late in the evening the nurse and a large man began lifting the sleeping children from their resting places. One at a time they were carried off the boat. The big, hairy man lifted Song from her place and climbed off the stern of the boat and up the dock. Song kept her eyes shut and her little body relaxed. There was a large white van at the top of the gangway with the side door open. Through squinting eyes, Song saw several of the other girls lying quietly on blankets on the floor of the vehicle. The big man laid her roughly on the floor next to one of the girls and motioned to a man standing near the back of the van. He nodded his understanding. Song knew she had to find a way to escape, now.

The man standing guard was not especially tall but he was very stocky; large, squat and muscular wearing a black turtle neck sweater and dark jeans and boots. He turned from the van and, cupping his hands to his face, struck a match and lit a cigarette. Song moved as quickly as she could and, without making a sound, slid out the side door and around to the front of the van. She silently slipped away, shielding her flight with other cars parked in the lot.

She huddled behind the front tire of a car parked on the other side of the mole, forty feet or so from the van, and peeked over the fender. A moment later the nurse walked up to the muscular man at the back of the van and handed over another child and walked back down the gangway. When the man moved out of sight she fled between the cars and hid behind some trashcans alongside a restaurant that faced a busy street leading into a marina.

Ten minutes later she watched as the van with the two men inside pulled out onto the street and drove away. She was frightened. Alone and very frightened. She wanted to get away from the area but of course she had no idea where to go. From her vantage point she could see cars, many more than she had ever seen before. Big and shiny, driving about. She knew she was in a big city. And the people weren't Chinese. They were mostly white and well dressed. She watched them from behind the trashcans, wondering what to do.

Song remained behind the trashcans for over an hour. Then a long, blue car pulled up and parked. A young couple got out, laughing and holding hands as they walked into the restaurant. Song slipped from her hiding place and climbed into the back of the car and lay down on the floor. She fell into a light sleep in spite of trying mightily to stay awake.

Happy voices awoke her. The young couple had returned to their car. They talked in low tones as the young man started the car and pulled out of the parking lot. Song tried not to breathe, afraid that they might hear her. As they pulled into traffic, music began to come from the front seat. Song chanced peeking out the side window. She ducked her head down in shock. A giant man was standing on the sidewalk. Standing on the sidewalk staring down into the car. The image burned into her mind. He was at least five meters tall and had a great white beard and striped pants. It was all too much for the small Chinese girl. She was in a strange land with people she didn't know, a land where monsters roamed.

Victor had been kicked out of the small carnival, fired for stealing. He ended up in Hollywood still hoping for a career in show business. So far this gig was the closest he had come to breaking into the business. Ever the optimist, as the thousands of young men and women who came to the town were, he thought he might be discovered with this job.

He strolled back and forth in front of the newest hamburger stand to make a try of it on Marina Drive in King Harbor. USA Burgers was all red, white and blue neon with large front windows and bright chrome tables and stools reflecting the colored lights.

Victor walked back and forth on ten-foot stilts with long, slow strides. The red and white striped pants fluttered as he strode about. He scratched at the false white beard and adjusted the top hat. He smiled to himself. Uncle Sam hawking burgers. There was a certain humor in the whole deal and, at six bucks an hour; he would be able to pay some of the back rent he owed at the cheap motel.

Victor stared down into the blue sedan hoping to catch a glimpse of some bare leg. The young lady in the front seat was an eye catcher. He caught motion from the back seat out of the corner of his eye. He thought he saw a small child's face for just a second, a round little face with almond black eyes. Then he turned away and waved at a carload of teenagers who promptly hooted and gave him the finger.

*****

Song relaxed slightly as the young couple talked. They were too interested in each other to discover her in the back seat. She listened to the young woman as she sang with the music on the radio, apparently to the man at whom she was gazing adoringly. After riding for half an hour she felt the car slow, turn and then drive over a bump and stop in a dark area. After the car stopped, the young couple got out. Song laid on the floor in the back seat and waited in the darkness.

Song waited until she was sure they weren't coming back. After looking out the window to be sure no one was watching, she opened the door and started to get out. She thought for a moment and then took a sweater that was draped over the seat. Then she climbed from the car and looked around. She was inside a large structure, apparently a place to park cars. She could see the street through the barred door at the entrance. Song pulled the sweater on over her cotton pajamas, walked to the door and squeezed between the bars. She began walking down the street. At the end of the block she could see many cars driving very fast. There was a traffic signal light which she wasn't sure about. She remembered traffic lights from her brief visit to a big city in her homeland but she couldn't remember what they meant exactly. Tears formed in her eyes as she thought about her home and her family. Now she wasn't even sure where she was or how she'd ever get home. More than anything, she wanted to be in the little hut smelling the cooking oil as her mother made her family their evening meal and to be with her brothers and sisters.

Song pulled the large red sweater tighter around her and began walking down Sunset Boulevard, eyeing the pedestrians, the night people of the 'strip.'

Chapter 22

Jake exited the 405 freeway, as he did every night, at Sunset and headed west towards home. He reached over and turned off the radio on the unit car. His day was done and he was looking forward to a quiet evening at home. Dinner and some TV. It had been a busy day and he was more than a little tired.

The headlights picked up the young woman as the car swung into the curve of the narrow street, a mile or so from the freeway. She was waving feebly, standing beside a VW bug. Her face had what appeared to be blood, smeared around her nose and mouth. Jake pulled over, came to a stop a few feet in front of the Volkswagen and got out of his car.

"Hello miss, I'm a police officer, what's the trouble? What happened, are you all right?"

"Oh, I feel so stupid," the girl was young and attractive and Jake took her to be a student from the UCLA campus a short distance away. "My car broke down again and the hood came down and I bumped my nose and I'm late and..." The words came out in a torrent as she tried to explain.

"Well, I'm not much of a mechanic, miss, but let's see if I can help." Jake moved towards the back of the little car.

"Oh, oh I don't think it will start. My boyfriend usually has to work on it for a half hour or so to get it to run again." She held a paper towel to her nose. "Could I ask for a ride to," she pointed towards UCLA, "the school. My boyfriend will bring me back later and get it running, dumb thing."

"Sure, come on." Jake opened the door for the young lady and she got in with a grateful smile. They made small talk as the car headed towards the Westwood campus.

"Here. Here would be just fine." The girl said, pointing towards sorority row. Jake stopped just short of the intersection and she got out of the car, thanking him. He headed on home, feeling glad he'd been able to help the young girl.

He parked in the driveway and as he entered the house he knew he was going to have a quiet evening alone. Edie wasn't home and sure enough, there was a note on the kitchen table. Parents' night at school, she wouldn't be home 'till late. There was left over spaghetti and salad in the refrigerator.

After dinner he sat in the study and tried to read. "Better than the mindless crap on TV." he thought. But he couldn't keep his mind on his book. It kept returning to the Landers homicide and his missing partner, Marty Pritchard. 'Was Marty dead?' he wondered. 'If not, where was he? What did he know about Lander's murder? Good questions I'd like the answers to. This situation has to be tied to the burglaries,' he thought. 'I wonder how, exactly.'

Jake decided a nights sleep and a fresh start in the morning was probably a good idea. He headed upstairs for a shower.

There it was again. Something there, right at the edge of recall, nagging at him. Something someone said. A remark or a comment that he'd been trying to remember but couldn't. "What the hell was it?" he asked himself.

*****

Traffic was light and Jake made it to the division earlier than usual the next morning. He poured himself a cup of coffee and headed to his office to catch up on the never ending paper flow. He frowned as he took a sip of the black liquid. It was worse than usual.

The twenty four hour log for the previous day was sitting on his desk and as he sat down to read it Kelly came in with a fresh cup of coffee. "Try this, Lieutenant. That stuff you've got resembles battery acid." Jake thanked her as she walked out of the office.

Jake perused the report. The previous day had been relatively uneventful. A few armed robberies, several burglaries, domestic violence complaints, bar fights, shootings (mostly misses) and a significant number of arrests, mostly gang bangers. The Street Gang unit had been busy.

"Lieutenant," Kelly stood in the doorway, a clip board in her hand. "Don't forget, Mitch's coming by for lunch today."

"Right, thanks. And we've got a squad meeting in about twenty minutes. Remind the supervisors, will you?"

"Already done" she said, with a smile.

"Your efficiency continues to keep me in awe" he replied ".

The squad meeting went well. Jake filled his detectives in on the latest information regarding the murder of Landers and the ongoing search for Pritchard. Jake wasn't surprised to learn that the grape vine was functioning well and most of what he told them was old news. Nevertheless, he wanted them to hear it from him. He filled in a few details and answered a few questions. Then he presented a couple of commendations, reminded everybody to stop parking their detective units in the Captain's parking space and closed the meeting by thanking all of them for their efforts. He was proud of his crew and felt it was important they know it.

The rest of the morning went by quickly. Detectives came in the office from time to time, updating him on various cases and at twelve sharp Jake looked up to see Mitch standing in the doorway with a big smile on his face.

"Hi Lieutenant. Ready for lunch?"

"Yeah, let's go." Jake smiled at his friend.

After lunch Jake pulled the unit car next to Mitch's, let him out and then pulled in and parked behind the station. He was buzzed through the back door and walked along the hall towards his squad room and office. He said hello to one of the old time uniformed officers and frowned when the old cop didn't respond. That was odd. Jake hoped everything was all right. The old timer was a good cop.

As he stepped into the detective squad room everything went quiet. The normal noise came to an abrupt halt. Jake stared around the room. Most of his officers bent their heads and avoided his gaze. Jake looked across the room to his office. There were five men, including Captain Hughes, standing in his office. Kelly was sitting in a corner looking up at one of them, shaking her head no. As Jake moved towards them, she looked up at him and he saw a look of anguish in her eyes. The men followed her gaze. Jake recognized Captain Jack Hill from Internal Affairs, as he moved to the office door and pulled it open.

"Come in Lieutenant." Hill pointed at a chair in front of Jake's desk. "Sit there. This is," Hill pointed at a grave looking man in a dark gray suit, "Captain Rusk, LA Sheriffs."

"Lieutenant, I'm going to read you your rights." Rusk pulled a card from his suit coat and performed the ritual every cop was aware of but never thought they would hear directed at themselves.

"Now this," Rusk held a paper towards Jake, "is a search warrant we have executed for your office and unit car. We want the keys." For the first time Jake saw that his desk drawers were all open as was the door to his closet. He looked towards Captain Hill.

"What the hell is this?" Jake's voice reflected his outrage.

"You will have to surrender your badge, ID and your weapon. Give them your car keys. You are suspended pending the investigation of several felonies, Lieutenant." Before Jake could respond Captain Rusk cut in.

"Your home is being searched under authority of a separate warrant," He looked down at his watch, "right about now. I expect you to be at this location for an interview tomorrow morning at ten a.m., Lieutenant," he said, handing Jake a business card. The men, without another word, began filing from his office. The last man was carrying a clear plastic bag with Jake's tweed sport coat from the closet and another bag with a brown manila envelope in it.

"That's it. No explanation. Nothing?" Jake said, growing angrier by the minute.

"Well, there is one other thing," one of the other men said. "Get yourself a lawyer. You're going to need one."

Jake turned to Captain Hughes.

"Ed. What's happening here?"

"C'mon in my office. I'll give you what I have. They showed up about a half an hour ago and frankly, they didn't tell me a hell of a lot."

Jake followed the Captain into his office.

"Shut the door and sit down Jake."

Jake pulled a chair over in front of Hughes' desk and looked at him.

"What the hell's going on? What am I supposed to have done to warrant all this?" Jake asked.

"Well, as I said, they didn't give me all the gruesome details but apparently there's some woman who has accused you of assaulting her. Said you stopped to help her over on Sunset someplace and when she got in the car you attacked her, tried to sexually assault her. She maintains you punched her, giving her a bloody nose, among other things. She got an attorney and went to I.A.D."

"Really. Well, that's a bunch of crap. I know the female in question. I stopped to help her last night. She had a problem with her car. I gave her a ride to the campus. Dropped her off and that was it. I never so much as touched her. Why would she accuse me of this sort of thing?"

"I don't know Jake, I really don't. But there's more than her allegations. When I.A.D. showed up and searched your desk they found an envelope full of photos. Kiddie porn stuff. Naked children engaged in some sex acts. Do you know anything about that?"

"What! Kiddie porn. You can't be serious, Captain. You know me better than that. Pardon the trite cliché but somebody's framing me, big time."

"I respect you Jake and I don't buy any of this either. If this is a frame, and I'm not doubting you, it's a pretty sophisticated one, isn't it? Who have you pissed off enough to go after you like this?"

"Nobody, Captain. I know I'm not the most loveable guy on the job, but this_"

"Well, go home and think about it. There's got to be an answer to this situation. Let me know if you come up with anything. In the meantime, don't go off on your own. You go out and start poking around and I.A.D. will pounce on you for interfering with their investigation. O.K.?"

"Yeah, sure. I know. If I get any ideas I'll let you know, Ed. I'd appreciate it if you kept me informed from your end."

"I will, Jake. Don't worry, this will get straightened out."

Jake got up, handed Hughes his badge and I.D. card and walked out. He went to his office, retrieved some of his things and spoke briefly with Kelly, assuring her there was nothing to the allegations. She told Jake she was certain of that and he headed for the back door to get his car. Half way there he realized his car had probably been taken downtown to headquarters to be processed for evidence. Besides, he was suspended. He couldn't take a car home anyway.

Jake walked back to the homicide unit and found Kilgore at his desk. Before he could speak, Kilgore got up and walked up to him:

"Jake, this is a phony deal all the way. Nobody in the unit believes a bit of it. I, we, know you too well to even consider this a remote possibility. Somebody's set you up."

"No shit. And they've done a pretty good job of it, Dave."

"Maybe. But the department will get to the bottom of it. If they don't, I will," Kilgore told him.

"Let's see what happens. Don't get involved, Dave," Jake told him.

"By the way, how about a ride home?"

"Sure. Let's go."

Jake and Kilgore talked about the situation en-route to Jake's house. As they pulled up in front, Jake again admonished Kilgore not to get involved in the matter. Kilgore agreed he wouldn't. As Jake began to get out of the car Kilgore grabbed his arm.

"Jake, let me know how I can help. Anytime."

Jake looked at him. "Thanks, Dave. I may take you up on that."

Chapter 23

It had been a day since Jake's suspension. He and Mitch were sitting in the cockpit of Mitch's sailboat looking across Alamitos Bay at Naples Island.

"Well, I wish there were something I could say, something to cheer you up." Mitch looked at his friend with real affection. "How's Edie taking all this?"

"Edie's a hell of a lot angrier than I am at this point. She knows this is all bullshit and can't believe the department thinks I could have done it."

"So lay it out for me, we'll think of something."

"Mitch, the whole thing is bizarre. Somebody set me up, somebody who obviously wants to screw me over. But why and who? I don't have the slightest idea. I haven't got any enemies that I know of. We all piss people off from time to time but not to this extent. Shit, Walter Burnett is the only guy on the job I know of who really dislikes me and he sure as hell wouldn't stoop to this. I don't know. I don't know who to trust on the department. Somebody set me up and nobody wants to be close to me." Jake chewed vigorously on a what had been a toothpick and was now a sodden bit of wood dangling from his mouth.

"The victim, who is she?" Mitch asked.

"She has an attorney. I guess she is going to go for civil action after the criminal stuff is out of the way. She's who she says she is. Student at UCLA. Appears to come from a good family. Dad's a mail carrier, I think. I can't understand what she's doing, why she's saying what she's saying." Jake shook his head again.

"The sheriff's investigators found blood in my car. Apparently, when I gave her a ride she let some blood get on the seat. But they also found some blood on the sport coat in my closet, that I wasn't wearing thc night I helped her, and I'd bet it'll match hers. Obviously someone put the blood on the jacket while it was hanging in my closet. Somebody inside the department has to be involved."

"And the envelope with my prints all over it. Kiddie porn! It hit the papers this morning. I'm going to be charged with kidnap with bodily harm and attempt rape and possession of child pornography. Can you believe it?"

"O.K. What's her story? She says she broke down and you pull over and than pull her into your car and she fights you off and you hit her in the face and break her nose and she escapes and what? Runs half a mile to the campus and calls the police? They have her blood in your car and on your coat, that you weren't wearing. They find an envelope in your desk drawer with kiddie porn photos and your prints are on the envelope. Anything else?"

"I don't think so." Jake answered. "My attorney says that's it."

"Do you like your lawyer? Is he a good guy?" Mitch asked with concern in his voice.

"Yeah, I've known him a long time, was on the job and went to law school, he's OK I'm sure."

"What does he say?" Mitch asked.

"Well it's mostly the blood evidence. That and my prints on that damn envelope. And the sport coat. I can't figure how someone got in my office. Had to be a cop. Someone who also told her where to be and when, in order to intercept me on my way home," Jake noted.

"Anyway, with all that I'm going to have a tough time in front of a jury trying_"

"Jury? Bullshit! We aren't going to let this go that far." Mitch said and then sat back and continued in a softer voice. "The supposed victim, she's the key. Somebody put her up to this and we need to find out who."

"How would you propose we go about doing that?"

"I haven't figured that out yet." Mitch said.

"Don't try figuring it out. Things will work out. Going after her won't help matters."

"Jake, I've got a feeling this whole thing is connected to your two burglars. I'm not sure exactly how but_"

"Funny you should say that, Mitch. I've had the same hunch. I think those two may have gotten involved in something more than simple burglary. I'd sure as hell like to find Marty Pritchard, if he's still alive. Unlikely as that seems."

"Yeah, I agree," Mitch said. "By the way, do you have any idea who the culprit is that put the blood on your coat and the envelope in your desk?"

"Someone who had access to my office when I wasn't there. Someone who could walk in and out without looking out of place."

"And who fits that description?" Mitch asked.

"Kelly, obviously, and Rene."

Before Mitch could reply, "What the hell!" Jake jumped and pulled his head away. A bird had landed on his shoulder. A black bird.

"Oh, mister crow." Mitch laughed. "Isn't that something? He's really made himself at home. Sleeps on top of the radio and eats dog food. He flies around the beach every morning and then comes back here and takes a nap. Look, he likes you."

Jake leaned back and stared at the young crow perched on his shoulder.

"How do you know it's a he. What's his name?"

"Well I don't really know, but if it's a he it's Russell Crow and if it's a her it's Cheryl. What else?"

The bird cocked its' head at Jake and flew to the back stay and perched there, staring down at the two friends.

"It seems to me that a black bird is a bad omen," Jake observed. He turned and looked at his shoulder. "And when it craps on your shirt you are truly in deep shit."

*****

It took Pritchard a full minute to realize where he was. He lay on his back staring at what appeared to be rotted wood strips just inches from his nose. His eyes were correct, he was nestled in the bow of the overturned whale boat on top of some very hard cork life jackets that were digging painfully into his back. He rolled over and climbed out from under the boat and stared around him at the mounds of junk. He felt as though he had been thrown away himself. Absentmindedly he scratched at his left hand and tried to figure out the time and which way to walk out of the yard, a real maze of wrecks and other used up equipment of the busy harbor.

As he wandered around he hit several dead ends and began to feel his anxiety level rise, even above the hunger pangs. He couldn't afford to miss Manny. Manny was his salvation.

He finally found his way to Anaheim street. He looked down several blocks and could see the intersection and a corner of the lunch stand where he would make the meet and finally have a car and some money. He felt dirty, hadn't had a bath in three days and was beginning to itch from his filthy condition. And food, some money would get him . . . he began to day dream about what he would order , finally deciding on a big steak and three, no four scrambled eggs. He shambled along the street and came out of his reverie over food as he came within a hundred yards of the lunch stand. There were thirty or forty, mostly young men and some old winos, standing about the outside of the building. Day laborers, most illegal migrants, waiting for a contractor to gather a few to work for a day at a dollar an hour. The winos waiting to get a few hours handing out fliers advertising a used furniture store or a pizza joint that makes deliveries.

Pritchard stood and looked for a vantage point to make sure Manny didn't bring someone with him. He felt sure, after all he had done for him, Manny would help. He finally walked to the intersection and crossed and mingled with the crowd of hopeful workers to be. Pritchard garnered nary a glance from anyone. He had a five day growth of beard, his diet of Cheetos and soda crackers had caused a least a ten pound weight loss and his cloths not only fit poorly but were themselves as dirty as he was.

He saw Manny pull into the parking lot in his ever polished several year old Cadillac Fleetwood and park a few yards away. Manny climbed from the car and looked around. His glance went right by Pritchard, not recognizing the detective in his gaunt and disheveled condition. Manny stood there expectantly as Pritchard watched him, forcing himself to be patient for just a couple of minutes to make sure everything was as it should be.

Had not Manny shrugged his shoulders and looked across the street, Prtichard would not have noticed the white van parked just down one of the dirt alleys. With a shock he recognized the two men seated in front as being, in all likely hood the same two from the '507'. He tried to melt further into the crowd, desperately tried to make himself invisible.

And everything stopped, nobody moved for what, it seemed to Pritchard, hours. The man's voice standing behind him almost frightened him into wetting his pants:

"Do you or not?" The man was wearing blue denims neatly pressed and standing with his hands on his hips.

"Me?" Pritchard asked his hand to his chest.

"Yeah you, do you want ta' hand out pamphlets, are you sober enough to walk? Six bits an hour and a bottle on tha' way back."

Pritchard thought as quickly as he could and decided this was his best chance for escape.

"Sure, yeah sure I'm not drunk.

"Climb in the back with the other guys." The man said pointing to a stake bed truck with five or six older men seated in the back. Without looking over his shoulder Pritchard did as he was told and spent the next six hours walking the residential area of Wilmington putting fliers in Spanish and English extolling the expertise of a Doctor Rodriquez Chiropractor and Industrial injuries specialist on parked cars and the front doors of houses.

The truck dropped him off at dusk down the street from the lunch stand and he made his way back to the whale boat clutching the free bottle of wine, a bag of three burgers and almost four bucks in his pocket. As he climbed under the rotted old boat he wiped his nose, he felt like he was coming down with a cold, felt feverish. In all likely hood caught from sleeping outside for as long as he had. Never mind a very poor diet.

CHAPTER 24

Jake spent another sleepless night, getting up before Edie and making the coffee. She came down as Jake was finishing his second cup. They chatted for a few minutes, mostly about the suspension and the circumstances surrounding it. Edie made no effort at hiding her indignation over the way the department was treating Jake. As though he was a common criminal. She suggested he retire after the situation was resolved but Jake ruled that out immediately.

"I'm not ready to pull the pin just yet, Edie. I like the job. I look forward to going to work and that's not going to change. I'm going back."

"What ever you think, but if it was me I'd tell 'em to kiss my--"

"Whoa, honey. Let's be a lady about this," Jake kidded.

"Well really Jake, you've given them twenty eight years of dedication and this is how they thank you. Those bastards!"

"Listen, Edie. The department isn't picking on me or trying to screw me over. They have evidence I did something and they have to deal with it appropriately. They can't just say 'Jake's a good guy so let's just forget this, it couldn't be true.' That's not the way things work."

Edie looked at Jake for a long minute. "I hope you're right. But it sure sounds like they're trying a lot harder to prove you're guilty than to prove you're not. I hope your faith isn't misplaced."

"So do I honey, so do I," Jake replied.

Edie left for work about thirty minutes later. Jake poured another cup of coffee and sat down to read the paper when he heard Mitch pull up in front. There was no mistaking the blown out mufflers on Mitch's old car. Jake met him at the front door and they walked through the house to the patio where they sat down.

"Jake, I've got an idea."

"I was afraid of that," Jake replied.

"No, seriously. I think we need to do a little investigating ourselves. There's two sides to this story."

"Nobody's more aware of that than I am, Mitch. I've asked Kilgore to check out the girl, the complainant. She's one of the keys to the situation. Actually, I'm more interested in who the inside player is though. Right now Kelly looks like a damn good suspect."

"I don't see it, Jake. She's as loyal as they come. Why would she be a party to something like that?"

"I have no idea. But stranger things have happened."

"No, it's someone else. I'm certain of it."

"Okay Sherlock. Who?"

"I'll have to get back to you on that one," Mitch admitted. "Listen, Jake. We haven't got much, but there is the '507' thing. Why don't we look into that? We've got nothing to lose. It could be connected to this whole thing."

"I can't see how but--"

*****

Jake had been sitting in his old Chevy pick up for at least three hours, down the block and across the street from the '507'. The little walkie-talkie lying on the seat buzzed for what seemed like the hundredth time. Mitch had brought two of them along. He used them when cruising in tandem with his boating friends. "Not a lot of range but keeps us off the ship-to-shore radio," Mitch had explained. The buzz got more insistent.

"What!" Jake said, getting a little impatient.

"See anything, yet? Over." Mitch's voice was tinny over the cheap set.

"Who else would I tell if I did?"

Silence from the other radio. After a moment, Jake pushed the 'talk' button again:

"Over." Exasperation evident in his voice.

"Ah...10/4." There was silence for a moment and then from Mitch, "Over."

Hours earlier Mitch had convinced Jake they should sit in at the '507.' After much discussion about how worthwhile the venture would be, they decided Jake should watch the front of the bar and Mitch, one block over, would keep the rear covered from the alley. As far as Jake could see the last three hours had been fruitless. The night people on skid row were much as they had always been. Perhaps the average age was a little younger than when he walked a beat in the area, but not by much. The aimless wanderings of the winos, the gum chewing cheap hookers and the shifting eyes of the predators were all familiar to Jake. He fiddled with the truck's radio one more time. The damned thing would only pick up one station and that was scratchy western music. Time seemed to have come to a complete stop.

"It's Bleek, I'll be darned." Mitch's voice broke the silence over the walkie-talkie.

"Bleak isn't the word, let's call it a night." Jake responded.

"What?" Mitch came back, his voice excited, forgetting to say 'over'.

"You said it's bleak. I agree. This is boring and pointless. I'm counting winos to pass the time." Jake radioed back, "Over."

"I said what? You what?" Mitch's voice high pitched.

"No, I said, I mean you said, "Jake paused, sometimes his conversations with Mitch deteriorated into nonsensical interchanges that ended up going nowhere. "You said this whole idea was without value, you said bleak, it was bleak, over."

"...and it's been years, I'm going to talk to him. Over." Mitch had been talking over Jake's transmission. Now it was Jake's turn. He spit out his toothpick.

"What the hell are you talking about?" Jake said, frustration evident in every word.

"Will you please calm down?" Mitch's tone condescending. "I just spotted Bill Bleek. He's in a Salvation Army uniform. He's working the bars like they do, got a woman with him too, in uniform!"

Jake remained silent.

"Over." Mitch finally said.

"And just who is Bill Bleek? Over." Jake said.

"He owned the '507'. When I used to hang out in there. I'll bring the radio with me, I'm going to talk to him. Over and stand by."

Mitch climbed out of the old Mustang and walked up to the couple standing near the rear entrance to a church that was across the alley from the '507'. He called out as he approached them:

"Bill! Dog gone, Bill, it's me." As he spoke, Mitch stretched out his arms in greeting. The man and woman in their gray uniforms with red piping turned and stared at him. The man was a little taller, by an inch or so.

"It's been years. Is it too much to hope? Look at you. You look just fine." Bleek stopped talking for a moment and looked Mitch up and down. "Why I believe you've gotten sober. Praise be, I think it's true. Is it?"

"Yep, nine years and a little."

Bleek held his wife's hand as he told their story, finishing up by saying that his CPA training was going to get him a promotion to Captain.

Meanwhile, Jake not knowing what was going on, decided to drive over to Mitch's location where he found him talking to the couple. Mitch introduced him to Bill and Esther.

"So uh, Bill who bought the old '507'?" Mitch asked.

"You know I could never understand that. An attorney came in one day and talked about the place with me and the next day came back and made a very generous cash offer. A corporation bought it. Frankly it was not a very good investment." Bleek stood there shaking his head.

"Now Bill, don't question the Lord's work." Esther put her hand on her husband's arm.

"What was the name of the company?" Jake asked.

"Goodness it's been so long, I can't remember. Is it important to you Mitch?" Bleek asked.

"Oh, who knows, it could be. What about the church?" Mitch asked pointing at the old structure, weathered and stained from the years of living downtown. "Do you know the pastor?"

"Yes, yes I do. He is a fine man. Reverend Throgmorton, from England you see."

"OK if I use your name, Bill? I think I'll stop by tomorrow morning and talk to him. " Bleek agreed readily and the four of them, Jake, Mitch, Bleek and his wife stood there on skid row at two thirty in the morning and talked of times gone by. As they parted, Bleek agreed to call Jake with the name of the company that had purchased the '507' and Esther grabbed Mitch and gave him a big hug with happy tears in her eyes. Jake smiled at Mitch's awkwardness at the moment.

CHAPTER 25

Just before lunch time the next morning Mitch was sitting in the Church vestibule with Pastor Throgmorton. A small rotund man in his late fifties with a ruddy face and full head of coal black hair, he seemed full of optimism and cheer in spite of what Mitch perceived as dreary surroundings. The church had that dry dusty smell of old books and stale furniture polish mixed with the muted sounds of the city traffic and light sneaking past the stained glass windows giving it a feel of agelessness. Mitch made some small talk and the Pastor said that Bleek had stopped by and told him about Mitch and how happy Bill was that Mitch was alive and well.

"He thinks the world of you. He and his wife Esther have been a real blessing to the people in this neighborhood." Throgmorton said with real affection in his voice. Mitch asked the Pastor about the bar across the alley and any back door to the church and who might use it to enter the bar rather than from the front entrance a block over.

"Yes," the Throgmorton countenance took on a thoughtful

look, "we leave the church open all night, one never knows when some poor soul needs to sit with our Lord. There are a few people that come through the church and make their way across to the '507' a few times a week or so. They always leave an offering and are never any trouble. Why do you ask?"

"It's more than likely some of these people might not be very nice folks. But not to worry Pastor. Thank you for your time."

Mitch walked down the church aisle between the pews and waved good bye over his shoulder.

"Oh," the Pastor called, "car, I remember there is one car I've seen they always park down the block. It's a big black one, with those shaded windows, maybe a Cadillac or a Lincoln. I hope that will help." He said as he waved good-bye.

*****

Jake jumped at the sound of the telephone. He had fallen asleep in front of the television. The stake out of the '507' had been tedious and boring and it left him tired enough to doze off. He looked at the clock as he reached for the phone, almost midnight.

"Hello?"

"Jake, it's Dave. I'm down the street, can I come by?" Kilgore's voice quiet.

"Sure, I'll be at the front door." Jake stared at the phone after hanging up. What could Kilgore want at this hour?

A few minutes later Kilgore's black Explorer pulled to a stop under the tree in front of Jake's house and Kilgore came quickly up the sidewalk. Jake greeted him at the door.

"C'mon, lets sit in the patio, want some coffee?"

"Yeah, OK." Kilgore had a serious look on his face.

Jake came out onto the patio with two cups of coffee. Kilgore was slouched on one of the colorful canvas chairs, his chin resting in one hand. He took the mug with a nod and sipped at the hot liquid.

"What's up?" Jake asked, sitting across from the detective.

"I've been down in Long Beach. You remember a cop named Piper?"

"Piper?" Jake rubbed his forehead. "Names familiar. Maybe. Big guy? Blonde, maybe?"

"Yeah, that's him. He remembers you." Kilgore sat there, staring straight ahead, thinking.

"And . . .?" Jake coaxed.

"He works intelligence now. We worked a deal a long time ago, couple of crazies hitting super markets. They jumped back and forth between our two jurisdictions. Wound up in a shooting. Piper and I took 'em down."

That was all that needed to be said. Kilgore wanted Jake to know that whatever he had to say would be solid information, that it had come from someone Kilgore trusted and respected. The two men sat there, Jake content to let Kilgore figure out how to present whatever he needed to say. Finally he looked directly at his boss:

"Your friend Mitch. Piper remembers him too." Kilgore was becoming more and more uneasy. He sat there, saying nothing.

"OK let's have it. Tell me what's going on here," Jake prodded.

"Your friend Mitch worked for the mob after he left the P.D." Kilgore paused and stared into the coffee cup in his hand.

"He worked for the New Frontier Hotel in Vegas, which is owned by the Montini crime syndicate out of Boston. There's a lot of stuff in his file at Long Beach. He was close with a dirty Vegas cop, a captain on the take. His job was security but all he did was escort big spenders and act as a bag man for old man Montini. The Feds filed a memo with Long Beach. The 'Uncle,' that's the old man, is the head guy. His name is Tuto Montini. According to the Feds, he took Mitch under his wing. There was some reliable intelligence that a couple of small time guys hit the pavement. Mitch was part of it."

Kilgore stopped and stared at Jake to see his reaction. Jake stared back, disappointment apparent in his stare.

"Go on."

"Out here on the west coast about five years ago, two of our guys eyeball him meeting one of the Montini enforcers in a bar up on Wilshire. Sitting in a booth, talking. I looked up the memo. It's good info. They picked the enforcer up at LAX and followed him to the bar. The subject talked to Mitch for a while and then took a plane back to Boston. They made Mitch with the license plate on the car he was driving. They also got good pictures. Sorry Jake. Your friend looks pretty dirty. I had to check. I had an uncomfortable feeling about the guy.

"I appreciate it, Dave. I really do. I guess I have to pick my friends more carefully."

"Well, I'm not saying he has anything to do with your present predicament but--"

"But he sure as Hell could have." Jake said, staring across the yard. "He sure as Hell could have."

Jake looked at Kilgore. While the number of those he thought he could trust seemed to be dwindling, Jake knew Kilgore was both an unwavering friend and a good cop. Before this was over, Jake began to realize, he'd probably test both aspects of their relationship.

Kilgore finished his coffee and said goodnight to Jake. He told him he'd be in touch; that he had some other things he wanted to look into and not to worry.

“Dave, don’t get too involved in this. Be careful. You have an excellent reputation with the brass. Don’t jeopardize it for my sake.”

“Jake, I’m not doing anything you wouldn’t do if our situations were reversed. I’m not doing anything wrong. I’m asking the same questions anyone looking at the circumstances would ask. If the brass has a problem with that well, screw it,” Kilgore said. “I know you’re getting a royal frame job here and, frankly, my curiosity won’t let me leave it alone, Jake.”

“Thanks, Dave,” Jake said as Kilgore walked down the sidewalk toward his car. Kilgore got in the Explorer and then got back out and walked back to Jake. He reached in his jacket pocket and handed Jake a small box. “I almost forgot. These are from the guys in my unit. They didn’t want you to run out.” It was a box of toothpicks. Kilgore returned to his car and drove off.

Jake walked back through the house and sat down at the kitchen table. Edie walked in and sat down with him.

“Who was that that just left? It’s kinda late for visitors.”

“Dave Kilgore. He dropped by to give me a little info he picked up.”

“Really. It must have been pretty important,” Edie said, fishing around for more.

“Well, yeah. It was, I guess. I can’t say I’m shocked but--”

Jake told Edie what Kilgore had found out about Mitch.

“So now what, honey? What are you going to do?” she wanted to know.

"Good question. I need to think about it. At this point I'm not certain. One thing's for sure though. I damn sure don't want him out there doing anything on my behalf."

CHAPTER 26

Joseph J. Ponticelli had a big resentment. He squirmed in the driver's seat of the police car trying to get his bulk in a comfortable position. Being back in uniform was bad enough. But with all the attendant gear, all the new stuff they'd added to the Sam Browne belt; the mace canister, portable radio holder and so on, being stuck in a black and white for eight hours instead of sitting behind a desk made him a very unhappy fellow.

He resented Lisa and he resented Lieutenant Roach for his predicament. From his point of view, his situation hadn't been of his own making. True, he did like a little extra 'poontang' from time to time. And Lisa the cocktail waitress did have magnificent breasts. In fact, they were so wondrous that she commanded an extra twelve dollars a shift at the bars where she worked. They also drew the attention of the lieutenant. Unfortunately, Joseph, being a tit man, succumbed completely to Lisa's attributes. It took six months for the lieutenant to realize that he was sharing his true love with Officer Ponticelli and only one day to transfer him to the morning watch, working midnight to eight in the morning, in uniform. The adjustment after twelve years in a detective assignment working the theft detail was, to say the least, difficult.

In spite of his resentment, Joseph was a good cop and at quarter to three in the morning he was cruising the alley north of Sunset Boulevard with the unit's lights off, looking for anything out of order. He shined his six-cell flashlight into the nooks and crannies of the trash cans and stairwells as he drove slowly along. He almost missed the small bundle of rags under the stairs behind EZ Cleaners. Song was having a nightmare and she cried out, flinging one thin arm out in self-defense. Joseph jerked the car to a stop and backed up. He stared at the little hand sticking out of the pile of rags. He quickly got out of the car, walked over and knelt by the girl. He took her tiny hand in his big paw and gently held it as he pulled the rags away from her face. She awoke and stared into the bright light, her dark eyes blinking rapidly. Then, frightened, she tried to yank her hand from his.

A half-hour later Song was seated on a wooden bench at the Hollywood station with a female officer seated next to her. The officer, realizing she couldn't communicate with Song, spoke in soft comforting words, hoping to ease her fears. Joseph was explaining to the desk sergeant how he found the frightened little girl:

"Look Sarge, this kid's not from here. I'm sure of it. Her clothes, the straw slippers and look at her pajamas. That cloth's more canvas than cotton. And she doesn't speak any English at all, I'm sure. This is a weird deal I'm telling' you. It's like she just stepped off the boat from Asia."

Kelly caught the last few words as she came up to the front desk. After Jake's suspension she'd been shifted back to a detective assignment on the morning watch. It had been exceptionally quiet and, other than an occasional phone call, she had been bored. Looking for something to occupy her time, she'd decided to go through some watch reports. She glanced at the little girl as Joseph leaned on the desk, talking to the Sergeant. Joseph looked over at the jail matron who was sitting with Song.

"Keep a good eye on her. She tried to jump out of my black and white twice on the way to the station. She'll rabbit in a second, given half a chance."

"Where'd you find her, Joe?" Kelly asked and Joseph explained.

"I'll take care of her," Kelly said as she walked over and tenderly touched the side of Song's face and softly said, "well little girl you're safe now. Let's see if we can find out where you belong." Kelly's voice and the touch seemed to further calm the little girl. Kelly took her by the hand and walked back toward the detective squadroom, saying over her shoulder, "Joe, I'll bet she's hungry. See if there's anything in the fridge would you?"

Chapter 27

In the making of porno flicks, the studio is similar in many regards to a legitimate enterprise, a normal movie making operation. The people or technicians are much the same. Key grip, editors, actors, and of course camera people, are all part of the crew. However, on the typical porno set there is, in addition to the usual folks, a coterie of lovelies known as 'fluff girls.' Belinda was one of the best.

Belinda, known in some circles as "Sweet Cheeks," walked through the parking lot of the mall with her purchases in a large canvas bag. She carried the bag every where she went insisting, to anyone who would listen, that the bag would save the rain forest if everybody used one rather than plastic or paper bags. She had tarried with a young clerk at The Boom Box and the mall lot was nearly empty as she strode rapidly towards her car. She fumbled for her keys and finally got the door of the old Volvo coupe open.

The blow landed squarely between her shoulder blades driving her forward into the car and knocking the wind from her with a whoosh. Before she could recover a strong hand was at her neck forcing her face into the soft fabric of the front seat. She felt as though she were going to suffocate.

"Keep your mouth shut and put your hands behind you, now." The husky voice spoke quietly into her right ear. She made a feeble attempt to struggle and the grip on her neck tightened painfully. So painfully that she quickly did as she was told, putting her hands behind her. They were tied tightly around the wrists and she was forced upside down onto the floor of the front seat. The car started and slowly drove out of the large parking lot. Her face rubbed harshly against the carpeting every time the little car bounced over a speed bump. Her fear was turning to hysteria and she started to plead with her captor:

"Please, what do you want? Please take my car, my purse. Don't…"

"Shut up or I'll gag you." The man's voice was calm and quiet. Somehow, that was all the more frightening.

After driving for ten or fifteen minutes, the car made a series of turns and came to a stop. The man got out of the car. A moment later she felt his hand in her hair and she was pulled roughly from the car. He forced her to walk through some grass to a tree. She was pushed against the tree in a sitting position. She looked around wildly. At first glance she thought she was in a park. Trees and a large expanse of grass with cement benches, a ghostly white in the light of the half moon, were all she could see. As she looked more closely, the headstones told her it wasn't a park, but a cemetery. Her fear jumped up another level and she began to tremble. Tears began running down her cheeks. The man was sitting on the end of one of the benches about four feet from her. He was large with a dark watch cap and dark clothing. She couldn't see his face in the shadows. He sat there silently staring at her.

"What do you want? Why are you doing this?" Her voice was shrill with fear.

No answer, he just sat there staring. His eyes reflecting the moonlight.

"Why won't you answer me? Please . . ."

Silence. After a moment she tried again:

"Listen, I have some money saved up. We could, you know, go to a bank. The ATM. I'll give you the money. OK? It's almost a thousand, OK?"

He just smiled and shook his head.

The silence seemed to go on forever and then he spoke in a frighteningly quiet voice.

"The Bengal tiger loves the kill. Especially so when the prey is a female antelope. The blood is richer you know. They rip open the stomach and feast there first" The man paused and coughed a cruel laugh before continuing.

She moaned and turned her head to the side. She was going to die. She knew it. She felt a calm come over her. A feeling one gets when all hope is lost.

"Oh please, please," she mumbled in a subdued voice. "What? What are you going to do?"

"What's the most important thing to you right now? Let me guess. Going home and getting tucked in by your mother, no doubt. Having her tell you everything is going to be all right. I'm going to ask you some questions." The man stood and moved to her, bending down and putting his face next to hers. "If you don't tell me the truth I'll know and bad things will happen to you here. Here in the graveyard." He paused, and then in a barely audible whisper, "You know that's true, don't you?"

She sobbed and nodded her head.

"Who told you to set up my friend?" The man was sitting on the bench again.

"Oh God, I can't. They'll hurt me."

"No, they won't. First, they won't know I talked to you and second, when I know who they are, they are going to be too busy to think about how I know them. You're in way over your head, Belinda. Think about it, who do you think is worse, me or them?" He sat back and stared.

"You don't understand. The attorney, they got me an attorney and he said . . ."

"Your attorney can do whatever he wants, this conversation is between you and me." The man paused. "He wouldn't tell me anything. Well, he did tell me where to find you."

"What?" She blurted.

“Your attorney took advantage of you. He is only interested in making money, he threw you to the wolves." He nodded at her encouragingly.

And she told him the whole story.

Her folks weren't wealthy and school cost money. A friend at school introduced her to Harry and he hired her. The first two weeks all she had to do was odd jobs, run to the all night market for paper towels or other stuff and pick up burgers for the people on the set. There's nothing wrong with sexy movies. She and her boy friend watch them. The movies were made out in the San Fernando Valley, always at night in a big warehouse. Blue Bird Studios. They paid her one hundred dollars a night, in cash.

Harry was director and producer. He was a nice guy, thought like she did, believed the government and the big corporations were evil. Wore a "Save the Rain Forest" T-shirt and everything. After a couple of weeks he told her she could be one of the 'get ready girls.' All she had to do was play with the male actors, get them hard before their scene and she would make three hundred dollars a night. She needed the money and what could it hurt? A hand job, no big deal. Oh and she would never do oral sex unless she liked the actor. Anyway, she became a 'fluff girl.'

A week ago Harry told her she could make some big money.

He told her about Jake. That he was a cruel man and all she had to do was file a complaint and then she could have all the money from the lawsuit and they would give her five thousand dollars as well. And the cop was a bad man, wasn't he? It was a chance to strike back against the establishment and so she did it.

So Harry smacked her in the face and made her nose bleed and she waved Jake down and then called the sheriffs from the UCLA emergency clinic.

"And that's all I know," Belinda looked hopefully at her interrogator. "Please, will you let me go?"

He asked her where the studio was and what kind of car Harry drove and some other questions and she told him. As he untied her hands he told her:

"Just go home and don't tell anybody about our little talk and you'll be OK." He helped her to her feet and handed her the car keys. She rubbed at her wrists and began walking hurriedly towards her car.

"Oh Belinda?" She stopped at the sound of his voice, without turning. "Your bumper sticker, Save the Whales? Your car is made in Sweden. They kill a lot of whales. Did you know that?"

She got in her car and drove away, with out looking back. She was still too frightened to get angry.

Mitch watched her drive off. Then he turned and walked across the cemetery grounds to the opposite side. He scaled the fence, walked to his Mustang and got in. As he started the car a big grin crossed his face.

"Well, Jake's going to be real glad to see me when I fill him in on this little caper. First, though, I think I'll pay a little visit to Harry and Blue Bird Studios."

Mitch put the car in gear and drove off.

"Yup. Jake's gonna be real glad to see me."

It was one AM and the traffic in the San Fernando Valley was light. The small fluorescent signs in the storefronts along Roscoe Boulevard were still lit, calling attention to a variety of enterprises, products and services. A few businesses were still open; Jack in the Box, a 7-11 mini mart and one or two gas stations.

Mitch revved up the engine in the old Mustang. The miss was getting worse and he had yet to diagnose the problem. Every time he took it to a mechanic the car ran perfectly. Thinking about this, Mitch drove right by Albany Street. He made a u-turn and then a right onto Albany, which brought him into a seedy residential area. There were bars on the windows and graffiti just about anywhere that paint would stick. Half the streetlights were burned out, or in some cases, shot out. Mitch drove slowly down the side street. What should have been an industrial area was instead small homes.

He pulled over to the curb, turned on the overhead light and looked at the directions he'd written down from the Thomas guide on the computer earlier that evening. The u-turn had confused him. He should have taken a left onto Albany.

Mitch turned off the overhead light and was preparing to pull out when an old lowered Chevy pulled up next to him and stopped, the loud exhaust murmuring as the four young men in the car stared at him. All four had red bandannas around their foreheads and the look, the hard look of gang bangers. Mitch gave them a wave and began to pull from the curb. Naturally the Mustang stalled and two of the gang bangers climbed out of the back of the low rider. Mitch reached between the seats and closed his hand around the handle of the .38 M&P Smith and Wesson he had stashed there, for reassurance.

"Good evening gentlemen, a little lost and an old car. Been one of those nights." Mitch smiled as he spoke to the pair.

"Where you from homey?" one of them asked.

"Up until a week ago I was doing time in Folsom. I'm down

here looking for an old cell mate of mine. Said he might have some work for me. I turned on the wrong street."

The pair stared without speaking and Mitch stared back, hardening his gaze. He had a slight smile on his face, showing no fear. After a moment one of them waved to the others and they got back in the car and drove slowly away.

Mitch let out a breath of relief. "Assholes. The only thing they respect is other gangsters, assholes like themselves." He cranked the starter. The engine fired up as though there had never been a problem. He made another u-turn and drove across Roscoe on Albany and into the industrial area he'd been looking for to begin with and where he expected to find the warehouse studio.

He found it a block and a half up. It was a gray, one story large building at the back of a moderately sized parking lot. One dim bulb above the loading dock the only light. The large group of cars parked at one end of the lot belied the building's unoccupied appearance. Mitch looked over the parked vehicles as he drove by. Except for a new Jag coupe, they were all non- descript, older models. He parked under some palm trees a few hundred feet down the street and began walking back towards the darkened building, checking to make sure his weapon was secure in it's position at his back, held in place by a leather holster sewn onto his belt. He was wearing a black leather jacket, jeans and his steel toed, Redwing work boots. He felt in the jacket pocket for the small flashlight and looked down as he flicked it on, seeing the glow from within the pocket. He was as ready as he could be.

The gate was loosely chained and padlocked. Mitch slipped through, scraping his face in the process. He moved slowly across the parking lot and, staying close to the wall, began to circle the building. Halfway around he still hadn't found either a door or a window.

"Who tha' fuck 're you?" The ugly man appeared from nowhere. He was a foot shorter than Mitch and a hundred pounds heavier. His round shaved head disappeared into his wide shoulders and the bunched up muscles of his arms stretched the t-shirt he was wearing. His eyes, half hidden in the flesh of his face, glared at Mitch. He was swinging a two-foot length of heavy chain as he stood there.

"Are you Harry? I'm sorry I'm late. Accident on the 405." Mitch was trying to think fast, this guy could eat him for a snack before lunch.

"So much for stealthy approach," he thought to himself. He should have realized they'd have security around the studio.

"What are you doing here?" the small giant asked in a gravely voice.

"Looking for the door." Mitch answered, looking over the man's shoulder to see if there was anyone else.

"Why do you want the door?" The man was still swinging the chain in a menacing manner.

"Well, champ, I want to go inside, I want to be an actor." Mitch had decided it was time to abort this mission. The sooner the better. The short man standing in front of him was not part of his plan.

"Wiseass? You like bein' a wiseass?" The man was working himself into an angry state. The chain was swinging in a larger arc.

Mitch figured he had about a second to go to plan B.

He took a half a step forward and brought his right fist from behind his back in a round house. Putting all his weight into the punch, he hit the man as hard as he could in the solar plexus. The blow had absolutely no affect on his adversary at all, none. Mitch did manage to get his left arm up in time to partially block the chain as it slammed alongside his head.

Plan C, run like hell. "My legs are longer than that midget s.o.b.'s," he thought as he raced for the fence. "Oh please start," he mumbled as fear lifted him over the fence. He sprinted to his car, which, mercifully, started right up.

Just before the on-ramp to the Hollywood freeway, Mitch looked in the mirror and saw that he was bleeding from a bad cut on his left cheek and that his eye was beginning to swell shut. It was also beginning to take on a green, blue and black hue.

"Could have been worse," he thought.

*****

Jake was in the waiting room of the Memorial Hospital emergency ward when Mitch emerged with a bandage on the side of his head and a very black eye. At five a.m., neither man looked especially happy.

"What happened?" Jake pointed at the bandage covering one side of Mitch's head.

"Uh, they had to sew it up." Mitch wasn't too sure Jake was

going to be to pleased about his activities over the previous twelve hours. He touched the bandage gingerly.

"Do you know what time it is? Sew what up?" Jake looked annoyed and frustrated.

"Um_ I don't know, four o'clock?" Mitch stalling, trying to get his thoughts in order.

What seemed like a good idea at the time, was now, with Jake standing there, perhaps a little impulsive.

"No. It's after five. What happened, what did they sew up?"

"Uh, my head. And I've got a hell of a headache. Let's go have some breakfast. I'm starved." Jake nodded his head. He knew Mitch well enough to know he wasn't going to get any answers right away.

"C'mon, we'll take my car, I'll drop you back off here later." Jake wasn't about to let Mitch go until he found out what was going on. Besides, Mitch might not be in any condition to drive.

As Jake's old pickup pulled out of the hospital parking lot, a black Lincoln Town car took up a position a half a block behind and followed.

The Denny's restaurant at Sixth and Long Beach Boulevard was busy with the normal five to six a.m. crowd. Early morning people on their way to work, a hooker or two finishing up late and three cabbies in a corner booth discussing the wagers they'd make later in the day with the cook, who also happened to be a bookmaker. Mitch slipped the hostess a five-dollar bill and they were seated in the closed area in the back of the restaurant, usually open for dinner only. Jake stared intently at Mitch, a toothpick moving rapidly from one side of his mouth to the other, a sure sign he was upset.

"OK. No more stalling, what happened, what's going on?" Jake leaned forward as he spoke.

"Well, it's a little complicated," Mitch explained.

"Uncomplicate it and give it to me straight." There was a hard edge to Jake's voice.

Mitch took a deep breath and continued. "Promise to let me tell the whole thing before you get pissed off." Jake nodded impatiently.

"I had a little talk with Belinda and I thought I better get a hold of Harry before she had a change of heart and warned him and then after dealing with a bunch of gang bangers, this huge little dwarf hit me with a chain and I'd just had it for the night and went to the hospital and called you." Mitch finished in a rush and sat there with a half- smile on his face.

"You what! Belinda? Tell me you don't mean the Belinda." Jake was incredulous, "and who is Harry?"

"Yeah, the Belinda. I wanted to talk to her. We went to a graveyard and. . .."

"You went where?" Jake looked around to see if anyone was listening. "You kidnapped her?"

"A graveyard, but there's no problem. I didn't kidnap her, exactly." Mitch held his hands up projecting his innocence.

"Not exactly! What the hell do you call it? You're probably going to jail for kidnapping! All done on my behalf, to help me clear up my situation. This should help a lot. We can share a cell, exercise together. It'll be great!" Jake was staring at Mitch in stunned disbelief.

Mitch looked back at Jake. "Look. Would you just hold on for a minute before you send us off to jail and let me tell you what she said?"

Jake nodded resignedly and Mitch related what Belinda revealed to him. He told Jake about the porno studio, Harry and the attorney who apparently orchestrated the deal to frame Jake. He went on to describe his failed attempt to check out the porno studio and finished with:

"So, Belinda is scared out of her wits. She knows she's in a no-win situation. She can't tell anyone. She can't tell Harry. He'd either rat her off to the attorney or kill her. She can't go to the police without exposing herself to prosecution for lying about her encounter with you. She is stuck in the proverbial spot between a rock and a hard place. When the time comes she'll have to tell the story to the department, but not until we figure out who's behind this and why. So I think_"

"Stop! What the hell do you think this is Mitch, some B-movie?"

Mitch stopped, "well, no. But_"

"How did you really get this broad to talk to you, Mitch? Use some good old Mafia tactics? Rough her up a little? Knock her on her ass, threaten to shoot her in the kneecaps, what?"

"What are you talking about, Jake? What Mafia tactics? Where did that come from?"

"Don't give me that shit, Mitch. There's a little something you forgot to share with me about your days in Vegas. A guy named Montini. You remember him. Little Italian guy. Mobster in every sense of the word. Don't tell me you've forgotten good old Uncle Montini. Or the two guys you allegedly took out for him."

Mitch stared at Jake for a minute. "No, I haven't forgotten Montini. But that was years ago, Jake. I haven't seen Montini or any of his people in a long, long time. If your source knows what he's talking about, he'll tell you that. He'll also tell you that I was working for the hotel, not Montini. I worked security. By coincidence, I happen to be at the right place at the right time and interceded when a couple of thugs went after Montini's niece. I don't deny the likelihood that both of them were whacked, but I didn't do it and I honestly don't know who did. I left Vegas right after that. Not on the run, just thought it was time to get out of there before I did get involved in something I'd regret. I was still a cop at heart, Jake. Still am."

"Frankly Mitch, I don't know what the hell you are. You've been in and out of jail so many times in the last twenty years you're more criminal than cop. You haven't got any business thinking of yourself as a cop anymore, Mitch. None at all."

Mitch stared at his former partner in disbelief. "I'm sorry you feel that way, Jake. I thought you knew me better than that."

"So did I. But this caper with Belinda doesn't help, Mitch. What were you thinking?"

"We both knew she was lying. I confirmed it and now we've at least got a lead on who's behind this situation. That's a step in the right direction, isn't it?" Mitch looked at Jake, waiting for an answer.

"Well, I guess you could look at it that way. But any hope of using Belinda as a witness at any point is out the window. You'll be damned lucky if she doesn't decide to sue you or press charges or something," Jake pointed out.

"Sue me! What's she gonna get. An old sailboat, an old dog and a one legged crow. Wow! She'll be sitting pretty."

"Are you sure she was telling the truth?" Jake finally asked. Mitch nodded yes. "Where does a porno ring fit? She says Harry is the main player. That doesn't ring any bells with me. And the warehouse, they are going to know someone's sniffing around after," Jake pointed at Mitch's head, "after you punched the guard."

"Aw, that'll be all right, I told him I wanted to be an actor. They got to have a lot of weirdoes coming around, don't they?" Mitch said.

Jake stared at him and said, "Well, at least one."

Mitch thought about that for a second and then grinned at Jake. Jake didn't smile back.

"Let's go. I'll give you a ride back to your car," Jake said, sliding out of the booth.

Down the street, the passenger in the black Lincoln looked through the tinted glass as he listened to the cell phone. On the fourth ring a man answered.

"Hello."

"Yes, it's me. He picked up a big guy at a hospital and now they're in restaurant for the last hour." Boris listened for a moment and then replied:

"Tall, white hair, black leather jacket and a bandage over left ear." And then, "yes, we will be there at noon. Sounds like the same guy as in bar, yes?"

Jake drove Mitch back to the hospital and pulled into the parking lot. Mitch directed him to his old Mustang. Jake hadn't spoken during the drive to the hospital and Mitch was uneasy as Jake pulled up and stopped behind his car.

"Listen Jake, I…"

"No, you listen Mitch," Jake interrupted. "I don't need this kind of help. I'm in enough trouble without you doing anything. With your help I'll be in a lot more. You seem to think we, you, can operate like it's still 1960. Well, it's not and this crap's out. Batting people around might be an acceptable job technique for you and the assholes you run around with, but I don't want any part of it."

"Jake, you don't understand."

"Bullshit! I understand perfectly. You forget, I was your partner for a lot of years. I know how you operate. But, over time, people generally change. Evidently, you haven't."

Jake looked at Mitch who sat silently, staring out the windshield. "I'll see you around Mitch. Go back to sailing your boat. Maybe after this situation gets resolved, assuming it does, we might talk. I doubt it. I think you're dirty, Mitch, I can't afford to take another chance with you. At best you let people down, that's your history."

Mitch got out of the car and then turned to say something more to Jake. Jake stepped on the gas and the cars forward momentum slammed the door shut as he drove off. Mitch watched Jake drive out of the parking lot. "Well, shit," he said, "I think I'll have to go find Harry Becker by myself. I'm not going to let Jake down."

*****

Detective Steve Change had his badge clipped to the pocket of his black leather jacket and held his ID card out for the Sergeant as he walked up to the front desk. He was almost as broad as he was tall and his eyes were as black as his hair. Under his jacket he carried two Smith and Wesson nine-millimeter pistols in a double shoulder holster rig. In addition, he had a Chief's Special thirty-eight in an ankle holster. Most of the officers in his squad were similarly armed. He was part of the Chinatown detail. He was second generation American Chinese and, in some circles, considered a traitor to his people.

The sergeant directed him back to the detective squadroom. He walked down the hall to the detective division and spotted Kelly and Song sitting on the old leather couch against one wall of the large room.

"Hi Kelly. It's been too long." His smile was genuine.

He and Kelly had worked a black and white a long time ago when they were both fairly new on the job. She smiled and said, "thanks for coming right over, Steve, I definitely need some help here." Kelly explained what she knew about the little girl sitting next to her as Steve looked at her. He then began talking to Song in Chinese. Their conversation, along with a lot of hand gestures, went on for some time. Kelly listened to the sing-song melody of the talk with interest. She watched as Steve knelt in front of the girl, talking softly in a gentle lilt. He finally turned to Kelly.

"Well, as near as I can tell she was brought here on a big boat from mainland China. An Army man bought her from her father." Steve paused and rubbed his face. "She's a peasant girl, Kelly. The dialect is a little strange to me and she has never been to school. So I know I'm not going to make much sense here." Kelly nodded her understanding and Steven continued. "Her father worked in a deep hole. She says she was happy that the money the family got would make her mother's life easier. So the Army guy put her on this big boat with nine other kids. A nurse was with them. She kept them sleepy while they traveled on the boat. The trip lasted a long time and then they were put on a smaller boat with a white man. He took them,

I guess, to a harbor somewhere along the coast here. Then, somehow she escaped. She says she rode in a nice car for a while and then walked a long way. She's been wandering around West L.A., eating out of trash cans and hiding during the day. Poor kid."

"What do you make of all this, Steve? You guys have any intell' about anything that matches her story? I mean, what do you think?" Kelly asked.

"I don't know. Could be an illegal adoption deal. Could be sweat shop, although I don't think so. She's too young and she says the other kids were the same age." Steve stopped and thought, "doesn't make any sense to me. Though there are frequent rumors about child prostitution. But so far we've never come up with anything to substantiate them."

"So she got sold in China and brought to the states and ran away. That's it?" Kelly asked.

"Well, here's a clue to work on," Steve said, half jokingly, "whatever harbor the little boat was in when she got away, she says she saw a giant guy with a white beard and a big hat."

"A giant guy?" Kelly asked.

"Yeah, she said he was three times taller than her father. That would make him fifteen feet or so tall. But remember, I can only understand about every other word she says."

Kelly stared at the little girl as she sat on the sofa sipping the soup Joseph had found in the lunch room. There was something about her that brought back not altogether pleasant memories of Kelly's childhood.

"OK. I'm going to keep her with me tonight. Maybe somebody in your squad has some idea what's going on with her." Kelly wrote down her home phone on a piece of paper. "Here's my home number. Could you ask around and give me a call tomorrow at home?"

"Sure Kelly. I'll talk to the guys in the morning and give you a call either way. I gotta go. It's good to see you Kelly. Maybe lunch one day?"

She nodded yes and Steve left. Kelly walked over and sat down with the little girl she now knew was called Song. She patted her on the knee, smiled and said, "Well, Song, no more eating out of trash cans for you."

Chapter 28

Harry Becker was a very nervous fellow. He had two good reasons, one long-term and one immediate: he was greedy, and he was horny. Harry thought he was smarter than he was and he was convinced his failures were not of his own making; the fault always lying with someone else. He was also absolutely certain that the world was against him. Of course, his use of amphetamines worked to enhance all these feelings.

Harry had no illusions about his station in life. His small movie production company had experienced enormous growth for several years. He had struggled to break into legitimate moviemaking to no avail and had finally found a niche in the porno industry.

Then one day an attorney and a rather large and totally intimidating thug had come to him and persuaded him that it would be in his best interest to sell the company to a man they represented. Since Harry was also a coward, he put up little resistance. They gave him a reasonably fair price and agreed to keep him on the payroll and allow him to continue running things. Harry knew he really had no options, although he lied to himself about it.

The man that called him almost weekly with new directions made it very clear there would be no questioning his orders. Harry noticed that the company had several new employees who didn't treat him with the respect he thought he deserved as the boss. However, Harry had heard for years that the 'adult' movie industry was being infiltrated by the mob; organized crime, as the feds liked to call it and Harry opted not to press the issue.

On this particular evening, Harry stood in front of the mirror in his office at the studio, evaluating his appearance. He saw himself as rather dapper. He was a bit below average height and used lifts in his shiny, over the ankle boots to increase his stature. At forty- two years of age, his hair was beginning to show some gray and he used Grecian formula to subdue that trend. He was very proud of his hair and went to the hairdresser at least twice a week. He had a pompadour much like Elvis had which he kept neatly in place with an ample application of butch wax.

Harry considered the silk suits he had specially tailored as his trademark. The suits, in a variety of pastel colors, fit his small frame loosely. He wore matching colored shirts, open at the neck, with a number of gold chains hanging from his neck. With his greasy hair, colorful clothing and excessive gold jewelry, Harry looked exactly like what he was. A procurer and porno film maker.

Satisfied with his appearance, he left the studio, got into his Jag convertible and drove through the valley heading for the Sunset Strip and some nightclub action. It was a warm night and even though he was feeling pretty good, he took a 'black beauty' from the glove box and washed it down with some coffee he bought at a gas station where he'd filled up. The pill kicked in just as he pulled off the 405 freeway onto Sunset.

Harry was a bar hopper and not much of a drinker. He bounced from bar to bar along the strip, barely finishing his drink in each establishment. He'd say hello, talk briefly with some of the other patrons he knew and if nothing interesting developed he'd move on. During his foray he took two more of the potent little pills, believing they transformed him into a smooth talking and totally irresistible charmer with the ladies. Or the 'quiff,' as he referred to them. An Englishman he'd met once used that phrase and Harry thought it lent an air of class to his persona.

Around midnight he decided there was no action on the strip

and headed back to his car for the drive home to Venice Beach. It was a warm night and with the top down, he decided to take surface streets and turned onto La Cienega.

That was when Mitch lost Harry. He'd followed Harry from the time he left the parking lot of the studio. From bar to bar, every where that Harry went, Mitch had been close behind. Kelly had checked business licenses and found out Harry's full name and a P.O.box, no home address. She also checked D.M.V. records and found that he drove a Jaguar. Mitch spotted the Jag in the studio parking lot and the rest was easy.

And now Mitch's Mustang chose Sunset and La Cienega to stall. He banged on the steering wheel in frustration and anger as Harry's Jag disappeared around the corner.

"C'mon, damn it. Start, you bucket, you rust bucket of bolts! This is important!" He ground the starter to no avail.

After the unpleasant conversation with Jake, Mitch decided he had to have a talk with Harry. He couldn't just walk away. Jake was his friend and if Jake didn't see it that way, well, he'd just help him anyway. That's what friends were for. Despite what Jake said, Mitch did still think of himself as a cop. Cops take care of each other and right now Jake needed help. That was that, as far as Mitch was concerned. Harry was obviously going to have to be talked to and Mitch felt he was just the guy to do it. Unlike Jake, Mitch didn't feel the constraints of the constitution should keep him from asking a few questions.

Just as the old Ford kicked over a police motor officer came tearing through the intersection on the yellow light, with a high pitched 'whoop whoop' of warning. Mitch gunned the V8 and swung hard left following, not daring to hope that Harry might be getting pulled over.

Harry wasn't being pulled over but he did slow down and give way to the red lights of the motor cycle that, by running a red light, brought Mitch back onto the tail. Mitch had little trouble staying with Harry for the rest of the drive.

Harry lived on the second floor of a very posh apartment house in Venice Beach. The lease was in the name of one of the corporations that owned several video stores that distributed the porno flicks made in studios like Bluebird. Harry pushed the door opener and the steel grates of the subterranean garage slowly slid open. Mitch pulled across the street as the taillights of the Jag disappeared inside. He slumped down in the seat and began watching for a light to come on in one of the darkened windows of the building. It didn't take long, second floor in the corner. Mitch was rewarded with a glimpse of Harry walking by the window a moment later.

Mitch reached in the back seat and took a blue canvas bag from the floor and climbed out of the car and walked quickly across the street to Harry's building. The bag contained a number of items gathered during a short shopping trip Mitch took to Hollywood that afternoon. It also contained an M&P stock, two inch Smith and Wesson which he put at the small of his back under the camouflage jacket he was wearing.

It only took a moment to slip the lock at the lobby door with a credit card and Mitch was inside and on the fancy elevator heading to the second floor. As the elevator started up with a jerk and a whine he took one last look in his canvas bag and smiled at what he thought of as his “interrogation kit.”

Harry was bouncing around in his apartment dusting the furniture. He was scrubbing diligently at an imagined spot on one of the multi-colored vinyl bean bag chairs in his living room. Harry had taken too many of the little black pills during his evening out and was 'tweeking' from the effects of the uppers. He was not thinking clearly and jumped at the sound of his doorbell.

"Yeah, who is it?" Harry shouted through the door.

"Special delivery for Mister Becker, sir." Mitch held the large express envelope he'd picked up at the post office. Harry stared at the red and white surface through the peephole:

"Slide it under the door."

"Yes sir." Mitch pushed a corner of the package under the door. "Sorry sir, it's too thick and besides, you have to sign for it."

"Shit!" Harry stared at the envelope peeking under the door. He couldn't make a decision. It seemed too late to be getting mail. He looked at the dust rag in his hand and couldn't remember why he was holding it. "Why so late? Why are you doing delivering so late?"

"The sender paid for twelve hour delivery sir, guaranteed."

That logic seemed irrefutable and Harry pulled open the door.

Mitch's body was tensed and as the door opened he came at the small man like a whirlwind. He hit Harry twice in the chest with a forearm, made all the stronger by the familiar rush of adrenaline, and brought his knee up into his crotch.

"Unh, uh." Harry fell backwards under the onslaught and sprawled on his back on the floor. Mitch knee dropped him and rolled him over and quickly duct taped his hands behind him and stuffed a sweat sock in his mouth. He propped Harry up in an armchair and sat across from him and stared with the most evil look he could muster and said nothing. Harry was trembling violently and making mewling noises through the sock.

"Mmf. Umf mmm." Harry's eyes were wide with fear and looking every which way in panic.

"Harry," Mitch spoke in almost a whisper and drew an ugly knife from the canvas bag, "Harry you are going to have one chance to answer my questions. Only one chance. Do you understand? This is a very serious business you've gotten yourself into and you are going to tell me all about it."

Harry stared at Mitch and then nodded his head yes. Mitch pulled the sock from Harry's mouth. The drugs had obviously distorted Harry's judgment:

"Who the fuck are you?" Harry said in a loud squeaky voice, "you're fuckin' with the wrong guy you mother fu...um'ff." Mitch pushed the sock back in Harry's mouth.

"Oh Harry, big mistake. What? You're mobbed up? You're a big wheel? Here Harry, let me show you what I'm about." Mitch leaned forward, almost in Harry's face, and spoke in a loud angry voice. "You don't know serious! Let me show you serious, you dirt bag."

Mitch took an aerosol can from the bag and, holding Harry by the hair, began spraying the left side of his head.

"This'll be cold, it's procaine. I don't want you passing out on me from the pain." Mitch took an evil looking knife from the bag, making sure Harry got a good look at it. Then he began sawing at Harry's left ear. Harry tried to thrash about. Mitch continued to saw, using the dull edge of the blade. Then he stopped and held the theatrical ear he had purchased at the shop in Hollywood, dripping with make up blood, in front of Harry's face. Harry passed out.

After a few minutes, Harry came to and, after looking around, immediately became aware of several important facts. Mitch was sitting back in the chair in front of him with bloody hands. A towel was wrapped around Harry's head, and sitting on a footstool between them, was another towel folded into a square. Mitch lifted a corner of the towel and Harry saw what looked like an ear, his ear he reasoned. He began to get nauseous and thought he was going to vomit. He started hyperventilating and, as he became light headed, Mitch leaned forward from where he was sitting. In a quiet, calm voice Mitch said:

"Time, time is important to you Harry. I ask and you answer and perhaps we'll be done in time for you to have that sewn back on. Or . . ." Mitch paused, "you can lose a few more parts."

"Please, please what do you want? Who are you?" Mitch had removed the sock again and Harry was, to say the least, open to discussion.

"I want you to tell me everything about framing the L.A. cop."

"No, no I didn't. I only did what I was told. Belinda, she, I mean he told me he needed one of the girls that would do something for a lot of money, I didn't know what. You're asking the wrong guy. Please." Harry looked at Mitch pleadingly.

"OK. I believe you, Harry. Tell me the whole story and don't leave anything out."

And Harry did. The fear and the shock and the amphetamines combined to overcome any fear he had of his bosses, at least for the moment.

He told Mitch about the way the people came to him and bought his small production company. How suddenly there was lots of cash. That he answered to someone who gave orders over the phone or by written message and that he was pretty sure it was the Mafia. An east coast family, he thought. About how he got a phone call and that he told Belinda to do as she was told. It wasn't until after that, that he knew she was part of a frame.

He told Mitch that he didn't really know who he answered to, but that the man, who ever he was, knew the movie business. Early on, he was told to hire two people who were there to keep an eye on things. Once in awhile, a real mean little Italian guy would come around and fuck one of the girls. The first time, Harry told him to get off the set and the guy slapped him around pretty good. After that, he realized he was just an employee and, what the hell, the money was good. He described the little Italian and Mitch made a mental note to himself that the guy's description seemed familiar.

"What else Harry?" Mitch held the knife up with a malevolent smile.

"Nothing I swear, nothing!" Harry thought for a second. "The building, the little building at the back of the studio. It was just a storage area. They remodeled inside and nobody, I mean nobody is allowed back there. Personally, I think they have a kiddie porn deal going there. They brought in two big video copy machines. I don't know any of the people. They're not in the legitimate exotic business like me." Harry looked pleadingly again at Mitch. "My ear," staring down at the towel on the footstool, "please, I've told you everything."

"OK Harry, you've been a big help. Here's what we are going to do. I'm going to cut you loose and we are going to go for a ride. I'm going to drop you off at an emergency hospital and they'll sew your ear back on. If you give me any kind of trouble I will stick this knife so far into your throat your head will fall off, understood?"

"Yes. Yes. Please let's hurry."

Mitch cut the duct tape from Harry's hands and picked up the towel holding the plastic ear. "Here Harry, you carry the towel. Make sure to keep it covered, it has to stay cold."

Mitch drove Harry to the Urgent care center twelve blocks away. He sat and watched Harry scurry to the entrance, cradling the towel in his arms, his head wrapped in the other towel. Mitch knew it was risky taking Harry to the hospital but he couldn't resist. He could just imagine Harry screaming at the nurses and doctors that his ear had been cut off by a crazy man and showing them the bloody plastic ear, demanding they sew it on his head. Mitch actually considered walking Harry inside just to see the whole scenario unfold. Common sense told him it wasn't worth the risk.

Mitch felt in his pocket for the small tape recorder and turned it off. He headed for the freeway.

"Time to head for the boat," he thought. "I need to get a little rest and figure what to do next. Jake's gonna realize I'm really trying to help him when he hears what I've got. I hope he's cooled down since yesterday."

The sun was nearly up when Mitch got to the small marina where his boat was tied up. He pulled into the equally small parking lot and put his car in its assigned stall. As he walked through the lot toward the dock he noticed a black Lincoln Town Car in one of the other stalls.

"New tenants, I guess. I wonder what kind of boat they've got. Probably pretty nice, considering the car."

Mitch got to his own boat and went on board. Both the dog and the crow greeted him as though he'd been gone for days. He fed them both and went below to sleep.

Chapter 29

About the time Mitch got back to his boat, Jake was getting up from another restless night. Edie got up shortly after Jake and they shared a little small talk as Edie got ready for work.

Jake was scheduled to report to Internal Affairs later that morning for an interview and although it would be his first opportunity to formally deny the charges and explain the facts, he was nervous about the matter. Edie tried to ease his concerns with little success. As she walked out the door she wished him luck, then thought better of it and told him he didn't need luck. The truth was on his side, she reminded him.

"Yeah, I know. I wish the evidence was," Jake muttered to himself. He sat down to have another cup of coffee and read the paper. As he browsed through the news, his mind wandered. He realized that the sudden parting with Mitch was bothering him. He guessed they'd become closer friends than he thought.

"What the hell was I supposed to do?" he wondered. "The guys' tactics are out of the sixties. He's a jailbird and probably some kind of enforcer for the mob. He'd make a great character reference at my

Board of Rights."

Jake went back to his paper. After a few minutes, he put the paper back down.

"Damn. Why am I feeling guilty about this?"

Jake thought awhile. "Screw it, I've got more important things to worry about right now."

At ten o'clock that morning Jake reported to Internal Affairs on the fifth floor of the police headquarters building. Once known as 'The Glass House," because of it's square and unimaginative architectural style and the fact that it was wall to wall windows from the ground floor to the roof, on all four sides. It had been formally named Parker Center after the late Chief of Police, William H. Parker who was credited with reforming the L.A.P.D. in the fifties.

Jake walked into the Internal Affairs office and told the receptionist who he was. She asked him to take a seat. She called the squad room on the com linc and advised the person on the other end that Jake was there. As he waited, Jake looked around the outer office. Not much had changed since he'd worked Internal Affairs almost fifteen years before. He recalled a few of the cases he'd handled. The situations cops could get themselves into had never failed to amaze him. More often than not, their problems stemmed from the three things every recruit was warned about in the Academy: booze, broads and money.

After just a short wait a young sergeant, Jack York, walked into the reception area and introduced himself. He escorted Jake back to an interview room where York's partner, Ernest Franks, was setting up a tape recorder. Jake sat down and shoved a toothpick in his mouth. After the standard admonition was read into the recorder, York began asking questions. The interview lasted about two hours and when it was over Jake didn't feel as though he'd convinced the two sergeants that Belinda had been lying and the whole thing was a set up. He hadn't, of course, been able to tell them about Mitch's 'interview' of Belinda. Not unless he wanted to lay Mitch out and subject him to arrest. Pissed off as he was, Jake wasn't ready to do that.

As Jake got up to leave, York stood and walked out with him. They stepped into the hall and York closed the office door behind him.

"Lieutenant, I only know you by reputation. But based on what I've heard, I find all this a little hard to believe. Is there anything at all you haven't told us that might help. I'll work as hard to prove you're innocent as I will to prove otherwise. If there's anything--"

"No, there isn't. If I had anything I thought would help I'd tell you. Right now, all I have is my word."

They shook hands and Jake walked to the elevator. He rode down to the first floor and left the building.

Jake drove through downtown traffic to the freeway and was home in about forty minutes. He spent an hour on the phone with his attorney, Frank Lacey, filling him in on the I.A.D. interview and discussing the possibility that he would be indicted for the charges he was accused of. Lacey was not encouraging and Jake felt it was probably inevitable. They scheduled a meeting for two days later and ended the call.

The afternoon ground on, Jake bored and worried. He tried to keep his mind busy and off his predicament, but without much success. Then, about three thirty, the phone rang. Jake picked it up. "Hello."

"Jake. Don't hang up. It's me, Mitch. I have something for you. Some information you need."

"Do tell. Where did it come from? Who did you have to kill?" Jake asked sarcastically.

“Nobody,” Mitch said in a tone that suggested he thought Jake was serious. "I didn't kill anyone. But I had a long talk with the guy I told you about, Harry Becker. What an asshole! He confirmed what Belinda told me. He got a call from his boss, some mob connected guy, who had him put Belinda up to the whole deal. He's scared shitless of this guy."

"Who is the guy, the boss?' Jake asked.

"Some mug who gives Harry his marching orders. But Harry says this guy gets his directions from a big boss. Someone he doesn't know. A bigshot who wishes to remain anonymous. "

"What did you do to this guy to get him to tell you all this, Mitch?" Jake asked.

"Nothing, Jake. Not really. I just fooled him into thinking he'd lost an ear. That's all, Jake. Honest. Why don't we meet so we can talk over our next move? I think we're getting somewhere with this, don't you?"

"What's this 'we' crap? You think we're partners?" Jake asked.

"Well, no. But what else have you got going for yourself?" Mitch replied. "I'm trying to help here, Jake. I know you're pissed about the Belinda thing but get over it. We need to move on. Let me help. I've found out a lot of stuff you need to know."

Jake thought for a moment. He had nothing else going for him, that was for sure. If he met with Mitch maybe something helpful would come of it. 'What the hell have I got to lose,' he thought. "O.K. Mitch. Let's meet somewhere."

"Good. Do you want me to come over?"

"No, let's meet at your boat. I could use some fresh air. It'll have to be this evening though. I promised Edie I'd fix her favorite dinner. She's feeling the brunt of this as much as I am and I don't want to disappoint her."

"Yeah, I understand. Come on down when you can. I'll be here.

""I should be there by eight or so. See you then. And no more forays. Just wait on the boat."

*****

Arlo sat at his desk playing with the gold Mont Blanc pen and staring out the window, looking at the Santa Monica mountains in the distance. Loose ends, there were always loose ends. The missing detective, Pritchard, he was a loose end. He had to be found, and soon. Yes, he was a very loose end.

This friend of Jake Reed's was a loose end who needed to be dealt with, as well. Also, the sooner the better. There was no doubt he was the man at the '507,' asking all the questions. And he was certainly at the warehouse in the Valley. Arlo put the pen down and reached into the bottom drawer of his desk, brought out a cell phone and began making phone calls. The last one was to the pay phone at the '507.'

"Ivan," Arlo listened for a moment, and then, "the boat at the marina in Long Beach . . .we need to sink it. Be sure our friend is on board. Tonight." Arlo ended the call and put the phone back in the desk drawer. He called out to his secretary:

"I am having dinner with the Mayor and his wife this evening. Please call my wife and remind her."

*****

That evening while Arlo dined with the Mayor, Ivan drove the black Lincoln Town Car south, down the freeway to Long Beach. Next to him sat his brother and fellow emigre, from Russia, Boris. As they drove they discussed their plans for the evening. Nothing very complicated, really. That was the way Ivan tried to keep things when his brother was involved. Boris was a little slow. Not stupid, just not what you'd call a quick study. A thorough explanation was always a good idea. Ivan provided a step by step description of the coming events and Boris listened intently. By the time they got to the marina parking lot, Ivan was satisfied that Boris understood his part completely.

After confirming that Mitch's car was in the lot Ivan parked the Town Car. The two men got out and walked around to the trunk. Ivan opened it and removed two fishing poles and a tackle box that he handed to his brother. They walked across the parking lot and out onto the sand, trying to look like a couple of fishermen. No one was on the beach but Ivan figured that if anyone did come along the two of them wouldn't look suspicious. As they stood near the water's edge, Ivan pulled a small pair of binoculars from his jacket pocket and began looking at the boats in their slips, about one hundred yards down the beach. After a few moments he looked over at Boris:

"This will be quick and easy, I've found the boat. There is no one around. Come, we do it now."

Boris nodded and followed obediently, carrying the metal tackle box with him. They walked down the beach and up to the landing which led down to the slips. The two men stopped and Boris pulled a bottle from the box. He took the bottle, unscrewed the top and inserted some cotton cloth. He sloshed the gasoline inside the bottle around to thoroughly soak the cloth. Then he pulled out an old Zippo lighter and flicked it once to make sure it would light.

Looking around them one last time, both men started down the gangway and onto the dock. Most of the lights on the dock were burned out and the half moon provided most of what light there was. Ivan whispered to Boris:

"It's the one out on the end. It should have a number on the front of it. 6159." Boris nodded and looked down the dock. As the two men neared the boat they saw an interior light burning. They could see Mitch moving around inside. Ivan whispered,

"Look, the little door at the front, on top. It's open, throw it in there."

If he tries to come out of boat, shoot him." Boris nodded his understanding and moved ahead of Ivan, both men slightly crouched now.

Mitch was straightening the boat up. Jake would be there shortly and he didn't want him thinking he lived like some old reprobate. Between his old deaf dog and the crow who crapped where she pleased, keeping the boat's cabin clean and relatively odor free was not easy. He looked around. 'Clean enough' he thought. He sat down on the bunk in the main cabin and began to doze. Sleep had been difficult because of his stitched up ear. He had to sleep on his left side facing the dog that always slept in the bunk with him. It wasn't bad enough that the dog took up half of the narrow bunk but she had bad breath as well. A good night's sleep had been pretty elusive, lately. Just as Mitch began to nod off the crow let loose. She had been sleeping on her regular perch on the old TV at the rear of the main cabin. She sensed the two strangers on the dock and liked it not one bit.

Caw! Caw!

Mitch awoke to the sound with a start and looked out the forward port where he saw Ivan and Boris. Mitch knew they weren't boat owners from the little marina. He walked to the aft hatch, stepped up onto the lower stair and stuck his head out.

"Hey. What are you guys doing?"

Ivan, startled, cranked off a round from his pistol in the direction of the voice in the darkness and Boris hurriedly tried to light the Zippo, failing for the first several tries. This gave Mitch, who by now had ducked back down in the cabin, time to reach for the first weapon that came to his sleepy mind. He slid the hatch back and popped up just long enough to fire the Olin twelve gauge flare gun at the two men.

Thanks to nothing more than pure luck, the flare hit the bottle that Boris was so desperately trying to light. There was a whoosh as the gasoline ignited and Boris became a human Tiki torch. He began screaming and running in circles, swatting at the flames. Ivan rushed at his flaming brother and pushed him into the bay. Meanwhile, Mitch was below trying to remember where he'd put his old Smith and Wesson. While he was looking for the gun, lights began coming on in several boats and people began to emerge from below deck. Ivan decided it was time to make a hasty retreat and ran back up the dock.

Of course the noise, the minor explosion when Boris went up in flames, his screams, Ivan's gunshot and, no doubt, Cheryl crow's raucous cawing, compelled a number of good citizens to call the Long Beach Police Department.

*****

Jake drove south on the same freeway Boris and Ivan traveled over earlier. He reached the marina parking lot and pulled in, parking behind Mitch's old Mustang.

"I hope this isn't a mistake," he muttered, still worried about Mitch's approach to helping him. As he got out of his car, Jake heard what sounded like a gunshot.

"I hope that wasn't what I think it was," he thought. Since being suspended, Jake couldn't legally carry a concealed weapon and rather than ignore the rules he'd opted to go without one. "Probably firecrackers." As he walked across the lot in the direction of the marina he heard a second shot, louder than the first.

"What the hell...sounds like a war going on." He quickened his pace and as he rounded the corner of a small building which had blocked his view of the marina, he saw a man run up to the end of the dock ramp. The man turned and sprinted down the beach. Rather than follow his professional instincts and pursue the man, Jake decided he'd go down to Mitch's boat to make sure everything was alright. As he walked down the ramp and out along the dock towards Mitch's boat, Jake noticed someone in the water near the end of the dock. As he approached, Mitch stepped out of the aft cabin of his boat and jumped onto the dock.

He picked up a long pole that was lying on the dock and held it out to the man in the water. Then he noticed Jake walking up.

"Give me a hand here, Jake. This guys in bad shape." Mitch said. Jake looked at the man in the half light and could see that he was barely moving, flailing weakly for the pole.

Jake stepped over to the side of the dock, getting ready to jump in the water to help the man when Boris, finally grabbed the pole and held on. Mitch pulled him toward the dock. When he got within reach, Jake reached out and grabbed his arm. As he began to pull him out of the water Boris screamed. Jake realized that the skin on Boris' arm was sliding off, revealing the muscle underneath.

"Jesus, Mitch. This poor bastards burned to a crisp," Jake yelled. He let go of his arm and grabbed the belt around his waist and held on. Mitch stepped over and the two of them pulled Boris out of the water and up onto the dock. Boris assumed a sitting position up against a dock box. He was clearly in shock and said nothing.

One of the people from a neighboring boat walked up, took one look and said he'd call for an ambulance to go with the police he'd already called for. Jake and Mitch looked at each other. They stood up and Jake asked what was going on. Mitch began to explain.

As the two men talked, Ivan watched from the beach. He'd crept back to within fifty yards of where Mitch and Jake stood. Ivan realized he'd failed in his mission. The gray haired man was alive and well. That would never do. The 'Boss' would not be pleased. Ivan's attempt at an 'accidental death' had turned into a fiasco. And as for Boris, who knew what would happen to him, now that he was in their control.

Accident or no accident, Ivan concluded that he had to at least kill the gray haired man if he was to redeem himself with the 'Boss.' He sat down on the sand and braced his 9mm Berretta against his knee. He took careful aim and fired one round. Ivan, unlike his brother, was not a crack shot. The round skipped across the deck of a forty foot sloop and struck Boris in the temple. He died immediately. Jake and Mitch hit the dock face down and waited for a second shot, which never came. While they lay waiting, Ivan dashed for the Lincoln Town car and made his escape. When no further shots were fired for several minutes the two men concluded the shooter had fled. They got up slowly and looked around. Nothing. The screech of tires they'd heard emanate from the parking lot probably indicated the gunman's departure.

A short while later the police and an ambulance, which was no longer needed, arrived at the scene. The uniformed officers assessed the situation and requested the on-call homicide detectives. The scene was secured and they waited for the homicide team. Within 20 minutes the detectives arrived and began their investigation. Mitch described what transpired; how he'd lit up Boris with the flare gun after his accomplice fired a shot at him. How Boris wound up in the water and had subsequently been shot, apparently by his partner in crime. Neither Jake nor Mitch had any idea who Ivan was actually shooting at.

As one of the homicide detectives was examining Boris' body he noted a tattoo on the inside of his relatively unburned left arm. He examined it closely and asked his partner to take a look, as well. Jake, curious about what they were looking at, stepped over.

"What have you got?" he asked.

"This tattoo, it looks like Russian Mafia. This guy must have been a bad ass. What's he after your buddy for?"

"I don't know and I doubt if he does either. This is all mysterious as hell," Jake told him.

The first detective turned to his partner. "Call and see if any of the Organized Crime guys are working tonight. They'd probably like to see this. Maybe they know this guy."

"Yeah, okay. I'll check." his partner replied. He walked off the dock to the pay phone. He returned a short time later. "Piper's working. He's interested and said he'd be right down."

"Piper," Jake thought. "Now there's a guy I need to talk with."

As Jake stood watching the detectives going over the crime scene he wondered how many times he'd responded to similar situations during the course of his career. "A bunch," he thought. He also realized how much he'd missed being on the scene, in the thick of things, since he'd been suspended. He hated being on the outside looking in.

Jake looked away from the detectives when he noticed Mitch emerge from the front hatch of the boat. He was carrying something Jake couldn't make out. Mitch stepped out onto the dock and walked toward Jake. As he drew near Jake could see that Mitch was holding his crow nestled in his hands.

"My crow, Jake. The bastard shot my crow. She's dead." The shot that Ivan fired at Mitch had gone through the side window of the forward cabin and struck poor Cheryl, killing her. Tears welled up in Mitch's eyes.

"I nursed her back to health, Jake. I should have turned her loose, back to the wild where she belonged. Now look at what's happened to her. Poor Cheryl."

"Mitch, if you hadn't saved her she'd have been dead long ago; lunch for some cat. You extended her life and she paid you back by saving yours. You did a good thing. We'll give her a proper burial."

"Yeah, I guess you're right. Hey, I've got an idea. We'll bury her at sea. You and me. We'll sail out past the breakwater and wrap her up and send her to her maker. Okay?"

"Sure. Count me in, Mitch," Jake replied.

The detectives continued their investigation at the scene. The photographer showed up and began taking pictures. An obvious old timer, he needed little direction as he moved about, getting every aspect that would be needed to complete the investigation. Another crime scene technician, the print man, arrived and began dusting the few places that might provide some trace prints.

As the photographer was finishing up and preparing to leave, Piper strode onto the dock. He said a quick hello to the two homicide detectives and then asked the photographer if he'd taken photos of the dead man's tattoos.

"Yeah, sure," he replied. "I'll send you prints of everything, if that's alright with these guys," he said, gesturing to the homicide team.

"Fine. No problem," one of them replied.

Jake stood out of the way while Piper knelt down and studied the dead man carefully. He looked at the tattoos closely, gingerly turning the burnt and peeling arm. He checked his neck and pulled the top of his shirt open to take a look at the chest. As he looked he spoke to one of the detectives:

"Jerry, would you let me know when the post (post mortem exam) for this guy is scheduled. I'd like to be there to see what other tattoos he's sporting. He's a hard core Russian Mafia asshole. I'm pretty sure I have him in file already. I'll check when I get back to the office."

"I'll let you know. It'll probably be the day after tomorrow. The Coroner's running about a day behind," the detective replied.

Piper stood up and looked around. "Well, hello Mitch," a hint of disdain in his voice.

"Hello Mark. How are you?" Mitch responded, an edge on his voice that suggested he wasn't going to take any crap from Piper, just in case he planned on giving him any. Mitch was still upset about Cheryl and not in any mood to be screwed with.

Before Piper could respond Mitch turned towards Jake. "You probably remember Jake Reed. He used to be on our, uh, your department before he left to join the L.A.P.D. He's a Lieutenant. He's in charge of Hollywood Station now."

"Not quite the whole station, just the detective division," Jake quickly explained. The two men shook hands.

"How are you, Mark? Long time since we've seen each other."

Piper smiled. "Jake. I remember you well. We worked a car together a couple of times, as I recall."

The two men began talking over old times, laughing about a few situations they recalled. Mitch stood by, listening but not engaging in the conversation. He preferred not talking about that period of his life. Jake realized why Mitch was silent and didn't try to draw him into the conversation.

After about ten minutes, Jake and Piper had pretty much run out of reminiscences. Piper told Jake he was at the end of his watch and the two men shook hands. Piper turned to leave and Jake followed him down the dock. When they were out of earshot, Jake asked Piper what he knew about Mitch. As they continued walking, Piper gave Jake a capsulized version of what Jake had already heard from Kilgore. By the time they got to the lot where Piper had parked his car, Jake sensed that Piper seemed to be laying it on a little thick; assuming a lot of negative things about Mitch because he personally disliked him.

"Tell me something Mark," he said. "Do you think Mitch is connected with the Mob? Directly, I mean."

"I'll be honest with you, Jake. I don't like Mitch. Not a bit. As far as I'm concerned, he's an asshole. He drank himself off the job because he had no self -control. He's a jailbird, a con man and, who the hell knows what else. That says it all, in my book. But, frankly I doubt that he's anything more than a guy who hung around a few Mafia types and wound up in the files. He's not their kind of guy."

"Okay, Mark. That's kind of what I suspected. Thanks for the info. By the way, Mitch has been sober for a hell of a long time. He hasn't been in jail in years. He's trying to do the right things. Maybe you ought to give him the benefit of the doubt."

"There's no doubt, Jake. He's an asshole."

"He's a close friend of mine, Mark. A friend who's put his ass on the line for me. More than once. Think what you want, but spare me any further opinions. By the way, he thinks you're a real nice guy."

Jake turned, walked back to the dock and out to the end where Mitch was sitting on a dock box. As he walked up, Mitch suggested they go aboard the boat. Once on board and below deck, Mitch reminded Jake why they had planned to get together. He wanted to tell him about Harry.

Chapter 30

It was nearly midnight when the two men finished discussing the evening's events, as well as the revelations provided by Harry the previous evening. They had been unable to put the pieces together, however they agreed that it was likely all connected. Finally, Jake stood up and extended his hand to Mitch. The two men shook hands firmly. Jake looked at Mitch for a moment, saying nothing.

Then, "Mitch, I appreciate what you've done to help me. I know you're well intentioned. I have to tell you the truth. There is intell that you were possibly connected to the Montini family. I'm not saying you are." Jake held up his hand to stop Mitch from interrupting. "You are trying to help but you're not. Everything you have found out is useless, can't be used in court. And people are dying. I'm not saying you caused that but you're older now. You not as sharp as you were." Mitch nodded slowly:

"Maybe so. Yeah you might be right about that"

"Not maybe. I am right. You are going to get yourself killed. Don't you get it?"

"Look what are you saying? What do you want me to do."

Mitch asked.

"We do it my way, Mitch. No more midnight rides to the local cemetery, no threats, no ass kickings, no dime novel detective work. Got it?"

"Yeah, I got it Jake."

"Don't do anything without discussing it with me first. Can you do that, Mitch?"

"Sure."

"Good. Now we both need some sleep. It's been a long day. Go crawl into your vee-berth with that old mutt of yours. I'll call you in the morning." Mitch nodded his agreement. Jake climbed the stairway to the boat's cockpit. He stepped over the side rail onto the dock. Forty minutes later he was home and crawling into bed. As he rolled over on his side, Edie cuddled up behind him.

"Hi honey. Glad you're home. How's Mitch?" she asked sleepily.

"Oh, he's fine. But it was a rather eventful evening," he added.

Edie started to roll over and reach for the light, obviously expecting to get all the details.

"Whoa, hold on," Jake said, reaching behind him and pulling her back up against him. "I'll tell you all about it in the morning, which incidentally isn't that far off."

"Okay," she whispered, cuddling closer. They were both asleep in minutes.

*****

At 5:30 a.m., the phone rang. Jake, accustomed to calls at odd hours of the day, picked it up on the first ring. For a moment he forgot his situation and assumed it was a callout, probably a homicide. He quickly realized it wasn't and said, "Jake Reed."

All he heard on the other end was heavy breathing. "A wacko," he thought.

One more try, "Hello, who's this?"

As he was about to hang up he heard a weak, strained voice attempting to speak.

Finally, "Lieutenant."

"Who's this?" Jake ran his hand through his hair and across his face.

"It's me, Lieutenant. Marty Pritchard. I'm scared. I'm sick, can't do this anymore. I, promise will ya' promise…" Jake could hear breathing, rasping on the other end of the phone.

"Promise what, Marty? Where are you?"

"Oh no, can't tell, they'll get me. Ya' gotta help me, please."

"Marty, you're in big trouble. Your best bet is turn yourself in, you know that, man! Use your head," Jake said.

"No, can't. Can't go to jail." Pritchard paused. "Can't. I'll make you a deal, Lieutenant. I'll tell you everything and you help me. Promise me, don't tell anybody."

"Tell me what?" Jake asked.

"Oh shit! Call ya' back." The connection broke. Jake stared at the phone and tried to digest what Pritchard said.

Meanwhile, Pritchard melted into the shadows of the yard. He'd used the pay phone at the bus stop in front of the yard entrance. A black and white unit car had turned the corner and slowly cruised down Anaheim Avenue. Shaken, Pritchard made his way back to his hiding place and fell into a feverish sleep.

Jake got up and put the coffee on. He was fully awake and no longer interested in sleep. He sat in the kitchen sipping the strong, black coffee and staring at the copper pots and pans hanging over the stove. 'Marty Pritchard, alive. Where the hell was he? Where's he been and what did he have? What does he want to tell me?' Jake wondered. He looked at the clock, a grinning black cat on the wall with its tail serving as a pendulum. Edie explained it was retro. Sometimes she got a little carried away with her decorating ideas. Jake waited for Pritchard to call again. By six thirty he concluded it wasn't going to happen right away and he picked up the phone and called Mitch. He answered after a few rings:

"Hello." Mitch sounded cheerful.

"Mitch, it's Jake."

"Hey, Jake. Good morning! Hold on a minute, the damn dog's eating my corn flakes." Jake could hear Mitch scolding the dog. Then he got back on the phone:

"You'd think that a dog that got bailed out of the pound only minutes away from the executioner would have a little more respect for her savior, wouldn't you? How are you this morning? What's up?"

"Come on over, will you? I've got some coffee going. Guess

who called me about an hour ago. Marty Pritchard. Alive, but not well. He sounds sick, almost delirious. Anyway, get over here, O.K.? My old truck's not running again, and we may need to go meet him, where ever he is."

"Yeah, sure. I'm on my way."

"Bring the dog if you want," Jake said, and broke the connection.

At about the same time, Pritchard slid from under the old boat and made his way back to the pay phone. He felt relatively safe now that the other denizens of the area were up and about. He was just one of the many derelicts. He searched the pockets of the dirty canvas jacket for the change he'd put in one of them, finally finding the coins.

He stood at the phone trying to remember what he wanted to say to Jake. Over the last two days he realized it was getting harder to think, to concentrate on what he was doing. He held on to the post the phone was attached to. He was dizzy most of the time now. It was hard to stand. He felt like he was falling all the time. As he started to dial, he stared at his hand, at the wrist. The purple sores were seeping a yellowish fluid and he knew there were more sores on his chest and back, doing the same thing. They weren't especially painful but they itched a lot. The phone only rang once and Jake answered:

"Hello."

"It's me." Jake recognized Pritchard's raspy voice.

"Marty, where are you? Are you drunk?" Jake asked.

"Sick, don't feel right…" Pritchard's breathing labored as he tried to gather his thoughts.

"Look, you don't have a choice, you have to turn yourself in, I'll help you as much as I can."

"No! I can't. Won't. They'll get me. They killed Landers, cut him up. All his fault, I told him. Bad. Trouble we'd get in big trouble. His fault."

"Pritchard!" Jake interrupted the rambling, "where are you? I'll come to you. I won't do anything until we talk. You sound sick, you need help."

"Yeah, I need help, Jake, help. I'm hiding, they can't find me. Under a boat in the junk yard. In Wilmington. B and S Yard on Alameda, O.K.? Come alone, promise?"

"I'm going to bring a friend, Marty. He's an ex-cop, an old friend. We can trust him." Jake waited for Pritchard to respond.

After several seconds:

"O.K., I'm real hungry. Will ya' bring something to eat, and a gun, bring your piece O.K.?"

"Yes, I'll bring some food."

"Yeah, food. I'm going back to the boat, Lieutenant. See ya,' yeah, see ya' soon." Pritchard broke the connection, went around the corner and pushed through the hole in the fence surrounding the junkyard. He staggered through the maze of old cars, boats and assorted marine hardware to the old boat he'd taken refuge under. He crawled under it and went to sleep.

Jake hung up the phone. 'I hope we can find this guy before he takes off again. Or dies,' Jake thought.

Mitch knocked on the front door just as Jake finished making two cheese sandwiches, putting them in a paper bag along with a bottle of orange juice. He walked out the front door past Mitch and said:

"Come on, I'll fill you in on the way."

*****

Mitch pushed his car up to seventy miles an hour as they raced down the 110 Freeway, heading to the harbor area of Los Angeles.

"Be careful you don't get a ticket," Jake said. Mitch smiled.

"What, with you in the car. Professional courtesy and all that."

"Apparently you've never been stopped by the C.H.P. They write everybody. And don't forget. When I got relieved from duty they took my badge and I.D."

"Oh yeah, I did forget," Mitch said as he slowed to sixty-five.

"He sounds sick, I mean really sick, delirious." Jake said. "I hope we can find him.

"Don't worry, we will. I know Wilmington well. I've prowled through a lot of the junk yards looking for boat parts."

Mitch moved to the right lane as they approached the Anaheim Avenue off ramp. It was a little after seven in the morning and the traffic was all going the other way as people made their way into downtown LA, on their way to work.

"I'm pretty sure I know the yard." Mitch said. "Got a bunch of old boats and marine stuff. I bought some winches there once, got a good deal. New stuff costs so darn much. The minute you say boat, just double what it costs." Jake looked over at Mitch and realized his rambling was a way of keeping things level. Keeping it calm 'til you get there, he used to call it when they worked together, such a long time ago. Jake stuck a toothpick between his lips. 'Maybe these things are my way of staying calm,' he thought.

Mitch pulled up to the entrance of the yard and then changed his mind and parked around the corner on the side street. They got out and walked along the old board fence bordering the junkyard, pausing to look through the cracks into the yard.

"Well there's at least ten hulks in there. What do you think?" Mitch asked.

"I think we climb the fence and see if we can find him." Jake answered.

"Yup." Mitch said pulling off his old wind breaker and hanging it on a nail that protruded from the old fence. As Mitch began to climb up, his shirt rode up and Jake saw that Mitch had a revolver in a holster stuffed inside his pants at the small of his back. As he reached the top of the wooden fence, Mitch looked over his shoulder at Jake and saw the look he was giving him.

"C'mon, watch out for splinters," Mitch said, hoisting himself over the fence. Jake decided not to say anything about the weapon and climbed over as well.

They found Pritchard beneath the third boat they searched. He was huddled near the bow of the overturned old hulk. The stench was almost unbearable. Pritchard hadn't bathed in a long, long time. His clothes were filthy and stained with a mix of blood and feces. The bouts of diarrhea occurred while he was asleep, as often as when he was awake.

"Marty, it's Jake." Both the men were kneeling and looking at Pritchard laying there. He opened his eyes and stared at them without recognition. He pulled at the old canvas jacket trying to cover his head and face and began mumbling. The sores were visible through the days old growth of beard. His arms, exposed beyond the jacket cuffs, showed more of the purple and yellow pustules. He was still recognizable, although barely. He had lost at least thirty pounds and his skin had a yellow cast to it. His greasy hair hung down over his forehead. His eyes, red rimmed and sparking with a high fever, tried to focus on Jake and Mitch.

"Pritchard. Marty, it's Jake. We're here to help. Do you understand?" Jake said.

"Help, yeah help," Pritchard croaked and reached out one arm. "Lieutenant, it's you!"

"OK Marty, we're going to get you out of here, get you to a doctor. Come on."

Jake nodded to Mitch and they moved forward, gingerly taking the sick man by the arms helping him from under the boat. He stood there between them and then mumbled something and pulled free. He staggered backwards several steps and then, with his arms windmilling, fell over backwards into a rusty puddle and lay there with his stringy greasy hair floating at the surface

The old man sitting behind the desk in the old shack that served as an office for the junkyard would best be described as grizzled. His bib overalls hung loosely on his gaunt frame, his gray hair was uncombed and matched his wild eyebrows. He stared over a pair of store bought reading glasses at Mitch without saying a word.

"Smelling salts, do you have any smelling salts?" Mitch said for the second time. The old man slowly shook his head no. "What about ammonia? Do you have any of that?" The man pointed to a door with a sign that said bat- room. Mitch pulled the door open and amongst the cleaning supplies took an old rag and poured a generous amount of fluid from the bottle of cleaning ammonia and, waving thanks, hurried back to the prone Pritchard.

They had lifted him from the puddle and carried him out of the yard and onto the sidewalk. Jake stared down at Pritchard laying there and said:

"We have to call this in. I'll call Kilgore and the paramedics."

"C'mon Jake, let's just take him to Harbor General in my car. Maybe he'll come around and tell us what the hell's going on," Mitch said.

"No. We have to do this the right way. He's wanted on a felony and may be a witness to a homicide. We don't have a choice here. You watch him and I'll find a phone."

"Right over there, the other side of the bus stop, there's a pay phone," Mitch said, pointing. Jake walked off toward the phone.

Mitch knelt down next to Pritchard and looking over, saw that Jake was at the phone. He took the saturated rag and held it over Pritchard's mouth and nose.

"C'mon asshole, wake up, wake up." As he breathed in the shocking fumes, Pritchard began struggling to avoid the rag:

"Mmf, mmf!" He pushed at the cloth. Mitch took the cloth from Pritchard's face and threw it into the weeds alongside the fence.

"Jake, he's come around, get over here!" Mitch yelled.

Jake ran back and both men knelt, looking at Pritchard with concern.

"Marty, we're here to help, you're going to be OK. The medics are on the way. What, what can you tell us? Who did Landers? What did you guys get yourself into?" Jake said. Pritchard looked around wildly, his eyes glassy with fever. He began mumbling erratically:

"Son of a bitch, he was fuckin' his own kid. His own kid and sure . . .always the big wheels, I tole' him. Oh yeah, I tole' him . . . bad, it's a bad idea. Don't fuck with the wheels, but no, not him, mister smart guy, oh fuck! They cut his head off, oh no. Who the hell, who did we think . . .he fucked his own kid, dead and the TV, saw it and now he's walking around with no head. Note didn't help him. Told him, I did, told him and the note . . . " Pritchard began laughing hysterically and then stopped suddenly and stared straight up at the blue sky.

"Is he dead?" Mitch asked, as Jake grabbed a dirty wrist, looking for a pulse.

"No, but he's got a real fast pulse, gotta be way over a hundred." Jake looked up at the sound of a siren. "Here come the troops."

Within two minutes a squad car and a City fire department truck were on the scene and shortly after that two detective units arrived. Jake explained to them how they found Pritchard. He, at one point, looked around to confirm something with Mitch and saw he was gone. A few minutes later he reappeared from within the yard. Jake gave him a quizzically stern look, but said nothing.

A half an hour later they finished telling the detectives at the scene what they knew and prepared to leave. They walked around the corner to Mitch's car. As Jake climbed in the passenger side Mitch said:

"Hold on a second." He walked over to the fence and picked up a paper bag and then got in the car. "OK, let's go."

"What's in the bag, Mitch?" Jake looked over as Mitch put the car in gear and began driving off.

"Oh, some stuff."

"Stuff?"

"Well yeah, some stuff I found under the boat and uh, some stuff, some odds and ends Pritchard had in his pockets. I didn't look too close. We can look at it when we get back to your place.

"Evidence. You've removed evidence, Mitch. You can't do that! Damn it!" Jake glared at Mitch. "This is just what I was talking about. You think this is thirty years ago when we used to play fast and loose with the rules."

"Sure, well I'm not going to tell anybody, I haven't even told you yet. Let's just look at it and then we can turn it in and I'll say I found the bag later. That I went back to find my keys. Lost my keys and didn't know it 'til later." Mitch paused, "OK?"

Jake sat there a minute, mulling the situation over as Mitch pulled onto the 110 Freeway.

"Let's stop at Harbor General, that's where they're taking him," Jake said.

*****

Harbor General was a block and a half off the 110 Freeway at Carson Street. As the county hospital, it was responsible for the indigent and those who couldn't afford health care. It sat upon two square blocks of county property. Other than the gray, brown main building the facility was a mixture of Quonset huts and odd buildings, all obviously added as the need dictated and with no thought for aesthetics. Patients and staff moved about the grounds. The patients with no direction, the staff, most with clip boards under their arms, with purpose.

Jake and Mitch made their way to the emergency ward and searched for a nurse who could steer them to the doctor in charge. They understood Pritchard was officially in custody and could not be spoken with, but emergency nurses and cops had a special bond and Jake hoped to take advantage of that. The Head Nurse was located and, after making a call, she found Doctor Ostroki. He had an accent and stood in the hallway looking this way and that as he explained to Jake and Mitch:

"It's rare. He has a whole list of complications, pericarditis, endocarditis, and abscesses. He should have been treated days ago with antibiotic therapy. As I said, it's rare. Spirillum minus, common in Japan, not here. Is there anything else? I'm very busy."

"Doc," Mitch said, "could you just put it all a little simpler? We're not doctors, I'm an old sailor and he's a dumb cop," pointing at Jake who raised his eyebrows at being referred to as dumb.

"Uh huh," The doctor responded, "He was bitten, probably by a rat. The sore is still open. The abscesses are the worst, his brain is involved as are his heart valves. He was found in the harbor area. No doubt a rat from overseas." The doctor looked back and forth at the two of them. "You touched him? Go to your own physician and get a series of antibiotic shots." He reached in his pocket and handed them each a card. "Have your doctor call me if you wish. Good bye now." He turned and began hurrying down the hallway.

"Doc," Jake called after him, "is he going to be all right?"

"No," the doctor said over his shoulder, "he'll be dead within two or three hours," and he disappeared around the corner.

Actually, Marty Pritchard died a little over an hour later. In a comatose state, he never uttered another word.

Mitch pulled into Jake's driveway and shut off the car. It was nearly noon. Mitch suggested they go in the house and call the hospital to find out what was happening with Pritchard. They got out and walked toward the front door.

"I expect we'll learn he's dead, Mitch. The doctor made that pretty clear. Damn, I wish he'd called me while he was still lucid. I could have helped him and I probably could have learned a few things about what he and his partner were involved in. And, who else is, or was, involved. Now we might never know exactly what those two were up to."

"Yeah," Mitch said, "and what it all has to do with your current situation. That would be good, too."

"Yes, it would. I'd sure like to know what, if anything, they had to do with getting me suspended. Maybe nothing, but the possibility is there. C'mon, let's get a cup of coffee."

They went in the house and Mitch sat down at the kitchen table while Jake put a pot of coffee on the stove. Jake walked through the house, threw his jacket on the bed and went into the bathroom where he found a note from Edie taped to the mirror.

"The woman really knows me," he said to himself. The note told him that Kilgore had called and wanted Jake to call him at the office. Jake walked back to the kitchen and told Mitch and then went to the phone. He reached Kilgore immediately and they spoke briefly.

Jake hung up and sat down at the table with Mitch. "Kilgore's got some info he wants to give me. He talked to his contact at the bureau, the guy who's been helping him dig up the corporate structure that owns Blue Bird Studios. He wants to meet for lunch. Want to come along?"

"Are you kiddin'? That could prove interesting. I've got my suspicions. Now we'll see if I have any intuition left, any instincts."

"Instincts? You pickled your instincts years ago," Jake said. "Anyway, he's going to meet us at Little Joe's. Let's go, driver. Kilgore's a busy man, we don't want to keep him waiting."

Jake turned the coffee off and they left immediately. In thirty minutes they pulled into the parking lot adjacent to the restaurant. Kilgore was waiting, standing near the front door chatting with the owner. He looked surprised to see Mitch with Jake but said nothing. They were escorted to a table in the back of the restaurant in a small banquet room. Before they sat down Jake said "Mitch, Dave and I have to talk for a few minutes. Excuse us, will ya?" Mitch got up and left the room.

Jake told Kilgore what he'd learned regarding Mitch and his past activities and indicated his inclination to let it ride for the time being. Kilgore understood Jake's position and agreed to do the same. Jake called to Mitch and he re-entered the room and sat down.

"So,how are things at the station, Dave?" Jake asked.

"They're okay, they'll be better when you get back to work," he replied.

The waitress came and took their order. She returned a short time later with pasta for Jake and Mitch and a cup of coffee for Kilgore. As they ate they talked.

"Anything new on the Hilltop case?" Jake asked.

"Actually, yes. We're pretty sure Darryl Sherman's our man. Everything fits, including his weird behavior when he was in jail down in Orange County. It's just a matter of time."

"Good, real good. Have you spoken with her parents lately? It would be good to give them something to ease the pain a bit."

"Yeah, I spoke with her father yesterday and he seemed to be relieved, at least a little. The poor guy's still really devastated. It's been a while. I thought he'd be a little better by now."

"Well, you guys have done your job well. That's all you can do, Dave."

"We do what we can. Anyway, let me bring you up to date on what I've come up with. You're going to find this real interesting, Jake. Chuck Holtz from the bureau got back to me last night. He's the guy I told you about who has worked White Collar crime for years, mostly in the L.A. office. Really knows his stuff when it comes to figuring out corporate structures and connections; stuff like that." Kilgore took a sip of water, glanced over at Mitch and than continued:

"He agreed to help me dig up the information on Blue Bird Studios. Once we started on it he got all involved. He said he'd never looked at a corporation that had so many twists and turns. In his view, the whole thing was set up to protect corporate officers from being identified with the seedy side of the business. In fact, he's going to open an investigation into the organization and see what they're really up to. The corporation operates a variety of apparently legitimate businesses, including Blue Bird. They have about twenty Adult Entertainment locations throughout the L.A. and Orange County area, selling porno videos, sex devices, stuff like that. They also own over forty dry cleaning establishments. Perfectly legitimate little neighborhood cleaning shops. Nothing nefarious.

"The corporation also owns several bars, some high class and some not so high class. One in particular you'll find interesting. You mentioned the '507' once. They own it."

"This corporation owns the '507?'" Jake asked. "A sleazy little hole in the wall like that. That seems a little strange to me."

"Agreed. But they do," Kilgore replied. "Obviously they've taken diversity to a new level."

"Or a new low," Jake said. "Have you been able to identify any of the corporate bigwigs?"

"There's a couple of guys in New York that are V.P.'s, more for show than for any real hands-on function. According to Holtz, they're loosely connected with the mob. Associates, so to speak. Never arrested but flakey, nevertheless. Here's something interesting though. One of the dry cleaning shops has as leasee a holding company owned by Arlo Calarsi"

"What! Arlo Calarasi," Jake replied, looking over at Mitch.

"I'm not surprised," Mitch said calmly. "I had a hunch he'd turn up."

"Dave, this is real interesting. Mister Big Time Hollywood guy. The Mayor's good buddy. He's got connections all over the place.

In fact, I've seen him at some Department functions with none other than Chief of Detectives, Walter Burnett."

"Really. Our beloved Chief of Detectives is buddy's with this guy? I guess we have to assume he doesn't know everything about Arlo, huh?"

"I guess we should give him the benefit of the doubt," Jake replied, "but he ought to check out his friends a little closer."

"Or maybe he does know about the guy, but thinks everyone else doesn't," Mitch observed.

"He's got a point, Jake" Kilgore said. "Who knows what the nature of that relationship might be. We know Burnett wants to be Chief. Maybe Arlo, if he really is a big shot movie industry mogul and a friend of the Mayor, is his sponsor."

"Well, either way, we need to dig into this. There's more going on here than a questionable friendship," Jake observed. "The '507,' Belinda Burnham, Blue Bird Studios and Arlo Calarasi are all connected. Add to that the fact that Arlo's house was on the list of potential burglary location's Pritchard and Landers were considering hitting and things really get interesting." Jake said.

"Yeah, don't they," Mitch replied. "Where do you want to go from here, Jake?"

“Well, there's another question that rears it's ugly head, isn't there? Who the hell were those two assholes that tried to send you and your boat to the bottom the other night? It's hard to believe that isn't connected somehow, right along with my current situation."

"I'll follow up on that with Piper, Jake," Kilgore said. " He's had time to run them through his files. He should have a full work up on them both."

"Thanks, Dave. I appreciate that. I appreciate everything you've done, in case I forgot to mention it."

“I know. I have to go. I have to be at the Coroner's Office in fifteen minutes for an autopsy. We had a homicide the other night, Thursday, over on Hollywood Boulevard, west of La Brea. Two gentlemen of the alternate life style got into a tiff. One of them chased the other onto the roof of the four-story apartment building they lived in. They were both naked and screaming at the top of their lungs. Put on quite a show for a large group of people who were holding a luau on the roof of the apartment building next door. Anyway, the chaser had a huge butcher knife that he ultimately managed to plunge into the chest of the chasee. All this right in front of fifty or so witnesses. Then the suspect pushed the dead guy into the pool and returned to the apartment they shared and waited for us to show up. A self-solver."

"Never a dull moment in Jollywood," Jake said. "I'll get lunch, Dave."

They all stood and shook hands. Kilgore shook hands with Jake and stared at Mitch for a moment before he exited the restaurant. Jake and Mitch stopped at the register to take care of the bill. Jake replenished his supply of toothpicks and they walked out.

They drove back to Jake's house and as Mitch pulled to the curb he told Jake he had to go.

"What, have you got a hot date?"

"As a matter of fact, I do," he said. "And when you're as old and worn out as I am, it takes time to get ready. But then, I don't have to tell you, do I?"

"Real funny," Jake responded. "Is she able to walk on her own or does she use a walker?'

"We're talking about Kelly here so watch your tongue."

"Is that right. She hasn't figured you out yet, huh? I'll have to speak to her."

"Now that she's given in to my charms, it's too late. There's nothing you can say. But I'll tell her you still think you're her father. She'll appreciate that."

Mitch waved and drove off. Jake walked to the house, thinking about the relationship that had developed between Mitch and Kelly. An unlikely match, he thought. But none of his business.

Jake went in and immediately placed a call to his attorney. He left a message and within ten minutes Frank Lacey, called him back. Jake brought Lacey up to date on all that had happened. When he was through Lacey asked him what he was going to do and Jake admitted he wasn't sure yet. He explained to him that he hadn't had time to consider all the information he had. Jake told him he expected that however he proceeded, Kilgore would probably be involved in helping him.

"You know, Jake, with all the information you've come up with, including those two Russians, Harry Becker, Belinda and now Arlo, you ought to consider going back to I.A.D. and giving them what you've got."

"Well, you may be right but I certainly can't tell them what

Mitch got out of Belinda. I mean, considering his less than legal tactics, once they talked to her they'd be getting a warrant for his arrest. But I suppose I could give them some of this. The I.A. sergeant I spoke to seemed uncharacteristically interested in getting all the facts about this situation. York was his name, I think."

"Sergeant York. Just like the hero in World War I. Give him a call, Jake and let him in on things. What could it hurt?" Lacey suggested.

"I'll think about that, Frank. Thanks for the advice. Guess that's why you get the big bucks."

"Yeah, that's it. And Jake, be sure that if you set up a meeting with York you let me know. I need to be there. O.K.?"

"O.K. I'll be talking with you. Bye."

*****

Late that afternoon Jake put in a call to I.A.D. and left a message for Sgt. York to call him. Then he walked to the store to pick up what he needed for dinner. If nothing else, his hiatus from work had allowed him to improve his cooking skills and expand the list of dishes he was able to prepare fairly competently, much to Edie's delight. As he walked in the front door after coming from the store the phone was ringing.

"Probably the good sergeant," he thought. He was surprised to hear Mitch's voice on the other end.

"Jake, it's me. Listen, I just spoke to Kelly. Called her to confirm our date. I told her about Pritchard and the corporate stuff we got from Dave. Ya' know, Arlo and all. She got kinda funny, sounded like she was crying or something. Anyway, she said we, meaning the three of us, have to talk. She wants to get together this evening. She's really upset about something and apparently it can't wait. I don't know what's up but can we meet somewhere? I'll pick Kelly up."

"All right. How about if I come down to the boat? Around nine, after Edie and I have dinner."

"Fine, see you then. Bye."

*****

Edie arrived home a little earlier than usual and she and Jake had a pleasant dinner together. Jake told her all the latest developments and she seemed a little more upbeat about the situation being resolved soon. She realized how agonizing the suspension had been for Jake. His reputation and status were on the line and now it looked as though some progress was being made to resolve things. After dinner Edie volunteered to clean up. Jake decided to ride his motorcycle and left immediately for Mitch's boat.

As he rode down toward the beach he thought about what Mitch had said. Kelly was upset, maybe even crying. "What was that all about," he wondered. As much as he hated to think it, there was still some doubt in his mind about Kelly. Someone put all the incriminating bits of evidence in his office and she was still as good a suspect as anyone. Jake had gone over the possibilities a dozen times and had yet to develop a better suspect than Kelly.

"Maybe she was ready to cop out, tell them why she did it," he thought. "At least if she did, they could move on. Someone else would have to be involved and she'd have to tell the whole story. We'll see."

Jake pulled into the parking lot of the marina. "I hope this visit isn't as exciting as the last one," he said to no one in particular, as he walked toward Mitch's boat.

*****

Right on time, Mitch pulled his old Mustang into the 'loading only' zone in front of Kelly's apartment complex. He barely had time to get out of the car before she came striding down the stairs leading from the lobby. She pulled the passenger door open and said:

"C'mon let's go." She was wearing jeans and an old ribbed sweater. Her hair was pulled back severely in a bun at the back of her head and she was wearing little, if any, make up. She sat in the seat staring straight ahead as Mitch pulled away from the curb.

"Uh, I thought we could go down to King Harbor. Have dinner where we had our first real date. I thought it might be fun. The last few days have been a little rough on everybody, know what I mean?" Mitch said, looking over at Kelly, who still stared out the windshield. He decided not to ask her why she wanted to meet with him and Jake.

At the restaurant, Mitch managed to race around the car and open the door for her. They'd ridden in silence all the way to the dinner spot. As they entered the restaurant Mitch put his arm around her shoulder and felt her stiffen at his touch. The maitre de' led them to a quiet booth with a view of the inner harbor and the traffic crawling along on Harbor Drive. He handed a menu first to Kelly and then Mitch and wished them a happy meal. Kelly put her menu down without looking at it.

"Hi folks! Can I start you off with a drink?" The waitress was blond, slightly overweight, with large breasts trying to push their way out of her Hawaiian Sarong. She had a happy, vacant look on her face as she stood there with a pad of paper in one hand and a pencil in the other.

"Give me a glass of white wine and a small dinner salad," Kelly said.

"I'll have a plain coke with a lime, a shrimp cocktail and a bowl of your clam chowder, New England style please." Mitch smiled at the young waitress. As she walked away swinging her hips, Kelly said with an edge to her voice:

"Think she's cute?"

"Ah c'mon Kelly, she's funny. That's all, she's silly just like most of the kid's today." Mitch sat there for a moment staring at Kelly. Her face was drawn and she wouldn't meet his eyes. Instead she stared down at the table cloth, making small circles on the white cloth with her fork.

They sat there, neither of them speaking, until their food and drinks were brought to the table. Mitch took a bite of the cold shrimp, munched approvingly and said:

"Kelly," taking her hand in his, "I'm not your enemy, I'm your friend. So please tell me what's wrong. You can't tell me anything worse that what I've done or seen. I'd never judge you, you know that." She looked at him and her eyes became moist. She shook her head back and forth as she pulled her hand from his. He took her hand back and said in a strong voice:

"Nope, you gotta tell me, I'm here to help. Now come on, level with me. What's wrong?"

"Oh, damn, I've really screwed things up, Mitch." Her voice was low. "You're not going to like what I'm going to say." She sat there as though gathering herself and then:

"You know I told you I was raised by a foster family? Well, really my grandparents, on my mother's side brought me up. My mom was a showgirl and I guess pretty wild. She didn't want much to do with the family." Kelly put her fork down and began to speak more rapidly.

"My grandparents told me my real father was a cop, married of course and, you know, back then abortions were hard to get and dangerous, so they talked my mother into going through with the pregnancy and they said they would raise me. A couple of years ago my mother showed up and we've been trying, trying to work things out." Kelly looked at Mitch with a sad look.

"My mother's name is Maureen. She married a guy named Arlo. Married him about thirty years ago. She likes her life. Rich, high society. How was I supposed to screw that up?"

"Arlo? The Arlo I'm thinking about?" Mitch asked, a shrimp halfway to his mouth.

"Yeah, he's my stepfather. He is a hard man, mean. I don't like him and he doesn't like me. It's difficult for my mother. She has to sneak around half the time to see me." Kelly took a deep breath.

"So the guy that committed suicide is your, what, your brother?" Mitch asked.

"Yeah, my half brother. I only met him a few times. We didn't really hit it off. He was a strange kind of guy."

"So far Kel I'm not seeing a big problem here. What else?" Mitch said.

"Well for starters, I didn't tell Jake any of this. You know, when he went to the scene and after. It didn't seem important. And Landers and Pritchard. I should have said something then. But I thought they were bad cops, burglars, who'd just go away. No reason to say anything."

"What about this guy Arlo? What kind of guy is he?" Mitch asked.

"Like I said, we don't get along. Arlo looks squeaky clean but he's involved in something. I don't know what exactly. For all I know he could be a big time dope dealer or something. He's got money invested in a lot of things other than the movie business. I have an uncomfortable feeling he might have something to do with Jake's trouble. I kept quiet because of my mother, mostly. And I felt sorry for Andy. He was kinda pathetic." She looked at Mitch, "I never told him, I never told Jake. How could I have been so stupid? He trusted me and I blew it."

Mitch motioned to the waitress and when she brought the

check he put some bills on the table and said:

"OK, let's go tell him. It's a little after nine."

They pulled out of the parking lot and turned left from Harbor Drive onto Beryl Ave. Kelly looked at the search lights piercing the night sky, announcing the grand opening of the latest fast food emporium. Her mind was too busy to notice Uncle Sam, obviously promoting something or other, on stilts swinging one long leg after the other, reeling up the side walk on his way back from a smoke break.

They rode in silence across the Palos Verde Peninsula on their way to Long Beach and Mitch's boat and Jake.

Mitch didn't ask, but he sensed she hadn't told him everything.

*****

It was ten minutes to ten when Mitch and Kelly pulled into the marina parking lot.

"Jake's already here. That's his motorcycle," Mitch said. Kelly nodded her head and they walked down the gangway to Mitch's sailboat. Jake was sitting in the cockpit staring at the lights reflecting on the calm water of the bay. He turned and looked at them as they approached.

"Hi Mitch, how are you?" He looked toward Kelly and nodded. "Kelly." he said. "I got here early." He looked back over the water. "It's peaceful, Mitch. Sometimes I can see why you live on a boat."

"Hey Jake," Mitch climbed over the rail, "here Kelly, let me give you a hand." Kelly moved to the cockpit and sat across from Jake. "You guys want some coffee?" Mitch asked. "Only take a minute?" Jake and Kelly both looked at Mitch standing in the companionway and nodded their heads yes. Mitch pumped the alcohol stove and lit the burner and the warm odor of the stove drifted up to the cockpit.

"Well Kelly, want to tell me what's on your mind?" Jake looked at her with that serious look all the detectives in the division knew. Kelly reached into the pocket of her jeans and pulled out a sheet of paper. Without a word she unfolded the paper and handed it across to Jake. He held it at arms length and squinted.

"I can't read this. Mitch, have you got a flashlight?" After a moment Mitch handed up an oil lamp and Jake held the paper close to the yellow flame and read the note. He read it through and then read it again, more slowly.

To my loving parents Arlo and Maureen,

By the time you read this I should have arrived at an advanced stage of decomposition. The accompanying smell may be a little offensive, especially right here in your little love nest. I'd love to be able to see your reactions. Not that I expect any remorse from either of you.

You, dear father, are devoid of feelings for anyone except, of course, yourself. You are a sick, perverted son of a bitch who destroyed my childhood for your own pleasure. I actually thought that what you were doing to me was normal. At least for the first few years. I thought you loved me. I really did. You hurt me, but I was sure it was alright. You were my father, after all. When I began to realize it wasn't alright, not exactly normal, you showed me a tape. Andy and Arlo. Remember? The tape of the two of us? I wonder how many times that's been reproduced. It had the desired effect, didn't it? Kept me quiet all these years. I began to realize that I was as perverted as you are. But not for long. I'm going to Hell but at least I won't have to look my children in the eye.

I want to thank you Mother. I don't know if you knew what was going on with your husband or not. If you did, then may you rot in hell along with that bastard you're married to. You were supposed to protect me from bad things. If you didn't know then I guess you didn't care. Either way, you failed miserably at motherhood. I'll take solace in knowing you now have to wonder if your dear husband will kill you to keep you from exposing him.

As for my wife and children, they're safer living without someone who's probably harboring the same twisted desires that you have, Father. My wife looks at me like she thinks so, too. I want to spare them the agony you visited on me, you bastard!

Thanks for nothing.

Your Loving Son, Andy

When he finished Jake looked up at Kelly.

"Where did you get this Kelly?" His voice low.

"At Landers' apartment the day we went there. He had it stashed in his bedroom." Kelly looked down at her hands folded in her lap.

"Why? What? Your reason, Kelly. What is your reasoning?" Jake said, his voice almost a whisper.

"I, I just wasn't thinking clearly. I didn't think the note was that important at that point. I was thinking of my mother." Kelly said. "And then when all the other stuff came up I wasn't sure what, I mean, I still can't think how it's all connected to you. Anyway here I am, I'm trying to make it right with you. I know you know how much I respect and admire…"

"And everything's OK? Sorry Kelly, not a chance." Jake paused. "This piece of paper may clear up a multitude of mysteries. But it damn sure doesn't change anything where you're concerned. You're obviously involved in planting all that crap in my office. The kiddie porn, the blood on the jacket, the whole deal. Now I find out you're guilty of withholding evidence in a murder investigation and you're trying to save your ass. Not going to happen Kelly. This goes to I. A. in the morning." Jake looked over at Mitch. "Take her home, I'll talk to you in the morning."

"I'll get home by myself." Kelly stood up. "I was dead wrong Lieutenant, but I didn't participate in framing you and I don't know who did." She sighed. "But I think I'd believe the same thing if it was me." Without another word, holding her hand palm out at Mitch, she stepped off the boat and disappeared into the darkness at the gangway.

"With friends like us who needs enemies?" Mitch said as he came on deck with two mugs of his horrible coffee. "The note was from the guy who committed suicide? Andy? What does the note say? He was her stepbrother, she only met him once."

"How do you . . ." Jake started to say.

"Whoa Jake, she told me tonight at dinner. Didn't tell me about the note though. Just that Maureen was her mother and only came back into her life a few years ago. I think she's, oh I don't know, trying to get her mother's acceptance; some abandonment issues and things. You understand. It was a tough situation. She obviously was torn between protecting her family and her duty as a cop. She had a lot of inner conflict and soul searching to resolve."

"Don't give me a bunch of psycho babble. She's as wrong as she can be. You've been sleeping with her and you're judgment is, to say the least, clouded," Jake said.

"Now who's using psychology, Jake? I don't think she planted those pictures in your desk and she has nothing to gain by giving you that note. Nothing I can see, anyway but a possible jail sentence. What does the note say anyway?" Jake handed the note to Mitch. "No, just tell me. I can't read it out here." Jake looked at the paper.

"He says basically that the old man, Arlo, molested him when he was a kid. Maureen never protected him from the son of a bitch and he obviously hated them both. It looks like he was beginning to worry that he'd turn out to be a pervert like his old man. And he obviously wanted to leave them with a nasty mess in their bed when they returned home." He shook his head slowly. "Sad, sick situation."

"So Arlo was doing his own kid," Mitch said.

"Seems as though." Jake rubbed his face.

"You know what Jake?"

"What?"

"We should sleep on this. My head's too full. We still don't have anything like proof, do we?" Mitch said.

Jake looked at Mitch. "Are you kidding? What the hell do you call this?" Jake asked, holding up the note." She confiscated a piece of evidence that is, to say the least, pertinent to a murder investigation. The murder of a cop, by the way. Crooked or not, he was a cop. Why she decided to give this to me, I can't tell you. But I can tell you this: I don't buy her story that she was trying to protect mother. She's up to her ass in this whole situation. Even you can see that, Mitch."

"Maybe you're right but I can't believe she'd do anything to set you up. There's a lot more to the story. There has to be. Before you call I.A.D. in the morning why don't we meet for breakfast? Sleep on this and let's see if we come up with anything. O.K.?"

Jake looked at Mitch. "No, Mitch. No more meetings to talk things over. There's nothing that needs to be discussed. I've got a pretty good idea of what's going on and I'm through sitting around waiting for I.A. to figure it out. I, we, have a lot of information that, unfortunately, we can't give them because of the way you got big pieces of it. But it's still good information. I'm going to do what no one else seems inclined to do; get this mess resolved. I've waited too long, already."

Jake climbed off the boat onto the dock. He turned and looked at Mitch from the dock. “By the way, Mitch. You better look for a new squeeze. This one's trouble."

Chapter 31

Kelly had to wait almost an hour for a cab. She'd walked almost ten blocks from the marina to a pay phone next door to a small cafe that catered to the beach crowd and closed at four in the afternoon. She stood in front of the dark building waiting for the taxi. A drunk cruised by her twice, offering her a ride. The third time she told him to 'fuck off,' flashing her gold badge at the same time. He did not reappear.

Finally back at her apartment, she took a long hot shower and then sat with a cup of tea, curled up in her favorite old easy chair and thought about her meeting with Jake and Mitch. Somehow, the stress of the last few weeks seemed to be over. No more secrets. At least none that were troubling. With a sigh she climbed into bed and for the first time in what seemed like a very long time, she fell into a deep slumber.

Her bedroom window faced the inner patio of the horseshoe shaped apartment building. At a few minutes past three in morning, the neighbor's tomcat began to howl a warning at some interloper, pulling Kelly from her sleep . She got up and sat by the window, legs curled under her and looked down into the shadowed patio, plants reflecting the dimmed night lights surrounding the area. The tom, his fluffy tail standing tall, pranced across the area, proudly having warned off another challenger. He disappeared into the plants at the far side of the ornate fountain that was trickling water from the top into the base.

The peace and quiet, the time of night and the first rest she'd had in some time allowed Kelly's mind to 'percolate with her subconscious.' At least that was the way Mitch explained it two hours later, while sitting in the cabin of his boat as she explained what had suddenly occurred to her.

*****

"The straw slippers, Mitch. I was just sitting there looking out the window thinking about that little girl. I could see her perched on the bench at the front desk, at the station. Her little feet with those slippers. Then, those damn pictures. Before you and Jake came back from lunch that day, they showed me the pictures. They wanted to know if I'd ever seen them before. All those little girls, all those little girls with those grown men. They were Asian and in one picture the same kind of slipper was on a coffee table. Straw. It was so unusual I remembered it!"

Kelly was excited. She sat opposite Mitch holding a cup of hot chocolate. She'd awakened him, whispering through the forward hatch above where he slept in the V berth. He was so shocked he sat up and bumped his head on the bulkhead.

"So I bet it's not only child porno, it's a child procurement for a bunch of sickos!" She stopped talking and stared straight ahead, her expression all cop. Then she resumed telling Mitch all the details about the girl. Finishing up with, "and with everything else going on I just never connected it, never told you. Don't you think it all ties together?"

"Uncle Sam." Mitch said.

"What? What do you mean, Uncle Sam?" Kelly asked.

"The new joint at King Harbor, remember? They are using a guy dressed up as Uncle Sam on stilts to advertise. That's what the girl described she saw when she got away from the boat." Mitch reached over and picked up the phone, pushing his sleeping dog out of the way.

"What are you doing?"

"Calling Jake." Mitch said dialing and a moment later, "Jake, it's me. Listen don't call I.A. about Kelly until you talk to me." Pause and, "no, she's here now." Pause and, "of course I'm interfering again, I'm habitual, remember?" Pause and, "no. I don't want to tell you over the phone but, if you aren't here in an hour, she and I are going to set sail for the South Pacific," and, "well then do me this one favor. Don't make the call to I.A. about Kelly until this afternoon." Mitch turned to Kelly. "He really thinks you planted the pictures in his office, Kelly. But he won't talk to Internal Affairs until this afternoon."

Mitch and Kelly sat staring out the ports. The early morning light, barely discernable over Saddleback Mountain to the east.

"Time to get to work," Kelly said. "Probably won't get to say that much longer. In fact, that may have been it, at least as far as the police department is concerned."

She climbed the steps out of the cockpit of the boat and quickly stepped onto the deck and then onto thc dock. "See you later," she yelled back over her shoulder as she headed up the dock. "I'll call you."

*****

The call came in at seven thirty-five the next morning. Kelly in extra early, decided to begin cleaning out her desk. She figured by 2:00 o'clock that afternoon she would be relieved of duty on suspension pending criminal charges.

"This is Detective McBride."

"Hi, I'm Officer Wang, with the Asian squad? Hear you got a little kid with a weird story, Steve filled me in."

"I do, there's something wrong and I . . ."

"Listen. It won't do any good for me to try to talk to her, her dialect is totally foreign to me."

"Damn, I was hoping . . ." Kelly trailed off.

"There is something, though," Wang said. "Her story about the army guy in China. Every once in awhile we get a rumor about a Red Chinese General. Literally translated from Chinese, he's called 'fiendish white ghost.' A year or so ago an agent from the feds contacted us. He said he was with the State Department. He came around and asked if we had any intell' on this guy. I got nothing from him and all I could tell him was we'd heard rumors we couldn't confirm."

"About what?" Kelly asked.

"About these kids being brought over from Asia. I'm not sure why but a lot of scenarios present themselves."

"What does your gut feeling tell you?" Kelly asked.

"Well, what with two boats, rumors that someone is buying these kids from their parents, and that a minister is presumably the boss over here..."

"Minister? What do you mean Minister?" Kelly interrupted.

"Yeah, she used a word Steve didn't understand. It means men that carry crosses from far away. It's kind of Chinese slang for the missionaries from years ago that came to the Chinese mainland. She, Song, thought the white guy that took the kids was a missionary," Wang explained. "She added that he was too mean to be a man of God."

"So?" Kelly prodded.

"So, who knows. But I'll tell you what it isn't. It isn't an adoption deal. Too much money involved, what with the boats and all. And it doesn't figure to be a sweat shop deal. The kid's are too young. So a wild guess would be...I don't know. Something illegal. We'll continue working on it."

"Okay. Good. If you hear anything let me know will you? She, well she seemed so forlorn, know what I mean?" Kelly said in a low voice.

"I will. We're putting out feelers. Someone out there knows what's up. Maybe we can get them to tell us," Wang answered. "But don't expect much, O.K.? The Asian community still doesn't have a lot of faith in us. Particularly the recent immigrants. As far as they're concerned we're just like the police they have to deal with back home. You know what I mean?"

"Yes, I know what you mean. But please do what you can, will you?" Kelly hung up the phone and sat there playing with a pencil and trying to sort through her feelings. Way in the back of her mind there was a thought trying to get her attention. She picked up her phone and dialed Mitch at the boat.

*****

"Hey Tiger, how ya' been boy?" Mitch reached down and

scratched the old, scruffy, brown dog behind the ears. "Where's your old man?" The dog wagged its tail. Mitch walked towards the boat in the slip a few feet away.

Mitch had driven across Palos Verde Hills to avoid the early morning traffic from Long Beach to King Harbor. It was a pleasant drive; the morning sun behind him, the early day giving promise of good weather. Catalina Island was clearly visible from the 'Hill,' the channel calm and blue. He and Kelly had made a plan. Mitch would go to King Harbor and see what info he could dig up from the boating community and Kelly would talk to the China Town Squad and talk to Song again.

Mitch had tried to convince Kelly there was a connection between the little girl's plight and what had happened to Jake.

"Look at it this way, Kel," he'd told her. "The porno studio sets Jake up with the rape charge, at least according to Belinda. Somebody plants child porno in his desk. Child porno with Asian kids, for crap sakes. And now we've got a Chinese girl that escapes from a fairly sophisticated set up involving bringing kids to the States. It all connects, I'm telling you."

Kelly had disagreed. "Too much of a reach, Mitch," was all she could say. She agreed to the plan only because she felt it was a separate case worth pursuing on its own merits.

*****

"Burt, you aboard?" Mitch banged on the hull of the Choey Lee, an old wooden sloop. Burt was one of the old timers in the harbor. He and Mitch had more than sailing in common. Burt, at one time in his long life, had been a cop. He'd never told Mitch where or when.

"Who is it? Whad'da you want?" Burt stuck his grizzled old head up though the aft hatch with a scowl on his face. "Hey Mitch! How are ya? What brings you over here? Come on, come on, come aboard. I've got a pot of joe on the stove."

Mitch waved 'no thanks' to the coffee as he climbed over the side of the boat. Burt's coffee was a legend. Some people said a cup could kill you and two was even worse.

They sat in the cabin of the proper wooden boat and brought each other up to date. They talked of weather and waves until Mitch finally brought up the reason for his visit. He provided Burt with the entire story of his reunion with Jake and everything that had transpired since.

"See, Jake's a fine fellow and a great cop so I've stuck my nose in it."

"Sounds as though you've fucked it up as much as helped," Burt said, referring to Mitch's novel methods with some of the people he'd encountered.

"Aw, I've been all through that with Jake. They never would have testified for him anyway. They'd be copping out on themselves. 'Sides that, can't you picture that little weasel Harry rushing into the hospital yelling about his ear?" Both men sat there smiling at the thought.

"So you think the boat that's been bringing in these kids is ported here, do you?" Burt asked.

"Yeah. You know this harbor better than anyone, Burt. Any thoughts, any ideas about what boat might be doing some smuggling, making pick ups; off shore from the way I figure it."

"Well there is this one sleaze." Burt rubbed his beard. "You know the type. Daddy left him a big sport fisher, a Bertrum. Forty-six feet and got the range sure enough. A real nothing, that guy. Hanging around the bars, bringing every slut in town to the boat at all times of the night. Had a handful of gold chains around his neck and not enough decency to bait a hook."

"Had?" Mitch asked.

"Yup. They found him floating the other morning. Seems as though he drank too much, fell overboard and drowned himself." Burt's expression indicated that he thought that was probably just as well.

"Can you tell me anymore about him?"

"Nope," Burt said as he stood up and went to the ship's radio and turned it on. He waited a moment for the set to warm up and then took the mike and said:

"King Harbor patrol, this is the Wayward Rat, over."

"Good morning Burt, this is King Harbor." The tinny voice came back immediately.

"Right. Is Charlie still on duty?" Burt replied.

"Yes. He's on patrol. Dead sea lion on the beach. Over."

"Ask him to come by," a pause and then, "over." Burt turned

off the radio without waiting for a reply.

"Charlie?" Mitch asked.

"He took the report on the drowning. Sure you don't want some coffee?" Burt held up a chipped cup. Mitch, with great reluctance, nodded yes. He marveled at the way Burt seemed to give orders to the harbor police.

They sat quietly in the cabin for almost fifteen minutes before the sound of a burbling engine idled up to the stern. A moment later a young, well built man in uniform of dark blue shorts and a white shirt with epaulets and a shiny badge, stood in the aft companionway.

"Good morning Burt, what's up?" The young officer asked, a smile on his tanned face.

"Morning Charlie," Burt answered gesturing to Mitch, "a friend of mine, used to be on the job." Charlie looked at Mitch appraisingly and nodded. Burt came right to the point:

"We want to board the Bertrum. Likc to look things over."

"Well, it's still in impound. But homicide signed off yesterday. It's officially an accidental drowning," Charlie said. "Can't see a problem. Let's go."

Burt's slip was across the entrance from the fuel dock and right next to the harbor patrol office. They walked down the dock to where the sport fisher was tied up and boarded.

*****

Kelly sat in the coffee shop nervously tapping her nails on the Formica table. It was quarter past two and Mitch was late. She'd had a relatively productive day. The China Town Squad had found a young woman, an artist, who spoke Song's dialect. Kelly felt her investigation was moving forward smoothly. Not that breaking a child prostitution ring would redeem her career. She knew she was finished; her police career over. But she liked the idea of going out in style and, in the back of her mind, she was still trying to figure out who within the ranks had planted the pictures in Jake's desk. She hoped to make things right between the two of them.

The only snag in her day had come at the foster home where everything came to an abrupt halt. Edna, the stern looking housemother, refused to allow Song to go with them, insisting on a warrant. In fact, Edna wouldn't even allow them to talk with the young Chinese girl. It took almost two hours of phone calls to the brass before someone in authority directed Edna to let Song accompany the two detectives.

"Hi Kelly. Sorry I'm late but the trip was worthwhile I think." Mitch sat down at the table with a smile on his face and began, without pause, to tell Kelly of his day. Finishing up with:

"But I still can't figure out what Burt's background is. I've asked him a couple of times and all he ever does is smile and change the subject." Mitch reached into his jacket pocket and brought out a photo. He held it out to Kelly. It showed a man in his early thirties standing with his arm around some floozy he'd probably picked up in some waterfront saloon. They were standing on the stern of a powerboat.

"This is the guy that owned the boat and drowned last week. I'd bet he had a little help. It was no accident. Burt handed me this picture as I was leaving, took if off the boat, sneaky old fart."

Kelly took the picture and stared at it for a moment and then reached into a manila envelope and handed Mitch a drawing.

"Looks like a match, don't you think?" she said. Then she explained how the China Town Squad had found a woman who spoke Song's dialect. She was an artist and had drawn composites from Song's descriptions of the boat's captain and the supposed minister.

"Song said he was dressed in clothing like a minister but she was sure he wasn't a man of God. She's seen some missionaries in China and said this man wasn't like them. Here's a picture of him."

Kelly handed Mitch a second drawing. It portrayed a dark man around fifty years old with curly black hair going to gray at the temples. He had a cruel mouth and dark eyes, set rather close together.

"Well, he doesn't look like a minister, does he?" Mitch said staring at the picture. "Looks like he could be Greek or Italian." Kelly nodded in agreement.

They picked at their food and tried to talk. There was a distance between them and Mitch didn't feel especially interested in closing it. Finally, they agreed that they needed to continue trying to find out who planted the pictures in Jake's desk. That was pretty much up to Kelly.

On the sidewalk outside the coffee shop, Mitch tried to give Kelly a hug good-bye and was met with a sad smile and the old 'hold your purse in front of you.' They said they would talk to each other the next day. Each walked away sensing a passing.

*****

At quarter of six in the morning the street in front of Hollywood Station was almost deserted. The sun was just beginning to illuminate the light layer of smog that promised to intensify as the day began to warm. Kelly sipped at a lukewarm cup of coffee as she made her way from the parking lot to the rear entrance to the station. She stopped at the foot of the stairs and stared at the same old bag lady who made her way past the station every morning, looking through the trashcans that bordered the sidewalk. The woman had on the same worn, gray overcoat and baggy nylons that hung like dirty rags around her spindly ankles. With a sigh, Kelly pushed the ringer at the rear door and advised the officer on the front desk she wanted entry.

The detective offices were empty. The day squad would not be arriving for at least another forty minutes. Kelly flopped at her desk and stared in the direction of Jake's office. Her mind kept going over the day the Sheriffs and I.A. came to Jake 's office and suspended him. She stared down at her desk at the list of names she, with Mitch's help, had put together. She took a pencil and scratched the first name off the list. She smiled to herself, thinking of Mitch's reaction when she suggested that his insistence on including Kilgore on a list of persons who might have framed Jake was guided by jealousy rather than any logic. She probably never should have told him that she and Kilgore had been an 'item' at one time. As she looked at the rest of the names no one stood out. These were all good people. People who could have accessed Jake's office.

Kelly stood up, stretched and yawned. A cup of coffee seemed in order. She hadn't slept, it seemed, for more than a half hour at a time for several days. As she passed Jake's office enroute to the coffee maker in the rear of the squadroom, she noticed a stack of personnel files on the desk. The acting C/O, Lt. Gillis, had been looking through the files, trying to get to know the detectives in the division. "Well, give him an 'E' for effort," she thought.

Kelly continued to the coffee maker and put on a pot. She waited while it brewed and then took a cup with her back to her desk. She sat down and rested her head on her arms. How, she wondered, was she going to figure out who planted the stuff in Jake's office. Who'd set him up?

Today would probably be her last day as a cop. Jake had surely reported her to I.A. last afternoon. Withholding evidence in a homicide. That was going to be bad enough, but Jake's belief that she framed him was worse. She hadn't done it but Jake didn't believe it. That hurt and she didn't see how she could convince him otherwise. And she needed to tell Mitch it had been fun but she had to move along and thank you very much.

"Hey Kelly! You sleep here last night?" The voice startled her awake. She'd drifted off while thinking about her problems. She looked up to see the first of the squad arrive for work. Ed Marquez and an old timer named Fitzgerald.

"Uh, no. Just came in early to beat the traffic. Good morning." Kelly said.

"Sure," and with a nasty grin Marquez said, "have a good time last night? Maybe ya' ought to take the morning off." Fitz laughed and both men headed to the coffee pot.

Kelly glared at Marquez. Then, loud enough for both men to hear she said, "I guess when you're not getting any, Ed, then thinking about it is all you've got."

Fitzgerald laughed and slapped Marquez on the back. "You asked for that, Ed."

CHAPTER 32

Jake had taken the long way home after leaving Mitch at the boat. He cruised along the coast for several miles before turning inland toward home trying to clear his mind. After riding along the boulevard for several miles he turned off and rolled through the darkened neighborhood and pulled into the driveway of his place. He parked the bike in the garage and went inside. Edie was still up and obviously relieved to see him. She always worried when he was on the motorcycle, especially at night. They kissed hello and walked together to the den where they sat next to each other on the overstuffed, leather couch.

"Well, you're not going to believe this," he told her. "I'm beginning to feel like I'm living in a dime novel. Talk about bizarre events. If I put this in a book, all the stuff that's happened in the past couple of weeks, I'd be accused of having an overactive imagination. I've never been involved in an investigation that's as complicated as this is getting to be."

Jake told Edie about the evening's events. He showed her the letter and explained why he was convinced of Kelly's involvement.

Edie asked him what he was going to do.

"I'm going to Internal Affairs with this mess and then I'm going to talk with Captain Hughes. Ed's a good guy and, as far as I know, he hasn't written me off yet. He needs to know what's going on. Then I'm going to work. It's pretty obvious this thing's not gonna get resolved soon. It needs a little push. I'm going to light a fire under it and see what happens."

Jake and Edie chatted a while longer, discussing, among other things, the upcoming selection of the new Chief of Police. Walter Burnett was still the odds on favorite.

*****

Jake was up early the next morning, thanks to the phone call from Mitch. Mitch's strong plea convinced Jake to hold off on contacting I.A. until the afternoon. He planned to meet with Ed Hughes at the station and then head downtown to talk with Sgt. York at I.A.D. He sat at the kitchen table sipping a cup of coffee and reading the paper. The lead story in the second section was the soon-to-be-selected new Chief of Police. Walter Burnett, the apparent darling of the news media, was prominently mentioned. Charles Collins was mentioned, as well, but he was obviously the dark horse in the race. At least as far as the news media was concerned. "Too bad," Jake thought.

As Jake got up to get his jacket and leave, the phone rang. His first thought was that it was probably Mitch and he was tempted to let it ring. After a moment he picked it up and was relieved to hear his secretary, Rene, on the other end.

"Hi Boss. How you doing?"

"Hi Rene. It's good to hear your voice. I'm doing alright. How about you?"

"Okay, I guess, but I wish you'd come back to work. Everybody misses you around here. Me the most. What's going on with the I.A.D. investigation? They've been around here interviewing everyone. But you know, those guys won't tell us anything."

"Well, I like to think they're doing things right. Trying to get to the truth of the matter, as they like to say. Time will tell. How are things in the division?" Jake asked.

"Screwed up, but with your duly appointed Assistant C/O in

charge what else did you expect? Are you sure that Lt. Gillis has a degree in management? The guy seems lost without you."

"I'm sure. And if you give him your unwavering support I think he'll do fine. You know, whip him into shape in your usual diplomatic way."

"Well, I'll try but it would be a lot easier if you'd just come back and straighten him out yourself. He's something to behold when he conducts a squad meeting. The troops give him a real bad time; in a friendly way, of course. Oh, and speaking of squad meetings, I've been catching up on my filing. It's easy to get behind when you have to baby sit the acting boss, along with everything else. Anyway, I've got a bunch of commendations I'm getting ready to put in the concerned detective's personnel packages. I know you like to read them to everyone at the squad meetings first and you always have them initial them, right? So we know they've been read?"

"Yeah, right. They don't like to admit it but they appreciate a little pat on the back in front of their peers."

"Who doesn't?" Rene responded. "So any of these that aren't initialed, you want me to save for your next squad meeting?"

"Well that assumes there will be a <u>next</u> squad meeting, doesn't it? I like your positive attitude, anyway. How long have the commendations been kicking around? Are they getting dated?"

"No, not really. Actually there's only a couple. One just came in and the other came in about a week before you… I mean, well, before you got, you know…railroaded."

Jake could tell Rene was getting teary eyed. "The one that came in before I went on my forced sabbatical's getting a little dated. It probably should be filed. Who's it for?"

"Boogie Newton, the desk man."

"You mean Boogie, 'have I used up all my sick days yet' Newton? He got a commendation? I find that hard to believe. Who commended him? Mrs. Newton?"

"No. Actually some citizen found him 'moderately helpful.' I guess that means he didn't fall asleep while talking to her on the phone. I might add, Boogie's a little miffed. He told me that he actually attended the squad meeting that day expecting you to read his commendation and you didn't."

"Well, I probably didn't, now that you mention it. He never attends squad meetings because he stays behind to cover the desk and the phones. I've never seen him at a squad meeting."

"He says he attended that day. Got Ed Marquez to cover. Well, I guess Ed actually volunteered so Boogie could be there."

"Really. That doesn't sound like the Ed Marquez I know. How would he even know Boogie got a commendation?"

"I don't know Boss but apparently he did. Anyway, should I have Lt. Numbnuts,er...I mean Gillis read it at the next squad meeting?"

"Sure, do that. Tell Boogie I owe him one. I've got to go but I'll talk to you soon. In fact, I'll see you soon. I'm dropping by the station in about an hour to talk to the Captain. Are you available for lunch?"

"I'll make myself available."

Jake hung up and, after grabbing his jacket from the closet, left the house and headed for the station.

As Jake cruised along the Hollywood Freeway he thought about his conversation with Rene. After he'd been relieved from duty he'd considered who had had the opportunity to get into his office and his desk. Kelly was the obvious choice. Rene was out of the station the entire morning and Boogie Newton, although near by at the desk, just wasn't the type to be involved in anything like framing Jake. Anyone who knew him knew that Boogie, although a little different, was as straight as they come. Jake trusted his instincts on that one. But Ed Marquez. Now that was another matter. Jake didn't trust Ed Marquez. Not a bit. Jake had made it a habit to watch Marquez like a hawk. His work performance was marginal and his skills as a detective supervisor were nearly non-existent. He was a back slapping, glad hander who wanted everyone to like him. As such, whenever one of his subordinates screwed up, Ed felt it was his job to cover it up rather than mete out any discipline. Of course, all the detectives who worked for him thought he was just great. Jake had addressed that issue with Marquez on more than one occasion and had taken disciplinary action once. It didn't have the desired effect, as Marquez drifted back into his usual pattern.

"Well," Jake thought. "It wouldn't surprise me to find Ed Marquez right in the middle of this little mystery. How could I have overlooked that jerk? Pritchard and Landers were his boys." Jake pondered the possibilities as he drove through traffic to the station. Marquez might be the one who set him up but he damn sure wasn't on his own. Ed didn't like him but he didn't have the balls or the smarts to do it by himself. Besides, Marquez didn't dislike him enough to go to such extremes. At least Jake didn't think he did.

A car horn beeped behind him, he had been lost in thought. He made a quick decision, a gut decision. He would wait one more day before calling I.A. down on Kelly's head.

Jake pulled into the station lot and, from force of habit, parked in the Detective C/O's spot. When he realized what he'd done he backed out, narrowly avoiding a homeless woman who had been wandering through the lot. He picked another stall, parked and went into the station.

As he entered the building, Jake found himself a little uncomfortable, not sure what kind of reception he might get from officers in the station who knew him. But he made his way to Captain Hughes' office without encountering anyone he knew. He said hello to Hughes' secretary and asked if the Captain was in. She nodded hello and told him to go right in. Jake walked into the office and found Ed Hughes at his desk. He smiled warmly, stood up and shook hands with Jake.

"Jake. I'm glad to see you. Dare I ask how things are going? How's Edie?"

"She's fine Ed. Thanks for asking. As for me, I'm alright, too. But I'm getting real tired of hanging around waiting for I.A.D. to figure out what the hell's really going on. As I've said before, Ed this whole thing is a set up. I hope you know me well enough to continue believing that."

"Jake, I have no doubt whatsoever that the allegations against you are bullshit. If I.A. does their job checking out, what's her name…Belinda, she may not look quite as innocent as she seemed. As for the stuff they found in your office, well…I don't know how it got there, but I don't believe you had anything to do with it. That having been said however, the whole thing still presents a problem, doesn't it?"

"Yeah, Captain, it does. But since I've had all this time to sit around and think about it, one thing is perfectly obvious. Somebody wants me away from the job and preoccupied with my own problems. Out of the loop. If I were here, working, what would I be doing? The answer's obvious. Digging into the Landers and Pritchard case. I know Homicide is handling that, but there's a lot more here than just the murder of a cop. Somebody's worried shitless about something. Something I might dig up if I was here working."

"Like what, Jake? Do you have anything specific?"

"To tell you the truth Captain, something interesting has developed that has caused me to re-think my initial suspicions a bit. Anyway, I can see you're busy so I'll get out of here and let you get back to work. Hopefully this will all be resolved soon. If I come up with anything I'll let you know.

"You didn't drive all the way in here just to reassure yourself that I was still in your corner, did you?"

"No sir. Actually I drove in to take Rene to lunch," Jake lied. He walked out of the office, patted the envelope he had in his inside breast pocket and thought, "I'll hold on to this just a while longer. Maybe Kelly's not the bad guy, er…girl, after all."

Jake walked down the hall to his office. When he walked in Lt. Gillis was sitting at Jake's desk. He looked up, saw Jake and got up immediately.

"Just keeping the seat warm, Jake," he said. "Good to see you. Are you back? Have you been returned to duty?"

"Don't get your hopes up pal. You're still the man. I just came in to take my, your secretary to lunch. Assuming you can spare her for about an hour."

"Hey, you're still the boss around here. I think so and most of the troops feel the same way."

"Most, huh? I can guess who the exceptions are. Anyway Gene, I'm anxious to get back. It's all up to I.A. now. They seem to be moving at their usual pace."

"You mean indiscernibly?"

"Exactly." Jake turned to Rene, seated at her desk. "Ready to eat?'

She got up and walked to Jake. Without saying a word she wrapped her arms around him and gave him a big hug. "It's so good to see you," she said. "Let's go before I get all emotional."

"Oh please, not that," Gillis said. "After you talked to her on the phone this morning, Kelly told me she had to go down to the ladies lounge to compose herself."

"Really. I'm touched." Jake said, eyeing Rene.

"Don't get carried away. My reasons for the extended stay in the lounge had more to do with 'the curse' than my conversation with you," Rene replied.

"Yeah, yeah. Tough exterior but underneath a real softy," Jake retorted. "Let's go."

They walked past Kelly's unoccupied desk on the way out.

"Where's Miss McBride this morning?" Jake asked.

"She's been coming in early. She checks to see if there's any adjutant stuff to do and then she teams up with the detectives working on the Asian girl case. She's been helping them a lot."

"Asian girl case? What's that about?" Jake asked.

"I don't know much about it, Jake. You'd have to ask Gillis," Rene replied.

They walked out of the station to the parking lot. As they walked to Jake's car a couple of detectives from the robbery unit spotted Jake from across the lot.

"Hey, Lieutenant. When you coming back? Our morale's in the tank. The place ain't the same without you." Both were grinning from ear to ear.

"I was thinking about coming back tomorrow but that was before I remembered that you two were still working here. And I use the term 'working' loosely," Jake replied. He waved and opened the door for Rene. They drove out of the lot.

Jake and Rene agreed the Village Café would be a nice quiet, out-of-the-way place where they could talk. Jake drove up Beachwood into the hills to the little neighborhood eating spot. Once inside and seated in a booth they chatted for a few minutes about the latest gossip around the station, Rene's kids, who the next Chief was likely to be and Rene's kids. Rene was a proud parent who loved talking about her kids and Jake enjoyed her motherly boasting.

Finally, Jake asked her how things were in the division.

"They could be better. Lt. Gillis is trying real hard but like I told you, he has a way to go. I know he means well; that's the only thing saving him from a full-blown mutiny. I have noticed though that after they had a chance to think about it, most of the detectives in the division believe you got set up. It's obvious to most of us."

"Well, thanks for that, Rene. I'm glad to hear it."

They finished their lunch and Jake drove them back to the station. As he pulled in the parking lot Jake asked Rene to do him a favor. "I don't want to go back inside right now but I need to talk to Kilgore. As soon as you see him, ask him to give me a call. Either at home or on my cell phone. As soon as possible, O.K.?"

"No problem Boss. I'll have him get hold of you right away."

"Thanks. See you soon. Take care of those kids," Jake said.

"You know it. Thanks for lunch."

Jake waved and drove off.

Fifteen minutes later Jake's cell phone rang and Kilgore was on the other end.

"Hey, Jake, they just announced the new Chief. It's Walter Burnett. I can just imagine how pleased you are."

"Shit!" was all Jake could muster up.

"Anyway, what's up Lieutenant? Rene said you wanted to talk to me."

"Dave, I'm going to need your help. A lot of things have developed that I'm not inclined to go to I.A.D. with. I'd like you to look into a few of them for me. Can you do that?"

"Name it Jake. Whatever you need."

"Let's meet somewhere. I don't want to discuss this over the phone."

Twenty minutes later Jake and David Kilgore were drinking coffee in the parking lot of a small donut shop on Santa Monica Blvd. Jake told Kilgore about his suspicions regarding Marquez. He also told him about Kelly's relationship to Andy, the note she'd taken from Landers' apartment and the conversations they'd had since then. Jake told Kilgore that he frankly wasn't sure about Kelly but that he had to admit Marquez appeared to be a more likely suspect for planting the false evidence in his office. Kilgore agreed.

Kilgore also agreed with Jake that if Marquez was the bad guy it was at somebody else's direction. He would have to be squeezed hard to find out who that somebody else was. Unless they could put Marquez in a serious bind he wasn't likely to tell them anything. They discussed various possibilities, none of which seemed likely to produce the desired results. Jake suggested Kilgore go through Marquez's personnel package to see if there was anything useful. Getting it might prove difficult, however. The packages were regarded as highly confidential and access was generally limited to the Division C/O. Finally, Kilgore told Jake he wanted to think about it. He had a few ideas he wanted explore. He told Jake he'd be in touch.

After they parted company, Jake drove towards home. He thought about calling Mitch when he got home. The devious mind of

Mitch could probably create a plot to persuade Marquez to cooperate. However, knowing Mitch it would probably involve jail time for both of them. "I'll work on this with Dave," he thought. "Better to leave Mitch out of it."

*****

Kilgore arrived back at the station and went to his desk where he sat browsing over follow-up reports and mulling over the situation. He was confident Jake was right about Marquez. Jake's assessment of Marquez was similar to his own. As fellow detective supervisors, Kilgore had seen Marquez in a variety of situations. In Kilgore's opinion, Marquez's integrity and leadership left a lot to be desired. Kilgore felt Ed was fully capable of taking part in a plan to frame Jake and Marquez had made no secret of his dislike for him. Except from Jake, of course. "What a slime ball," Kilgore thought. "He's overdue. I wonder if Kelly would like to help me with this?"

Late that afternoon Kilgore saw Kelly walking through the squad room. He beckoned her over and asked what she was doing there so late in the day. He knew she'd been coming in early; usually before anyone else was in. Kelly explained about her involvement in the Asian girls case. It had been one of those days. Lots of leads and, since she had nothing else to do, she decided she'd just keep at it. Kilgore advised her not to overdo it and she agreed.

As she started to walk away Kilgore said "Kelly, how about giving me a hand with something?"

"Sure, Dave. What is it?"

Kilgore motioned her to sit down in a chair next to his desk. The squad room was almost empty and the few detectives still working were across the room from Kilgore's section so they could talk without being overheard.

"Listen, Kelly. I spoke with Jake today and he filled me in on what's transpired over the past few days. I know about the note, your involvement with the suicide, Andy, and the concern that exists in Jake's mind about you. But something else has developed that appears to take the heat off you and place it squarely on Ed Marquez."

Kilgore went on to explain how Marquez had conveniently arranged to stay behind during the squad meeting. When he finished she looked at him, anger apparent in her eyes. "That son of a bitch!

He's a snake!"

"My thought exactly. We think alike. How would you like to help us get him?"

"Us. Who's us?" she asked.

"Jake and me. We're certain that Ed didn't set this up on his own. He doesn't have the brains."

"Or the balls," Kelly added.

"Yeah, that, too. Anyway, we need to get Mr. Marquez in a position to be persuaded to tell us what the hell is up. You can help. As the division adjutant, you can go into the C/O's office anytime without anyone thinking anything about it. That gives you access to the personnel packages."

"Yeah. I have a key. Jake gave it to me."

Kilgore went on to explain to Kelly what he wanted her to do. She quickly agreed.

*****

The next morning Kelly pulled into the station parking lot before dawn. The bag lady was early this morning. She was sporting a new hat, one she had found the night before. The old fashioned pill box was tilted at a jaunty angle over one eye and she moved alongside the station with a definite stagger in her gait. She must have had an especially good night as she was pushing a relatively new shopping cart, one front wheel wobbling and squeaking. Kelly waved the old lady over and handed her a dollar bill. It was half past five. Plenty of time for her to proceed with the plan she and Kilgore had put together the night before. She wasn't sure there was much to be gained but she was glad to be doing something that might help. The fact that Kilgore trusted her enough to include her in the effort lifted her spirits appreciably. The fact that Jake didn't know of Kilgore's decision was okay with her. At least for now. He'd realize soon enough that she was on his side. Apparently he hadn't yet gone to I.A.D. with the letter. She wondered why, then let it go. Right now other things occupied her thoughts.

The detective squadroom was silent and almost dark, the only light from a desk lamp at one side of the room. Kelly went straight to Jake's office and to the desk. The personnel files were not there, where she'd seen them the day before. She began searching the file cabinet. Nothing there. She stood in the middle of the room, one hand under her chin and looked around the office. There, under a chair in the corner, a cardboard box. She pulled open the top and found the files stacked inside. She rifled through them, pulled Marquez's from the stack and moved to the copy machine at the other end of the office. It took almost ten minutes to copy the contents and then return the file to the box and refasten the top.

Still no one in the squadroom. She decided to check Marquez's desk. She walked quickly across the room and sat in his chair. She and pulled open the top drawer. There was nothing of any consequence. Just the normal pens, pencils and paper clips, a newspaper clipping a few months old and notes scribbled on the odd pieces of paper. Files, follow-up reports, his time book and various department forms. She thought briefly of copying some things, but after looking over at the clock she realized she was running out of time. It was almost six thirty and detectives would begin arriving by seven.

She went rapidly through the rest of the drawers, down to the last one on the bottom right side of the desk. It was locked. She pulled the drawer directly above it all the way out and reached in and tried to jimmy the locked drawer from the inside, to no avail.

"Oh well," she thought. "Maybe next time."

She looked around the room. "What else?" she asked herself. She thought for a moment. "His locker." She hurried back to Jake's office where the divisional key box was located. The box had a master key for all the lockers in the division. Expecting to find it locked, she nevertheless figured it was worth checking. She walked in the office and there was the door to the key box standing open. Hanging in the lock was a ring of keys. "Good old Lieutenant Gillis. He's not too swift but he means well."

Kelly quickly removed the master locker key and dashed out of the office. She took the stairs up to the locker room two at a time. When she reached the second floor she realized she had no idea which locker was Marquez's. She ran back down the stairs to Jake's office and looked at the list on the inside of the key box door. "Number 89," she gasped as she turned and ran back up the stairs. It only took her a minute to locate the locker and open it.

"I hope this is worth the heart attack I'm about to have," she mumbled to herself, her heart pounding in her chest. She began looking through the items on the top shelf. Mostly papers, some uniform accessories, shoe polish, a rag. She shuffled through the papers. Phone messages, mostly, business cards and a bank deposit slip. The name on the slip wasn't Marquez's, however. It was someone named Denise Tucker. $2,000.00 had been deposited in her account, bringing her balance to a nice, fat $11,889.00. "Lucky her, whoever she is," Kelly thought.

"Wait a minute. Denise, Denny. Could be." Ed, Mr. Happily Married Man, Marquez had had a girlfriend for years whom he bragged about to all his cronies. Kelly, definitely not one of his cronies, had nonetheless been subjected to his 'macho man' ranting about 'Denny,' the hottest broad in Hollywood.

"It's got to be his girlfriend. Where does she get that kind of money?" Kelly wondered. "I seem to remember Ed saying she was a waitress or a hostess, something like that." Kelly thought about it for a second and then put the slip in her pocket.

Meanwhile, Ed Marquez pulled into the lot, parked and walked toward the station back door, altering his route slightly to confront the old lady.

"Hey you crazy old bag" he said," Go crawl back in the alley where you belong!" The old lady's mere presence rankled Marquez. Whenever he saw her around the station he made sure to give her a hard time; not that she ever gave any indication that she cared.

"Well, what else might we have here," Kelly said in a whisper as she felt around the back of the locker shelf. She pulled a rag to get it out of the way and when she did a small object fell to the floor. She picked it up and found it was what appeared to be a cheap earring. "Must be something Ed wears when he dresses in drag," she laughed. She stuck it in her pocket along with the deposit slip.

She looked at the clock on the locker room wall. "Better get out of here. If any of the guys find me here it might be hard to explain what I'm doing in the Men's Locker Room." She hurried out and back down the stairs. She returned the key to it's hook and walk quickly to her own desk. She sat down just as Marquez walked into the squadroom. He stared at her for a moment before saying:

"Early again Kelly? What are you trying to do, make points with the lieutenant?"

"No, he already loves me. I just came in for a few things and to drop off a note to Gillis. I'm taking an overtime day." Kelly held up a piece of note paper. Marquez stared at her for a moment and then with a nod turned and walked away. Kelly took a deep breath. She got up, put the note on Gillis's desk and headed for the door. Two steps from the door, she heard her phone ringing and ran back to grab it.

"Mc Bride." A pause and then, "what do you mean she's gone?" Edna, Song's house mother, was calling, ranting that Kelly did not have authorization to take her today. "Calm down, Edna, we didn't pick her up. How long has she been gone?" A pause and then, "have you called her case worker?" Kelly assured Edna that she would notify the squad and they would find Song. "And please call me if she comes back."

Frustrated with this new development, Kelly picked up the phone and called Mitch.

Mitch absent mindedly reached over and put his hand on the old dog's back and began rubbing her fur. He stared out over the bay watching a sleek, black cormorant dive and surface, dive and surface after the small silver minnows that abounded in the waters this time of year. His mind played at what information they had about Jake's problems. He reached down into the cabin and held the drawing of the other man the Chinese artist had drawn from Song's description and let his mind wander.

Child porn in Jake's desk, the girl that accused Jake worked at a porn, legal, but porn none the less, studio. Said studio had the little weasel as a front man and who knew who really owned it. Kelly says all the photos were of Chinese, or at least Asian, kids. The boat and the dead owner in King Harbor and the minister who wasn't a minister. Two dead detectives who apparently were trying to shake down Arlo. Arlo probably abusing his son who's Kelly's half brother, and Kelly Arlo's step daughter. He had to admit that way deep down inside he held a little doubt about Kelly, hiding the suicide note was stupid, knowing her need to connect with her mother made sense and still…

Mitch picked up a piece of 180# sand paper and began working it back and forth over the ash and mahogany tiller, bringing out the grain of the two woods, the maple and honey colors standing out against the bronze fittings. His mind wandered to the Montini connection. Jake said the FBI agent mentioned a tie between Arlo and the family. Mitch shook his head, didn't make sense, the old uncle would never be involved in kiddie porn. Anyway all his interests were on the East Coast. It just didn't fit. The phone in the cabin began ringing, interrupting his thoughts.

"You've reached the boat," Mitch said.

"Mitch, it's Kelly. Pick up the phone if you're there."

"Hey Kelly, what's up?" Mitch asked.

"I didn't know you had an answering machine."

"I don't"

"But, what, oh never mind. Listen, Song ran away and I have to meet Kilgore and I'm worried about her and ..." Kelly's voice trailed off.

"How do you know?" Mitch asked.

"How do I know what?"

"That she ran away," Mitch answered.

"The house mother called the station, wanted to know if we took her with out authorization. She's been gone for at least eight or nine hours."

"Yeah, but how do you know she ran away?" Mitch asked again.

"Oh, well I thought about that, that somebody grabbed her. Doesn't work. How would they know where she was? And Edna says Song took money out of her purse, almost fifty bucks, and she's good at getting away, remember. She got away at King Harbor."

"Yeah, well the way you talked about the kid she didn't sound like a thief, do you think?"

"No, she isn't but she's, I don't know, scared and..."

"Look, Kel," Mitch said, interrupting, "she probably did run away. What do you want me to do?"

"I can't miss this meeting with Kilgore. Would you nose around where they found her the first time? Over around Sunset near La Cienega? I talked to the squad and all they can do is put it out as a watch report. They're satisfied she's a run away," Kelly said.

"O.K. Kelly, I'll snoop around. What's the meeting about? I haven't talked to Jake since yesterday."

"Oh, I can't tell you right now. I'll talk to you later. I've got to go, O.K.?" Kelly hung up with out waiting for an answer as Mitch said:

Mitch sat there for a few minutes staring at the piece of sand paper he was holding and then stood up, grabbed his leather jacket and giving the dog a pat said:

"Good girl, watch the boat, I've got to find a little girl." The dog wagged her tail and settled down on the cabin roof and dozed contentedly in the morning sun.

*****

Kelly got up and made her way to the station parking lot. She got in her car and removed the copied personnel file from under her jacket. She took the earring and deposit slip out of her pocket and set them on the seat. She glanced at her watch. Ten after seven. She had plenty of time before meeting with Dave Kilgore.

As she pulled out of the station parking lot she saw the old bag woman. She was sprawled out on a bus bench. The newspaper covering her was moving slowly up and down to the old lady's breathing.

As soon as Kelly got home she called David Kilgore and told him what she'd managed to find. She told him she had the personnel file copy which she was going to go through as soon as they got off the phone. When she told him about the deposit slip he quickly confirmed that Denise Tucker was, indeed, Marquez's girlfriend 'Denny.' "The guy can't shut up about her. He's going to blow his marriage over this Bimbo. I'd bet on it," Kilgore said.

"Well, if she's got the big bucks…" Kelly kidded.

"She hasn't got any bucks. She's a waitress. Ed says she's all body and no brains."

"Unless she's a hooker, of course," Kelly offered.

"I don't think so. I met her once. I don't think she's the type. Maybe Ed's depositing money in her account. Then the question becomes 'where does he get that kind of money' and in love or not, why would he put it in her account?"

"To hide it from the little woman," Kelly said.

"That's hell of a hunk of change for a cop to be stashing. I doubt if he earned it working off-duty jobs."

"Off-duty jobs. Ed Marquez? He barely manages the on-duty job the city pays him for. That guy wouldn't work a second job if his kids needed shoes."

"You're right Kelly. Therefore…meet me at Little Joe's about four-thirty. I don't want to talk about this on the phone. Bring the slip and the earring along. I'd like to look at them."

"I don't think the earring's anything, Dave. It looks cheap."

"Well, bring it anyway. I want to look at it," Kilgore said.

"Okay, see you at four-thirty."

Kelly got to Little Joe's early and was waiting when Kilgore arrived. Kilgore looked at the deposit slip and the earring. The earring in particular seemed to pique his interest.

"Kelly, did you notice the bent prong on this? It looks like there were two others that have broken off. My guess is they held a stone of some sort. What do you think?"

Kelly looked closely at the earring. "You're right. There must have been a stone. I wonder what kind."

"I never noticed before but you two make a lovely couple."

They looked up to see Jake standing a few feet away.

"Hi boss. Sit down. I forgot to tell Kelly you were going to meet us here." Kilgore apologized. He had forgotten.

"It's okay Dave. That is, if it's okay with Jake."

"Listen Kelly. Dave called to tell me what you've been doing. Helping him...helping me. It was his idea to ask you to help. I'm glad he did. After what I've learned about Marquez and his actions on the day of the squad meeting, well..."

"Thanks Jake. But I'm probably not going to be able to help much longer. I took today off to avoid I.A. and I haven't answered my phone or checked my answering machine for the last thirty six hours. But they'll catch up with me, probably sooner rather than later."

"Don't be so sure, Kelly. I still have the letter, haven't called I.A. yet. You have a few more days. I'm going to have to hand it over at some point but I'd prefer doing it along with the solution to this caper, including the murder of Landers and the identity of any other crooked cops."

"Speaking of which," Kilgore interjected, "let's discuss how we're going to nail Marquez. Here's what we have so far, Jake." Kilgore showed Jake the deposit slip and the earring while Kelly described where she'd found them. Kilgore pointed out the broken prong and the likelihood there was a stone in the earring. Jake told them he also knew about Denise Tucker. Jake had had a run in with Marquez over her several months before. Marquez had been spending extended lunch hours with her at her apartment, sometimes being gone for several hours. Jake had advised him to knock it off and Marquez had gotten indignant, going so far as to tell Jake it was none of his business. Jake advised Marquez that the city paid him for working eight hours a day and that made it his business. Marquez realized he'd taken the wrong approach and tried to appeal to Jake's emotional side, explaining that he was deeply in love. Jake advised him to 'be in love' on his own time, not the department's.

"Okay, we all seem to agree that Ed's probably the number one suspect. If he stashed the stuff in my office he did it for someone else. He doesn't like me much but he hasn't got the imagination to dream up and carry out something like this. He'd just go out to the parking lot and slash my tires or something if he was that pissed off."

"I agree," Kilgore said. "But who'd put him up to something like this?"

"Dave, I'm convinced this is connected to the burglaries Landers and Pritchard pulled off that got them both killed. They ripped off the wrong house, the wrong guy and paid for it. It looks to me like the wrong guy was Arlo Calarasi."

"Arlo," Kelly said. "Why Arlo?"

" The letter you gave me, Kelly. What did Landers have in mind for that? My bet is it was blackmail. Obviously he and Pritchard found the note when they burglarized the house. They broke in, wandered around and found your step brother, Andy. He'd left the note for Arlo and your mother. Landers, being the brains of the operation, saw an opportunity to get a few dollars out of Arlo by revealing the contents of the letter in which his own son accuses him of sex abuse. He must have called Arlo, told him what he had and when he met with him, Arlo killed him."

"Seems strange that Arlo would kill him, if he did, without getting the note first," Kilgore observed.

"Yeah, I agree, Dave. But given the condition of Landers' body, the indications that he was tortured pretty sadistically he…wait a minute. What if Landers was killed after he gave up something else he had; something else he took during the burglary? Maybe he was saving the note to use later."

"This all sounds possible, I guess. But I never pictured Arlo as the kind of guy who would do anything as drastic as this, as drastic as killing someone. Especially a cop. I mean, he's got a bit of a mean streak that I've seen from to time but killing someone…I don't know,"

Kelly said.

"Well, I don't either," Jake replied. "But I'd bet Arlo's on one end of this little plot and Ed Marquez is on the other. And, there's obviously someone else in the middle. Marquez is the guy we go after first. One way or another, he's going to lead us to whoever else is involved. My bet is it's Walter."

"So where do we go from here?" Kilgore asked.

"Kelly, I want you to go back through all those burglary reports and see if there were any earrings reported stolen that match the one we have. Remember, there was a stone of some sort, so any earring that had a stone of any significant value is worth checking out. Dave, you and I are going to have a little talk with Denise. But before we do I'm going to call a friend of mine who works for the I.R.S. With a little subtle pressure, perhaps Miss Tucker will tell us where she got all that money. Marquez, I'm guessing."

"Okay, boss. I'll start going through the reports as soon as I get back to the station. Oh, by the way, I have Marquez's personnel file in the car. Well, copies of it anyway. The actual file is back in the C/O's office. Do you want it? I went through it and nothing jumped out at me. All the usual stuff, minus commendations, of course. Ed hasn't exactly been a rising star, career wise.

"Yeah, I'd like to look at it. Maybe there's something in it that would be helpful. By the way Kelly, ask Rene to make me a copy of the commendation for Boogie Newton, will you? I'd like to look at it."

"No problem, I'll get it and bring it the next time we meet."

"Thanks, both of you. I appreciate your help."

They left the restaurant after Jake paid the bill. In the parking lot they chatted briefly before Kelly left.

"When can you go with me to see Denise, Dave?" Jake asked.

"How about tomorrow morning? I don't have much going until the afternoon."

"Sounds good. How about 8 o'clock at my place? Denise lives out on the Westside."

"I'll be there," Kilgore replied.

Chapter 33

Mitch pumped the brakes on the old Mustang as it gathered speed on the downgrade of the 405 freeway approaching the 5, cursing under his breath. He had to get the brakes fixed; his car was becoming a death trap. He swerved across two lanes of traffic, cutting off an old man in a Mercedes and barely making the off ramp to the 5. He accelerated into the traffic pattern, ignoring the loud blast of the semi's horn. He looked down at the list on the seat beside him as he headed into the San Fernando Valley.

There were fourteen bookstores, adult entertainment as they were, oh so politely called. First on the list was one just off the freeway on Roscoe Boulevard. He turned right at the end of the off ramp and went under the freeway, looking to his right. The store was only a half block down Roscoe, the front painted in bright blue and yellow colors with a large red sign announcing: Videos! Rent or Buy! And 'adult toys' in smaller letters. Mitch found a parking place a few doors down and sat in the car for a minute to gather his thoughts.

He didn't think for a minute that Song had run away. Unless Edna the house mother was a witch and was going to cook the little girl, there was no reason. And if she had split, well, she seemed able to take care of herself. What made more sense to Mitch, what his gut told him was that she had been snatched by the bad guys and the porn stores were the best lead. They sure as hell wouldn't take her back to King Harbor.

Mitch shrugged his shoulders. There were a lot of ifs in this deal and checking the porn outlets seemed as good a way to start as any. Jake and Kilgore and Kelly were off on their own and Mitch felt a little left out.

He climbed out of the old convertible and pushed through the heavy velvet curtains into the sex shop. He stood there a moment, letting his eyes grow accustomed to the dark and his nose to the smell, a sweet thick odor, somewhat akin to incense. In the center of the large room was an elevated counter with a very fat man seated on a stool surveying the few customers browsing through the videos arranged by subject matter on shelves branching out from the center. The fat man had curly red hair and a perfectly round face that he continually wiped with a damp cloth. He stared at Mitch with no expression in his eyes. Mitch nodded and began walking around the store, stopping to pick up and look at an occasional video.

The covers pretty much revealed the contents of the tape inside. Wonderful artistic expression. A woman on her hands and knees with her large stern facing the camera and looking over her shoulder with an inviting smile. The title: Butt Buddies. Another cover had two nude women in an embrace, titled Fur Bidden Love.

After fifteen minutes Mitch walked up to the raised platform.

"How ya' doing?" Mitch asked the large man who appeared to be in his mid forties. He gave a brief nod and pulled a stick of red licorice from a jar and began chewing on it without a word. A dribble of red spittle seeped into the creases of fat on his face.

"Good, good. Looks like you're doing OK," Mitch continued. "Listen do you have any other rooms. You know, any more special films or even stills. Something a little more exotic, shall we say?" The man just stared. Mitch looked around the room and pointed at four doors that were adjacent to one anotherat one end of the room. Each displayed a picture of a scantily clad woman.

"Like what's behind those?"

"Live, behind a window, three bucks for three minutes," the man grunted.

"Uh_ how old are they?" Mitch paused. "I uh, I'm looking for, well, youth, the innocence of youth. You know? I mean you get my drift?"

"You a cop?" The fat man asked.

"Yeah. Yeah I'm a cop. But we have needs too." Mitch answered. The man grunted again and waved his hand in dismissal. "We don't do that stuff. Go to Sweden."

"Thanks pal, I'll do that." As Mitch turned to go he said over his shoulder, "that candy is very fattening, if you haven't noticed.

As Mitch pushed through the door the obese man reached under the counter and picked up a phone.

It was noon and Mitch was half way into the valley now. He had crossed five stores off his list with about the same results as the first one. They were all set up pretty much the same.

Lots of videos, four or five live girls behind doors and, in the last two stores, hand cranked viewing machines with a sign announcing 3-D movies. Twenty five cents for two minutes. Each of the stores had several men sitting at the machines slowly turning the little handle on the side, faces pressed into the viewfinders. And every two minutes scrambling in their pockets for another quarter.

Mitch pulled up to the next location on his list. It was a large building split into two businesses. On one side a beer bar, the other the video store with the same color scheme as the others. A sign announced parking in the back. Mitch pulled in and walked around the side of the building and into the beer bar. There were only two patrons. Two old men sitting several stools apart and a woman behind the bar reading a gossip magazine. Mitch took a deep breath. He still loved the smell of these old neighborhood bars. Stale beer, tobacco smoke and Lysol all mixed in perfect proportions. He looked around and decided this was just what it looked like. A local watering hole and nothing more. He gave the woman a thumbs up and walked out and went next door to the porn palace.

It was the same set up. Seven or eight customers, plus whoever was behind the doors with the live entertainment. The raised platform with a young man standing up leaning on the counter watching the forlorn men browsing for something that really didn't exist . The young man's head was shaved bald and he had what appeared to be a necklace made of large ball bearings around his neck. It looked tight enough to constrict his breathing. He wore a pair of dark sun glasses that, given the subdued lighting in the room, must have rendered him close to legally blind.

Mitch, after perusing the same material for ten minutes, decided on a slightly different approach. He walked up to the young man and held a ten dollar bill in his hand, resting on the counter. He looked up at the man who reached out and took hold of the bill. Mitch didn't let go.

"I'm looking for something a little out of the ordinary. Think you might be able to help me?" Mitch said.

"Fag stuff in the corner over there," the young man said pointing with one hand and
tugging on the bill with the other.

"No, not that. Not whips and chains either. I'm looking for, oh_ art. Yes art, the study of the young. The vibrancy of youth. Do you understand? I would pay dearly for what I'm looking for. Dearly!" Mitch tried to talk an octave or two higher.

The young man looked around and then leaned across the counter.

"That's serious shit man, you gotta be careful, ya' know?" Mitch nodded and released the bill and reached into his pocket and put another ten spot on the counter. The young man scooped it up and nodded. "Go have a beer. I gotta make a phone call. Come back in fifteen minutes, OK?" Mitch nodded and said:

"I'll just wander around here if it's all right with you."

"Sure. It'll be a couple a minutes," the man said with a smile.

A half hour went by and Mitch was beginning to think he'd drawn another blank when the man at the raised counter motioned him over. Leaning over the counter he said in a quiet voice:

"Outside, in the rear parking lot. There'll be a little guy named Elmo. He's driving a Buick, a gray Buick. He can help you." The young man straightened up and looked away.

Mitch headed out the front door, feeling the old .38 pistol snug up against his back. He stood in the sunshine for a minute looking around, letting his eyes get used to the light. Nothing seemed amiss and he walked around the building past the beer bar and into the parking lot. The gray Buick was parked at one end of the building, the back bumper close to the wall. A small, non-descript man in his late forties leaned against the front fender. He was wearing a sort of Alpine hat with a feather and a rather bright blue sport coat. He looked as though he should be sidling up to someone at the racetrack, touting a winner. Mitch nodded to the man and walked toward him:

"You Elmo?" The small man nodded and said:

"Yeah, I specialize. You interested?"

Mitch nodded and patted his back pocket saying:

"Yes, you might say I'm a connoisseur and I'm prepared to pay if the quality is what I'm accustomed to."

The man looked around the parking lot and then motioned to the back of the Buick.

"Take a look-see. I think you'll like my product. Keep it in the trunk, you understand." As he spoke he moved to the back of the vehicle and opened the deck lid. Mitch moved around beside the man and looked into the trunk. As he bent over, time stopped and the earth spun away from beneath him. A comfortable blackness followed the hard, sharp pain to Mitch's head.

Chapter 34

"Yah fuck!" Tony slapped the large Russian across the face. Boris stepped back and rubbed the side of his face. He stared at the floor, mumbling.

"Bite, she bite me." He held up his right hand. "When I grab her she bite hand."

Tony looked over at the man sitting in the corner of the office.

"He hit the kid didn't he? That's where she got the bruise, right?" The man nodded. Tony turned back to the sullen Boris. "She's fuckin' merchandise. Five large tomorrow! And you put a mark on her." Tony raised his fist, "I oughta', fuck!" He walked over and sat down behind a desk and motioned to the man in the corner to come over and take a seat in the chair across from him.

The man stood and moved slowly across the room. He was huge. Well over six feet and in excess of two hundred and fifty pounds, everything about him was big his head, his hands. His ears were large and protruded from the sides of his head. His eyes, set a little too close together were black and hollow, lacking any expression whatsoever. His voice was surprisingly high for his bulk.

"She'll be O.K.., Tony. A day or two and you won't be able to see the bruise at all." He twisted his large head around and looked at Boris, "where'd you get him? Ain't he a Russki? How come Tony?"

"He came recommended. He's good for some things." Tony unwrapped and lit a cigar. He took a draw, blew the smoke into the air and then held the cigar and stared at it. "Vivi, I asked you to come out to the west coast because you're family and I can trust you." Tony paused and Vivi nodded slowly. Tony continued, "we have a good thing going out here. It doesn't interfere with anything my uncle may have an interest in. You understand?" Vivi nodded.

"The guy you grabbed. We need him to speak to us and tell us things he might not want to tell us." The big man sat and stared and then nodded again.

Tony stood up and walked around the desk and put his hand on Vivi's shoulder, "I would like you to stay out here for a week or ten days. I will be sure it is worth it for you. You will go home with your pocket full. O.K?"

"Sure Tony, you've never been known to fill your own belly alone. Whatever you say."

"As far as my Uncle. There is no reason to trouble him with this business. He's old and needs no trouble. Understood?" Tony said.

"Sure Tony, I understand," Vivi answered.

"Boris," Tony said, "look at the girl and sailor boy. Make sure they are still tied up." Boris walked over to the steel door against the far wall of the office, pulled back a bar that held it closed and opened the door. "And don't kick them around. I want him awake when we get back, you un'erstand?" Boris stared into the room and muttered that he did.

"Good, keep an eye on them. Vivi and I gotta go into the city," Tony looked at his watch, "we'll be back in about three hours." He motioned to Vivi and they left. Boris shut and locked the door and sat down and began to read a Russian newspaper.

*****

Mitch was becoming more and more agitated. Every time he tried to order a whiskey instead of the watery beer in front of him, the bartender with the blond wig would begin singing 'People' in a falsetto voice and dance 'Shuffle off to Dixie' to the other end of the bar. When he tried to wave the barkeep back he found his hands were crazy glued to the bar. He kept trying to scream but it seemed to stick in his chest.

Mitch slowly came awake, or more precisely came to, and felt the regret of having had a drink and throwing away his sobriety. It took a few moments to realize he'd had a 'drunk dream' and another few to have the feeling of relief that it was just a dream. He started to sit up and found he couldn't, and in trying his head began to throb painfully. He was lying on his side. As he became more and more aware of his situation he realized his hands and feet were tightly bound and a piece of tape was across his mouth. He opened his eyes and found he could only see out of one eye, the other being swollen shut. He also noticed that his ribs hurt like hell.

He lay there and took stock of his situation. It was not an unfamiliar circumstance. It was much like the old days when he would come to in a drunk tank with no recollection of how or why he was there. The last thing he could remember was walking towards that guy in the parking lot. Reno? Leeno? What the hell was his name? Beeno? He slowly moved his head around to look at his surroundings. A small amount of light was seeping down from a very dirty skylight a good twenty feet over his head. There was a metal fire door at the far end of the room and no windows. The room was bare except for some shelving against the wall, opposite the door. The walls were cinder block and very high. A sound came from a corner of the room. He turned his head in that direction.

The small girl was curled up in a ball with her hands tied in front of her. Mitch knew immediately that it was Song.

An hour later Mitch had pretty much given up any idea of getting loose. The duct tape seemed to be wrapped around his hands and wrists in several layers. The same at his ankles however a piece of line had been attached there. It stretched to his wrists and held him, his backed bowed, in a hog tied condition. He had tried stretching and pulling at the bonds for at least half an hour and nothing felt any looser. The skylight now emitted no light other than an occasional flash of headlights as a car went by on a nearby road.

Mitch's ribs hurt like hell where he'd been kicked, but the blows to his head had been glancing and done no real damage. His mind felt clear. He figured he and Song were in the cinder block building at the rear of the porn studio. The building he'd seen on his previous foray to the valley. He looked over at the dim shape of the little Chinese girl huddled in the corner. She was leaning against the wall with a blanket around her shoulders. As he stared at her a car drove by and Mitch could see her eyes, glistening black, staring at him.

"Look kid, it would really help if you could," Mitch whispered, "oh I don't know, call the cavalry, the cops or maybe untie me. I've run out of ideas here." Mitch twisted around and held his tied wrists in her direction. "I think we have a real problem, you and me, I don't think those people like us." Mitch stopped whispering as the sound of the metal bolt at the door scraped at the hasp. He closed his eyes and remained motionless.

"and don't kick them around, ya uner'stand." Mitch heard the voice from the other room and the reply from the second man, who stepped into the room briefly and then went back out. The light against Mitch's eyelids faded as the door was closed and locked again. He lay quictly absorbing thc voicc. Thc affcctcd, raspy quality, thc cast coast accent. He recognized the tone and pitch. "It's Tony, fucking Tony," he thought. He laid his head on the cement floor and pulled against the tape.

Mitch heard her before he saw the motion. Song was crabbing across the floor. When she was next to him she positioned herself so they were back to back. He could feel her small hands pulling at the tape around his wrists. He moved his arms as best he could to help. For five minutes she struggled with the bindings to no avail. Her fingers weren't strong enough, the tape too tight. Mitch looked over his shoulder at the girl who stared back at him, breathing hard through the gray tape covering her mouth.

And then she bent her head to the cement floor and began moving her face back and forth across the rough surface. For a moment Mitch thought she had lost it, thought she had become hysterical. Then he realized the little girl was trying to pull away the tape covering her mouth. And a few minutes later he felt her tiny teeth at his wrists chewing at the tape. It took less than three minutes and with a tearing sound his hands were free. He rubbed his shoulders and arms to get the blood flowing, sat up and pulled the tape from his ankles and then freed the girl. He put his hand gently to the side of her face.

"Good. You did good." He took her by the shoulders and moved her back to where she'd been sitting in the corner. "Shh. Just stay here. Let's see if I can find a weapon or something." The girl seemed to understand. Mitch lightly placed the tape back across her mouth to make it appear untouched. Then he began walking the perimeter of the darkened room. He searched as much by feel as sight. Metal shelving was bolted against one wall. Mitch counted eight high. He tried pulling one of the brackets loose but they were bolted too tightly and after a minute he continued feeling his way along the walls. He was getting edgy. At any time the thugs in the next room could come back and he was basically defenseless. He stood in the center of the room thinking. Nothing. There was nothing but the shelves and they were bolted together too well to pull apart.

He sighed and began a circuit around the room again, feeling along each shelf as he moved. On a bottom shelf, back in a corner he found a piece of plywood. It was about a foot square and slightly rotted. He held it in both hands and pulled it against his knee. With a soft crack the wood broke in half. He wedged that piece against a corner of the shelving and broke small pieces off several times to fashion a crudely shaped stake. He ran his fingers along the splintered wood trying to figure out how much of a weapon he had. It wasn't much but it would have to do. Now for the chance to use it, he thought.

Boris finished his newspaper, sat back in the chair and took a deep swallow from the vodka bottle he had in his jacket pocket. Boris was not a happy man. 'Sailor boy,' as Boris referred to Mitch, had caused him no end of trouble. In his mind 'sailor boy' was the reason Boris accidentally shot his cohort. Arlo and Tony had both lost respect for Boris because of his failure to remove Mitch from the picture. And of course the detective's head that was found in the bag, well, that wasn't his fault but it did reflect on his professionalism. As he sat reflecting, Boris was building a strong resentment against Mitch. He took another swig from the bottle and got up. He walked to the store room door, pulled the bolt open and looked into the room.

The girl was in the corner and Mitch was lying on the floor on his side, his eyes closed. Boris felt the gun in his back pocket to make sure it was secure and walked into the room. He looked again at Song. He then bent over Mitch, grabbed him by the front of his shirt and began pulling him into a sitting position.

"Up, you. Wake up you fuck." Boris shook the apparently unconscious Mitch.

The sharp plywood stake struck Boris in the throat, just below the adam's apple. Mitch pushed against the flat edge of the wood with his palm as hard as he could. His thrust was strengthened by fear as much as anger. He could feel the wood splintering against the small bones in Boris' neck. Boris grabbed at his throat with a wet scream and fell to his knees. Mitch kept pushing at the piece of wood. Boris grabbed Mitch's wrists, growling like an animal. Mitch felt the strength in Boris' hands and reached behind Boris' neck. With one hard push of the stake he drove the makeshift weapon deeper. Boris went limp and fell over on his side, exhaling his last breath.

Exhausted, Mitch got to his feet and walked over to Song who had been fearfully observing the struggle between the two men. He picked her up, hoisted her onto his right hip and ran to the doorway. He looked into the empty office and saw his old .38 pistol sitting on the desk. He scooped it up as he moved across the office and into the warehouse.

Seeing no one in the storage area, he headed for the large metal doors at the far end of the building, running for all he was worth. When he got to the end of the building he pushed open a smaller door built into the larger metal doors and walked through. He found he was looking into the parking lot of Blue Bird studios. Across the lot he saw the chain link fence and the gate to the street. A few tall poles with floodlights cast shadows on the lot.

Mitch began making his way across the lot towards the gate, trying to stay in the shadows. Halfway across the lot a voice shouted at him.

"Hey! Hold it right there." The squat man he'd encountered on his last visit came running toward him. He was carrying the same chain in his right hand, swinging it slowly. "Oh, you again," he said, a big grin on his face. Then, "what's with the kid?"

"Look pal," Mitch said. "She and I are leaving and my suggestion to you is to take your chain, shove it up your ass and get out of my way." The man was not moved.

"No way. You're comin' with me fuck face." The man moved forward as Mitch reached under his shirt and pulled out the revolver.

"I did my best to explain, stupid." Mitch, from five feet away, fired one round into the man's thigh. The big grin became a grimace as the big man dropped quickly to the ground, screaming with pain. He raised his hands in front of his face and begged Mitch not to shoot him again. Though tempted, Mitch turned, raced to the gate and pushed against it, shoving it open.

Still carrying Song, he walked quickly towards Roscoe. He stayed off the sidewalk as much as possible, walking in the shadows of the brush and small scrub pines. Roscoe Avenue was a block away and Mitch could see cars driving by in both directions. As he got within a few yards of the street he saw a large black sedan stop and signal for a left turn onto the street. Mitch faded back into the shadows of some bushes and waited for the car to make the turn and go past them.

Mitch looked around and got an idea. All he had to do was get across Roscoe and he thought he could find some respite, a place to hide, regroup and find Jake.

Mitch got to the intersection and looking both ways, ran across Roscoe and into the residential area. He shifted Song to his other hip. Up ahead of him he could see a small group, six or seven men, standing in front of one of the houses that lined the block. Mitch slowed to a walk and stopped about five feet from them. They stood staring at him. They were all wearing oversized starched and pressed khakis and Pendleton shirts.

"Remember me? I was in your neighborhood a while ago?" Mitch held the girl and waited.

"You got blood all over you, Ese'" The young man put his hands in his pocket and looked at Mitch.

"Yup." Mitch said, looking down at his shirt, "some assholes are trying to hurt this kid. I think they'll be here pretty soon. I don't want them to take her. They sell kids to perverts, ya' know, sickos."

"And what Ese'? You an Angel?" the apparent leader of the group said.

"Naw, if I was I'd fly away. Some things are just wrong. I could use your protection and a phone for just awhile."

"And you'd pay?" the young Mexican asked while the rest of his group stood listening. Mitch paused for a minute and then said:

"You don't want money. Not for this. But I would be in your debt." Mitch stared directly at the young man. "And I always pay my debts."

The man nodded, said something in Spanish to the rest of the men and motioned for Mitch to follow him. They walked up to the front of the house and through the front door. Several young Mexican women were playing dominoes and drinking beer. The home smelled of cooking, of boiling meat and onions and peppers and hot oil. The TV was on a Spanish speaking station and a plaster cast of Jesus on the Cross was mounted prominently on the wall above the fireplace mantle. The man said something in Spanish and the women went to Mitch. With soft voices they took Song from his hip and, while making a great fuss over her, went into the warm kitchen. The young man flopped into a overstuffed chair and motioned at Mitch to sit on the adjacent couch.

"There's the phone, Mister Angel," he said, gesturing. Mitch sat down and looked at the clock on the far wall. Ten thirty? It couldn't be ten thirty. It took Mitch a moment to realize the clock was one of those joke clocks that run backwards. It was one thirty in the morning. He dialed Jake's home number. After five rings, Edie answered:

"Hello?"

"Edie, it's Mitch. Is Jake there?"

"Oh Mitch, Hi. Yes, but he's asleep. He's exhausted. Could you call him back in the morning?"

"Umm, no, I don't think so Edie. It's, ah it's kinda' really important." Mitch paused. "Ah really important, Edie."

"OK, Mitch, I'll get him." While Mitch waited, one of the young men stuck his head in the front door and said something to his leader.

"Mitch?" Jake in a sleepy voice.

"Yeah it's me Jake. Got a kinda situation here." The young Mexican interrupted:

Your friends? They driving a black Lincoln?" And before Mitch could answer, "they come by twice now. They're looking pretty hard for you."

"Mitch?" Jake's voice slightly testy.

"Yeah, I'm sorry. Aah_ I got the kid. Song." Mitch said.

"You what? Where did....what time is it." Jake asked.

"Um, about one thirty. Look. This is a real mess. I don't have my car and I'm out here in the Valley and I need you to get out here quick and get us. Let me explain when you get here."

"Where's here? What kind of mess, not that I'm surprised. And what are you doing with the child? She belongs in protective services, not with you." Jake sputtered.

"Jake we are in the neighborhood across Roscoe from the porn studio. I'm a little banged up and I'm sitting in a gang leader's house. I don't have my wallet so, I can't take a cab. And protective services didn't protect her. She got kidnapped. So let me give you the address and will you get over here, pronto? "

"Mitch I told you . . .oh never mind, what's the address?"

Mitch asked the man for the address and then repeated it for Jake.

"OK. It'll take me a half hour. There won't be any traffic."

"Jake? You better bring a weapon. I think it's a little hot out here." Mitch suggested. He heard Jake mumble something as he hung up the phone.

*****

"Did 'ja see that?" Vivi asked nodding with his head to the driver's side window.

"What?" Tony asked.

"I don'no. Thought I saw something in the bushes. Probably a cat."

Vivi pulled the black Lincoln up to the gate of the Studio and beeped the horn one short blast. After a minute Tony opened the door:

"I'll get the gate. I don't know where that fuck is." He climbed out of the car and pushed the closed gate open. After the car pulled through he closed the gate and climbed back in the passenger seat. Vivi drove the car thru the parking lot toward the rear of the main building. Suddenly the headlights illuminated the squat man lying on the ground, holding his leg.

"What the fuck? Stop the car!" Tony jumped out and stood over the prone man. "What? What happened to you? What're you doing?"

"The bastard shot me," the squat man said.

"What bastard? Who the fuck are you talkin' about?"

"Same guy, boss. Same guy as a coupl'a weeks ago. He was carryin' a kid when he came around the corner." The man grimaced. "Came around the corner and I tried to stop him and he shot me in the leg. Shit!"

"How long ago?" Tony asked.

"What? Three, maybe four minutes. They went out the gate."

Tony turned and began running towards the cinder block building, waving over his shoulder to Vivi to follow. With a screech of the tires the Lincoln skidded up to the entrance at the same time Tony got there. Both men came through the door at the same time with guns at their side. They could see light coming through the open doorway of the office.

"Boris. Boris, you in there?" Tony yelled pushing Vivi in front of him. There was no answer and the two men made their way to either side of the office door. Tony motioned to Vivi:

"See what's up. I'll cover you."

Vivi moved into the room and then walked across and looked into the open doorway of
the storeroom. He looked back over his shoulder at Tony:

"They're gone. Well, Boris is here. But I think he's gone too."

Tony came to the doorway:

"Gone? What the... oh fuck!" He stood staring at Boris' body. "That asshole, I told him to be careful. Shit!" Vivi pushed Boris' body with his foot.

"He's pretty dead, Tony. What now?"

Tony was thinking quickly.

"OK. You said you thought you saw something on the street. Let's go back and see if it's them. They ain't gotta a car, they can't be far." Tony reached into a closet in the office and removed a short barreled shotgun.

"Here take this. We'll do 'em both if we have to. Oh, and tell numb nuts to get in here with some gasoline. He's only hit in the fucking leg, he can walk." Tony took a large black suitcase from the closet and began emptying his desk. Vivi moved quickly to the car, carrying the shotgun in his left hand.

Vivi drove around for a half an hour and was finally satisfied he wasn't going to find Mitch or the girl. He went west on Roscoe and turned right heading towards the studio. The gates were open and he pulled the big car back to the cinder block building and parked adjacent to the doors. Tony came out carrying the large suitcase and threw it in the back seat. The squat man limped behind him with a towel wrapped around his leg. Tony turned, reached into his pocket and drew out a roll of bills:

"Here, get out of L.A. somewhere and get in a motel. Then call the '507' and tell 'em where you are. I'll get a doctor to you there, O.K.?" The man nodded yes and took the bills.

"Wait a minute," Tony said and took the bills back and

pocketed a few and returned the rest. "Get going." He turned to Vivi:

"C'mon, we're going to clean this mess up. We gotta hurry now," Tony ordered, walking back into the building.

They walked through the storeroom area where stacks of videos filled the shelves and into the office. Tony had dragged Boris' body into the office where it was lying face up on the carpet. Tony picked up one of the two-gallon cans and began splashing gasoline over the corpse. Boris' mouth was half open and Tony made a point of pouring some of the liquid directly into the mouth until it spilled over onto the cheeks.

"There, you fuck. One last drink." Tony turned to Vivi, "grab that can and let's get outta here."

As they made their way through the warehouse, each of them splashed gasoline on the stacks of videos. When they got to the door, Tony lit a book of matches and threw it into a puddle of the gas. It lit with a small whomp and Tony swung the metal doors shut. They climbed into the Lincoln and drove onto the main thoroughfare.

"Where to Tony?"

"A pay phone. I'm gonna have Arlo meet us."

"The fire Tony, there'll be cops all over. Your uncle isn't gonna like that," Vivi said in a low voice.

"Naw, it'll be O.K. The building's gonna hold the fire inside and that video stuff'll burn good and hot. The place is under a separate lease, not tied to Blue Bird in any way. Dummy corporation. The owner of record's been dead ten, maybe eleven years. It's a dead end."

"What about Boris? They're gonna know he was burned up," Vivi said.

"So what? What are they going to know? Fucker sneaked in the country, got no records. As hot as that fire's going to be all they're going to find is his fucking teeth. All they are going to know is he was from somewhere other than these United States. No worries, I guarantee." Tony sat in thought for a moment, "and the kid? I don't think she ever saw me. She was always knocked out."

"O.K. Tony. Look here's a gas station, they'll have a pay phone."

*****

Mitch sat on the couch waiting for Jake. It had been twenty minutes since he talked to him on the phone.

"That blood, that all yours?" The gang leader asked. Mitch looked down at himself and shook his head no. The man nodded slowly:

"These kids they selling, all illegals?"

"Far as we can tell," Mitch answered. The young man nodded again and said nothing.

Mitch was trying to think through the evening. He wasn't sure how much to tell Jake. He didn't want to lie but on the other hand, he didn't want to get Jake in a compromising position either. Mitch shook his shoulders and stretched. The violence was finally touching him. Bringing up a lot of old stuff. He could feel it across his chest and seepimg into his mind. A long time and he still had that energy. Get him near the wrong situation and violence came a calling. Intellectually he knew it made no sense but still there it was. He could see the look on the Russian's face as he pushed the splintered wood into his throat, hear the gurgled growl. And the chain man, how is he going to explain that to Jake. 'So after I killed the Russki with a piece of wood I shot the shit out of mister fireplug with my old #38. Oh, well I was carrying it and when they snatched me they left it on the desk and I grabbed it as I was running away.'

He really needed more time to think than he had before Jake was going to arrive.

"Your friend is here." Mitch looked up at the leader.

"O.K., we're going to go now. Can I have a piece of paper?" He took the paper and wrote on it. "Here's my name and here's how to reach me. I have a debt to you." The Mexican nodded once and took the paper.

Song came out of the kitchen. The young women had given her a bath and dressed her in clean clothes. She was wearing a white peasant blouse and a flowered skirt with a pair of huaraches. Her black hair was piled atop her head, held in place with a small plastic broach. Mitch took her hand and they walked outside to Jake's waiting truck.

"Jesus, Mitch. What happened to you?" Jake seemed very unhappy. "I know I 'm not going to like the answer but fill me in."

"Well, maybe we better get out of the area first Jake. I don't want to push our welcome here." Mitch pointed at the group of men staring at the truck.

"Right." Jake said, pulling away from the curb, making a U-turn and heading towards Roscoe. Without looking at Mitch he said: "Now tell me what happened. All of it."

"It's kinda' involved but here goes. Kelly asked me to find Song. She said she ran away, but I didn't believe that and. . . "

"What do you mean you didn't believe that?" Before Mitch could answer both men turned to the sound of sirens.

Speeding down Roscoe were several fire trucks and behind them a unit car. At the intersection where Jake and Mitch were stopped the units all turned left and headed down the block towards the porn studio location. Above the treetops the glow of a large fire could be seen. The tar and shingle roof had finally caught from the heat of the base construction of metal. Jake looked at Mitch. Mitch shook his head slowly and with that silly grin on his face, he scratched at the side of his head.

“There it is,” Mitch said pointing down the street past the porn shop. It was after three in the morning and there was no traffic on the street, the only business open, a 7-11 across from Mitch’s old Mustang. Jake made a U-turn and pulled behind the car and turned off the truck. Jake turned in the seat, stuck a fresh toothpick in his mouth and stared at his friend:

“I know you are tired and you look like hell but you have to tell me what happened.” Mitch stared out the windshield. He wasn’t sure how much to tell Jake.

“Can’t it wait, just a while, Jake? I need to think and, besides, I’d just as soon not go over everything while she’s sitting here,” Mitch said, nodding over the seat at Song who was curled up in Jake’s jacket. Jake agreed.

They stayed for a few more minutes and then Jake drove them home. Mitch carried the sleeping girl into the house, much to the delight of Edie, who pulled the child into her arms and shooed the two men from the room. They left Song with Edie and drove back to the Valley to get Mitch’s car. On the way, Jake waited for Mitch to begin an explanation of the evening’s events. When he didn’t, Jake, exasperated, spoke up.

“O.K., Mitch. Let’s have it. I want to know what the hell happened.” Jake pointed at Mitch’s pants. “That’s blood. The kid looks traumatized, there’s a major fire and who the hell knows what else. Now fill me in.”

"Well, sure Jake. See, Kelly called me and asked me to look for Song who, she said, ran away. I didn't believe that. It just felt wrong, didn't figure. So, rather than jack myself around driving around Hollywood, I…" Mitch shifted in his seat. "I figured the best place to start was with the porn shops on the list. The people running them have something to do with these kids being brought here. I went…"

"Wait a minute, what list?" Jake interrupted.

"The list of porno shops we found that were connected to Blue Bird. You know, the whole corporate thing with Arlo."

"Yeah, O.K. Go on."

"I started going into them, one by one, trying to score some kiddie porn. I figured if someone said they had some and wanted to deal I could squeeze them about child prostitution. I mean, if they're selling that stuff they'd probably have a lead we could use, right?"

Jake nodded slowly. "Yeah, I guess. Interesting how your mind works." They pulled up and parked behind Mitch's car.

"What I figure happened is, I'm working my way through the Valley, going to each store. So, they wait for me to show up at this," Mitch pointed down the block, "this one. The manager tells me to wait, there's a guy that might have what I want. Then this greasy looking fuck walks in and tells me to meet him in the parking lot. He opens his trunk and the next thing I know, I'm taped up and lying in the dark."

"Tell me again why you didn't believe Song ran away," Jake said.

"I don't know. It just didn't make sense. But I've got a question for you." Jake raised an eyebrow:

"Uh huh, what would that be?"

"Why are you downplaying this Song thing? Everything you and Kilgore and Kelly are doing seems focused on Burnett. He and Arlo are joined at the hip. Arlo's running the porno studio and the kidde porn and selling kids to sickos. We get him and we get Walter. One falls and the other one goes with him. All you seem to want to do is get Walter."

"Mitch, Walter is the key. We pull Walter down and he gives up Arlo," Jake said.

"Maybe, but we're getting close to Arlo. Look, they're closing doors, cleaning everything up before we get there. That boat in King

Harbor, they drowned the owner…"

"Mitch, you don't know that. There's no proof," Jake interrupted.

"C'mon Jake, the guy picks up a bunch of kids off shore and a minister that isn't a minister picks the kids up and Song gets away and the guy drowns. Do you really think that's a coincidence?"

"No, you're probably right, but like you said, Redondo Beach P.D. has seen no evidence of any crime. It's a dead end."

"And Song? They snatched her from that so-called 'safe home' you guys stuck her in. How the hell did they find out where she was?"

"Walter's probably a good guess," Jake replied.

"Yeah, he probably is, now that you mention it," Mitch said, obviously thinking that over. "Anyway, they're cleaning everything up so there is no path to them. And you seem focused on chasing Walter."

Mitch lit a cigarette. He stared out the passenger window and then blew a stream of smoke into the night air. Jake broke the silence:

"Mitch. We are doing this thing the right way. As far as the kids go, the China Town Squad is working on that, so leave it alone."

Mitch kept staring out the window, "yeah, O.K."

"I mean it Mitch. You've been a great help, but it's time for you to back away. Go sailing. Kelly's going to need somebody to lean on. She's probably going to be prosecuted for withholding evidence."

Jake avoided telling Mitch that his investigative techniques left a lot to be desired and could ruin any case that Jake was trying to build against Walter and Arlo.

"Fine. Yeah, O.K. fine, I'll go sailing." Mitch reached for the door handle, "anything else?"

Jake's countenance took on an angry look. "Are you going to tell me what happened at the studio?"

"The Russian, the other one, was there along with two other guys I never saw. The kid got me loose and I, uh…hit him with a stick and we ran like hell. I guess the other two came back and torched the place to get rid of all the porn, kiddie porn. I suppose that's another dead end now, right?"

"Yes, for now. That's it?" Jake stared intently at his old partner.

"Yup." Mitch climbed out of Jake's truck, "I'm going to the boat and clean up and get some sleep. Let me know how it's going."

Jake watched Mitch climb in the old Mustang. After a minute of cranking, it started and he drove off. Jake shook his head. He didn't think his old partner was going to stop meddling. A deep sense of foreboding came over him.

CHAPTER 35

Mitch woke up after only a few hours sleep. His body was stiff and sore from the rough treatment at the hands of his kidnappers the day before. The sun was just clearing Saddleback Mountain as he climbed off the boat and headed up the dock to the shower. He stood under the hot water, thinking until it turned cool. He probably should have told Jake that he thought he recognized Tony's voice the night before at the warehouse. He should have told him about the other dead Russian and the squat little guy with a bullet hole in his leg, too. But the way Mitch figured it, that would just result in a lot of wasted time answering questions from a bunch of detectives that wouldn't accomplish as much as he could with a phone call.

After he pulled on a pair of worn jeans and a sweatshirt, he fed the dog and took her for a morning walk along the beach. Mitch worked out the details of what he was going to say. He got the dog back aboard and she settled down for her morning nap. Then he walked over to the restaurant a quarter block away.

"Hey Sherry," he said to the blonde waitress who'd been a fixture in the place for years.

"Morning Mitch. Are you going to have breakfast?"

"Naw, just coffee. Is the boss around?"

"Er…no, he's not going to be in today, why?" she asked.

"Well my phone's on the fritz. Thought maybe I could use yours," he said, handing her a ten dollar bill. "There's for the coffee, I don't need any change."

"Oh, you don't need to do that," she said pocketing the bill, nonetheless. "Sit over there. I'll bring you the phone."

Mitch looked at the clock on the wall. With the three hour time difference it would be a few minutes after ten in the morning on the East coast. He pulled a paper from his pocket and began dialing. It took twenty minutes for him to connect with the woman he was trying to reach:

"Hi. It's Mitch."

The soft voice sounded delighted:

"Mitch! God! How are you, arc you OK?"

"Yeah darlin', I'm fine and you, how are you?" Mitch asked.

"Great. Couldn't be better." They talked for a minute or two. Mitch told her about living on the boat and the dog and still being sober.

"So, haven't touched the stuff in a long time," he finished.

"Do you miss it?" she asked.

"Oh sure, once in awhile. You know the mind has no memory for pain. Listen I need you to do something for me."

"Sure Mitch, what is it?"

"I need your uncle to call me. I'm sitting in a little restaurant near the boat. I'm using their phone." There was a long pause and then:

"Well, OK Mitch. Give me the number and I'll see what I can do." He read off the number and then she said:

"Be careful. I don't need to worry about you do I?"

"No, no everything's fine. Look, I'll just sit here for awhile and wait. The waitress is letting me use the phone," Mitch answered.

"OK. Take care Mitch."

Ten minutes later the phone rang.

"Hello." Mitch answered on the first ring.

"Mitch?" The voice was deep.

"Yes."

"Hold on," and a moment later a different voice:

"Good morning."

"Good morning. It's been awhile. Thank you for returning my call," Mitch said.

"It's nothing." The voice quiet.

"There are some problems out here. I have a friend, a good friend. He has a problem," Mitch said.

"I have heard some things."

"I was a, an unwilling guest last night. I recognized one of my hosts as someone from a long time ago. May I speak frankly?" Mitch asked.

"As I know, you will anyway. Go ahead."

"This person I remember, and another I only know by name, have been involved in a business with children, pictures and more. They have a select clientele that desires children. I know you would not condone or tolerate these activities. I'm calling you before anyone. I have not told my friend of this."

"Do you feel this places me in your debt, this, this information?"

"Not at all. I think we can benefit each other. My friend is very stubborn and very skilled. He will find the truth of things quite soon. My thoughts are only that you, with all due respect, might wish to take some action to protect your good name. I only want to have these children put into my care," Mitch said. After the briefest pauses:

"Good, you are still the man I thought you were. Someone will be in touch with you shortly."

*****

Kelly arrived at the station at her usual time, 7:00 a.m. And as usual, the little bag lady was in her spot in the parking lot. "Well," she thought, "I guess Ed hasn't managed to scare her away yet. He's sure got a thing about her. I wonder why she bothers him so much."

Kelly thought about it as she walked in the station and back to the detective squadroom. Rene was at her desk going through the department mail that had come in earlier that morning. She was a remarkably efficient secretary, Kelly thought. Jake was lucky to have her. More than a few Captains had tried to get her to leave the division and come to work for them. She'd refused them all because of her loyalty to Jake. A loyalty that was returned in kind by Jake who trusted her completely and made her job as pleasant as possible. They were a good team. In fact, if Jake could have his way, he'd often joked, Rene would be the Assistant Division C/O. Her common sense and job knowledge made her well qualified. Unfortunately, her status as a civilian employee precluded that assignment.

"Good morning, Rene. Hard at it, I see."

"Well, when you've got to do your own work as well as you know who's…" she said, glancing over her shoulder in the direction of Jake's desk, where Lt. Gillis was sitting, reading the paper.

"Well, we all have our burdens…"

"Honey, this is more than a burden. If he comes up with one more goofy idea to add to my workload, I'm going to go in there and gangster slap that grin off his face. Then they can suspend me until Jake comes back to work."

"Speaking of our friend, can you run off a copy of the commendation Boogie got? He wants to take a look at it."

"It's right there in the 'to be filed' box on top of the file cabinet. Would you mind digging it out and running it off?" Rene asked, a slightly haggard look on her face.

"Of course," Kelly replied, as she grabbed the box and started to go through it. After a minute or so she found the letter. She ran off the copy and put the original back.

"Thanks, Rene. Guess I better get to my own desk and see what's waiting for me."

Kelly walked a short distance to her desk and began going through the few items she found in her in-box. Finding nothing of importance to take care of, she reached into her lower desk drawer and pulled out the copies of the burglaries that she and Jake had correlated with the address list they'd found in Lander's apartment. It reminded her of finding the letter Andy had written and the fateful decision she'd made to conceal it from Jake.

"Talk about your lapses in judgment," she thought. "That was a beauty."

She began going through the reports, searching for earrings on the 'items stolen' list. Three of the reports listed earrings however the description of one set clearly eliminated them from consideration. The other two looked possible. Kelly picked up the phone and called the first victim's residence. She wasn't home but the maid who answered said she'd have her call as soon as possible.

Kelly called the other victim, Dolores Davies, and found her home. As soon as Kelly told her who she was the woman asked if her property had been recovered. Kelly explained that she had what might be one of the earrings, minus the stone. The woman was clearly disappointed.

"I wonder if I might come over for just a few minutes so you could look at what I've got and tell me if it's yours." Kelly asked.

"Certainly dear," she replied. "Come right over. I'll be here."

"Thanks. I'll leave right now."

Kelly got a set of keys for one of the plain pool cars and left to go see the woman. It took her twenty minutes to drive up into the hills to the residence on Stone Briar Way. The lady she'd spoken with on the phone opened the door before Kelly was halfway up the walk.

"Good morning," she said. "I assume you're detective McBride, the woman I spoke with on the phone."

"Yes I am, Mrs. Davies," Kelly replied, removing her I.D. card from her purse and showing it to the woman.

"How nice. A lady detective. The force needs more women you know. We can certainly detect as well as any man, don't you think, dear?"

"No question about it," Kelly answered.

"Come in dear. I've had Clarice make a pot of coffee. We can sit outside in the courtyard. It's a lovely morning."

Kelly followed her through the house. It was furnished in Old English, matching the Tudor styling of the exterior. Kelly was very impressed.

"You have a beautiful home, Mrs. Davies," Kelly said.

"Thank you dear, but please call me Dolores. Mrs. Davies is far to formal and, besides, it reminds me of Mr. Davies. Someone I'd rather not dwell on," she said, opening the door to the courtyard and ushering Kelly through and over to an umbrella covered table with a glass top. They each took a chair and sat down.

"I'm sorry. Has your husband recently passed on?" Kelly asked in as consoling a tone as possible.

"Oh no, dear. The, pardon my language, asshole, recently left me for some woman he met over the internet. Can you imagine? The internet! How common can you get?"

"How sad," Kelly said. "I'm sure he'll come to regret that decision."

"My lawyer's seeing to it. He'll rue the day he went online. For the rest of his life, hopefully."

Just then the maid, Clarice, came out the door and into the courtyard with a pot of coffee which she served to the two women. As soon as she left Kelly asked Mrs. Davies, Dolores, to look at the earring . She took it from Kelly and looked at it closely.

"It looks like my earring setting . But it had a rather large ruby in it when it was taken."

"Yes, I know. That was reflected in the report. Whoever stole it apparently pried the stone out and probably sold it. But you're sure this is the setting?"

"Yes, quite sure. The earrings were very unique. They were designed by a jeweler in Beverly Hills. One of a kind. He threw the mold away so no others could be made," Dolores said proudly. "My former husband gave them to me on my fiftieth birthday."

"That's very nice. Can you tell me the name of the jeweler? I'd like to talk to him."

Mrs. Davies excused herself and went into the house for a few moments. When she came back she handed Kelly a piece of paper on which she'd written: Coronet Jewelers, 777 Rodeo Drive. She'd also included the phone number. "Here you are, dear."

Kelly thanked her and told her she was going to work on the case until it was solved. Kelly finished her coffee and excused herself. Dolores escorted her to the door and Kelly waved goodbye as she walked toward her car. As she got in and started down the hill she thought about the unique nature of the earring. If it was a one of a kind, it would really put Ed Marquez between the proverbial 'rock and a hard spot,' she thought, gleefully. How would he explain his way around that?

Kelly headed for Beverly Hills. The drive took about half an hour, traffic being what it is in that part of the Los Angeles area. She drove around the block several times before finally parking in a red zone and hanging the radio mike over the rear view mirror, the universal sign to the local meter maid that the vehicle was a police car and presumably on 'official business.' Kelly walked up the block to Coronet Jewelers and went in. The store was small but well stocked with what looked to Kelly like very expensive jewelry. At the back of the store stood a stocky, well dressed man whose appearance told Kelly he was a security agent rather than a jewelry salesman. The bulge in his jacket indicated to her he was armed. He smiled but remained where he was as a second man stepped from an office near where the security man was standing and approached Kelly.

"Good Morning. How may I help you?" he asked.

Kelly identified herself and told the man why she was there. He looked a little disappointed, obviously hoping she was a customer.

"I'm Roger Dubois. I own the store and design the jewelry. May I see the earring, please?"

Kelly handed him the earring and he examined it quickly. "Yes, I created this setting. Obviously there was a stone inserted in it when I sold it."

"Yes, I assumed as much," Kelly replied, a bit put off at the man's rather arrogant demeanor. "Was this and its' mate a unique, one-of-a-kind pair?" Kelly asked.

"Why…yes," he replied, somewhat hesitantly. "All, er…most of my jewelry is custom designed and unique."

"Including this one? Look, Mr. DuBois. I don't care one way or another but I need to know if there could be more than one set of these earrings."

"Well, there could be. I guess I could check."

"Do that, Mr. DuBois. I really need to know. Just between you and me."

"I'll be right back. Please wait here. Look around, you may see something you want. I'll give you a very reasonable price. And please call me Roger."

Roger went back to his office. Kelly looked over at the security agent who smiled at her. She smiled back and began browsing around, occasionally gasping at the prices on the displayed items. "There must be a million dollars worth of stuff here," she said to the agent.

"Around a million and a half, I'm told," he replied. "He caters to a very wealthy clientele."

"Obviously," Kelly observed. "Most of mine comes from the costume jewelry counter at the local discount department store. I guess I need a sugar daddy."

Kelly and the agent chatted for a few minutes before DuBois returned. He had a catalog of information regarding his store's inventory that he was perusing.

"Uh, I've checked my records and it appears I may have made

more than one set of these earrings," he explained, holding up the one Kelly had given him.

"How many more?' Kelly asked as she took the earring from DuBois.

"Well, twelve all together. Eleven more. I don't know how that happened," he said defensively.

"Your secret's safe with me, Roger. But in the future, when you tell your customer an item's one-of-a-kind, I'd suggest you make sure it is. 'Mistakes' like that can be bad for business."

"Yes, you're right. I appreciate your discretion, Miss McBride. I really do." All of the arrogance had gone out of his voice.

Kelly said goodbye and waved at the security agent who smiled back, obviously enjoying Rogers' attitude adjustment.

Kelly walked back to her car in time to see a meter maid completing a parking ticket and shoving it under the wiper.

"Thanks a lot," Kelly said. "I guess you missed the fact that this is a police car, huh?"

"Nope. But we ticket everyone here, in Beverly Hills," she replied.

"Well, good for you. Have a nice day," Kelly said before the meter maid did.

She drove off and headed for the station to talk with Kilgore.

The drive to the station was relatively quick, in spite of traffic. She parked in the lot and went inside, returning the keys to the pool car keyboard. She looked over to Kilgore's desk and saw that he was there. He was talking with one of the homicide detectives who worked for him. She went to her desk and began taking care of some paperwork, keeping an eye on Kilgore at the same time. The detective finally got up and returned to his desk and Kelly immediately called Kilgore on the com line.

"Kilgore," he responded.

"Dave, it's me, Kelly. I've got something I'd like to run by you when you have a minute."

He looked over in her direction and nodded. "I'll come by your desk in a minute, I need to make a phone call first."

Kelly went back to her paperwork and a few minutes later Kilgore walked up and sat down next to her desk. "What's up?" he asked.

She told him about her visit with Dolores Davies and to the

Coronet Jewelry store. "The only problem is the earrings weren't as unique as we hoped The jeweler admitted that he made twelve sets of them. He sold them as one-of-a-kind but they really weren't. My asking made him nervous as hell, too."

"I'll bet it did. So, they're not unique, huh? Well, Ed Marquez doesn't know that, does he?" Kilgore grinned at Kelly.

"That's true, he doesn't."

"Thanks Kelly. You do good work. I've got to call Jake. I'll tell him about the earrings. See you later." He got up and walked back to his desk, glancing over at Ed Marquez, who was on the phone.

"Probably talking to his girlfriend," Kilgore thought. "Well, stand by, Eddie boy. You've got a big surprise coming your way. Soon."

*****

At eight that morning David Kilgore had called Jake. Jake was already up and finished with the paper when the phone rang. He answered on the second ring and they spoke briefly, agreeing to meet at a coffee shop near where Denise Tucker lived, at ten. As soon as Jake hung up he grabbed his phone book and looked up the number of Richard Birch, a friend who worked for the Internal Revenue Service. In a few minutes he had Birch on the phone.

"Richard, this is Jake Reed. How are you?" The two men chatted amiably for several minutes before Jake told him why he'd called.

"Listen, I need a favor. I assume you're still well connected with your ring of tax evasion crusaders." Jake was referring to the fact that most successful I.R.S. agents had sources that kept them apprised of various schemes and schemers trying to avoid paying their fair share to Uncle Sam.

"You might say that," Birch replied. "I do my best to protect you, the honest taxpayer, from getting screwed by those who try to…"

"Yeah, yeah. I've heard that speech before," Jake interrupted. "Listen, Richard. Can you find out, unofficially of course, what the deposit history of someone has been? I have their bank name and account number."

"Piece of cake, Jake. When do you need it?"

"Right now."

"The banks don't open for another 45 minutes."

"Well then, how about in an hour?"

"I'll see what I can do. Give me your number and I'll call you back," Birch said.

Jake gave Birch the information on Denise Tucker and then gave him his phone number. Birch quickly recognized that the number wasn't a department line. "Where are you, Jake? I don't recognize that number?"

Jake explained that he was at home and then provided Birch with a hasty explanation of his situation. Birch didn't hesitate.

"Jake, I know you well enough to know that the charges are bullshit. If this info is going to help, well…I'll do whatever I can."

"Thanks, Richard. I appreciate that. We'll have to get together for a beer soon. On me, of course."

Birch agreed, assured Jake he'd get back to him as soon as possible and hung up.

True to his word, twenty minutes later Birch called back.

"Jake, Richard. Here's the information you asked for. Denise Tucker currently has a balance of $11,049.88. She has a steady history of deposits every two weeks over the past four years. Probably a paycheck. Usually about $600.00. Not exactly making the big money, is she? Anyway, about ten months ago she starts depositing large, well large for her, sums of money. Sometimes as much as $3,000.00. My source tells me the deposits are in cash and the last one was about a month ago. I did a social security number check and she doesn't show any other source of employment to account for the money. I checked to see if she declared the money she deposited last year on her tax return. She didn't. Interesting, hey?"

"Very. Listen Richard. This is real helpful. Can you hold off on confronting her about last year's taxes for awhile? She may prove to be very helpful if I can brace her first," Jake asked.

"No problemo. I've got plenty of cases on my desk and they're all bigger than this one, believe me. Just let me know when I can drop a dime on her and get her attention. O.K.?"

"Definitely. Thanks, Richard. I'll be talking to you."

Jake hung up and left to meet Kilgore.

Jake and Kilgore pulled into the parking lot at the same time and went in the coffee shop. After ordering, Kilgore said "Jake, I've got the information on the earring. Kelly found the owner in about an hour and she's already been out to speak with her. She lives up in the Hills. Very well-to-do. She was under the impression her earrings were one-of-a-kind. At least that's what her husband told her when he gave them to her. She told Kelly where her husband bought them and Kelly checked with the jeweler. He hesitantly admitted that he'd actually made twelve pairs, not one."

"Well, there's a real surprise. A dishonest jeweler," Jake said jokingly. "And in Beverly Hills, no less."

"Yeah, what's the world coming to?" Kilgore replied. "Anyway, Ed Marquez doesn't know they aren't unique. I had Kelly check the burglary report. Mrs. Davis, or something like Davis, the victim, said at the time that the earrings were unique and there were no others like them. So as far as Marquez knows, they are. That assumes, of course, that he read the burglary report."

"Well, before we talk to Ed let's see what his girlfriend can tell us. The more we can jam him with the better."

Jake told Kilgore about his conversation with Richard Birch. "The bank deposits stopped about a month ago. A few weeks after the last burglary. If Ed was involved in doing the burgs or just steering our two thieves to lucrative locations, he was certainly getting a share of the profits. That could explain the deposits in his girlfriend's bank account. It hides any incriminating evidence and Ed's wife doesn't get her hands on any of it."

"Yeah, and it makes Ed look like Mister Big in the eyes of his true love, Denise," Kilgore added. "He's probably feeling pretty smug right now. The money's safely tucked away and the two guys who can cop him out are dead. No wonder he's been so relaxed, lately. Things have worked out real nicely for Marquez.

"Yes, haven't they. Let's see if we can screw them up," Jake said with a grin.

They left the coffee shop and drove in Kilgore's police car the few blocks to Denise Tucker's apartment building. The front security door wasn't locked however an inner door allowing access to the building's residential units was. They entered the lobby and checked the resident list posted next to a phone hanging on the wall. They found Denise's number and Kilgore dialed it. After three rings a sleepy, female voice said, "hello" and Kilgore replied: "Hi Denise, David Kilgore here. I work Hollywood Detectives. I need to talk to you about something important. Can I come up or would you prefer to come down to the lobby?"

"What's it about?" she asked.

"I'll tell you all about it but I'd prefer to do it in person. Are you going to come down here or should I come up?"

The lock on the door buzzed indicating Denise opted to have him come up. She said "Apartment 311," and hung up the phone.

The two men walked through the door and climbed the stairs to the third floor. Her apartment was mid way down the hall. Kilgore knocked and after a moment Denise opened the door. Kilgore showed her his I.D. card and badge and she invited them in. She was dressed in a silk robe that did little to conceal her ample bosom and a stunning pair of legs. Ed Marquez hadn't exaggerated.

"I didn't get your name," she said, looking at Jake.

"Jake Reed," he replied.

"I thought you…, I mean do you work at Hollywood, too?" she said.

"You know I do, Denise. I'm sure Ed has filled you in on my situation."

"Ed, Ed who?" she replied, looking as innocent as possible.

"Let's cut the crap, shall we? Ed Marquez has been boasting about you for years. I won't repeat all the details. But most of the guys in the division feel like they know you pretty well, if you know what I mean."

"Well, maybe I do know Ed Marquez. I think he mentioned that you were in a lot of trouble. Suspended or something?" she said, still trying to look innocent.

"Not nearly as much trouble as you are, Denise," Kilgore replied.

"Me. I'm in trouble? For what? For knowing Ed Marquez?" she asked defensively. "I haven't done anything. Unless going out with a married man is a crime. He has a very unhappy marriage but he can't leave his wife. She's bedridden you, you know." Denise looked at them, obviously hoping for a nod of understanding.

"Yeah, right Denise. She's bedridden and I'm one of the Seven Dwarfs. Ed's wife is quite healthy. In fact, she works out regularly at the Academy gym. He's feeding you a line of bullshit, just like the line he's using on his other part time squeeze. You better face facts, Denise. You've been had. And now he's really put you in a tough spot."

"What do you mean? What tough spot?" she asked.

"Well, how about tax evasion for starters. How about receiving stolen property? My guess is that when we return here with a search warrant we'll find an item or two that was taken in a burglary. Has Ed given you any jewelry over the past few months?" Jake asked.

"Tax evasion! Stolen property! What are you talking about? I pay my taxes. I don't have any stolen property, at least not that I know about."

"Tell us about all the money that's been deposited in your account over the past year, Denise. Where did that come from? You've got over eleven grand in the bank on a waitress's salary. Some of which, by the way, you forgot to mention on your tax report for last year."

"Gifts, gifts from Ed. He deposited that money in my account."

"And left you hanging out to dry when the I.R.S. audits your statement. How nice of him. Of course from his point of view that's better than him having to explain it to the tax man; or his wife," Jake replied.

"What about other gifts, Denise. Has he given you any little trinkets?" Kilgore asked.

"He did give me a bracelet. He won some money playing poker at some casino and he spent it on me, on a bracelet. I'll get it." Denise left the room for a moment and returned shortly with a gold bracelet that she held out to the two men.

Kilgore took it and examined it carefully. "Looks like the real deal. The stones look like diamonds. If they are, this thing is worth plenty. There are at least twenty of them."

"What will you bet we can find that listed on a burglary report?" Jake said.

"You mean it's stolen?" Denise asked, looking slightly worried.

"Yes, Denise. In all likelihood. That's what we were talking about when we mentioned 'receiving stolen property.' Do you mind if we take this along so we can check it?" Kilgore asked.

"No, I guess not. What happens to me if it is stolen? Are you going to arrest me? Even if I didn't know it was stolen."

"That's up to you, Denise. If you tell the truth and don't try to cover for anybody, like Ed, for instance, you can come out of this unscathed. If you lie, you're probably going to jail. It's that simple. You decide," Kilgore explained.

"I won't lie to you," she said, tears beginning to well up. "I'm not a bad person. Really, I'm not. If Ed's breaking the law like you say, he didn't tell me about it. And if he gave me stolen stuff then he's a jerk."

"I'm glad you see it that way. Now, what else has he given you? Anything?" Jake asked.

Denise nodded and walked back to the bedroom. The two men followed. She began going through a jewelry box on her dresser, picking out several items. She handed them to Jake. "Most of these, I think. I can't remember for sure. There might be others but…" She began to cry. "I can't believe this is happening. Why did he do this? I thought he loved me."

"Take it easy, Denise. We all get taken in at one time or another," Kilgore told her.

"We have to go now. We'll check this stuff to determine if any of it's stolen and we'll let you know. O.K.?"

Denise nodded. "O.K."

As the two men prepared to leave Jake spoke to Denise, "listen, I appreciate your help. I know you're upset but don't call Ed. Things will work out much better for you if you don't. Do you understand?"

"Yes, I do. I hope you're right. By the way, did you say he has another girlfriend?"

"I'm afraid so, Denise," Kilgore replied.

"Bastard."

Jake and Kilgore drove back to the coffee shop and pulled into the parking lot. They sat in the car and discussed their next move.

"Well, now we've got something to go on," Jake said. "The first order of business is to check the stuff Denise gave us. When you get to the station, Dave, give it to Kelly. She can do that. She's got all the reports. And keep an eye on Marquez. See if he shows any sign that he knows what's up. As soon as Kelly's checked the reports and identified the items that are stolen we can brace Ed."

"I can hardly wait," Kilgore said.

The two parted, leaving in their respective vehicles. Jake drove home, thinking about their next move. A little before noon the phone rang.

"Jake, it's Dave. Good news. Kelly checked all the items and it looks like every thing but a cheap watch is stolen. She says some are positive i.d.s and a couple she's going to have to have the owners look at to be sure. Ed's been in the office all morning. I've been keeping an eye on him and he looks like his usual disinterested, uninvolved self. He doesn't appear to be aware that he's in deep shit, yet so I guess Denise hasn't called him."

"Good. It'll be a nice surprise, won't it? It probably wouldn't be a bad idea to call Denise and tell her how much of the jewelry she got from her boyfriend was stolen property. Point out to her that she's in serious jeopardy of being charged with 'receiving.' That ought to encourage her cooperation."

"Good idea. I'll do it right away. How do you want to go about confronting Ed?" Kilgore asked.

"Well, I've got an idea. I know that if I call him and tell him I want to meet with him he'll either refuse or come up with some excuse to avoid me. But I think he'd respond to Fuzzy Lander's mother, don't you?

"Yeah, probably. But what makes you think you can find her and that she'd go along with you if you do?"

"I already know where she is and I'm quite sure she'd love to help me. Ask Kelly to give me a call, will you? I'll call you back in a little while." Jake hung up the phone.

In just a few minutes Kelly called. Jake thanked her for checking out the jewelry he and Kilgore recovered from Denise. She told him she was glad she could help. She also told him that she'd checked out the letter that was sent to Boogie. The person who allegedly sent it didn't exist.

Jake told her he wasn't surprised and then he told Kelly what he had in mind for Ed Marquez.

At four o'clock the same afternoon, Ed Marquez sat at his desk with his feet up and his hands laced together behind his head. He was trying to decide whether he should go home or call his wife with an excuse for not coming home. If he went home it would be a dull evening in front of the television, avoiding, as much as possible, any conversation with Helen, his wife. Being around her was, for Ed, an experience he preferred to avoid. He no longer found her attractive, in spite of her physical fitness regimen. Her constant urging that he quit drinking and smoking and, as she put it, "shape up," was getting old.

"I swear, if she wouldn't get half my pension, I'd dump her in a minute," he thought. "I'd go over to Denise's for the evening but the dumb broad hasn't been home all day. I wonder where the hell she is?"

As he sat thinking, his phone rang. He considered not answering it, pondering the possibility it might be Helen. On the other hand, it could be Denise. Ed picked up the phone.

"Burglary, Marquez," he said.

"Mr. Marquez?" a woman asked.

"That's what I said, lady. What can I do for you?" he asked. The voice sounded like an old woman's.

"Mr. Marquez, this is Frank Lander's mother."

Ed sat up in his chair, obviously surprised. "Mrs. Landers. This is a surprise. How are you? You must be doing better than you were."

"Yes, I am. At the time of my boy's funeral I was quite ill, hospitalized. But I'm much better now. I came to Los Angeles to retrieve some of Frank's, I guess you called him 'Fuzzy,' anyway, to retrieve a few things. I'm at his apartment. I was wondering if you could meet me here. There's something you'd probably be very interested in. I don't know whether I should turn it in to the police or what."

"Really. What is it?" Marquez asked.

"I'd really prefer to show you," she replied.

Marquez thought for a moment. 'What the hell could she have found that the investigating officers missed?' he wondered. 'I better get over there before she does decide to turn it, whatever 'it' is, over to the investigators.'

"I was just getting ready to leave, Mrs. Landers. I'll come right over. I should be there in about ten minutes."

"Alright. I'll wait here for you," she said.

Ed got up and headed out of the station to the parking lot. Walking towards his car, he glanced around the lot.

"Well, where is the old bag?" he wondered. The homeless woman was nowhere in sight. "Good. Maybe she finally croaked."

He got into his car and headed off for 'Fuzzy's' place. As he predicted, about ten minutes later he pulled up in front of the seedy apartment building.

"What a dump," he thought. "Fuzzy could have done better than this. Especially after we got our 'off-duty' jobs," he chuckled to himself. He walked in the building and up the stairs to the second floor apartment. He knocked on the door and said, "Mrs. Landers, it's me, Ed Marquez." He heard footsteps and then the door opened.

Marquez was visibly startled as Jake opened the door.

"Hi Ed . Come on in," Jake said, grabbing Marquez by the arm. Before he could offer much resistance, Kilgore stepped to the door and took Marquez's other arm.

"Yeah, c'mon in Ed. There's a friend of yours here who'd like to say hello. They pulled him into the room. Seated on the couch across the room was Kelly. Next to her sat the bag lady from the station parking lot.

"Hello Mr. Marquez. Delighted to see you. I know you're always so pleased to see me. Oh, and I'm not really Frank's mother, you know. Just a little joke I helped these nice people with."

Kelly stood up. "Come along, Betty. Time to go. Let's get something to eat." Kelly escorted the old lady toward the door. She winked at Marquez as she passed.

"Yeah, I'll be going now, too," Marquez said. "This was real funny but…"

"You're going nowhere, Ed. We have a lot to talk about," Jake said. "Thanks for the help, Kelly. And thank you, Betty. You were great." The two women left the apartment.

"You might as well sit down, Ed. This is going to take a while," Kilgore told him.

"Fuck you, Dave. What the hell do you two think you're up to. I ain't staying here for a minute. You don't have any authority over me," he said, looking directly at Jake.

"That's right, Ed. I don't."

Marquez started to move toward the door. Jake grabbed him by the front of his shirt, spun him around and pushed him backward onto the couch.

"Listen to me, you asshole. You've caused me a lot of grief over the past few weeks and now I'm going to return the favor. You're in trouble up to your fucking eyeballs. You can play tough guy, which we both know you aren't. Or you can sit and listen. Then when we're through you can tell us what you know." Jake chewed vigorously on his toothpick.

"And if I decide not to… what then?"

"When we get finished, let's see what you think, shall we?"

Marquez rolled his eyes. "Yeah, sure. Whatever you think. You don't worry me in the least."

"Well, let's see if we can change your mind, Ed. How's this for starters?" Jake threw the earring that Kelly found in his locker. Marquez instinctively reached and caught it.

"What's this?"

"A little bauble that was found in your locker. It's one of a kind and it was taken in the burglary of a home in the Hills. The owner identified it. Also found in your locker, Ed, was a deposit slip for your girlfriend's bank account. Deposited by you, according to her. $3,000.00. She says you deposited a lot of money in her account. She also says you gave her a lot of little baubles; baubles she gave to us. Guess what? Except for a cheap watch, which you probably bought, all the rest are stolen. Taken in burglaries by your detectives and, in all likelihood, by you."

Marquez stared straight ahead, obviously pondering his situation.

"Here's something else, Ed," Kilgore said. "You set Jake up. You arranged to be the only one at the desk during the squad meeting that day. Boogie Newton's commendatory letter, the one that caused him to attend the meeting, was a phony. Sent by a non-existent person from a non-existent address. Probably you."

"That's bullshit. Why would I do that?" Marquez asked.

"You did that because someone told you to, Ed," Jake said. "I'd like you to tell us who that was. Someone in the department had you do it because they wanted me out of the picture, worried about my career and away from the station. Somebody concerned about what I was going to dig up during the investigation of the burglaries, Lander's death and the suicide of Andy Calarasi. Obviously Fuzzy picked the wrong person to try to blackmail and got killed for his efforts. They'd have probably killed Marty if they could have found him. But he resolved that problem for 'em, didn't he?"

"Oh, and then there's the matter of a couple of thugs trying to kill a friend of Jake's and torching his boat," Kilgore added.

"I know nothing about that," Marquez said quickly.

"Yeah, but you know plenty about all the rest of it, don't you, Ed?" Jake said.

Marquez sat sullenly, saying nothing. Then he looked at Jake and Kilgore. "If I help you out, tell you what I know, what then?"

"The only thing I can promise you, Ed, is that with or without your help I'm going to find out who, besides you, set me up. I'm also going to find out who killed Landers, something you should have a profound interest in. That is, unless you were involved in that, too; a possibility I haven't ruled out."

"No way, no way would I kill 'Fuzzy.' You know that, Jake. You know me. I'm not that kind of guy. I'd never kill a cop."

"O.K., fine Ed. But the assholes you're hanging around with obviously don't have any qualms about it. Give Dave and I everything you know. Convince us you're not involved and we'll go after who is. Or, you can sit there and act stupid. We'll figure it out anyway, sooner or later. The only difference will be that when this is over, the D.A. will go after you with a vengeance for your failure to cooperate."

Marquez thought about it for a moment. He realized his options were limited. 'Why should I go down alone?' he thought. 'I might have done a few burglaries but all the rest of this shit, it wasn't my idea.'

"O.K. Jake. Let me lay it out, at least as much as I know." Jake and Kilgore sat down across from Marquez. Kilgore got a notebook from his inside jacket pocket and prepared to take notes.

Marquez loosened his tie. He leaned forward, resting his elbows on his knees. He looked at both men and began. "About six months ago Marty, Fuzzy and I started doing burglaries, mostly up in the Hills. The deal was I'd look up the addresses in the Vacation Check log. I'd pick out the homes in the high rent district and give the addresses to Marty and Fuzzy. They'd do the jobs and then we'd meet and split the goods. Mostly jewelry…well, you know that. We'd fence some of the stuff and keep the rest. I gave some to Denise. She didn't know the stuff was stolen. She's kind of dumb. The rest I fenced, usually electronic equipment. I put the money in her bank account, most of it, anyway. I didn't want the old lady asking me where I got it. She's the suspicious type. Better she didn't know."

"Who else in your unit was involved?" Kilgore asked.

"No one else. Just us three. No one else knew what we were doing," Marquez said. "I swear to you, it's true."

"Yeah, O.K. Who's idea was it to start pulling jobs in the first place, Ed?" Jake asked.

Marquez stared at the floor. "Mine, I guess. I had the hots for Denise and there was no way I could get her attention without spending money on her. She's a kinda high maintenance broad, if you know what I mean. Fuzzy, Marty and I had been working together for a long time. We knew each other and I figured they'd go along for the money." Jake and Kilgore stared at Marquez, their disdain obvious. Marquez continued.

"Well, one night Marty and Fuzzy go to this house up on Evergreen Terrace, up above Sunset. Arlo Calarasi's house. You guys know the place. They do their usual thing and while they're walking around the place they go into a bedroom, on the second or third floor. It's a really big house. Anyway, in the bedroom they find the stiff in the bed. They figured he'd committed suicide. Shot himself. A young guy who, you know, turns out to be the son. Calarasi's son. They clear out of there fast. It kind of shook both of them up. We get together later and they tell me what happened and we decide to lay off for awhile . The news coverage of the suicide and who his old man was and all kinds of shit made us all nervous. The next thing I know, Fuzzy and Pritchard don't show up for work. I figured the two of them made a huge score; a stash of cocaine or maybe a safe full of money, and forgot to mention it to me. Fuzzy had no family and Marty's wife was getting a divorce so it wasn't too hard to believe they'd taken off. You know the rest after that, Jake"

"I know that Fuzzy's head shows up in a dumpster. I know why, but I don't know who killed him. Are you telling me you don't know anything about that?" Jake asked.

"C'mon Ed. Give us the rest," Kilgore said.

"I can't give you what I don't have, Dave. I was as surprised as you were. Frankly, it scared the shit out of me. Doing burglaries was one thing, but Landers getting killed… I don't know."

"Did it occur to you that Landers' demise might be connected to the suicide, to the last job you guys did?" Kilgore asked.

"Yeah, later it did."

"Later when?"

"Well, later."

"Later, like when you set me up?" Jake asked angrily.

"Yeah. I guess so. But that wasn't my idea, Jake."

"I can believe that. Too complicated a production for you to come up with, Ed."

Marquez looked indignant for a moment. Then he grinned slightly and nodded. "You're probably right, Jake," he agreed.

"So who did, Ed. Who set it up and got you involved?"

Marquez stared at the floor for a couple of seconds. Then he looked up at Jake. "Your old friend, Walter Burnett," he said.

Kilgore and Jake looked at each other, each trying to decipher what the other was thinking. Jake turned back to Marquez.

"You're telling me that the Chief of Detectives, the guy who thinks he's soon going to be the Chief of Police, asked you to set me up to be fired and prosecuted. Maybe to go to jail?"

"Yeah, that's what I'm telling you. And he didn't ask me, he told me. I put the stuff in your office but I didn't have anything to do with the broad over on Sunset. I don't know anything about that; it was someone else."

"But you don't know who?" Kilgore said skeptically.

"That's right, Dave. I don't know who. Believe it or don't. That's the way it is."

"Assuming that it's all true, Ed, why would you do it for Burnett, or anyone else for that matter?" Jake asked.

"A couple of reasons, Jake. Number one, I don't like you much. You know that. The other, bigger reason is I owed Walter."

"Owed Walter! Kilgore responded. "What for? What the hell did he do for you to warrant screwing Jake over like this?"

"I went through Ed's personnel package the other day," Jake said. "I noticed Burnett's name on a few things. Early in your career you and Walter were real buddies, weren't you? He was your supervisor. Signed several commendations. Prepared your ratings, got you promoted."

"That's true, he did," Marquez replied.

"So you figured you owed him for that?"

"No, it was more than that. When I came on the job Burnett and I were partners. He was my training officer. We, I, got into a situation one night. I shot a guy we'd arrested. Had him in the back seat of the police car. I was fucking around with my gun, trying to scare him into talking about some crime. I don't even remember what it was about, exactly. Anyway, the gun went off and hit the guy right in the face. Killed him, obviously. I was scared shitless. Figured I was going to lose my job, go to jail. Walter handed me a 'throwaway'' gun to drop on the seat next to the guy. We got our story together and he helped me get through the interviews. By the time we got done, I had a commendation in my package for heads-up police work in saving both our lives. So, when Walter asked me to do what I did I figured I was in no position to tell him no."

"So he told you what he wanted you to do and you got it together. The bloody jacket, the pictures," Kilgore asked.

"The jacket I took care of with a small vial of blood he gave me. He gave me the pictures to plant, too."

"The letter to Boogie Newton…"

"Yeah, I wrote that, too."

"I still have a hard time believing Walter Burnett is involved in this caper. What the hell would motivate him to put you up to this? Why would he possibly give a damn about that suicide investigation? And as for Landers and Pritchard, he'd certainly want to know the extent of their activities. I spoke to him personally about the investigation. He was …wait a minute." Jake thought for a minute, pulling the soggy toothpick from his lips. "When I saw Burnett at the Academy, at George Ryan's retirement party he said something that was a little curious. What was it?" He pondered for another moment. "If I recall correctly he said something like…something to do with extortion. It didn't click at the time. Maybe Landers and Pritchard were trying to extort Walter. I remember thinking at the time that Walter didn't seem overly avid about capturing those two. He left me with the impression that if they just went away, it would be fine with him. I assumed he was concerned about bad publicity about a couple of his detectives hurting his shot at the Chief's job.

"The extortion thing seems unlikely," Kilgore said. "How do you extort a Deputy Chief? Those two wouldn't have the balls to try something like that. I just don't see it."

"I agree," Jake admitted. "It does seem a little outlandish."

"You said Burnett furnished you with the pictures. Where would he get that kind of stuff?" Kilgore asked.

"From his good buddy, Arlo, obviously. Which means that Burnett and Arlo are better friends than I thought," Jake said. "Burnett is obviously aware of Arlo's business activities, including the porno business, and who the hell knows what else. The extortion Burnett was referring to was the extortion of Arlo. If Burnett was willing to go as far as he has, according to Ed here, then he and Arlo are joined at the hip."

"Yeah, I think you're right," Marquez said. I think he did get the photos from Arlo. He had several of them and I got the impression he kind of enjoyed them. He looked them over pretty good before he gave them to me. I never knew he went for that kind of crap. Little kids. What a sicko."

"Well, there's one big problem with this scenario. We've got a detective who is an admitted burglar telling us that a Deputy Chief, one who may soon be the Chief of Police, is involved in a criminal conspiracy. Who do you think is going to be believed?" Jake asked.

"The answer to that is obvious, I guess," Marquez replied. "But I have a little something that might persuade you to believe what I'm telling you. When Walter gave me the pictures, four of them, he'd handled them all. He told me to be sure to wipe them clean before I planted them."

"Four. There were only three pictures in the desk," Jake said. "You kept one. For insurance."

"That's right, Jake. And I forgot to wipe it clean. I figured it might come in handy someday to have a kiddie porn picture with Walter's prints all over it. If I'm going under, Walter's coming with me. He's abused our friendship, the bastard. I don't owe him anything, anymore."

"I'd like that picture, Ed. Where is it?"

"It's in the trunk of my car. You can have it."

The three men left the apartment and walked down the stairs and out of the building. They went to Marquez' car and he opened the trunk. He removed a large manila envelope from a box of papers and opened it up. He tipped the envelope on end let an 8"x10" photo slide out. He took it gingerly by the edges and handed it to Jake.

Jake looked at it and turned it so Kilgore could see it. "Oh, lovely," Kilgore said, obviously disgusted at what he saw. The photo showed a young Asian girl, not more than twelve or thirteen years old, orally copulating a middle aged man while a second one was having sexual intercourse with her from behind.

"So Walter goes for this kind of stuff, huh?" Kilgore said.

"The prints will tell it all," Marquez replied. "You'll see that I'm not bullshitting you guys."

"If you're right, Ed, I'll take great pleasure in nailing the bastard. But the big question remains. Why would he put you up to this? What did he tell you?"

"Nothing, he just told me do it. No explanation offered and when I tried to ask he got hot. I let it go."

"Okay. We'll talk more, later. For now, I want to know if

we've got Walter's prints on this filth or not," Jake said. "Dave, I'd like you to take this to the lab and get someone you trust to print it. Someone who will keep quiet about whose prints they find."

Kilgore took the photo and carefully placed it back in the envelope. "Shouldn't be a problem," he said. "Tracy Capps is a good friend. She'll do it and forget it. I'll call you as soon as it's done. Where are you going to be?"

"We'll be at my place. Ed and I are going to have dinner together and talk things over. Does that work for you, Ed?" Jake asked, staring deliberately at Marquez.

"Do I have a choice?" Marquez replied.

"Sure you do, Ed. Do you want red wine or white wine? We're having fish so the white is probably more appropriate."

"Yeah, fine. Whatever," Marquez replied.

"I'll call you," Kilgore said as he got in his car and drove off.

"Hop in, Ed," Jake said, gesturing to his old truck which was parked a few yards away. They both got in and drove off.

*****

Mitch sat in the Mustang tapping his fingers on the steering wheel to the rhythm of the currant hit music on the FM station. He'd been parked in the library lot off Sunset in West L.A. for almost a half hour. The library closed at nine PM and there was only one other car in the dark lot that looked as though it had been there for a week or more, the windshield was dirty and leaves from a nearby tree were strewn over the hood. Headlights swept through the rear window of Mitch's car as two vehicles pulled into the lot one after the other. A white van pulled up on the driver side of Mitch's car and a sedan parked next to the van.

A large man pulled his bulk from the van and walked around to stand beside Mitch's window.

"You Mitch?" Mitch nodded and the man threw a set of keys onto Mitch's lap and turned and walked to the sedan which immediately drove out of the lot.

Mitch got out of his car and looked in the passenger window of the van.

"Whoa!" He hadn't seen the person seated in the front seat with a black hood and duct taped into the bucket seat. Mitch opened the door and pulled the hood away. The woman was obviously Asian, she stared fiercely at him with coal black eyes and pulled against the tape holding her tightly to the seat. Mitch stared at her for a moment and then looked into the rear of the van. A group of children were seated and lying down on two matresses in the bed of the vehicle. They stared open eyed at Mitch.

"OK kids, everything's going to be alright now." Mitch tried as best he could to sound kind and caring. He climbed into the van behind the steering wheel and looked over at the woman glaring at him. He leaned over and pulled the hood back over her head and started the vehicle and pulled out of the lot onto Amber Avenue and then turned right onto Sunset Boulevard.

As he drove slowly along Sunset he kept looking in trhe rear view mirror at the children. They sat quietly. Two of the little girls held hands. He sensed all the children were frightened, 'as well they should be.' he thought. 'And now what?'

His plan was working just fine. Uncle Montini had done just as he promised. The children were safe and unharmed and delivered to Mitch. Only one problem. What to do with them now; he hadn't figured out that part of the plan. If he called Jake he would have to explain how he came to have them to begin with and that didn't seem like a good idea. Kelly wasn't answering his calls and he knew she had her own problems what with being prosecuted and losing the badge. Pulling up in front of a police station appealed to him but once again there needed to be some explanation as to who the kids were and Mitch didn't want to have to try to answer a bunch of questions. He could picture some cops trying to understand why he had a taped up Chinese woman and nine children in a van he didn't own. Not an option.

Another half hour of indecision and aimless driving went by and Mitch found himself within a few blocks of Hollywood Station. Mitch pulled to the curb under some trees a half block from the department parking lot and sat there watching the driveway. Every once in awhile a black and white would pull slowly out of the lot and cruise slowly down the street. He knew it was only a matter of time before some suspicous cop pulled over to see what he was about. He took a deep breath and exhaled. He made up his mind. He would dump the kids and nurse at the station. Wasn't going to say a word to anyone. Figured Uncle Montini would mete out quicker and more efficient punishment to Tony and Arlo than any court was able to do.

"Kids. I can live with that." Nodded his head while he spoke to his image in the rear view mirror.

When the next unit car drove out of the parking lot Mitch started the van and pulled into the lot and parked near the rear entrance. Taking at last look at the children, now all asleep, in the rear he climbed out and locked the door. Jumping the wall next to the parked van he began strolling down the sidewalk without looking back. He intended to find a payphone on Sunset and call the station and tell them of the van and kids in their lot. He looked at his watch it was a little after two AM.

Once on Sunset he turned right and after a few blocks found a phone in front of a closed liquor store. He reached in his pocket and put two dimes in the slot and dialed the division.

"Hollywood station, Officer Gerk, how may I help you?" The cop sounded like he was a teenager.

"Her'ro, prease to rook at white van in your parking lot." Mitch held a piece of
tissue over the mouth piece and tried to affect an accent in order to fool the tape recording he knew was taking place.

"Pardon me sir?"

"White van in your parking lot, lots of kids inside, all kidnapped."

"Sir what is your name,where are you?" The young cop asked.

"Rook, never mind that, go get kids. They are right outside, OK?" Mitch said.

"Sir, I need your name."

"God dammit just go out and get the kids and the Chinese broad is a suspect so don't let her leave." Mitch grimaced, he'd broken out of his accent.

"Listen Officer, call the China Squad downtown and maybe Lieutenant Reed OK? I gotta go now, bye." Mitch hung up and began walking, walking away from the direction of the station. He figured he'd done more than enough, unless the rookie on the phone figured the whole conversation was a prank.

Three blocks further down he knew the call had been successful.

"Hey buddy want to hold it right there?" The cops flashlight beam was aimed at his face as the cop got out of the patrol car.

"Sure Officer, what's up?" Mitch said shielding his eyes from the light. The cop walked up and took Mitch's arm in a firm grip and turned him around and patted him down while asking:

"You don't have any weapons do you?" The cop turned Mitch around and stepped back as the other officer walked up behind Mitch and stood there about ten feet away.

"No, nope, don't believe in them. What did I do?" Mitch answered.

"Well it's pretty late for a walk where are you headed?" The lead cop asked.

"Oh, had a fight with my girlfriend and she told me to get out of her car, you know how it goes." Mitch said.

"Uh huh and where are you headed?"

"Well, I'm going to get my car so I can go home." Mitch said.

"And where would that be?" The cop asked.

"Well, Long Beach, boat, I live on a sailboat in Long Beach."

"I meant your car, let me see your ID please." The cop said.

Mitch pulled out his wallet and handed his license to the officer.

"Why don't you take a seat on that bench, Mitch, it will be just a minute or two." Mitch did as he was told and the cop walked back to the unit car, turned the spot light on the seated Mitch and sat in the front seat and picked up the mike. Mitch knew he was running a record check. The other cop still stood in the same spot. After a few minutes the older cop got out of the car and walked over to Mitch:

"You've been arrested quite a few times Mitch, have you been drinking to night?"

"Nope, don't drink any more."

"Yeah, well I kinda' believe you. You haven't been booked in a long time. Where's your car?"

Mitch told him it was in the library parking lot that he and his girlfriend met there at her request as it was a first date and she didn't want him coming to her home until she knew him better.

"And what would her name be?" The cop asked.

"I only know her first name, Ellen." Mitch said.

"Uh huh." The cop said as he wrote on a 3X5 card. "Well, we can't hold you Mitch so you're free to go. But why don't you give us a phone number in case we want to reach you."

Mitch did as he was asked and with a small wave began

walking down the street. After a few steps he heard the old cop say:

"Be careful, Mitch."

Chapter 36

As Jake was getting dinner ready with Marquez sitting at the kitchen table with a sullen look on his face, the phone rang. Jake looked at Marquez,

"That should be Dave. Wonder what he's going to have for us," he said.

"You'll see I wasn't 'B.S ing' you, Jake." Marquez said.

Jake picked up the phone. Kilgore spoke immediately. "Jake, Dave. Burnett's prints are all over the photo, just as Marquez said. Positive make. We've got him, the bastard. Tracy's sworn to secrecy. She won't say a word until we want her to."

"Okay Dave, good. Where can I reach you for the next hour or so?"

"I'll be at home. Assuming, of course that I don't get a homicide call out. I haven't had dinner with the little woman for a week and we both need to re-connect. But don't hesitate to call me. This is getting to be fun and I don't want to miss any of it."

"Depend on it, Dave. Talk to you later." Jake hung up the phone and looked at Marquez. "You're info was good, Ed. Walter's prints are there. It looks like he screwed up and I'm going after him."

"And what about me, Jake? Where do I go from here?"

"I'll tell you where you go, Ed. You go home. Think things over. Talk to your wife and get yourself a good lawyer. You're in deep shit. In a few days you're going to have to talk to I.A.D and tell them the whole story. Come clean and hope the powers that be give you a break. If you can convince them you were intimidated by Walter's authority, maybe you can save yourself some jail time. I don't know what else to tell you at this point. That is, of course, except to suggest that you not decide to take off."

"No way. At this point taking off would only make things worse. I need to work things out with my wife. She's a good woman; she'll stick by me. It's time to drop Denise. She's a beauty but she costs too much to maintain, if you know what I mean."

"Yeah, I can imagine," Jake responded.

Both men heard a car horn honk in front of the house. Marquez got up and put down his beer. He looked at Jake. "I know this isn't worth much, Jake, but I'm sorry I did what I did. I realize I've hurt the reputation of a lot of good cops and made the division look bad. I didn't think about that when I got into all this shit with Fuzzy and Marty. I was pretty stupid. I guess I let a great pair of legs and some big tits overload my brain."

"It looks that way, Ed. But your life's not over. Let's see how things work out."

"I'll see you, Jake." Marquez turned and walked to the front door. As he opened it Jake said: "Remember Ed, cooperate with I.A. and give them everything. Help yourself."

Marquez smiled and walked out. Waiting in her car in front of the house was his wife. He got in and they drove off.

Jake picked up the phone. It was time to put in a call to Deputy Chief Charles Collins. He called the department information number and was connected to Collins' office after a few moments. Collins wasn't there, having already left for the day. Jake called the Headquarters desk and asked the detective on duty to contact him and have him call Jake. The detective said he'd handle it and about thirty minutes later Collins called.

"Hello Jake, Charlie Collins here. What's going on? I thought you were relieved from duty."

"Yes sir, I am. But I have something that's extremely

important, both to me and to the department, that you need to know about."

"It would be more appropriate for you to go to your own boss, Jake. Walter Burnett is the Chief of Detectives. At least until the day after tomorrow."

"Normally I'd do that, Chief. But this involves Walter Burnett. It's not good and it has to be acted on immediately."

"Can you come to my office in the morning?" Collins asked.

"This can't wait until morning, Chief. I need to see you now. Believe me, I'm not overstating the importance of this."

"I'm sure you're not, Jake. I know you well enough to know that. Let's meet at my office. I'll be back there in half an hour."

"I'll see you there, Chief. Thanks." Jake hung up briefly and then picked up the phone and called Kilgore.

Kilgore answered on the third ring. "David Kilgore."

"Dave, Jake. Sorry to interrupt whatever you're doing. Can you meet me in Chief Collins office in half an hour?"

"Sure. Going right to the top, huh? Kilgore said.

"Well, with Burnett about to take over the Department I figured we'd need someone with some clout and the balls to act. Collins seemed like the guy to me."

"I couldn't agree more," Kilgore replied. "I'll see you there in half an hour.'

"And Dave, bring the report your print tech prepared. And the photo."

"You got it," he replied. "Oh, by the way, Jake. It may not be necessary but I sent one of my teams out to keep an eye on Ed Marquez, just in case he decides to skip between now and the time I.A.D. gets to him."

"Probably a good idea. I'll make sure I.A. is out there tomorrow."

Both men hung up. Jake grabbed his jacket and headed for the door. As he opened it Edie was standing there. "Well, you must have heard me coming," she said.

"No, Honey. I didn't. I was just leaving. I'll call and fill you in later. Things are looking up." He kissed her and walked briskly to his truck. As he opened the door he turned back. "I'm sorry but you'll have to fend for yourself for dinner."

"Oh no," she said smiling "How will I ever manage. Call me."

It took Jake twenty minutes to drive to the Police Administration Building. He parked in the lot and walked through the front door and up to the desk where a uniformed officer was seated. Jake identified himself and explained where he was going. The officer held him up momentarily while he called Chief Collins' office to confirm that Jake was expected. After a short conversation with Collins the officer gave Jake a visitors pass. "Sorry Lieutenant, but since you don't have your I.D. card or badge you're going to have to wear this," he explained.

Jake told him he understood, thanked the officer and walked to the bank of elevators across the lobby. He took an elevator to the sixth floor and walked directly to Chief Collins office. He entered the outer office and saw Collins sitting at his desk. Collins got up and met Jake with a handshake.

"Jake Reed. Good to see you."

"I hope you still feel that way in an hour. You're not going to be happy about what I have to tell you."

"Sounds pretty serious, Jake. Let's get to it," Collins replied. Jake realized he'd made the right decision in coming to Collins. He was a man of unquestioned integrity, intellect and professionalism. Quiet by nature, he had never been a self-promoter, preferring to advance in the organization on his ability. At 41, he was the youngest Deputy Chief on the job.

"Chief, one of my detectives, David Kilgore, is going to be here in a few minutes. He's been involved in what I'm going to tell you about since the beginning. I'll give you all the background leading up to the last few days and Dave can fill you in on the latest developments. O.K.?"

"Sure, Jake. Go ahead."

Jake began with the disappearance of Landers and Pritchard. He explained their activities, burglarizing upscale residences in the Hollywood Hills using the Vacation Check book as a guide. Collins was writing notes on a legal tablet he had in front of him.

"Hmmm. We'll have to come up with a better system for that, won't we?" he commented.

"Yes sir," Jake replied. He went on, explaining about the suicide of Andy Calarasi and the apparent burglary of the residence by Landers and Pritchard after Andy had killed himself. He reminded Collins who Arlo Calarasi was although Collins didn't need any reminder. He'd met Arlo once at a dinner where Arlo had been a guest of Walter Burnett. Although he was well known as a movie producer, Collins had an immediate dislike for him and wondered at the time why Walter had befriended him.

Jake explained that Landers and Pritchard apparently took some items from the home, including things they felt they could use to extort Arlo. Among those was the note that Jake got from Kelly. Jake described the content of the note in detail. Collins raised his eyebrows when Jake explained the circumstances surrounding the receipt of the note and Kelly's reasons for failing to hand it over when she found it.

"Her mother is married to Arlo Calarasi?" Collins exclaimed. "That's a hell of a coincidence, isn't it?" "Yeah, it is a little bizarre" Jake agreed.

"She's going to have to face department charges for her little misstep," Collins said.

"She realizes that, Chief. We've already talked about it and I've called I.A.D.," Jake assured him.

Jake advised Collins of the disappearance of the two detectives and the efforts taken to locate them. Collins indicated he was aware of the disappearance. Jake described the day they found Landers remains in the dumpster and the search that ensued for Pritchard.

Jake told Collins about his conversation with Walter Burnett at the Academy and the slip Burnett made which failed to register with Jake at the time. Then he described his encounter with Belinda Burnham and the ensuing events that resulted in his being suspended. Collins advised Jake that when he heard of the suspension he was shocked and extremely dubious about the entire incident. Although he said he'd discussed it with Burnett at a staff meeting and Burnett assured him the charges were probably true.

"I'm not surprised. When I tell you the rest of this saga you'll see why," Jake told him.

As he was about to continue there was a knock at the door. "That's probably David Kilgore. I'll get it," Jake said as he got up and walked to the office door. He opened it and Kilgore entered. He had a large brown envelope with him.

"Come on in, Dave. I've been bringing the Chief up to date on the situation."

"Detective Kilgore. I don't believe I've had the pleasure." Collins rose and shook hands with him"

"My pleasure, sir. Nice to meet you."

"Dave's my Homicide Coordinator, Chief. They don't come any better." Jake said.

Collins nodded approvingly and Jake continued.

"Anyway, after I was set up and suspended I considered what the hell to do next. And, of course, I wondered who wanted me out of the division bad enough to go to all that trouble. While I was thinking that over, a close friend of mine by the name of Mitch Thacker.
decided to help me." Jake then gave Collins a quick history of his relationship with Mitch since the early sixties. He also filled Collins in on Mitch's arrest record. He wanted Collins to have all of the facts, good and bad.

"Mitch contacted Belinda," he explained, "and persuaded her to come clean. She told him how she got involved in the situation and admitted that it was all staged. She put the whole thing on a guy named Harry Becker, a small time porno producer."

"Sounds like you cleared that up pretty well. How is it you're still not reinstated?" Collins asked.

"Chief, the approach Mitch took in getting the cooperation of Belinda Burnham was right out of the sixties, if you know what I mean," Jake said. "We had her story but we couldn't do anything with it, at least not then." Jake went on to explain what they'd learned about Becker and Blue Bird Studios and also the tie in with the "507".

He told Collins of the events on Mitch's boat the night the two Russians tried to kill him and torch his boat. Finally he described how Marquez had become the prime suspect in setting up Jake's office for the search that revealed the kiddie porn photos and the blood stained jacket. He and Kilgore described the way they, along with Kelly, snared Marquez and got him to cop out, telling them that Burnett put him up to it.

"That brings us to the envelope Dave has," Jake said. Kilgore handed Jake the envelope and he opened it, removing the photo and the fingerprint technician's report. "This picture is one of a set. The rest of them, three others, are the one's that were planted in my office. According to Ed Marquez, all four were given to him by Walter Burnett who, according to Marquez, told him where to plant them. Burnett also gave Marquez a vial of blood, Belinda's blood, to put on my jacket. Marquez did as he was told with one exception. He kept one photo that he said Walter had handled. He wanted a little insurance in the event Walter tried to turn on him later. This photo is the one Ed gave us. Dave had it printed and Burnett's prints are all over it. The tech's report is here with it." Jake handed it to Collins.

Collins took the picture and examined it. "This is pretty sick stuff. The girl looks like she's about twelve. And Walter's prints are all over it, huh?"

"That's right, Chief."

He looked at Jake for a couple of seconds. "Remarkable. You're telling me that the next Chief of Police, the guy who's going to be sworn in the day after tomorrow, has orchestrated a frameup to get you fired and maybe thrown in jail. I have to admit I don't find it entirely implausible. My respect for Walter has diminished considerably over the years, for a variety of reasons. But this is way out there. Assuming it's all true, and I'm not doubting what you've told me, the obvious question is 'why'? What possible reason would he have to do this?"

"Chief, Walter Burnett and Arlo Calarasi are good friends; apparently very good friends. Calarasi, through a variety of both sham and real business ventures, has set up an elaborate corporate maze that includes a number of saloons, the "507" is one of them, the Blue Bird Studio that produces porno, a number of porno shops, a legitimate film studio for which Arlo is best known and a string of dry cleaning establishments. Walter Burnett is a partner of record in twelve of the dry cleaning businesses. After seeing this photo I'd venture to say that he has an interest in the porno, as well. I'm certain Burnett's actions were at the request or direction of Arlo. Arlo is a bad man. I can't prove it yet but I'm convinced he or his thugs killed my detective, Fuzzy Landers. Landers tried to blackmail Arlo with something he and his partner found in Arlo's house the night they burglarized the place. I don't know what they had exactly, but if the content of the letter Kelly found in Lander's apartment is any indication, it must have been pretty ugly. Anyway, after Landers gave whatever it was to Arlo, Arlo killed him. Or had him killed. When that happened, Lander's partner, Marty Pritchard hit the road. He was obviously scared shitless that he'd suffer the same fate. He went into hiding and stayed that way until he was near death. By the time I got to him, he wasn't able to tell me much. While he was on the loose however, I suspect that Arlo was more than a little concerned that we'd find him and learn of his involvement.

"You know Jake," Kilgore said, "now that I think about it, when we were in the bedroom at the suicide scene the T.V. was on. So was the VCR. But there was no tape in it. My bet is that our two burglars took the tape. And I'd bet that tape has something on it that Arlo didn't want anyone to see."

Jake thought a moment. "You may be right, Dave. I wonder what the hell is on that tape to motivate Arlo to kill someone over it. At some point we need to find it. Anyway, I think that after Arlo killed Landers he told Walter about the extortion attempt and he probably told him about Lander's fate and the fact that Pritchard was still out there somewhere. Around that time I ran into Walter at the Academy and spoke to him about the investigation into the two missing detectives. Landers hadn't been found yet. I made a point of telling him how determined I was to find them. His response left me with the impression that if they just went away, it would be okay with him."

"Let me interrupt," Collins said. "You're suggesting that Walter was told of the murder of your detective, what's his name, Landers, and that he did nothing about it. I have a hard time believing that. Why would he protect Calarasi? Business partner is one thing but abetting a murder is another. It doesn't figure."

"I agree, Chief. If that's all they are. But I think it goes deeper than that. I think it goes deep enough to put Walter at Arlo's mercy. The photo speaks volumes about Walter's tastes. He obviously knows what Calarasi's involved in and may well be sharing in the proceeds. Public knowledge of that relationship would not only rule out Chief of Police, it would probably get him ousted from the department. Calarasi undoubtedly reminded Walter of this and who knows what else. They've been buddies for a long time."

"This guy Marquez, he's fully cooperative?" Collins asked.

"Yes sir. He came clean with us," Jake said, nodding at Kilgore. Jake went on to explain Marquez's reason for doing what Walter asked.

"Apparently Walter's been operating under his own rules for a long time. It's obviously time to change that," Collins said. "The first thing I need to do is get in touch with the Mayor. He's certainly not going to want to swear Burnett into office when he hears what we've got to tell him. After that I'm going to reinstate you."

"I'd appreciate that, Chief. I'd like to get back to work."

"Sounds like you already have, Jake."

"I mean officially," Jake replied.

Collins reached for the phone. Jake interrupted him.

"Chief, are you sure you want to call the Mayor? He and Burnett are pretty good friends. And part of the reason they're good friends is because Arlo and the Mayor are good friends. The Mayor may be an honest politician but he may also feel obliged to call Arlo. That would put this investigation in serious jeopardy, to say the least."

"Yeah, you're right, Jake. How do you want proceed with this? It's got to be quick, before Walter is sworn in."

"I agree, sir. I think we've got enough to go to the D.A. The physical evidence and Marquez's testimony should be enough to get a warrant. If the D.A. can get the Grand Jury together for a special session tomorrow we may be able to get a secret indictment."

"I think you're right. Let's go with it. But first lets get you reinstated. Does Captain Hughes have your badge and i.d. card?"

"Yes, as far as I know."

Collins made a couple of phone calls; one to I.A.D. and one to Ed Hughes. "You're reinstated Jake. Get to work and keep me posted. I don't want any more surprises. O.K.?"

"O.K, Chief. Thank you. No surprises."

Jake turned to Kilgore. "Dave, get in touch with the D.A.'s Command Post. We need to talk with their boss as soon as possible, tonight. Have him call here, just in case we need to have the Chief talk to him." Jake turned to Chief Collins. "We may need your clout, Chief. Just in case the D.A. doesn't appreciate the gravity of the situation. He is an elected official. I'm always a little dubious about which way they're going to jump when voter approval motivates their decision making process."

"I have to agree, Jake. Although Jack Bradley has been a real stand up guy, so far. We'll see."

During the next hour Jake and Collins talked about the case, discussing the best way to proceed. They agreed that if the Grand Jury failed to issue an indictment they would have to advise the Mayor, to preclude Walter's appointment. Assuming the indictment was issued, Walter would be arrested immediately. He was their best hope for putting together a case against Arlo.

"Speaking of Arlo," Jake said, "we should put a surveillance squad on him soon, before he gets wind of what's happening. I'm not sure what he's likely to do when he learns we've arrested his partner,

Walter, but I want to be able to put my hands on him."

"I agree. I'll have the squad on him beginning tomorrow morning," Collins replied.

The phone rang and Collins picked it up. "Hello, Jack," he responded to the caller, obviously the D.A. "How's the prosecuting business?" After a moment of small talk Collins got to the point of the call. He and Bradley spoke for several minutes and then Collins handed the phone to Jake. He introduced himself and answered a few questions from Bradley.

"I'll be there at ten a.m.," he said. "Thanks for your help." Jake hung up the phone. "Sounds to me like the people elected the right guy. He's ready to go after Walter and anyone else who's involved. We're going to talk at ten and with any luck get in front of the Grand Jury by one

Jake stood and shook hands with Collins. "I appreciate you're help with this, Chief. I'll keep you posted every step of the way." He turned to Kilgore. "Let's go, Dave. We've got a lot to do in a short time."

The two men left.

*****

Hey Larry, check it out."

The man sitting, dozing on the passenger side of the car opened one eye. "Huh? What is it?"

"Look who's taking a trip."

The other man opened both eyes and looked down the tree lined residential street. Although the sun was barely lightening the morning sky, he could see the man walking briskly to the car parked at the curb. Behind the wheel sat a female. At least it appeared, from their vantage point, to be a female.

"She just pulled up," the first man, Homicide Detective Anthony Ricci said.

His partner, Tom McCardle, chuckled. "Well, well. I'm very surprised. I thought he promised he wasn't going anywhere. Jake's going to be very disappointed."

The two men watched Ed Marquez, suitcase in hand, as he opened the car door and threw the bag in the back seat.

"Let's go," McCardle said. Ricci started the car and

accelerated rapidly down the street. Before the driver of the other car, who not surprisingly turned out to be Denise, could pull away from the curb Ricci pulled diagonally in front of her. He and McCardle got out of the police car and walked around to the passenger side of the car.

"Good morning, Ed. Getting an early start on the day, I see," McCardle said.

"What the hell are you guys doing here? What do you think you're doing? Get the hell out of the way."

"Get out of the car, Ed. You aren't going anywhere," McCardle told him.

"Stay out of this Tom. It's none of your business. It's between Jake and me, nobody else."

"That's where your wrong, Ed. You disgraced the whole division, from what I hear. You're not going to just go away with some bimbo like that's the end of it. Now get your miserable ass out of the car Ed. Or don't, and allow me the pleasure of dragging you out in front of your friend there. Your choice."

Marquez sat there for a few seconds, obviously weighing his options. He finally reached for the doorjamb to pull himself out of the car. Just then his wife, Helen, came out the front door of the house under a full head of steam. She was in slippers and a bathrobe, obviously having just gotten out of bed. "Aw,shit!" Marquez said, "Here we go."

"You son of a bitch," she yelled, waving her fists in the air. "You sneak out of the house and think you're going to run off with your tramp of a girlfriend. You son of a bitch." Helen, tears streaming down her face and fists clinched, tried to get to Marquez to hit him. McCardle stepped in front of her and held her flailing arms. "He's not worth the effort, Helen. Believe me."

Helen continued shouting and crying, glaring at her husband and then Denise. "How can you do this?" she asked, looking at Denise with hatred in her eyes. "How can you just drive up, right in front of my house and drive off with my husband?"

Denise had no response and the look on her face suggested she was asking herself the same question. Marquez got out of the car and looked at his wife. "Sorry, Helen. There's nothing else to say." He looked at McCardle and Ricci. "Let's go."

Ricci took Marquez by the arm. "Do I have to hook you up, Ed or are you going to go along with the program?"

"No cuffs, Tony. Just get me the hell out of here."

McCardle, meanwhile, spoke briefly with Helen. He tried to explain what was going on with her husband but she was, to say the least, disinterested. "He can kiss my Mexican ass," she said. "The next time I see that bastard it'll be in divorce court. When I get through with his sorry ass his pension won't be enough to keep him in beer. We'll see how long goldilocks hangs around after that."

McCardle turned back to the car and reached into the back seat where Marquez had thrown his suitcase. "I'll take this with me if you have no objections, honey" he said to Denise. She shook her head and he removed it from the car. McCardle walked around to the police car and got in the back with Marquez. "Home, James," he said to Ricci and they drove off, headed for the station. "I'll bet Dave's gonna be delighted to see us with you in tow, Ed" Marquez said nothing, staring out the window.

Half an hour later they pulled in the lot. "Hey, Tom. Isn't that Jake's car parked in his stall? Do you suppose he's back to work?" Ricci asked.

"Looks that way." He turned to Marquez. "How about that, Ed? Good news, huh?"

"Yeah, wonderful," Marquez replied.

They parked and went in the station. They entered the squadroom and walked past Jake's office, glancing inside. There sat Lt. Jake Reed.

"Hey lieutenant, good to see you back. How was your vacation?" McCardle joked.

"Funny, Tom, real funny. What's up with Ed," he asked, nodding at Marquez.

"Apparently Ed was about to go on a vacation, too." The two detectives explained what transpired earlier that morning. Jake listened to the explanation and then turned to Marquez.

"Well Ed, why am I not surprised? No matter how skeptical I am about you, you always manage to exceed my expectations. Sit down. We have some things to talk about."

Marquez walked into the office and sat. Jake wasted no time telling him what he thought about his apparent effort to run off with Denise. Instead he explained what had occurred the previous evening in his meeting with Chief Collins and the appointment with the Grand Jury that morning.

"You're going with us Ed. You and I and Dave are going to the Grand Jury and tell them what we have. You're going to tell them what you told me regarding Burnett and the frame up. Your degree of cooperation will determine what happens to you next. You know how the system works. Give up everything you've got and then we'll talk with the D.A. and see what he can do for you. Try to get cute and you'll spend the rest of your life in the joint. You know I'm not bullshitting you, Ed. You're in no position to try to cut any deals. Agreed?"

"Yeah, sure. Let's go," Marquez replied.

Jake called David Kilgore on the com line and in a few minutes he came into the office.

"Good morning, Ed. I heard you were thinking of taking a few days away from work. I'm glad you changed your mind."

Marquez ignored the sarcasm, staring at the floor.

"Let's go," Jake said, standing and heading to the door. Kilgore and Marquez followed. "We'll be back in a few hours, Rene. We'll be at the Grand Jury hearing room. If you need to reach me, call the D.A.'s office."

Rene said, "Okay boss. Good luck." She looked up at Marquez as he walked past. She said nothing, however the look on her face made it clear to Ed that the wish for good luck did not extend to him.

As Jake walked past Kelly's desk she looked up at him and then got to her feet. "Lieutenant, I need to speak with you. It's important."

"I know it is, Kelly. However, what I'm doing right now is, too. We'll talk as soon as I get back."

Jake, Dave and Ed Marquez drove downtown to the D.A.'s office in less than a half an hour. They parked and entered the Central Criminal Courts Building, identifying themselves to the security officer at the door. Jake slipped his credentials back in his pocket and patted them, happy to have them back in his possession. The three men went directly to the eighth floor and contacted the Deputy District Attorney assigned to their matter. His name was Jeff Luger.

After introductions, Luger wasted no time getting to the point. "I spoke to my boss, Jack Bradley, late last night. He told me, generally, what's up with this case. We need to discuss it in detail, obviously. I have to warn you, though. We may not get in front of the Grand Jury today. They have a full schedule and may choose to put it off until tomorrow. We'll know better as the day progresses."

"Did Mister Bradley tell you how crucial it is that we get this done today?" Jake asked.

"Yes, he explained the ramifications and I can appreciate your position. However, I can't tell the jury what to do. I have no control over them, as you know."

"I understand," Jake replied. "We'll have to see what happens."

"If we can't get before them today, can't you just advise the Mayor of the situation and ask him to delay the appointment of Burnett?" Luger asked.

"We can, of course. But if we do, when Burnett is told there's a good possibility that he'll talk to a co-conspirator involved in this situation and we'll lose a bit of advantage we have."

"I understand," Luger replied. "I'll do what I can. Now, lets go to my office and discuss this situation."

They walked down the hall and into Luger's office. For the next two hours they talked, providing Luger all the details leading up to the present. They showed him the photo and the Fingerprint Technician's report. Marquez was surprisingly cooperative, obviously realizing he was out of bargaining chips. He promised to tell it all in front of the jury.

The day wore on. No call from the Grand Jury room by one o'clock so the four of them went out for lunch at a nearby café. When they got back they learned that the jury had just left for lunch. The waiting continued into the late afternoon. Finally, at four thirty, just as Jake was briefing Chief Collins by telephone, the Grand Jury liaison called. They were ready to proceed.

The four men proceeded to the hearing room and Luger went in. After about thirty minutes he came out of the hearing room and sat down with the three men. "They're ready. Detective Marquez, you're on. I assume you know how to testify. Answer directly, tell only what you know. Look them in the eye. I don't want any screwing around, Ed. You understand?"

"I understand," Marquez replied.

"Let's go," Luger said, and the two got up and entered the hearing room.

Jake and Kilgore sat for about an hour and then decided to wait in Luger's office. They sat there for another hour before Jake finally persuaded Kilgore to go home. Jake assured him he'd call as soon as anything happened. Kilgore reluctantly agreed and left, heading for home and dinner.

It was nearly eight thirty and Jake was gnawing on his fourth toothpick when Luger and Marquz walked back into the office. Marquez looked like he'd been pulled through a knothole. Luger looked only slightly less haggard. "Well, how'd it go?" Jake asked.

"Time will tell," Luger said. "They're mulling it over."

"Mulling it over!" Jake said. "What's to mull over? It's pretty straight forward, isn't it?"

"To you and me, yeah. But these folks are having a little trouble believing a corrupt detective," Luger said, looking at Marquez. "Especially when he's accusing a Deputy Chief who's about to become the new Chief of Police."

"What about the photos, the prints?" Jake asked.

"That's what's going to bring us the indictment, eventually. They just want to think about it for a while. They'll indict." Luger assured them.

"Yes, but when? In about twelve hours the Mayor's going to pin the Chief's badge on that jerk unless we grab him first."

"I understand that, Jake. But I can't force them to move. If I try, they're liable to get difficult. I don't want that."

"No, I don't either," Jake agreed.

The men waited together for another hour and then the liaison officer called to tell them that the jury was going to call it a night. Before Luger could protest the officer assured them they understood the gravity of the situation and that they were going to reconvene at seven the next morning. Luger hung up and explained the situation to Jake. The two men said good night and left for home.

When Jake got home he took a quick shower and crawled in bed. Edie was awake and asked him how things went. He explained briefly and assured her he'd give her all the details the next day. They both drifted off to sleep.

CHAPTER 37

The pager went off with a loud buzz as it vibrated on the beat up bedside table. Vivi sat straight up in bed and pushed the old, black hooker away from the erection she'd worked so hard to create. He grabbed the pager and looked at the single number displayed on the face. He immediately got up and began pulling on his shirt, at the same time throwing a ten dollar bill at the forty year old woman.

"Here, now ged-outta-here." She dressed hurriedly and slipped from the room. Vivi lived in one of the cheap 'by-the-week' hotels in downtown L.A. It didn't include the luxury of a phone in the room. He walked down the hall with a handful of change and dialed a number from memory. After two rings he said his name, listened for a minute or two and then said:

"I understand." Vivi hung up and ten minutes later he was in his rental car heading west on Wilshire.

Tony sat in front of the TV set in his modestly furnished, one bedroom apartment in Westwood. He had no idea what program was on. He was deep in thought. He knew trouble was on the way. It wasn't the police he was worried about. It was his uncle. He'd thought about it and the only problem left that he could see was the children and they were secreted in a house in the Valley. Oh, and there was the little girl who escaped with Mitch. He sighed. Getting rid of the children wouldn't be easy. It wasn't like a simple hit. One body, one hole in the ground and some lye.

"Shit!" He swore to himself, this was very complicated. Arlo wasn't a factor. He could say nothing without implicating himself and that cop didn't know anything about him other than that he represented some out of state investors.

The doorbell interrupted his thoughts. Tony moved to the window and peeked through the curtains. Vivi stood at the door. Tony slid open a drawer under the coffee table and put a Chief's Special .38 revolver in his waistband under his shirt before he opened the front door:

"Vivi, my man. What are you doing here?"

Vivi pushed the door open and walked into the living room.

"Tony, I have a message from your uncle." Vivi spoke as though he had memorized what he was saying. "The only way to make things right with your family," Vivi said, setting a small case down on the coffee table and opening it, "is to have Arlo go away. You are to use this first, for pain." He pointed to a knife in the case. "Then finish the job with this," he said, pointing at a forty-five derringer alongside the knife. "Do you understand?"

"Vivi, how much does my uncle know?"

"Take care of Arlo, Tony." Vivi shook his large head slowly back and forth.

"Vivi I, I…" Tony stopped and plopped down on an easy chair. "Do you think it'll be O.K?"

"Do as you're told and everything will be all right."

Tony told him he wouldn't fail and to 'please tell Uncle 'it wasn't my idea. Arlo set the whole thing up.' Vivi nodded his understanding and, closing the case on the table said:

"The gun, of course, is not traceable." Saying that, he moved his large bulk to the door and left with not another word.

*****

Jake was up at six the next morning. He had a glass of orange juice and a bagel and grabbed a banana as he headed for the door. "I'll see you tonight," he shouted to Edie who was just getting up. She wished him good luck as the door slammed.

At the same time, Walter Burnett was standing in front of the full-length mirror in his bedroom. He'd just put on his dress uniform and he was admiring himself, pleased with the commanding image he presented. Yes, he would be a great chief, he thought. He relished the opportunities that his new position bestowed. There were, undoubtedly, a few people who were justifiably worried about their future with the department. Walter had already compiled a mental list of those who would merit his attention and the negative side of the ledger was considerably longer than the positive one.

Walter had a long memory, especially for those whom he felt had screwed with him over the years. Jake Reed, of course, was right at the top of the list. Too bad he'd already been dealt with, Walter thought. He would have particularly enjoyed torturing Lieutenant Reed with an assignment to a nice mundane desk job somewhere. Walter gazed at himself for another moment and then turned away from the mirror when he heard his wife coming. As Millie Burnett, his wife of thirty-seven years, entered the room she looked at Walter admiringly. "You look wonderful, dear. You're going to be the handsomest Chief the city has ever had."

Walter looked back at himself in the mirror and silently agreed. "Thank you. Are you almost ready? We should be leaving pretty soon. I'd like to get there a little early and chat with the Mayor before the swearing-in." Dolores assured him she would be ready momentarily.

As soon as Jake arrived at the station he went to his office and called Luger, who'd been in since six thirty himself. He told Jake the Grand Jury had reconvened at seven as they said they would. He was waiting for them to call and he assured Jake he'd call him. Jake hung up and called Collins office to brief him. After the briefing, Collins told Jake to come to his office. Assuming the Grand Jury handed down an indictment, the two of them would go directly to the Mayor. Hopefully, that would occur before the scheduled nine thirty ceremony. Jake left the station and was in Collins office by eight thirty. They both waited, resisting the urge to call Luger. Finally, at ten after nine Luger called. The Grand Jury had indicted Walter for conspiracy.

Chief Collins and Jake left immediately for the Mayor's office, arriving a few minutes before nine thirty. They walked into the reception area and Chief Collins identified himself to the clerk at the desk. He asked to see the Mayor immediately, explaining that it was urgent. She picked up the phone and spoke with the Mayor's personal secretary. After a moment she hung up. "I'm sorry," she said. "The Mayor has just left for the Council Chambers. They're swearing in the new Chief of Police in just a few minutes. But you must have known that."

"Let's go," Jake said, turning for the door. Collins followed him out of the office and down the long hall towards the Council Chambers. "Maybe we can get to the Mayor before he puts himself in an embarrassing position."

Mayor William "Bill" Miller was in his second term as the Mayor of Los Angeles. He enjoyed the job and was fairly popular among those who bothered to vote. Selecting a new Chief for the department had been an interesting experience for him. It was the first time a new Chief had been selected in over twelve years and the campaigning from within and without the department had been rather more than he anticipated. In the end however, the selection of Walter Burnett was pretty simple. Burnett had managed to avoid any negative attention during the course of his rather uneventful career and Arlo Calarasi, one of Mayor Miller's major campaign contributors, had assured him Walter was the best man for the job and that was good enough for him.

Jake and Collins arrived at the chamber door and pulled it open. Once inside they looked around. The room was packed with dignitaries from city and county government. Walter was at the back of the room, standing next to the Mayor who was beaming with pride, apparently delighted with his choice for Chief of Police. Next to the Mayor was Walter's wife ; a big smile on her face, as well. As Jake and Chief Collins tried to push their way through the crowded room, Mayor Miller stepped to the podium. The room hushed as he began to speak. "Ladies and gentlemen, I have a few remarks I'd like to make regarding our new Chief of Police, however, first things first. I'm going to swear Chief Burnett in and then I'll share with you my reasons for selecting him."

As Walter prepared to assume his new position he swelled with pride. A career long goal had finally been attained; he'd made it to the top. He was the Chief. He could hardly believe it. He looked around the room, realizing that he was now among the elite in city government. His importance couldn't be overstated. He'd arrived. As he surveyed the room, noting who was there, he saw Deputy Chief Charles Collins. 'Smart move,' he thought. 'He wants to be sure I see him and know he's one of my supporters. Maybe I'll let him run the Detective Bureau,' Walter thought. Then Walter saw Jake. Before he could consider what he was doing there the Mayor said: "Walter, I'm going to administer the oath." Walter turned to face him as his wife stepped to his side and put her arm through his.

As Walter stood with his hand raised, waiting for the Mayor to proceed, he sensed someone approaching. The Mayor looked to his right as Chief Collins hurriedly walked up. He stepped between Walter and the Mayor, leaned over and whispered in the Mayor's ear. The Mayors reaction to what Collins had to say was evident immediately. He paled as he listened and then looked at Walter. "This is going to have to wait, Walter," he said.

"What's going on here? What are we waiting for?"

"You to get out of jail, Walter," Jake said, as he took Walter tightly by the arm.

"Jail! What the hell are you talking about? What are you doing here? You're suspended."

"Not anymore I'm not. I've been reinstated, Walter."

"Reinstated. Who reinstated you?" Walter asked.

"I did," Collins said.

"What's this all about, dear?" Millie asked.

"It's all about a Grand Jury indictment, Mrs. Burnett. But that's only part of the story. You'll have to get Walter to show you all of the kiddie porn he's been enjoying." Jake turned to Walter. "Let's go Walter, you're under arrest."

"Are you nuts? You can't arrest me. I'm the Chief of Police."

"Not yet you aren't," Collins said. "And it doesn't look like it's going to happen any time soon."

Jake took Walter by the arm and they began walking toward the rear door of the chamber. The scene became somewhat chaotic as people, stunned and confused, tried to learn what had happened. The media members in the room were yelling at the Mayor, trying to get an explanation as Jake, Walter and his wife and Collins exited.

In the hallway, Walter stopped and pulled his arm free from Jake's hold. "What the hell is going on? I want an explanation, now!"

"Sure, Walter. Here it is. You've been indicted by the Grand

Jury for conspiracy. You engineered framing me. You set it up. That much we know for sure. Before we wrap this up I suspect you're going to be charged with a variety of other things involving you and your buddy Arlo. Now let's go."

Walter looked stunned. "You better have your facts straight, you asshole. You've got nothing."

"I've got Ed Marquez, Walter. And I've got a picture of a little girl engaged in sex that has your prints all over it. If I was you, I'd get a good lawyer."

Walter's wife looked at him, stunned. "Oh Walter," she said. Then she slapped his face, turned and walked off.

From the back of the chamber, Arlo stood watching as the Mayor and Walter entered the room. The swearing-in ceremony was about to begin and Arlo was anxious to see Walter, his business partner, assume the position of Chief of Police. He'd played no small part in Mayor Miller's selection of the new Chief and now his efforts were going to pay off. With Walter in the Chief's spot the sky was the limit. As Arlo looked around the room, happily mulling over the opportunities that lie ahead, he was startled to see Jake Reed enter the room accompanied by a man he took to be another cop. "What the hell is he doing here?" Arlo wondered. "He's got a hell of a nerve showing up for this."

Arlo watched as Jake and the other man approached the podium where the Mayor and Walter were standing. He saw the man with Jake talk to the Mayor and the reaction from the Mayor was obvious. He was clearly upset. As Jake and the man walked toward the door with Walter it was clear that it was in spite of Walter's objections. The Mayor stepped to the microphone and clumsily explained that there would be a delay in the swearing-in ceremony and then excused himself and left the room.

Arlo considered all that he'd just observed and concluded that the delay in Walter's swearing-in and the presence of Jake Reed meant trouble. Trouble for Walter and trouble for him. Arlo left the Council Chambers quickly and headed for the parking garage. As he pulled out onto Main Street and headed north toward the freeway a man seated in a blue Pontiac parked at the curb said: "Our boy is out and headed northbound." The microphone concealed in the visor picked up his words and transmitted them over the short wave radio concealed in the trunk.

"Roger, I've got him. Looks like he's getting on the freeway, westbound.
Probably headed for Hollywood."

After allowing Walter an opportunity to speak briefly with Millie and giving her the keys to the car, Jake and Chief Collins escorted him to the nearest stairway that they took to the underground parking garage. They walked to Jake's police car in silence. Jake got in the driver's side while Collins and Walter got in the back. Jake drove out of the garage and directly to the Police Headquarters Building. Jake parked in the space that Walter had recently vacated when he prematurely moved into the spot reserved for the Chief of Police. The three men got out of the car and entered the building, going directly to the elevator. A few moments later they walked into Collins office and went to the inner office. Before closing the door, Collins asked his secretary to make a pot of coffee. "and, no calls please, Bonnie," he told her. She nodded. "Unless it's the Mayor, of course," he added.

Collins closed the door and the three men sat down at a small conference table. They looked at one another. Walter appeared dazed.

"You know, Charles," he said. " I hope you have your facts straight. This asshole," nodding at Jake, "is a loose cannon."

"Really. I find Lieutenant Reed to be pretty credible. For that matter, Detective Marquez seems to be quite believable, as well. Is he a loose cannon too?" Collins asked.

Walter snorted. "Ed Marquez. There's a hell of a source. I don't know how he got on the job."

"No, but you know how he managed to stay on the job, don't you Walter?" Jake said.

"What the hell is that supposed to mean?"

"I think you know," Jake said, "but let's get to current events, shall we?"

"Fine with me. I'd like to know what's going on here, beginning with my alleged indictment. Oh, and by the way; don't forget to advise me of my rights."

Jake looked at Collins and he nodded. Jake recited the standard admonishment to Walter that included his right to counsel, his right to remain silent, etc. After he finished Walter thought for moment.

"Now I'd like to know what I've presumably been indicted for and on what evidence the indictment was obtained." Walter was obviously over the initial shock of his situation and ready to determine just how much trouble he was actually in.

Collins began to explain the charges the Grand Jury handed down. He described the testimony provided by Marquez and was explaining the fingerprint evidence when Bonnie tapped lightly on the door and then opened it.

"Sir, the Mayor's on the phone and wants to speak with you right now. He stressed 'now'. He sounds slightly upset."

"Only slightly? I suspect he's a little more than slightly upset. They probably just pulled him down from the ceiling." Collins picked up the phone.

"Hello Mr. Mayor, Charles Collins. I was planning on calling you in the next few minutes to provide you with a more thorough explanation of this situation. Would you like me to brief you over the phone or shall I come to your office?" Collins listened for a few seconds.

"I can be there in ten or fifteen minutes, however I'd like to speak with Chief Burnett first. Can you give me an hour or so?" He listened. "Well, if that's what you want, I'll be right over."

Collins hung up the phone. He looked exasperated and a little puzzled. "As you no doubt gathered, Mr. Mayor has spoken. He wants me in his office now. He also says you," looking at Walter, "are relieved of duty and assigned to your home. You are to leave now."

"We're not finished talking with him yet," Jake said. "I'd like to know if Walter has anything to say about the charges. We need to…" Collins interrupted.

"Hold it, Jake," he said. "I agree with you, however the Mayor was emphatic. I don't know why the hell he's taking that position but I intend to find out. In the mean time, Walter walks."

"Don't get too upset, gentlemen. I have no intention of talking to you about anything. I'll be consulting with my lawyer who, I'm sure, will advise me to remain silent. So, if there's nothing further…" He got up and turned towards the door.

"Hold it. There's a little matter of a Grand Jury indictment here," Jake reminded Walter. "You're not going to walk out of here until you've been booked."

Collins smiled as shock registered on Walter's face. "Come now, Walter. You don't think the Mayor has the power to override a Grand Jury indictment, do you? You know better than that."

Jake stepped over next to Burnett. "Walter," he said, "Are you going to come along peacefully or am I going to have to cuff you?" Jake had a poorly concealed grin on his face.

"Fuck you," Walter replied.

Jake nodded towards the door and said, "Let's go." Both men walked out with Collins following. They got on the elevator and rode down to the jail floor. The elevator doors opened and Jake and Walter got off.

Collins held the door. "Jake, take him to the Watch Commander's office to process him. Don't go through the booking cage."

"I'd planned to do that, sir. Low key all the way."

Collins nodded and let the door close. Jake and Walter walked to the Watch Commander's office. About an hour later, after Jake finished explaining the situation to the Watch Commander and completing the booking process, he left the jail and headed for his office.

'It's good to be back to work,' he thought.

CHAPTER 38

While waiting for Collins to arrive at his office, Mayor Miller contemplated the devastating turn of events. He'd spent weeks considering his selection for Chief of Police and now, after selecting Walter Burnett, he turns out looking like a fool. Now he'd need to explain to the press and to his constituents what happened. Worse, he'd have to defend his selection or at least explain how a candidate for the job could wind up indicted without him being aware of it.

'I trusted Walter,' he thought, 'and look what that got me. That son of a bitch! And Arlo. I trusted him, too. He assured me Burnett was the right guy for the job. Big donor or not, he's definitely on the shit list, as far as I'm concerned'.

Mayor Miller thought about that for a minute and then picked up his phone. He consulted the directory on his desk and dialed a number. Arlo, who'd just arrived home from City Hall, answered on the fourth ring.

"Well, Arlo, what do you think about this turn of events? Your boy, the guy you assured me was pure as the driven snow, the best choice for Chief you said. Now your boy is sitting in the slammer trying to raise bail. Indicted, Arlo, indicted!"

"Calm down Mr. Mayor," Arlo said. "How was I supposed to know Walter would get himself into a situation like this?"

"You're his friend, his business partner. You should know everything he's doing, everything he's involved in. Shit, Arlo, this is bad. It makes me look like I don't know my ass from a hole in the ground. I never should have listened to you. My political career's in jeopardy."

"Nonsense, Mayor. This'll blow over. Pick a new Chief. Explain that you were too trusting. That you assumed a well-thought of veteran like Walter was above reproach. By next week it'll be old news. Appoint this guy Collins and move on."

"Well, maybe. Collins does look like a perfect choice now that he's stepped in and handled the matter with Burnett."

"Sure. He's a hero. Took action to deal with a bad cop. Everyone will love him."

"We'll see, Arlo. But regardless of what I do, in the future please refrain from getting involved in these situations. I appreciate your support as an upstanding citizen, however I need to make these appointments without any outside influence. O.K.?"

"Whatever you think, Bill," Arlo said.

The two men said goodbye and hung up.

*****

Walter looked around the room as he entered. Several phones were located on a long counter, each separated from the next by a divider that extended to the ceiling. Several of the phones were in use by jail inmates. Walter stepped to one that wasn't and sat down. He dialed a number and after several rings a male voice, speaking in a tone just above a whisper said "Judge Wyatt's courtroom. Court is currently in session. This is Bailiff Hepler."

"Bailiff, this is Chief Walter Burnett from the police department. I need to speak with the Judge as soon as possible. When will he be available?"

"As a matter of fact, Chief, he's adjourning now. Please hold on."

Within a minute or two the Judge came on the phone. "Walter.

How are you?" he asked.

Walter explained that he wasn't particularly well at the moment. He gave the Judge enough particulars to understand his situation and then asked him if he could arrange to have him released from jail. The Judge, stunned at what he had been told, agreed to look into the matter and see what he could do.

Walter thanked him and hung up the phone. He got up and a jail officer motioned him to the door and then escorted Walter back to the holding tank. Forty-five minutes later the jail officer returned and informed Walter that he was being released.

"Well Chief, you obviously have some friends in high places. We don't normally get ' own recognizance' releases for felony arrestees. Who the hell do you know?"

"Nobody," Walter responded, "I shouldn't have been arrested in the first place."

"Yeah, right. Just another innocent man framed for something he didn't do. Tell it to the judge."

"I already did," Walter replied. "That's why I'm getting out."

*****

Twenty minutes later Walter was in the car with his wife Millie, driving home. She'd said nothing since he got in the car. In fact, she almost hadn't agreed to pick him up when he called but then thought better of it. 'Give him a chance to explain himself,' she thought. So far he'd made no attempt to do that. As they pulled into the driveway Walter said, "We'll talk later. First I have to take care of some business."

He got out and walked into the house, leaving Millie to fend for herself.

"Not so much as a thank you," she observed as she got out of the car and walked to the house. "You've really screwed up this time, haven't you Walter?"

As she closed the front door the phone rang. Walter answered on the second ring. It was Arlo.

"Hello Arlo. How did you know I was out of jail?" he asked. Arlo began to offer an explanation but Walter interrupted.

"Never mind. Listen Arlo, we have to talk. I want to know what's going on. I'm in serious trouble and I didn't get here by myself."

"Of course, Walter. We're in this together. Don't worry, I won't let you down. Just stay calm and don't talk to anyone. If you do, it'll only make things worse."

"Unless you've got a plan that'll make all this go away, Arlo, I hardly think you're in any position to offer me advice. I need to do what I can to save my own ass. Can you help me with that?"

"Sure, Walter. Trust me. I know things look serious but…"

"Serious! That's putting it mildly, you asshole! I've been booked. I've been printed and photographed! I'm facing felony charges! Things don't <u>look</u> serious, they <u>are</u> serious! And who do I have to thank for this? You, Arlo."

"Stay right there, Walter," Arlo said, his voice taking on an icy tone. I'll be right over. We better talk face to face."

"No, not here. I'll meet you somewhere." Walter thought for a moment. "How about the '507', in about half an hour?"

"Alright. But make it an hour."

Both men hung up. Walter stood there, pondering his conversation with Arlo. He wasn't at all sure he wanted to meet with Arlo, now that he thought about it. Arlo had a penchant for violence, only recently revealed, that scared Walter.

"Walter, what's going on. Please tell me. Don't leave me out. I want to help, if I can," Millie said.

Walter shook his head. "Believe me, Millie, you can't. But there is one thing I want you to do. Pack a few things and go to your Aunt Louise's place in Monterey. If I don't have to worry about you for awhile it'll be easier for me to do what I have to do here. Will you do that?"

"I guess so but I'd rather be here for you. I heard you talking to Arlo. I knew he'd have something to do with all this. I've never liked him, as you know. I know you've done something wrong, Walter but Arlo's behind it. I know he is, isn't he?"

"Yeah, Millie. He's a good part of the reason, but I'm a big boy. I could have avoided all this. Maybe I need to accept that and do the right thing. Now get some things together and let's get you on the way to your Aunt's place."

Millie hugged Walter. "I'm sorry I slapped you dear. I still love you. I'll try to understand and be as supportive as possible. If you want me to go, I will." She turned and went to the stairs where she stopped and looked back at Walter. “Please be careful…and do the right thing. It’s never too late to make things right.”

Walter smiled. “I love you, too Millie. I always will. Thanks for staying with me.”

She smiled and went up the stairs.

Walter sat down and thought about his conversation with Arlo. One thing he knew for sure. He definitely wasn’t going to the ‘507’. Walter had come to realize that Arlo Calarasi was a ruthless and violent man. He also realized that although he’d been a cop for over thirty years, he feared Arlo. He feared him a lot and had no desire to confront him.

Walter waited for Millie to get ready to leave. When she finally came down the stairs, he walked her to the car. He kissed her goodbye and told her to drive directly to her aunt’s. “Call me the minute you get there,” he admonished. She assured him she would and drove off, waving.

Walter returned to the house and picked up the phone. He dialed and waited. After several rings the phone was answered. “Jake Reed, please,” he said. In a moment Jake picked up the phone.

“Jake, this is Walter. We need to talk.”

“You sure you want to talk with me, Walter?”

“Yeah, I’m sure,” Walter replied. “Aside from my attorney, who would surely tell me not to talk to you, you’re the only one I trust.”

Jake mulled that over. “Really. Where’s Arlo, now that you really need him?”

“At the moment, I really don’t give a shit where he is. Look, let’s cut the crap. I want to tell you what I know about the murder of Landers and…and the setup. All of it.”

“Meet me here, Walter.” Jake told him. “By the time you get here most of my people will have gone home. I’ll be in my office.

“I’ll be right down. Thanks,” Walter replied and hung up.

Walter hurried to his car, backed out of the driveway and drove off, rounding the corner just seconds before the black Lincoln Town Car pulled up in front of the house. Arlo got out and walked to the front door. He rang the bell and waited. No answer.

‘He’s already left,’ Arlo thought, ‘and probably not to go to the ‘507’. He got back in his car and sat thinking for a few moments. He knew Walter was scared. ‘Where,’ he asked himself, ‘would Walter go?' Arlo considered the possibility that Walter would just take off, go into hiding. It seemed unlikely but when people are scared they make unlikely decisions. 'Maybe he's in the house, hiding and waiting for me to leave. 'Or he may have blown his brains out rather than face jail.' Arlo got back out of the car and walked up the driveway to the two-car garage. He looked through a crack between one of the doors and the door jamb. He could see enough to determine that the garage was empty.

Arlo walked back to the Lincoln and got in. It was obvious Walter was gone. "Sure as hell he's gone to see Jake Reed," Arlo said aloud. "That cowardly son of a bitch will lay us both out." Arlo fired up the car and drove away.

The man in the blue Pontiac sitting at the curb a block away observed Arlo's actions.

"He's been in and out of his car twice now. It looks like he's leaving westbound," he said. Over his radio, a voice responded. "I've got him. He's turning north on Montgomery, number two lane."

Arlo drove fast, faster than he normally did. He had no time to screw around, he thought. If Walter has gone to Jake Reed he'll lay me out like a rug, he thought. He considered his options, all of which ended with him getting out of Los Angeles without going to jail.

"Maybe I'd better call Uncle Montini. He can arrange to get me back east. Or better yet, out of the country," Arlo said aloud. "That might be my best option. I'll call him from the house." Arlo drove up into the hills and in a short while pulled up to his driveway. He pressed the opener that was clipped to the visor and the big gate swung open. He drove up the drive to the front door, parked and got out, leaving the gate open for a quick departure. Arlo entered the house and walked up the stairs, assuming Maureen wasn't home.

'Is she ever?' he thought. 'Out shopping, as usual. Probably time to dump her, the goofy bitch. She's more trouble than she's worth and I don't need any company when I get out of here.' He looked around the house, at the furnishings and all the things his money and success had provided. He'd worked hard to attain the wealth and prestige he enjoyed. Now he was going to have to leave it all, give it all up he thought, as he entered the bedroom.

He went to the closet and pulled a large tan leather suitcase from the floor mumbling to himself:

"That fucking Walter Burnett. I never should have hooked up

with a cop. None of this would have happened. Before I go anywhere I have to take care of him." Arlo continued to mull over how he was going to accomplish that as he stuffed clothes into a bag on the bed.

"Better call Tony right now," he said as he stopped packing and reached for the phone. Tony was probably the quickest way to get to Uncle Montini, although that fact pissed Arlo off thoroughly. He dialed the number and waited as it rang. Finally an answering machine came on and said to leave a message. Arlo hesitated and then hung up without saying anything. 'I'll try him again in a few minutes.', he thought.

Arlo continued packing the things he needed, unaware of the figure who stepped through the doorway of the bedroom.

"Well, isn't this ironic."

Arlo turned at the sound of the voice and was stunned to see Andy's wife, Melanie, standing there. She was holding a small automatic pistol. Arlo stared at her for a second.

"Melanie. Hello. What are you doing here, my dear? It's wonderful to see you," Arlo said, warily eyeing the gun. "What's that for, dear?" Arlo was visibly frightened. "Melanie, you don't…"

Melanie fired the first shot, striking Arlo in the chest. He crumpled to his knees and reached out his arms as if to plead with her. She fired the second shot. It struck him in the face. He fell forward onto the floor, dead. She looked at him, apparently unaffected by what she'd done. She lifted the corner of the bedspread, wiped the gun clean of prints and threw it on the floor near Arlo's body. She walked down the stairs into the foyer, turned and headed for the kitchen.

Just as she reached the kitchen door, Maureen entered from the other side of the room. Contrary to Arlo's assumption, she hadn't been shopping. Rather she'd been secluded in her study at the opposite end of the house. She'd heard the shots and was coming to investigate. Melanie stopped and looked at Maureen. Maureen appeared momentarily confused and then a knowing smile crossed her lips. Melanie hesitated and then took a tentative step forward towards the rear door. Maureen nodded and stepped aside. Neither woman said anything as Melanie walked through the kitchen and out the back door. She crossed the yard and walked through the garden, to a partially concealed gate at the edge of the property. She opened the gate and walked through it into a small neighborhood park. The few people, mostly mothers with toddlers, who were in the park hardly noticed her as she crossed to the street. She walked a short distance to where her car was parked and drove off.

Maureen stood in the kitchen for a few moments. She assumed Arlo was upstairs, either dead or dying. Either way, she didn't want to see him just then. She decided to go shopping. A few moments later she drove down the drive, turned right and headed for Beverly Hills.

As Maureen turned off the side street and onto Sunset Boulevard, Tony was turning up the hill toward Arlo's house. 'I've been looking forward to killing this asshole for a long time,' Tony thought. 'This is going to be a real pleasure. Taking off Mr. Bigshot. He's had it his way for a long time. Now it's payback time.' Tony had decided not to bring the knife and gun Vivi had provided. Tony would strangle Arlo slowly and watch him as he died. Tony had actually had a climax once when he strangled a bookie and he enjoyed it immensely.

As Tony pulled up to the house he noticed the gate was standing open. 'Excellent,' he thought. 'Now I won't have to let the dipshit know I'm here.' He drove through the gate and up to the front door. He shut the car off and got out, leaving the door ajar. He walked around the house, looking for a way in without alerting Arlo to his presence. At the rear, near the pool he found the unlocked door Melanie had used to leave. He went in and began prowling about the house looking for Arlo. After creeping around for ten minutes or so he climbed the stairs and entered the master bedroom. There was Arlo, sprawled on the floor. A small puddle of blood had pooled on the carpet. Tony knew a dead man when he saw one. He surveyed the scene for a couple seconds.

"That son of a bitch. He committed suicide. I really wanted to kill him and he goes and commits suicide. The bastard." Tony stepped closer and kicked Arlo, just once, to demonstrate his disdain. Then he picked up the gun and looked at it. "Walther PPK. Nice piece," he said. Really nice." He fondled the gun for a minute and then, against his better judgment he dropped it in his pocket. A decision he'd come to regret. Tony walked out of the room and down the hall. He walked through the house and out the front door.

The surveillance units were parked throughout the neighborhood with one watching the house from about half a block away. They'd followed Arlo home and were waiting to see what his next move would be. As they sat, the squad leader, Jerry Stafford, felt the vibration of his beeper. He checked the number and then punched it into his cell phone. Two rings and then, "Jake Reed."

"Jerry Stafford here, Lieutenant. You called?"

"Yeah, Jerry. Where's our boy?"

"Padded down, at the moment. He came here about an hour ago and hasn't stirred. His wife was home when we got here but she just drove off. Right after she left some mug drove in and went up the drive. I guess he's inside."

"Well, I don't want this guy splitting on us. I've got enough to book him for right now. Keep your surveillance tight. If he starts to leave, go ahead and arrest him. Otherwise leave him alone for the moment. I'll get back to you soon."

"Okay, Lieutenant. Will do." Stafford got on the radio. "Everybody sit tight. We're going to be taking him down shortly, it appears."

Before anyone could acknowledge, the point man came on the radio. "The guy who drove up a little while ago is leaving. What do you want to do with him?"

"Let's jam him. Which direction is he going?"

A voice came back, "Left turn, down the hill towards the boulevard."

"Units four and six, you're closest. Get on him and I'll join you in a minute. Let's try to stop him before he gets to the boulevard. Every one else stay in place."

The two units acknowledged the directions and were on the vehicle quickly. As Tony stopped at the boulevard to wait for traffic, one unit pulled in front of him as the second drove up against his rear bumper. As the detectives in the front car both got out through the driver's door, Stafford arrived at the scene. The two detectives in the rear car got out and approached the vehicle and quickly removed Tony. One asked him for ID while the other patted him down.

"Whoa, what's this," the searching officer said, squeezing Tony's outside jacket pocket to deny him access to the gun that was there. "He's got a gun, partner." Before Tony could resist or argue, he was handcuffed and pushed over onto the hood of the police car.

"Why the gun?' one of the detectives asked. Tony said nothing.

"O.K. friend. You're under arrest for carrying a concealed weapon. Your car will be impounded, towed away. You're going to Hollywood station for booking."

"Yeah, big deal," Tony said, trying to appear blasé about the whole thing.

He was quickly loaded into one of the police cars and driven away. Stafford told the other unit to return to the house as soon as they could get a black & white to impound Tony's car. Stafford then drove to the station and went to the detective squad room to talk to Jake. He found him in his office, talking to Walter. Jake saw Stafford and stepped out of the office to speak with him and Stafford filled him in on what had transpired. Jake told him that Walter had been a wealth of information regarding Arlo's activities, as well as his own, and there was more than enough to book him. The two men agreed that Stafford and his squad shouldn't make the arrest as they were undercover officers who preferred keeping their identities confidential. Stafford would go back to the house and maintain the surveillance until some of Jake's detectives arrived to make the arrest. Stafford agreed and left while Jake called Kilgore on the com line. He filled him in and told him to take as many detectives as he thought he needed and to go make the arrest. Kilgore was more than happy to oblige.

*****

Jake returned to his office and continued talking with Walter. Kilgore rounded up two of his teams and briefed them quickly. They left the station together, in two cars. It took them only a short time to get to the house. They met Stafford up the street, away from the house, and assumed responsibility for the situation. Stafford assured them no one had come or gone at the residence since Tony left. Kilgore thanked him and Stafford left with his squad.

Kilgore deployed his detectives around the house to insure Arlo wouldn't slip away from them and as soon as the house was secured Kilgore and one detective went to the front door and rang the bell. No one answered. They rang once more and then knocked on the door. Nothing. Kilgore tried the knob but the door was locked. He left the detective at the front door and went around the house to the rear door where one detective was deployed. When he walked up the detective told him that he'd tried the door and found it unlocked. After advising the others to remain where they were over his handheld radio, Kilgore and the detective entered and began to search. After thoroughly checking the ground floor they went up to the second floor and in a short while found Arlo's body. Kilgore advised the other detectives of the situation and then went to the house next door where he used the phone to call Jake. Rene answered and Kilgore told her he needed to speak to Jake. Rene told him Jake was still talking to Walter and Kilgore asked her to call him out of his office so Walter wouldn't overhear the conversation. Rene agreed and soon thereafter Jake came on the line.

"Well, here's an interesting development, Lieutenant. We're inside the house. We've located Arlo in his bedroom. He's on the floor, dead. He's been shot at least twice, once in the face and once in the chest. I haven't called the coroner yet but photos and a lab team are rolling."

"Well, this situation just gets more bizarre by the minute, doesn't it?" Jake replied. "I don't remember if I mentioned it but the surveillance guys brought in a guy they saw enter and leave the house about a half hour ago. They jammed him when he left and found a gun on him. A small automatic, a Walther I think. You don't suppose he might have something to do with Arlo's demise, do you?"

"Wouldn't that be an easy one. I'll get a ballistics test done as soon as I can. I've got enough unsolved. I sure don't need another one. Are you coming to the scene, Lieutenant?"

"Yeah, I think I will. I'll leave Walter here with Kelly and be out shortly."

"Okay, I'll see you here." Kilgore said, hanging up.

Jake had no intention of letting Walter know that his cohort in crime was dead. Walter was speaking freely, primarily because he feared Arlo and wanted to lay him out as thoroughly as possible. He wanted him in jail on as serious a set of charges as could be brought, to preclude his getting out right away. If Jake told him Arlo was dead, it was likely Walter might reconsider and stop talking.

Jake went to Kelly's desk and told her about Arlo's death. She asked Jake if her mother knew or was involved and she appeared relieved when Jake told her it didn't seem likely. Jake then explained to Kelly why he didn't want Walter to know about Arlo. She understood and assured him Walter wouldn't find out. Then they walked back to Jake's office and Jake told Walter he had to respond to a homicide, not Arlo's of course, and he'd return shortly. Walter, being the former Chief of Detectives, understood Jake had to comply with department policy. Kelly suggested that she and Walter have lunch in the meantime. Jake assured Walter he'd be back in less than an hour and left.

*****

Jake responded to the murder scene and spoke with Kilgore, who had the situation well in hand. The photographer was busy recording the scene and a print specialist was dusting in all the places likely to produce anything of value. Nothing particularly unusual about the scene was noted. As Kilgore described it, it was just your 'basic Hollywood murder', only in this case they had a suspect in custody before they knew they had a dead body. With that, Jake returned to the station to resume his conversation with Walter. By late that evening Walter finished laying out everything. He'd described his relationship with Arlo from the first day they'd met up to the present.

"Well, Walter, it looks like we've just about wrapped this up. At least for the moment. Is there anything else you'd like to tell me?" Jake asked.

"As a matter of fact, there is. Right now, I'd like to be in your shoes, Jake. You're a good cop. You have a great career. You can go as far as you want to, Jake. You love what you do, you have the respect of your peers and you love the department. You're right where you should be, doing exactly what you should be."

"I, on the other hand, have none of that. I did once but I've thrown it all away. I made bad decisions; the worst being having anything to do with Arlo. I wanted it all and now, at fifty three, I essentially have nothing. Think of it, Jake. I was seconds away from becoming the Chief of Police. Christ, in retrospect, I'm not worthy of associating with the men and women of this department. How in the hell did I get so screwed up?"

"I'm afraid I can't help you with that one, Walter. Excuse me for saying so but you'll have plenty of time to think about it. I'm going to call Chief Collins and give him an overview of what you've told me and see how he wants to proceed. Would you like a cup of coffee while you wait?"

Walter nodded, "Yes, I would. I could use one."

Jake walked out of the office and asked Rene to get Walter the coffee. Then he went directly to Captain Hughes' office. With Hughes listening Jake called Chief Collins and briefed him on Walter's statements. When he'd completed the briefing, Jake listened as Collins advised him how he wanted him to proceed. The conversation ended with Collins thanking Jake.

"You're welcome, sir. And thank you for your help. Remember me when you become the next Chief of Police." Collins laughed and both men hung up.

Jake looked at Captain Hughes. "He suggests we book Walter for an additional charge of conspiracy and ask for a bail enhancement."

"Sounds good to me, Jake. Good job."

Jake left the office, strangely saddened by the turn of events. Although never a fan of Walter he couldn't help but feel a little sorry for him. He'd gotten in way over his head and when he finally realized it, he couldn't get out. Jake was even inclined to believe that Walter's insistence he never knew that Arlo was producing child porno was true, even though he admitted he liked to look at it. As for what he knew about the death of Landers, that remained to be seen.

Jake walked back into his office. Walter sat sipping a cup of coffee. "Ready to get on with it, Walter?" Jake asked. Walter stood up and threw the empty cup in the wastebasket. "Yep," he said, and both men walked out of the office and to the booking desk to add the further charges to Walter's case.

Jake returned to the office about fifteen minutes later and found Kelly sitting there, waiting. "We might as well get all the unpleasant business out of the way today, Jake" she said.

"Yeah, you're right Kelly," he said, closing the door behind him. "What's your status with I.A.? Have they finished with you yet?"

"No. I'm scheduled for one more interview tomorrow. First thing in the morning."

"Well, be honest with them, Kelly. Any false or misleading statements will make things worse."

"Worse! How could I possibly make things any worse, Jake? My career's over. We both know that. I can't tell you how much I regret that, especially the way I let you and the department down." Kelly handed Jake an envelope she'd been holding. "Here's my resignation, Jake. I hope you can forgive me for screwing up the way I did. I'm not going to fight the system. I think I've pretty well established that I'm not meant for this line of work."

"I'm sorry things have worked out like this Kelly. I think you had a bright future with the department. However facts are facts and they'll fire you if you don't resign. I hope things work out for you."

"Well, Maureen and I are going to try to rebuild our relationship."

"Good. By the way, you better get her to hire you a good lawyer. I'm going to have to present the facts regarding your actions to the D.A. I'll try to persuade him that your resignation resolves the issue but I can't guarantee anything."

"Thanks, Jake I appreciate that. Oh, and please tell Mitch to take care." Tears slid down her cheeks as Kelly looked at Jake. Jake reached out, put his arms around her and gave her a strong hug. "Good luck, Kelly."

Chapter 39

The next week or so were filled with the normal slow pace of the justice system. The courts moved slowly. Walter moved to Big Bear high in the mountains and left things to his attorneys to keep him out of jail for as long as possible.

Jake of course was welcomed back with great enthusiasm by the troops and received a promotion.

And other events began to unfold.

*****

The twin engined Beech craft banked in the clear blue air of the Nevada desert at about twelve hundred feet over the buildings grouped around the swimming pool and dropped to the small strip next to the 3 par golf course.

Two large men in suits drove a canopied golf cart alongside the aircraft as it taxied to a stop. The door to the plane swung open and a small elderly man with snow white closely cropped hair stepped out and shielded his eyes from the bright desert sun. Without a word to either man he sat on the rear bench of the golf cart and made a small motion with his hand and the cart pulled away and headed to the main building.

A man in his forties with slick backed hair and purple lensed sun glasses moved quickly down the steps of the entrance to the stucco building and took the old man by the hand in a greeting. The old man pulled his hand away and walked into the lobby saying over his shoulder:

"Where's my room?"

Without a word the man picked up a small leather bag and led the way to a suite just off the lobby rushing ahead of the old man. The room was sumptuous, a bottle of red wine sat on the table and a view window overlooked the pool and beyond, the green of the golf course with gray and purple mountains beyond.

"There will be a woman and man come to visit me. The man in a few hours," the old man looked at a diamond encrusted watch on his right wrist, "and the woman this evening. I'll have dinner in the room with her, now leave me alone."

The man nodded his understanding and withdrew. A few minutes later a soft tapping at the door caused the old man to look up from the papers he was reading:

"Come." A pretty girl, not much more than eighteen, entered the front room carrying several towels over one arm and a small bottle of warm aromatic oil in her hand. She smiled and raised her eyebrows in question. The old man got up from his chair and nodding walked to the bedroom puling off the sweater and shirt. He lay on the bed face down and she spread the oil across his back and began kneading his shoulders until he fell asleep. She quietly slipped from the room as the man napped.

Just before sunset the telephone next to the bed chirped softly. The man put the receiver to his ear:

"What?" and after listening for a moment, "Wait ten minutes and then show her in. We will have dinner in half an hour." Without waiting for a reply he hung up and walked to the closet and put a maroon silk robe on over his old mans body. Exactly ten minutes later there was a knock at the door. He went to the door and pulled it open:

"Maureen my dear, come in, come in." He took her by the arm and led her to the table set with fine linen and crystal. She turned to him and took his right hand in hers and raised it to her lips saying:

"Uncle it's been so long. I'm so happy to see you."

Yes, yes, sit we have much to talk about."

Uncle Montini and Maureen sat across from each other sipping the red wine and speaking of the old days, of Maureen being a show girl at the Las Vegas hotel, of her friendship with Montini's niece and the arranged marriage to Arlo. Montini put his wine down on the table and stared intently at Maureen:

"And your marriage it went well?"

"After the first year or so it was fine. He made no demands on me, he was satisfied with the arrangement, I did the charity thing and the parties and social necessities and stayed out of his way."

"You knew nothing of this business? This children business?"

"No." Maureen answered.

"Your son, a shame."

"He was weak. He got the worst of Arlo and I suppose, myself. There is little else to say."

"and now Arlo is dead and my nephew in jail charged with his murder." Motini said and Muareen nodded yes with no other response.

Montini picked up his wine glass and twirled the red liquid in the glass and then looked up:

"Tony is claiming he didn't do this deed. He wants my help."

"I can understand that." Maureen said.

"Well I think he may be safer in jail. That gun, that little gun I don't think Tony would use such a gun, do you?" Montini said.

"It does seem unlikely."

"Yes, unlikely. More of a woman's weapon I think." Montini's eyes hardened. "Did you kill Arlo Maureen?" She sat silently for a moment and then nodded her head yes.

"Well that's done then. He was using your son. Ugly. Is that why?" Maureen gave another brief nod her eyes downcast. Montini took a sip of his wine. They sat there silently until dinner was brought to the room. Montini had a small piece of broiled trout and some slivers of fresh fruit and Maureen the same. The silence continued as they ate. The young girl knocked at the door and was bade to enter. She removed the remains of the dinner as Maureen and Uncle Montini sat silently and then asked if they wanted coffee.

"Espresso." Montini said. The girl stepped outside the rooms and returned with two demitasses. She placed them on the table and withdrew. Montini put one in front of Maureen and sipped slowly from his own small cup. After a moment he spoke:

"You will take over Arlo's endeavors. You will fly back tonight in my plane. I want you to stay at arms length from the porn studio and stores and the unions. You know the judges we have an arrangement with and they will answer to your requests. I am going to have Vivi, you remember him?" Maureen nodded yes. "Good, he will act as an intermediary in any union business and the smut stores. Tomorrow morning I want you to see this public relations firm. Talk only with the name on this card." He handed her a business card. "We are going to make you the grieving and wronged widow. This will allow the mayor to save face. He is not with us but he is greedy for funds and time is on our side. You will stay active with the Hollywood types and continue the legitimate productions. Do you understand?"

"Yes. What of long range plans?" Maureen asked.

"In time. You will know in time. You are going to need a trusted assistant."

"Yes. Trusted. I think Kelly." Maureen answered after a pause.

"Kelly." Montini smiled. "A cop? Working for our organization?."

"She has been fired and is going to be prosecuted. She took the note to protect me, my feelings."

"Yes, good. She has a sense of family responsibility. Build the trust slowly." Montini said.

"Will I talk to you through the same attorney?"

"Yes. Do you have any further questions?" Montini stood up.

"No." Maureen stood as well and taking Montini's hand in hers touched her lips to the old man's hand and whispered, "Thank you."

"Yes, yes. I am going to rest now tell the man outside you wish to return to L.A."

Maureen nodded and picking up her purse turned and walked slowly to the door. Montini watched her as she left and than picked up the white enameled telephone on the desk.

*****

Tony climbed the stairs leading to his garden apartment on the West side. The sprinklers watering the landscaping misted across the walkways cooling the warm summer evening. A pleasantly sweet scent of flowers hung in the air. He walked into his apartment and sprawled on the couch kicking of his shoes and giving a big sigh, he stared around the richly furnished apartment.

He had been out of jail for a few days and the attorneys told him he needn't worry about jail time over the 'bullshit' charges of possession of a firearm. The murder charge had been dropped; no gunshot residual on his person gave Uncle's attorneys the leverage they needed. His sister had called and told him Uncle seemed a little disappointed but she felt everything was going to be alright. 'Oh Tony you know Uncle, family is everything'.

Tony took a cigar from the coffee table and, after all the ritual, took a deep drag and blew the smoke toward the ceiling. All in all he felt pretty good. He had a good stash of money, the cops hadn't connected him to Arlo and the kid thing and most importantly his Uncle seemed to have forgiven any supposed transgressions. Why not? It was obvious to anyone Tony was in the process over carrying out the order to get rid of Arlo. 'Wasn't his fault somebody beat him to it.' Tony gave little if any thought as to who that might have been. Whoever it was did him a favor as far as he was concerned. The muted door chimes interrupted his reverie.

As Tony walked to the door he reached behind some books on the alcove table and stuck the small caliber pistol at the small of his back. He looked through the peep hole and saw Vivi standing there. After a moment he opened the door.

"Hey Vivi, how are ya'?" Tony stepped back from the door. "Come in, come in."

"Evenin' Tony." Vivi moved into the room and pulled off his hat, a tweed fedora that seemed so out of character with his bulk and scarred face.

"Grab a seat." Tony pointed to one of the stuffed chairs and turned to the wet bar in a corner of the large living room. "Get cha' a drink?"

"Yeah, a bourbon if ya' gott'it." Vivi sat carefully in the chair his bulk straining the fabric. He took the proffered crystal hi ball glass and held it up before downing the half inch of amber liquid.

"So what's up Vivi?" Tony stood a few feet from the seated man.

"There's some things goin' on. Out in the desert." Vivi looked around the room and raised an eyebrow as if to ask, 'how safe was it to talk?' Tony nodded his understanding and shrugged noncommittedly.

"Well he wants you to go out there and uh, make arrangements." Vivi looked around the room again as if he felt constrained in what he needed to say.

"Let's go outside, the flowers are real pretty, have ya' ever seen the garden around my place?" With a look of obvious relief Vivi stood and nodded his agreement. On the walkway Vivi began in a low voice looking around to make sure no one was with-in listening distance.

"There's a big hotel in Vegas. Uncle has a friend, a Bishop in tha' church. They want to get outta' the business. It's all set up, he wants you there. Look it over. If it's good he wants to move back into the, that business. Wants it legal like."

"A Bishop? So this Hughes thing and tha' church right? And we got one of 'em in our pocket? Oh man! Vivi this is big, real big." Tony rubbed his hands together. "So what's next?"

"Uncle wants ya' to call him. I got tha' number. Wants ya' to use a pay phone."

"Aw fuck! Tha' cops still got my car, s'posed ta' get this week. Shit!" Tony was excited and anxious, 'Vegas' He loved that city and he'd be a player.

"C'mon we'll take my wheels, do ya' know a pay phone aroun' here?" Vivi said holding up his car keys.

"Yeah let's go. I know one." Tony started towards the stairs walking through one of the sprinklers slightly out of kilter spraying water onto the walkway. Vivi followed walking around the spray so as not to ruin the new shine on his shoes.

As the two men approached the stairs leading to the sidewalk Vivi took Tony's head in his big hands and lifted him onto his tip toes and duck stepped him to the edge of the steep stair case.

"Hey! Hey! What tha' fuck…" Tony flailed his arms trying to reach the pistol hidden at the small of his back.

"Uncle says 'bye bye'." Vivi gave a violent twist of Tony's head and felt and heard the satisfying soft crack as his neck snapped. He took the limp body by the seat of the pants and scruff of the neck and threw it out into space. The body hit about half way down the staircase and then flopped end over end coming to rest on the sidewalk in front of the staircase.

Vivi walked slowly down the stairs and over to Tony's body.

He bent over and pulled Tony's wallet from his pants pocket and removed the money and began to walk away and then turned and went back.

"Shit bag." At the same time giving the body a kick. Vivi turned and strolled down the quiet tree lined street with a small smile on his face. He still had over an hour before he had to pick Maureen up at LAX.

*****

At one twelve AM the white Beech craft touched down at Burbank Airport and taxied to a private hanger at the north west corner of the field. As Maureen stepped from the plane a black Mercedes pulled up next to the sliding doors of the large building and Vivi climbed out of the back seat and hurried towards her. He nodded to her and took the overnight bag from her hand. She walked in front of him to the limo and sat down in the leather interior. Vivi sat opposite her, the small jump seat barely holding his bulk.

"Tell the driver I want to go to Arlo's offices in Beverly Hills." Maureen said. Vivi turned and gave directions to the driver and as the separating window between the front and back began to slide up turned to Maureen and said:

"It's good you're back I . . ." Maureen held up her hand palm to Vivi and picked up the built in telephone and after dialing:

"Yes it's me" She paused a minute and then, "Yes Uncle, he was here and we are going to Arlo's office now. I will call tomorrow afternoon and thank you for a wonderful evening your trust in me will reap us both success, I promise." She broke the connection and turned to Vivi with a raised eyebrow.

"Vivi this will be the only time we meet directly." Vivi nodded his head and Maureen continued. "You run the porno business and take care of any union affairs. I will communicate suggestions through the attorney and on occasion you may talk with my daughter Kelly. She has our confidence. Do you see any problems?"

"No. She has left the cops?" Vivi asked.

"Yes, those days are over. I shall groom her and show her the clean end of our business. We are setting up a non profit corporation, proceeds from the porno shops will in part be funneled to there. We are putting all the porno business at arms length from the rest of the businesses." Vivi nodded his understanding.

"All right then." Maureen paused, "Drop me at the Beverly Hills office and then go to the bar downtown and bring all the books and records to the attorney's office the police haven't been there yet is that correct?"

"No, only his other office." Vivi answered.

The limo pulled to the curb in front of Arlo's building and as Maureen alighted from the car she turned and looked at Vivi for a long moment.

"It has been a long time, Vivi, I'm glad Uncle chose you." With that said, she walked quickly to the chrome doors of the building.

Maureen sat at Arlo's desk and stared at the portrait he had commisioned of himself some years ago. The picture dominated the room placed on the wall facing the desk and the oak doors. She smiled to herself. Everything was falling in place. The attorneys would have everything under her control within the week. The PR firm already had a luncheon date set up with the Mayor for tomorrow. There was more thing, she picked up the phone and dialed a number from memory.

'It's Kelly leave your number, thanks.'

"Kelly, it's your mother. Let's meet tomorrow afternoon. Call me in the morning."

*****

Each table at the little outdoor cafe in Westwood had its own red, white and blue umbrella. Maureen sat watching students from the UCLA campus strolling along talking and laughing. She toyed with the long spoon pushing the lemon slice around the glass of iced tea. Kelly was due any moment. She reviewed in her mind how she would approach her daughter with the idea of coming into the business. Of course no mention of the Montini family, given some time in the operation she was sure she would be able to show Kelly the wisdom of that connection. Uncle was establishing a network of influence on the West coast, almost all legitimate.

The PR firm and the attorney had moved quickly after Arlo's death. There was to be a picture of Maureen and the Mayor in the LA Times along with an article portraying her as a wronged wife. A devoted wife active in charities and unaware of the double life her evil husband was leading. It was great stuff, the stuff of Hollywood. The

Mayor went willingly along with the whole story. He washed away any dirt that might cling to him from his association with Arlo. A promise of continued support, financial support, to his political career was most helpful to be sure. It had taken over an hour in the attorney's office to sign all the documents making her president of a number of corporations. Now she was titular head of all the legitimate companies. Delicately with perfectly manicured fingers she took the lemon slice from the icy glass and put the tart peel to her lips.

"Hello mother, have you been waiting long?" Kelly plopped down in one of the wrought iron chairs across from Maureen.

"No dear, it's very pleasant sitting here." Maureen stared at her daughter for a moment. "How are you? How are you dealing with leaving your police job?"

"Oh, all right." Kelly pushed a lock of hair from he face and looked out at the sidewalk. "It's strange not having a badge and gun, I think I miss it, but I only resigned a couple of days ago."

"Am I to understand they are going to prosecute you?" Maureen asked.

"That's what they say, withholding evidence."

"And then what Kelly? Jail?"

"Oh I don't think so. I don't really know, more likely probation and some kind of fine or community service, something like that." Kelly answered.

The waitress came over and Kelly ordered iced tea and both women sat quietly for a few minutes. Maureen broke the silence:

"I'm going to speak bluntly. Arlo was an ass hole. After he got me pregnant with your half brother we never slept together again. I knew he was a cruel man but I always thought that cruelty was focused on business, legitimate business."

"Why did you stay with him?" Kelly asked.

"The kid and, frankly the lifestyle, I knew Arlo would fight me on any divorce. I left him alone and he let me do what I wanted, the charities, all the other things. We had an understanding." Kelly nodded.

"So Kelly here's what I have decided. I have instructed the attorneys to divest the business of any porno businesses and the proceeds will go to charities. I have taken over all the legitimate businesses and I need you to help me. I need someone I can trust to run things. I want you to think it over. You'll see, it will be fun working together, we'll be very successful." Maureen reached across the table and put her hand over Kelly's and smiled. "We will get you the best attorney in the state." Kelly sat there a moment and then with a sigh agreed with her mother.

Three weeks later the two women and a young girl met for lunch.

"Oh Song, congratulations! Now you are a citizen and soon you will be my daughter." Kelly smiled at the young Chinese girl.

The three of them, Maureen, Kelly and Song were sitting in a small park just off Santa Monica Boulevard in Beverly Hills. Cookies and cardboard cups of tea were sitting on the bench between them.

Two weeks earlier an amendment to a bill before Congress added by a Senator from New York had been voted upon in the affirmative granting Song citizenship. Uncle Montini, through an intermediary, sent his thanks the very next day. The State of California expeditied the application for adoption and word came through their attorney that all was in order. Coincidently, the day before, the daughter of one of the officials signed a one year contract with one of the major film studios.

Kelly turned to Maureen with a big smile: "Mother, now that you're a Gran' Ma' what would you like to be called? Grammy? NaNa? Or maybe Granny?"

Maureen, with a rather stiff necked posture, stared out into space for what seemed like minutes and then answered:

"Maureen."

*****

It was a quiet tree lined street in the Green Pointe section of Brooklyn, a few small stores and some nicely kept two story brownstones and one of those tiny parks at the end of the block bespoke of middle class serenity.

In the middle of the block a quaint little bakery run by two old spinsters offered fine pastries and imported coffees and espressos. Several small wrought iron tables with glass tops sat on the sidewalk under a red yellow and green awning with Two Sisters Bakery embossed at each end of the colorful canvas.

At one of the tables furthest from the entrance a small man with white hair wearing a starched white shirt and bright red suspenders sat taking small bites of a prune Danish with occasional sips of strong black coffee. He gave an air of satisfied complacency as people strolled by in the early afternoon sun.

A black Lincoln Town car was parked a few car lengths from the bakery with two men in the front seat. A yellow taxi cab pulled up behind the Lincoln and a man in his thirties got out spoke briefly with the cabbie and then walked up to the passenger side of the black car. The passenger climbed out of the car and nodded to the younger man who leaned close and spoke to him in a whisper glancing about several times. Without a word the older man nodded and turned dismissively and walked down the sidewalk stopping a discrete distance from the white haired old man enjoying his Danish. After a minute or two the old man, with a brief flick of the wrist, motioned the waiting man to come forward. The man came forward and leaned over speaking in almost a whisper:

"I am sorry to bring such sad tidings." He waited for the old man's barely perceptible nod to continue. "Your nephew Tony on the West Coast had a terrible accident last night he fell down a cement staircase and broke his neck. He is dead. I have been told the authorities will rule it an accident. I am saddened by your loss."

"Yes he was a god boy." The old man paused and still not looking at the man took a sip of coffee. "And the Chink. Can I expect that business transaction to be complete in the near future?"

"Yes sir within the next two days, three at the most."

The man took a bite of Danish and motioned for the other to withdraw.

*****

The General rolled from the satin sheets and reached for the chilled crystal goblet of pomegranate juice and looked through the open doors at the cobalt blue waters of the Caribbean. It was good to be alive. He had been staying at the villa for close to three weeks and had just decided to purchase the property. All his plans had come together. He was wealthy. No one knew his new identity or where he was. The government of China wasn't even the least bit suspicious his feigned death had been a model of perfection. He rose and pulled on a white silk caftan. He picked up a small silver bell shook it gently, enjoying the muted sweet tones summoning his servant.

His scream followed the sound of the shotgun blast that tore into his stomach. It took him a little short of ten minutes to bleed out. Ten painful minutes while the beautiful silk garment turned red.

THE END

EPILOGUE

"Seems to me this is the where things started a couple of months of ago." Jake said. He and Mitch were sitting at the very Café where they first reunited

"Yeah, you're right. In fact this is the same place <u>and</u> the same table <u>and</u> the same waitress. Kinda' weird, isn't it?"

"Mitch, the only thing weirder than that is the fact that the D.A. opted not to file any charges against you. You do truly lead a charmed life."

"Aw, not really Jake. I think the D.A.'s office just recognizes good police work when they see it. And of course, which of those assholes would testify didn't hurt."

"I have to agree, Mitch. That really was a hell of a piece of work. You should be proud of yourself."

"Thanks, Jake. Hold that thought. I'll be right back." Mitch got up and walked towards the restroom. While he sipped his coffee, Jake looked around and noticed a newspaper lying on the unoccupied table next to him. He picked it up and thumbed through the first few pages. An article on the third page drew his attention.

"Local Jurist An Apparent Suicide" Jake read the article:

Los Angeles Superior Court Judge Ronald J. Hansen was found dead Thursday in his vehicle, inside the garage of his home in Hollywood. Police reported that it appeared the jurist died of carbon monoxide poisoning and they are proceeding on the theory that Hansen committed suicide. Police would not speculate on the reason the jurist chose to kill himself, although Hansen's name had recently come up during the course of an investigation involving the trafficking of young Asian girls who had been brought to the United States for immoral purposes. The investigation centered on the late Arlo Calarasi who was believed to have been the principal suspect in the operation. Calarasi was found murdered in his palatial residence in the Hollywood Hills last month. His murder remains unsolved and Lieutenant Jake Reed, the Commanding Officer of Hollywood Detective Division, has remained closed mouth about that investigation as well as Judge Hansen's demise.

Mitch returned to the table and sat down. "What's so interesting?"

"Just reading about the Judge's demise. I'm sorry that bastard decided to kill himself. I would liked to have seen him squirm in court. He knew he was bought and paid for. Those videos Arlo made of 'his honor' with the two 12 year olds pretty well slammed the door on his declarations of innocence. In fact, when we confronted him with the tapes I thought he was going to have a heart attack on the spot."

"Yeah, it's hard to believe that a guy in his position would get involved in that sort of stuff. I guess everybody's subject to moral weaknesses. He sure gave in to his, didn't he?"

"That he did Mitch, that he did."

"And what about Tony? What happened to him? Is he still in jail?"

"No, he bailed out a few days ago. No GSR. Besides, the gun didn't fit that thug. He said he found it at the scene and I'm inclined to believe him. No self respecting gangster is going to carry a .25 auto. It's a girls' gun, not manly. He said Arlo was dead when he got there. He did admit he went there to confront Arlo over the beef with Montini, but not to kill him. I'm not sure I'm buying that, but it doesn't matter he fell down the stairs in front of his apartment and broke his neck." Jake stared at Mitch looking for a reaction. "You wouldn't have any ideas about that would you?"

"Me?" Holding his hands to his chest, "No. What do the reports say?"

"Accidental death, the steps were slippery from a water sprinkler."

"Well, that's that then, right?' Jake nodded slowly.

"Well, I guess justice is served. But who do you think knocked off Arlo?"

"We're working on that. I've got a few people in mind. We'll see what happens."

As the two men continued talking Jake, who was facing the window, noticed a white Mercedes Benz sedan pull to the curb across the street from the restaurant. Kelly exited the driver's door while a young woman got out on the passenger side. Jake watched as the two women walked across the street toward the restaurant.

"Here comes one of your old flames, Mitch." Jake said, gesturing toward the window.

Mitch turned and looked.

"Yeah, she could have had me at one time but she blew it. Probably coming to find out if she still has a chance. Poor girl."

"I'd say you blew it old buddy. She's got the big bucks now. Working for Maureen pays very well, I'll bet."

"Well, as I've said before Jake, there's more to life than money. Although a new boat would be nice. Maybe I'll give her another chance."

Kelly and the young woman entered the restaurant. Jake estimated the woman to be no more than 19 or 20 years old. Tall, thin, dark haired and obviously nervous as hell, Jake thought. They walked up to the two men and Kelly nodded.

"Hi Jake, Mitch. You guys are still hanging around this place, huh?"

"Yeah. Old habits are tough to break. How are you doing, Kelly? Not still pining for Mitch are you?"

"No, I managed to get over him, but it wasn't easy." she said, winking at Mitch.

"Who's your friend?" Mitch asked. "Are you going to introduce us?"

"Yes I am Mitch. I'd like to introduce you to your daughter, Amanda."

Mitch sat in stunned silence, temporarily at a loss for words.

Amanda spoke up. "Hello. I've waited a very long time for this."

She approached Mitch and he quickly stood up as she wrapped her arms around him. They both began to cry. Jake and Kelly stepped a few tables away.

"That was a wonderful thing for you to do, Kelly." Jake said. "Frankly I'd forgotten that you were trying to find Mitch's daughter. Where has she been living?"

"Florida, with her mother, who refused to give her any information about Mitch. Since I used department resources I'll say no more lest I get myself in trouble. Or more trouble, I should say."

"Kelly, this is the best thing that's ever happened to me," Mitch said, holding his daughter with both arms.

"I'm happy for you both," Kelly replied. "Now I have to go. Amanda, please call me when you're settled and we'll get together for lunch." Kelly walked to the door and opened it. She looked back at Mitch. "Amanda's a pretty lucky lady to have such a good guy for a father. Maybe you'd consider calling me for dinner some time."

" Well,, I don't know if I'll have the time" Mitch said with a smile, "Jake and I are going to be pretty busy working on the Arlo murder case." He looked over at Jake.

"Dream on, Mitch. Believe me, you'll have plenty of time."

CPSIA information can be obtained
at www.ICGtesting.com
Printed in the USA
FSOW01n0335230218
44767FS